A FIRST-CLASS TICKET TO THE STARS

"Truck Driver" by Robert Chilson—She'd taken on a payload and sworn to see it in orbit, but no one had warned her that spacejackers might have a different flight plan laid out for her and her cargo. . . .

"Pushbutton War" by Joseph P. Martino—When computerized weapons guarded the starways, was there any role left for a mere man in the game of war?

"The Last Shuttle" by Isaac Asimov—She'd go down in the history books as Earth's last shuttle pilot, but was she the herald of the end of an age—or the beginning?

"Between a Rock and a Hard Place" by Timothy Zahn—They'd found the ultimate way to commute via flying skyports, but now a skycrash might bring them all down to Earth far too soon!

Book your passage to the planets and beyond, with this and the other tales you'll find in—

ISAAC ASIMOV'S WONDERFUL WORLDS OF SCIENCE FICTION

SPACE SHUTTLES

Isaac Asimov's Wonderful Worlds of Science Fiction #7

Edited by
Isaac Asimov, Martin H. Greenberg, and Charles G. Waugh

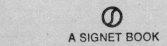

A SIGNET BOOK

NEW AMERICAN LIBRARY

SIGNET TRADEMARK REG. U.S. PAT. OFF. AND FOREIGN COUNTRIES
REGISTERED TRADEMARK—MARCA REGISTRADA
HECHO EN CHICAGO, U.S.A.

SIGNET, SIGNET CLASSIC, MENTOR, ONYX, PLUME, MERIDIAN
and NAL BOOKS are published by NAL PENGUIN INC.,
1633 Broadway, New York, New York 10019

First Printing, October, 1987

1 2 3 4 5 6 7 8 9

PRINTED IN THE UNITED STATES OF AMERICA

ABOUT THE EDITORS

ISAAC ASIMOV has been called "one of America's treasures." Born in the Soviet Union, he was brought to the United States at the age of three (along with his family) by agents of the American government in a successful attempt to prevent him from working for the wrong side. He quickly established himself as one of this country's foremost science fiction writers and writer about everything, and although now approaching middle age, he is going stronger than ever. He long ago passed his age and weight in books, and with some 250 to his credit threatens to close in on his I.Q. His sequel to *The Foundation Trilogy—Foundation's Edge*—was one of the bestselling books of 1982 and 1983.

MARTIN H. GREENBERG has been called (in *The Science Fiction and Fantasy Book Review*) "The King of the Anthologists"; to which he replied—"It's good to be the King!" He has produced more than 150 of them, usually in collaboration with a multitude of co-conspirators, most frequently the two who have given you MAGICAL WISHES. A professor of Regional Analysis and Political Science at the University of Wisconsin–Green Bay, he is still trying to publish his weight.

CHARLES G. WAUGH is a professor of Psychology and Communications at the University of Maine at Augusta who is still trying to figure out how he got himself into all this. He has also worked with many collaborators, since he is basically a very friendly fellow. He has done some fifty anthologies and single-author collections, and especially enjoys locating unjustly ignored stories. He also claims that he met his wife via computer dating— her choice was an entire fraternity or him, and she has only minor regrets.

Contents

INTRODUCTION: SHUTTLES

BY ISAAC ASIMOV

The word "shuttle" goes back to the Old Norse word *skutill*, meaning an arrow or a harpoon, a missile that travels a relatively short distance—from the person who hurls it to the target it strikes. The word "shoot" comes from the same source, and my own feeling is that the ultimate origin is onomatopoeic—by sound.

A narrow missile making its way rapidly through the air makes a sound like "shoosh" or "woosh" or "s-s-s-t," depending on the subjective interpretation of the person doing the hearing. From that, through a variety of changes, come "shuttle" and "shoot."

In prehistoric times, "shuttle" developed a markedly peaceful meaning—a development that always seems pleasant to me.

The art of weaving was invented before the days of writing, so we don't know the origins. Like most prehistoric inventions, later peoples, unable to imagine how mere human beings could think of such a clever thing, assumed that some god had granted the knowledge.

In any case, to weave you must begin with a series of parallel vertical threads, strong and tightly woven. (This is the "warp.") However, those parallel threads must be held together, and to do that, you place another series of threads, somewhat thinner, at right angles (the "woof"). Each thread of the woof goes over one thread of the warp, under the next, over the next, and so on. The next thread of the woof goes under, over, under, so that no two adjacent threads of the woof both go under or both go over a particular thread of the warp.

If the threads of the warp and the woof are then shoved close

9

together you have a two-dimensional set of threads that hang together and are much stronger on the whole than the individual threads are. You end with a piece of cloth, a textile material—light, porous, and much more suitable for keeping the body protected, clean, and comfortable, at ordinary temperatures, than furs or leather are.

The catch is that threading the woof along the warp takes a long, long time. Therefore, still in prehistoric times, the "loom" was invented. The threads of the warp were attached to each of two portions of the loom which could be pulled apart. This meant the threads of the warp would be alternately in, out, in, out. The threads of the woof could then be pushed through in a straight line, and when the pieces of the loom were joined together again, the woof would cross over, under, over, under the warp.

To increase the speed of operation, the woof is tied to a heavy object that is hurled across the width of the warp. This object is a "shuttle." After all, it is a missile and it travels a short distance. The shuttle carries the woof across the warp and then (with the loom separated in the opposite way) back across the warp, and then forward again and then back and so on, the loom always being manipulated so that the woof goes over and under the warp as it is supposed to.

Because of the backward and forward motion of the shuttle during weaving, the word "shuttle" gained a new refinement of meaning. Not only was it a missile that traveled a comparatively short distance but it was one that went ceaselessly back and forth over that short distance.

Thus, if some means of transportation travels from Point A to the not very distant Point B, then back to Point A, then back to Point B, and so on, indefinitely, it is a shuttle, too.

In Manhattan, for instance, there is a "subway-shuttle" that travels endlessly from Times Square to Grand Central Station, a distance of just about two-thirds of a mile, which is short considering that a number of subway lines in the city are twenty miles long or so. Naturally, people tend to economize on syllables, and the subway shuttle becomes simply "the shuttle" to subway users.

Similarly, once air travel became common, there were bound to be numerous flights between big cities that were quite close together. Thus, there would be a dozen flights or so each day between New York and Boston, or between New York and Washington. These are trips of about two hundred miles as compared with long-distance flights that can be three thousand or even ten thousand miles long. One speaks, therefore, of an "air shuttle," and those who often travel by air speak of "the shuttle."

The next extension is obvious to science fiction readers. Our first attempts in space were to place objects in orbit about the earth or to send an object to the moon and back. After that, we began to think of building a space station in orbit about the earth. It could be permanently occupied (in shifts) and serve as a base from which we could carry on long-term experiments, build space structures, and launch spaceships on long journeys.

Naturally, we would need some kind of space vessel which would specialize in traveling from the earth's surface to the space station and back, in order to bring in supplies, take off wastes, replace personnel, and so on. Since the space station would be considerably closer to the earth than the moon is, such a space vessel would be traveling a comparatively short distance—up, down, up, down, indefinitely. What would it be called? Inevitably, it would be a "space shuttle" or, to space hounds, "the shuttle."

Actually, the United States built a vessel suitable for such use long before it built a space station that could profit by that use. The first space shuttle, named *Columbia*, was launched on April 12, 1981, just twenty years to the day after the first human being, Yuri Gagarin, had orbited the earth. Four shuttles were eventually in operation, and by January 1986 some two dozen flights had been made with triumphant success.

Science fiction writers can write stories about such shuttles or about any devices that could represent comparatively short flights endlessly repeated. If we ever learn the trick of hyperspatial travel, we might conceivably talk of "the shuttle" between the sun and Alpha Centauri, or between the Milky Way and Andromeda. We might also have a shuttle between one end of a cylindrical space settlement and the other. The changes that can be rung, as you can see in the stories we have collected for this volume, are endless.

Of course, on January 28, 1986, the space shuttle went sour (only temporarily, I hope) with the explosion of the *Challenger*. But, you know, disasters of this sort, however horrifying and deplorable, are inevitable in any great and risky project.

My story "The Last Shuttle," included in this book, was written in March 1981, a month after the first space-shuttle flight, and was published in a Florida newspaper soon after being written. In it, I have a character point out that space-shuttle lift-offs are not necessarily trouble-free. "There was the case of Enterprise Sixty," she says, referring to an episode early in space-shuttle history.

Well, I got the name wrong, but I saw it coming, five years in advance. . . .

TRUCK DRIVER

BY ROBERT CHILSON

Ynga Lancaster hobbled awkwardly in her skintight pressure suit. It was inflated, so it didn't as yet grip her any more tightly than a stretch coverall, but the pads that filled out the concavities of her figure hampered her motion. Worse, they rounded her excellent figure out into that of a clumsily carved doll, one with features barely suggested.

Carrying her helmet under one arm and her flight orders and purse in the other hand, Ynga pushed open the door onto the ready line. It was chilly outside, with a hint of snow from a lowering sky. As a veteran pilot, her bird had been moved up near the building. She hurried toward it. Her pressure suit was permeable, designed to permit her to lose heat; and it wasn't designed for such extreme conditions as this. Though only a little below freezing—hot by the standards of shadows in space— the dense air carried her body heat away fast enough to make her shiver as she hobbled over the tarmac.

By earlier standards, the bird was a big one. It was a nuclear-electric aerospace plane capable of putting a hundred tons, not into Earth orbit, but into escape trajectory. In shape it was an arrowhead, with the trailing points extending somewhat behind the tail of the "fuselage." The main body, or fuselage, of the plane was perhaps half the wingspan; from there the wings thinned toward the tips. At the tip of each wing was a double electrojet, one above the other. These ramjets were each big enough for a man to take a running dive through without touching—and electrojets are vastly more efficient than thermal jets.

Along the leading edge of the wings were smaller jet intakes, the little electrojets that sucked air in to lift the wing. They could support the plane on hover with small or no load, or on air cushion near the ground with full load. Aft, on the trailing edges of the wings and body, were the exhausts of the turbo-electric jets that were used near the ground.

Paul Sitwell swung down from the flight deck and extended a clipboard. "Looks O.K., Ynga," he said with an attempt at heartiness.

She took the board, clumsy in her gauntlets, frowned at it. "What's wrong, then?" she barked.

"Wrong? Uh . . . nothing. I was just, uh, making sure. I mean, Mannie found a couple reds and he kind of, uh . . . and then I got behind—"

She ran her eye hastily down the checksheet, noting that everything had been marked if not checked. "O.K., O.K., don't tell me your troubles. Let me get out of this wind." She signed it clumsily. The flight techs supposedly checked everything after every flight, and there weren't many things that could go wrong with a nuclear-electric bird. Paul's job was merely to eliminate the waste of pilot hours in final checkout.

She swung gratefully into the warm bird.

The name of her plane was *Rival*. She looked around, soaking up the warmth for a moment, the comfort of her homey touches as warming as the plane's air conditioning. Bill, her husband, bless him, was not disturbed by the place of her birds in her life. She had added her own decorator scheme to the switches and buttons—in nail polish. The go-stick wore ruffled skirts, and a pair of Pete's baby shoes, gold-plated, hung from it where it extended from the board. She'd have had a picture of the two of them if there'd been room.

Activating the board, she gave the bird a spot-check, checked communications, told the voice in the tower that, yes, she had clipped her purse under the seat, made him admit that he had neglected to clock the fact that she was flying alone as usual, and switched on the visiplates. These birds, like all modern planes, had no ports; her view came from numerous thimble-sized ikons scattered over the hull in strategic places.

"*Rival* ready for the flight line," she informed the tower.

"So O.K., get that female kite out of the way and let a man through," Ernie Katz insisted.

Ynga grinned, seating her helmet and checking it. Ernie's bird was dubbed the *Manpower*; he even had a big UP sign painted on it.

Rival lifted a little as the jets along the leading edge pulled air in from above and blew it out below. In moments it was on air cushion. She halted its drift on the wind with the turboelectrics, turned it toward the flight line and wafted it along as gently as a leaf. Receiving final clearance, she tipped over the edge of the gentle ski-jump slope and blasted all the secondary jets at full.

By the time she had reached the bottom of this slope, *Rival* was airborne, definitely off air cushion, winging uncertainly over the east Texas flatlands like some misplaced condor. Its sharp nose and edges and extreme lines marked it as no submach barge, but a true eagle of the ionosphere, and it looked oddly out of place so near the ground.

The ground fell rapidly away, however, and by the time she crossed the Gulf Coast into cold winter sunshine, Ynga was ambling southeast at a leisurely 600. She concentrated on building up altitude. *Rival* had automatically throttled back on the jets that supplied lift to the flying wing, and they were now off.

A hundred miles or so south of New Orleans—half an hour from Galveston—Ynga had made 50,000 feet of altitude. She hauled *Rival* around to the south and glanced back in the side-mounted jet-view 'plates as the shock-diffusion pods were retracted from in front of the giant ramjets. They had been fully extended and the jets blocked off to reduce drag. Now, for submach speeds, they were fully retracted.

A good 600 miles per hour was more than fast enough to fire the big jets, even in air this dense. She hit the igniters and tensed involuntarily. The gale of dense, cold air howling through them had to be ionized and utilized in the split fraction of a second it was passing through.

The multiple electron beams, wrapped in concentric circles around the throats of the jets, started it. Their beams only penetrated air for a fraction of an inch—but that fraction was heated hotter than the solar surface. Air at that temperature is ionized, a plasma—and plasmas are electrical conductors. Behind the electron beams was a magnetic pinch. When a conductor enters a magnetic field, it is constrained to move, and this field was circular. The thin circle of plasma was forced inward, compressing the cold air within it to 15,000 degrees Fahrenheit. It came out of the exhaust much faster than it went in the intake, and the thrust was unidirectional; no nozzle was needed.

Rival vibrated to the fourfold kick of the big rams and Ynga relaxed; all had fired in the same quarter-second. She pulled the go-stick definitely back and headed for the high side of the atmosphere. At this level, there was no small danger that the dense air would blow out the jets. But by the time she had put another 15,000 feet beneath her, it was safe to go super.

Ynga clamped down on the throttle and grinned inside her helmet as the monster rams thundered. Pressure built up on her chest, and, flying by feel, she pulled back more on the go-stick.

Rival vibrated faintly and the thunder abruptly dropped to a murmur, almost a purr. Ynga held the stick back for a long time, topping out at 100,000 feet and 5,000 miles per hour. Very little sound was transmitted to sea level from this altitude, even at this speed and with this mass of plane. She held her speed down to a conservative level, though, until she had passed the tip of Florida.

Here she was treated to a *real* sight. Many big birds congregated here, thousand-ton aerospace planes, that took but an hour from takeoff to touchdown on an antipodal flight. They only went suborbital, and their ammonia tanks were frequently untouched on landing. But they could, with effort, put their full load in low orbit. At her speed she saw only those going her way at near her speed. She was on the Gulf leg of the equatorial flyway, and quite a few were going her way: trucks taking up raw materials to the factories in orbit.

They were slower on the start than *Rival*, however. She walked away from them, doubled her speed, added another 25,000 feet of altitude. Over the equator, she pulled back again. Climbing no faster than she had to to keep her jets firing, she racked up speed. At 15,000 miles per hour, she was unable to hold *Rival* down. The eagle had its eye set on near space. Centrifugal force alone threw her out. She fired her jets until they began to heat up from lack of working fluid; at the end they were firing at near 25,000 degrees.

The whole plane seemed to go limp when the big rams finally shut down. The Indian Ocean was just coming in sight past Africa. Ynga stretched, trying to relax. She checked a number of trouble spots, verified her course on the flight orders, reported again to flight control, settled back to wait.

It didn't take long. She was in suborbital flight, but there was no point in burning fuel near Earth. By the time she had half-circumnavigated the planet she'd be at apogee. She'd "burn" enough of the ammonia in her wing tanks to round out her orbit, wait half an orbit, and fire again to escape velocity and over. That would put her in Earth's orbit at less than orbital velocity—falling inward toward the sun. It'd take quite a while to impact on it, but she only intended to stay in that trajectory long enough to dump her load and pull out.

She'd been flying these radioisotope disposal drops for almost a year now. On the whole, she liked them, though they put her on overtime. Since they had been allowed to switch to one driver per bird, she only had to work the usual four-day week.

Being alone thus, Ynga was understandably startled when a hand reached past her to switch off the radio. She twisted around and had her eyes caught by a black hole in a very businesslike pistol.

The man behind it was in bulky space armor, not a skintight pressure suit. He grinned past a mustard-yellow mustache, his helmet transparent.

"Sit easy, Ynga femm," he said.

Motion caused her to twist in the other direction. Another man, smaller, also armed, was coolly seating himself in the copilot's chair. Mustard-mustache took the astrogator's seat on her right.

"Hot jets," he said sardonically. "Very. But we'll take it from here. You just have to follow orders and leave the worrying to us. Oke?"

She stared steely-eyed at him.

"Don't try anything funny, Lancaster," said the smaller man sourly. "We weren't born yesterday. Your husband, Bill, and the boy will answer if you do."

Ynga had to fight emotion for several seconds, was unable to speak—though not unable to note that the man was ignorant of the finer details. It suggested that he'd merely been briefed—and that there were a number of men in the gang. It was a well-laid plan—

"That's the trick, femm," said mustard-mustache, grinning confidently at her. He had rugged good looks, was too aware of it, too happy to have her at a disadvantage. Probably he even had one of those lapel pins under his sparmor: UP with Manpower.

The smaller man was the head, and the more sinister. Of course they were professionals, for hire. International business was a violent game. Though what corporation would want to steal a small aerospace truck like this was more than she could guess, or why. But she couldn't risk anything. These were pros. They'd keep their word.

"Give 'er the course, Joel," said the small man.

Joel tore her flight orders out of the holder and inserted his own. His clumsiness in his gauntlets—which he removed—and his general air of fumbling told Ynga that he was a stranger to flight decks, though he seemed to understand astrogation.

Ynga was only a truck driver herself, and knew only the basics, but as he explained the course, she understood. They proposed to fire at apogee of the present orbit, continue to fire for a quarter-orbit at low thrust, then fire hot, to escape velocity. There they'd dump the load.

That was dangerously close to Earth, though the quarter-orbit on low thrust would take them out a bit. Point was, they'd be adding to instead of subtracting from Earth's solar orbital velocity, dumping on the wrong side of the planet. The load of radioisotopes would fall outward, not inward.

How far she had no way of knowing, or where it would wind up. But, of course, it wouldn't be permitted to go far. In fact, a ship was probably already drifting along on a course that would take it near the load's orbit at the right time. That'd have to be within reach of its lead-"burning" electrorockets; they wouldn't dare go to fusion drive so near Earth. Fusion rockets had disastrous effects on the electromagnetic atmosphere, and it was illegal to use them inside Lunar orbit.

"What about—" She had to clear her throat. "My husband—?"

Joel laughed snickeringly.

The small man said, tonelessly, "A couple of the boys have him and the boy. They'll hold 'em until they hear from us, or until a certain time has passed. Don't worry."

Don't worry!

Joel asked her the ship's takeoff weight. She told him, adding numbly that she hadn't used any ammonia yet.

They sat, or floated, while *Rival* climbed silently upward as on some monstrous updraft. Ynga ignored Joel's sidelong glances and tried feverishly to think. They'd have her land the plane somewhere, and hold her until the ship had time to recover the cargo.

No doubt her trajectory would be traced when she varied from her flight plan, but the officials wouldn't think of following the load. They'd be concentrating on the plane.

They might be held quite a while. The load would have to be well away from Earth before it was approached. They might well simply kill her and Bill and Pete rather than hold them so long.

Joel hadn't put his gauntlets back on. And they were wearing armor instead of pressure suits. If she could spill cabin pressure quickly enough, bends would tie them in knots. They were breathing nitrox, by their voices. Her own pressure suit was molded of expansion fabric. Every fiber of it was a miniature balloon, open at one end. Under one atmosphere all were fully inflated, somewhat larger in diameter and quite a bit longer. As pressure dropped, they'd deflate, shrinking down to their normal size. At zero, they'd supply nearly an atmosphere of pressure. She'd scarcely feel a sudden drop—if it could be arranged.

"Does everything check out?" asked the small man with a hint of nervousness.

Ynga grinned inwardly; he'd been watching Earth shrink below them. Doubtless he'd been Out before, but it wasn't as immediate as this.

"Sure, weight's right on the nose, we're right on the curve they said," Joel told him absently, familiarizing himself with the astrogating instruments.

And with a sudden swoop of her stomach, Ynga had it.

Her hands were sweating in their gauntlets as they approached apogee. Her tension was not noticed by the hijackers; even Joel had finally given up his scrutiny of her for the majesty of space. They were approaching the night side of the planet, "twelve hours" from her takeoff point, but well off to one side. The sky immediately ahead and above them was that of midnight on Earth.

"O.K.," said Joel finally. He gave her the thrust figure again, set the bird's altitude himself—he had to have help in turning the plane, but he worked the instruments fairly well. Then he checked everything between glances at the visiplates while the small man fidgeted silently.

Joel gave her the go-signal from his own chron.

Ynga obediently hit the ammonia-tank heaters, followed through with the ramjet ignition sequence, then deliberately went around the board, hitting everything that would make a display. The board lit up like a caravan of Christmas trees. Joel and the other stared, bewildered and more than a little frightened.

She grinned a little, weakly, inside her helmet. Their expressions were much like Bill's when she tried to explain the workings of the aerospace planes that were her life, except that he usually looked bored. And he taught nuclear engineering at the General Nucleonics College.

The transmitted vibrations of the big ramjets, now rockets, hummed around them. Ynga's flying fingers touched the ammonia-tank vent-alarm cutoff, her stomach a ball of tension. Would it work *before* the alarm sounded, prevent it from sounding?

It did. She must have hit it just before it went off. She suppressed a sigh.

The red light flashed, of course, but so were plenty of others. She'd just have to keep them all flashing all the time the rockets were on.

Joel had given her a clear course through the Earthbelt, though they came closer than Ynga liked to half a dozen factory complexes. Space was crowded so near the planet, not merely with the factory and space city and amusement complex traffic, but from Luna and the asteroids as well.

Joel had taken possession of the radio switch, which he kept firmly off. It flashed angrily, adding its mite to the chaos of the board. Ynga's jaw set hard.

The sound of the rockets drowned out the hiss and thrum of escaping gas from the ammonia tanks.

The minutes ticked past like hours, but it was not long before Joel nodded and said, "O.K., up with her!"

Ynga pulled back and squeezed the throttles harder. *Rival* pulled directly away from Earth under three Gs, losing ammonia at a frightening rate. Ynga switched to space-scan radar and clidar. So far she didn't see anyone after them. But they couldn't violate all the rules, regs, laws and international agreements like this and get away with it.

Joel and his boss understood that as well as she did, and they were even more anxious to make it a quick flight. Their flight plan allowed for that. They weren't adding as much to Earth's velocity as Ynga usually subtracted on these flights. The load would drift outward slowly.

Ynga's thoughts kept straying to Bill and Pete. She couldn't stand much of that. Fiercely she concentrated on her own situation. She couldn't think of a thing that would be worth all this trouble to smuggle off Earth. Furthermore, every canister was carefully checked before it was sealed, and if it wasn't radiating, it'd look odd, to say the least. So, what radioisotopes would be valuable enough to warrant so much trouble?

Most big power plants were fusion. Small power plants, such as *Rival's* and her car's, were charged-particle nuclear-electrics. They used lightweight isotopes such as Carbon-14 and Strontium-90, subjecting them to terrific electromagnetic stress to cause them to break down at an accelerated rate. Isotopes with half-lives in the thousands of years could be burned out in a decade.

Such power plants were very cheap, because the fuel isotopes were easily made. Her cargo was supposedly of such spent fuel sticks. The only difficulty with them was that, though isotopes varied, alpha-emitters—alphagens—generally took a different excitation stress than betagens. The two couldn't be mixed in an "alphabetagen" with any degree of success. That was unfortunate, because the number of compounds that could be built could have been greatly increased. The fuel elements had to have the right electrical and mechanical properties as well as nuclear.

That left only the fissionable isotopes and gammagens.

Fissionables?

But fissionable power plants were far more expensive and far less efficient. The electromagnetic excitation used on alphagens and betagens didn't work on neutrons. The only thing they would be worth stealing for was bombs—

Burnout!

Ynga took a quick look at tank pressure and saw with a catch of her breath that they barely had fuel enough to get them back—empty. She switched off the tank heaters quickly, shut down most of the other displays. Then she hit the switches that opened the hatches. The loss of ammonia stopped when the heaters went off.

The big hatches were located between the giant dorsal fins that divided the flying wing into thirds. There was a row of smaller hatches outside these fins, but she left them shut. Radioisotope disposal was a bulk job, and her hundred tons had been made up in the big holds. When all these hatches were up, the ship had two more lines of fins running down its back. Ynga checked visually to see that all were all the way up.

Nodding absently, concentrating hard on her job to still her quaking spirit, she reached for the small rocket controls. These were designed to save bird turnaround time in space when bringing up cargo to factories. Blasting these tiny rockets caused *Rival* to move slowly, grandly "down" from under its burden. The cargo outweighed the bird itself by a large margin.

Once away from the big canisters, which began to spread slowly apart, she rotated *Rival* slowly on the gyros. "Upside down," and flying backwards, she warned them and fired the big rockets again.

She gave them ten Gs until she began to get hazy. Her captors blacked out—neither of them knew enough to have connected up the anti-G bands. The smaller man took it better; smaller people can take pounding better than big ones. One reason Ynga had made space pilot. But she was a good-sized woman, every bit as big as this small man. At a guess he could take as much as she.

He was a suspicious devil; he had a gun and a gimlet eye on her the instant her vision cleared.

When Joel awoke he turned ugly. The idea of blacking out while a woman held out didn't sit well with him. He said nothing, but he had no time to spare for the spectacle of the milk-shot blue planet swelling before them.

"Tell her where," ordered his boss.

Joel sullenly told her to put them down over the South Pacific and they'd tell her where from there. Sidelong glances told her he had his own plans after that.

Now that it was done, Ynga was weak and quivery. Her mind, hazy now, was full of Bill and Pete. Their freckles, engaging grins, and that little gap between their front teeth. Would she ever see them again?

These were professional industrial goons—spies, saboteurs, guards, or musclemen, as indicated, she thought feverishly. Industrial competition was cutthroat, but person-to-person violence tended to be avoided. Reprisals were too easy. They were out of practice. But Bill was only a professor. He wouldn't stand a chance against this kind of pro.

She remembered his earnest head bent over a nuclear physics journal so intently he never noticed the blue smoke pouring up from the defective toaster and hanging under the ceiling. He even wore old-fashioned horn-rimmed glasses. Said it got him half his promotions—made him look studious.

Studious!

Would they have him waiting there when she got down? There'd been time to get him and Pete halfway around the world—it would be after noon.

Maybe they were both dead.

Minutes filled with such reflections crawled with even greater deliberation. But at last they approached the planet. Ynga waited until the last minute to use her rockets. Then she barely had time to roll *Rival* over and set the proper altitude after she had emptied her tanks. They were coming into the air at a pretty steep angle.

It screamed around them. The impact made *Rival* ring like a bell and shy madly for space. Ynga fought the bird down, drove into the air again. A raging flame built up in front of the ikons along the leading edges. Joel and the other stared in fear and gripped their seats.

After the second impact they saw through a haze. Ynga clamped her jaw hard and bent *Rival*'s nose down steeply. Again and again the bird slammed into the upper atmosphere. Not even Joel's boss became suspicious until it was too late.

Ynga pulled back, leveled off, set the autopilot. She was gasping for breath, tasting blood, and seeing through a haze, head whirling. But she couldn't wait for her head to clear. Reaching over, she gathered up the two pistols, tucked them into the clip under her seat. The small man's helmet was ripped off first. She tapped him a couple of times above the ear to be sure, then brought his hands down and slipped the anti-G strap across between his back and his arms. His arms were free from the elbow down when the anti-G strap inflated, but caught between the arms of his chair where he couldn't switch it off—assuming he knew how.

She fixed Joel the same way. The bigger man was bleeding at the mouth. They could still kick at the control board, but she'd bet her life they wouldn't dare. The anti-G straps for the calves could have fixed that, but she didn't bother.

She also removed Joel's helmet.

By the time she had reached the South Pacific, they had recovered.

"Shut up!" she barked. Ynga was taut with desperate rage. At the very least she'd have revenge—

Joel was frothing. The other was very alert.

"I'm making the threats," she told them. "Where are my husband and son?"

Neither responded to the question.

Ynga grinned tightly and cracked the spill valves. Air fluted melodiously out through the whistles. A sound that would be recognized by anyone who watched adventure records.

They began to sweat, but the little man seemed determined to call her bluff. She grinned like a wolf. Both were singularly ignorant of aerospace flight. The air got thinner and thinner. Joel's monotonous threats grew thick.

They weren't yet gasping for breath when Ynga shut the valves.

"Tol' you," breathed the smaller man. "Jus' a bluff. Tough femm, b'not tough nuff."

"That's what I thought," said Ynga. "You'd never dare try to invade a private apartment. It was all a bluff."

She had to let out more air before they started to spill. The little man knew everything. Before he passed out he was babbling drunkenly that Bill would never see daylight again if anything went wrong. Nobody would ever find him on that seafarm. Shrewd questioning also gave her the proper code words to radio her arrival with. Some close checking of Joel's flight orders gave her the location.

She gave them more air and turned on course, ignoring the radio.

Ynga was quivering with exhaustion and tension and soaked with sweat, but she held herself in taut control. She couldn't depend on the authorities to get Bill and Pete out alive. On the other hand, the gang would be expecting her to come flying tamely in any time. She teetered indecisively between alternatives.

Finally she decided to go in. At least they'd be together.

When her captives awakened again they were grimly silent. Joel glared at her with real hatred now. She ignored that contemptuously. Approaching the seafarm at high altitude, she warned them: "You haven't seen the all nor the worst I can do while I've got you inside this bird. Try anything and you won't live to regret it—even if *Rival* is sitting flat on the water. Believe me."

They did.

That bluff should hold them until they were down—and they couldn't fly the bird anyway. She looked the farm over as she spiraled in, giving the code words. No comment at her voice; she'd expected to have to force Joel to give the words.

Chewing her lip, Ynga spiraled in, still high, still supersonic. She had the guns but she'd have to leave *Rival* and go hobbling in to use them—alone and under their observation. Couldn't be done. But if she pulled out and ran now, it'd be wet curtains for Bill and Pete—

She bumped up the magnification on the forward visiplates. They had a telescopic circuit to simplify docking in space. Searching the ground, desperately looking for a way out, she coaxed the big high-speed bird in.

"Come right in beside the dome—that wing can land on water, can't it?" asked ground impatiently.

"Check," she said automatically, putting *Rival* into a steep dive preparatory to leveling out on hover and skimming in to the clear water beside the watch domes.

Then she caught her breath.

A seafarm is essentially a series of tanks full of plankton. The mile-square tanks were merely thin plastic sheets supported at the upper edges by floats. The water in them was brought up by solar-powered pumps from as much as half a mile down. At that depth, beyond the reach of the sunlight, there are no plants to fix organic compounds, and the water is so rich with them they precipitate out. This rich water, brought up to sunlight and fed to plants, not only supplied a third of the world with food, but also supplied a third of the world's organic raw materials.

The process lended itself well to automation. The pumps were automatic, the plants grew naturally, fish rarely got into them—and in most cases would promptly have died if they had—and even harvesting was automatic. Pumps picked up the water, centrifuged out the plankton, and sent it along for pressing and drying. Men need only come by at intervals to collect it.

This farm did no processing. Thus, no permanent buildings were needed, only a few domes for the watchmen, who also made on-the-spot repairs. Permanent buildings would have been floating, submerged jobs. But since worldwide weather-conditioning eliminated hurricanes, nothing was needed for the watchmen but inflated domes floating on pontoons.

"Forgive me, Bill—Pete," she whispered as the big bird came in, and squeezed the throttles.

For a half-second she feared the big rams would falter. The howling gale of dense wet air pouring through them at this altitude was already causing them to run hot. The electromagnetic fields weren't able to keep the plasma away from the throats. Now she dived into thicker air, still at supersonic speeds.

But all jets are overdesigned. They held, running hotter and hotter—but they held. *Rival* was making better than 1900 miles per hour as she pulled out over the domes. In the climb, the jets finally faltered. The pyrometers tripped, the safety switches were thrown, and the plane quivered as its driving force vanished. *Rival* seemed half-dead, as sluggish as she felt, as Ynga whipped it into a turn on the turbojets, nose down again.

It was a slow turn. Out of it and making for the domes again, her teeth clamped on her lip at the havoc the single pass had raised.

The domes were down. Unidentifiable bits and pieces were scattered here and there. The body of a man was floating face down in the clear water beside the floats of the domes, apparently having been knocked off the company boat at the dock. It couldn't be Bill; Bill would never wear tartan plaid pants in "incandescent" red and green.

Ynga put *Rival* down hard and fast, her head snapping, the arms of the men, caught behind them, straining. Ramming the nose against the dock, she scrabbled up the guns, unhooked herself, started out.

Remembering the men, she hesitated, torn. After a moment, hefting a pistol, she stepped reluctantly back. Her face reflected her strain. The shock, on top of all the day's mental and physical shocks, was too much for the half-tough Joel. To Ynga's grim and everlasting delight, the mustard-mustached muscleman fainted.

She contented herself with tapping the head of his boss. He lapsed into unconsciousness readily. Then she was out and running across the dock.

The South Pacific sun hit her though the helmet, the glare arrowing into her eyes. Water lapped, flashed; white floats glared; even the sunpower screens reflected light apologetically into her face. The heat of the tropics smote through her sweat-soaked pressure suit. The salt sweat irritated the raw spots under it. After a few moments she slowed to a rapid, stumbling walk.

It took seconds of clawing at the collapsed fabric to find the door to the first dome. The plastic was set for translucence; it was light inside. She lifted it with her helmet. Three men lay sprawled unconscious, bleeding at the ears and noses, around an overturned card table. One breathed stertorously. Beyond, in another room, were two other men in bed. The plastic was dark here—the night shift. Fumbling past, she found the galley. Opposite it was an empty room with a chair and a big visiplate. The 'plate was overturned but still playing a Western record.

In the floor was an opened trapdoor.

Ynga caught her breath, almost plunged through it headfirst, trying to look. "Bill!" she called.

"Ynga! For God's sake! Do they have you? What happened?"

She could make out the sprawled body of a man—a body beyond doubt; his head was doubled under him. Fallen through the hatch, doubtless.

It was twenty feet down. After several moments of mental confusion, she placed it as a sub dock. A small sub was used to check the bottoms of the tanks for leaks or fish damage. The dock was for emergencies and doubled as a decompression chamber. Small subs are unwieldy on the surface.

"Bill! You all right? Wh-where's Pete? Bill!"

"O.K., here I am." She saw him looking up. No need to tie him up down there; there was no way out but this. "What do you mean, Pete? He's in school. Home, now," he added, looking at his chron.

"Th-they said they had you b-both. Oh, Bill! C-come on up."

"Let down the ladder. What happened up there? It sounded like a cannon down through this manhole."

Ladder, ladder. She peered under the plastic. "I—I don't see—"

"Built-in, automatic. Look at the edge of the hatch."

Ynga looked, saw a button with an L, hit it. The ladder spewed out of a mouth just under the hatch. A link ladder, with wide flat rungs but uprights of jointed links the size of matchsticks. It retracted to allow room to lower equipment down the shaft.

Bill came up quickly, stared, his height lifting the collapsed dome off her head.

Ynga explained quickly, leading him out, leaning on him for support. Twenty feet under water, he'd merely been almost deafened by the shock. Some of the gang were stirring as they clawed their way back out from under the light plastic. She gave Bill one of the guns.

He took it casually, almost absently. Behind his heavy, horn-rimmed glasses he wore an air of almost childish wonder with a dash of disdain for his erstwhile captors. He did not seem troubled even when they saw the small man glaring at them from *Rival*'s cabin door.

"It lacks a lot of being a competent gang," he said, ignoring her gasp. "Fanatics would be likely to hire third-raters to do their dirty work." The small man's head disappeared before she thought to raise her gun. Bill still seemed unmoved.

Rival had floated some thirty feet away from the dock.

After a moment they heard the whine of the turbines. "He must've been watching everything I did, studying the board," moaned Ynga. Bill pushed his glasses back on his rather blunt nose, shrugged clumsy hulking shoulders in the mannerism that made him seem so ineffectual and—studious.

The rudders on the giant dorsal fins swung hard over. The jets on one side sounded louder than the others. "Going to try to fry us with the jets—the damn fool," muttered Bill.

After a moment Ynga saw what he meant. A hundred-ton aerospace transport can't be handled like an airboat, much less like a rowboat. It obediently swung to the right, but came surging forward much faster. Bill backed away, hesitated. *Rival*'s swinging prow did not quite touch the floating dock—a great hawk moth brooding on its sins, ignoring the water creaming under its beak. She saw that it would make the turn and started to drag Bill away from the jet exhaust.

But he was off and running before she could speak. She saw his glasses bounce absurdly on his flat nose. He took off in an impossibly long leap—through the still-open door of the bird just as it began to recede from the dock.

Ynga's scream mingled with the sound of the jets.

He hit the deck in a sprawl, rolled completely over, losing his glasses. Then he was gone in the dimly lit interior.

Ynga hobbled frantically along the dock after the receding nose of the plane. She dipped one toe in the water, hesitated, not remembering—if she knew—whether her pressure suit would buoy her up, or drag her down. The gap was much too great to leap now, even unhampered.

"Bill!" she screamed.

Then the jets died.

"Bill!"

"O.K., what do I do now?" he asked her, appearing in the doorway.

In the sudden silence, her sob was as loud as a shout.

"The little guy?" she asked fearfully.

"Dead," he said, shrugging. "Brace up! It's been a rough day, and you've had the worst of it, but it'll soon be over. Just tell me how to get this bird back to the dock."

It took her a moment to catch her breath. "S-set everything on dead center," she said.

He frowned uncertainly.

"The go-stick." She could see the rudders. Below the plane, retracted on ground—she hadn't bothered—were their smaller counterparts. They had to be turned to dead center. The rudders hadn't enough bite in air to steer at low speeds like this, but those down in the water did.

With some fumbling, he managed to square them. "Now what?" he asked. She told him where to find the compressor turbine controls and how to turn them to start position. Hesitantly, he fired up some of the turbojets. The multiple scream pushed the plane forward slowly, slowly. It bumped the dock as she was hobbling down toward it.

Bill gave her a hand in.

He looked out at the deflated domes. Ynga followed his glance. Most of the living men seemed to be conscious. Motion was visible under the plastic. Three men sprawled across the domes' floats, holding their heads. No doubt they were all deaf—some permanently.

"No point in trying to hold them," said Bill. "They can be traced easily enough from the dead. And they're wounded.

Besides, they don't know who hired them. We'll call the authorities and let them handle it. Better call someone right away or you'll lose your license."

The little man was quite dead, with a broken neck. Joel was wide-eyed and sweating, conscious but still strapped in. They ignored him. Ynga took the pilot's seat, felt relief flow upward through her from it. Here she was in her own element.

The radio was blinking angrily.

She turned to the flight-control wavelengths and cut into a babel of voices, most of them angry. Some appeared to be patrolmen. Her explanation wasn't easy to make. She tried to be concise, but the incredulous interruptions slowed her. Some parts of it she held back; these wavelengths weren't secure, and flight control might talk to the press.

It was ten minutes before she got flight instructions, and they were promptly countermanded by a sharp voice which told them to sit tight. Minutes later a fast little courier screamed in—blue and green. UN Treaty Forces. They patrolled international water, air and space under the terms of the various treaties among the Blocs.

Their commander was a Japanese lieutenant with an almost British air. Joel and his boss were removed, with their guns, and their stories recorded. Ynga told them everything she had done.

"It leaves just one question," mused the patrolman, packing away his equipment. "Who's behind it all? One of the big corporations?"

"No," said Bill calmly. "The Lunar Separatists. They're the only group around that would be crazy enough to use nuclear bombs. I had plenty of time to think," he explained to Ynga. He gave the same reasons she had used in concluding that the cargo they had put in pickup orbit had to be either fissionables or breeder isotopes.

"Wait a minute," said the patrolman, eyes narrowing. "That's not under our jurisdiction, but we know pretty much where every gram of that kind of stuff is. None of the Armed Powers would let much of that stuff get away. And you need ten kilograms just for one crude bomb."

"Not anymore," Bill assured him. "I'm a research nucleonic engineer. It's not generally known, but the alphabetagen excitation problem's been cracked. You have to mix small percentages of fissionables into the fuel sticks, though. And the result isn't a nice, gentle, controlled rate of breakdown. Instead, virtually every unstable atom in the stick lets go at once."

"*Whew!*" whistled the lieutenant. "An alphabetagen bomb! So they had a few kilos of breeder isotopes, thorium or U-238, in one of the canisters. That'd give 'em enough fissionables for several hundred smallish bombs for sabotage." He grinned at Ynga. "They'll hate you, pilot!"

They were not held long after that. They were ordered back to Galveston, where further questioning would await them. Ynga was relieved by a report from flight control; a call to their apartment revealed that Pete was too engrossed in homework to come to the phone.

Bill seemed to hold his breath while *Rival* climbed skyward. When the big rams were off and the plane in suborbital above the atmosphere, she demanded, "Now you tell me how you managed to break that professional muscleman's neck—professor!"

"The company's physical fitness program—remember?" he asked. "Calisthenics, court sports, boxing, wrestling—and karate, savate, and whatever else we require to keep us interested."

"And you never told me! I worried myself almost sick. Just like a man!"

Bill laughed, looking up at the star-spangled blackness above. "They will hate you, too, Ynga," he said, at a tangent. "Having to sit and watch their swag float by just out of reach—they'll have plenty of time to brood on the wiles of women. They won't dare use their fusion rockets—not after everybody's been alerted."

She shrugged, as he had before, at the obvious. "Boiling off ammonia to reduce the plane's mass was obvious," she said. "Of course that puts the canisters in a faster orbit—one farther out. I'm only a truck driver, and a Terrapin at that, but that much astrogation anybody knows. It might even be a solar escape orbit."

He laughed again. "So smugly and calmly floating past, ignoring them—just out of reach. Just like a woman!"

"Serves 'em darn well right," she muttered vindictively, looking up at the sky. "Try to skyjack my truck, will they?"

HERMES TO THE AGES

BY FREDERICK D. GOTTFRIED

"What you're suggesting, Professor, is absurd."

"How can you say that, Dr. Tereskevitch, after what your cosmonauts found on the moon?"

The Russian glowered at Professor Lars Hansen. At least it seemed that way to the professor's young associate, Eleanor Mercer. Tereskevitch was commander of *Gagaringrad*, the first permanent Soviet space station. She suspected that he wasn't used to having his work challenged in his domain. Certainly not by Americans.

"Your reputation preceded your flight up. You Americans have a rather unflattering term—cracked pot or crashed pot or something similar. I'm never quite sure with your imprecise English."

Now he was being deliberately rude. Lars, however, merely shrugged.

"Still your government did agree to let this particular crackpot look at your find."

"Why do you keep insisting that anything was brought back other than some unusual rocks?"

"Can I ask the crew members themselves? They're still all up here in isolation—along with whatever it was they dug up."

The look Tereskevitch shot Lars Hansen was as withering as some Ellie used to receive when she had the temerity to ask questions in her freshman classes—from nearly every professor but Lars.

The Russian turnabout was as baffling as it had been unexpected. Everything was supposed to have been arranged. But instead of being welcomed upon their arrival, Lars and Ellie were treated as intruders.

That seemed to confirm the suspicion that *Gagaringrad* was more military than scientific. But another reason the Soviets were reluctant to permit outsiders aboard their station soon suggested itself. *Gagaringrad*, for all its technical innovations, proved crude in many respects. True, they could stand normally thanks to centrifugal force, but they were surrounded by nuts-and-bolts boilerplate. And all the considerable Soviet accomplishment in Earth orbit could not wipe out the fact that they had been beaten to the moon by some twenty years.

"I didn't consent to your coming," growled Tereskevitch. "Why anyone down there thought we needed an *American* paleontologist is more than I can understand."

"Perhaps because my theory finds more credence among your people than my own," said Lars. "*Your* colleagues sent for us, Doctor. They want it confirmed—especially considering the alternative."

Good for you, Lars, thought Ellie.

Tereskevitch pursed his lips. "You would have it that our lunar expedition found a *body* on the moon?"

"Uh-huh. At least, that's what their transmissions indicated—until you clamped down security."

"And you further insist that this—this creature, or whatever you call it, is millions of years old?"

"I'm only guessing, but I have good reasons for believing so."

"Sheer fantasy! Millions of years! Do you seriously think, Professor, there'd be even a trace of such a thing after so much time?"

"In the vacuum of space, yes—with all the body fluids evaporated, shielded from radiation, no decay, nothing to disturb its rest."

"But you'd have us believe that this creature is not extraterrestrial? That it's some sort of man?"

"No. Not if it dates back some 65 million years. This marks the transition from the Mesozoic to the Cenozoic era in Earth's geological history. In other words, from the age of reptiles to the age of mammals."

"Professor Hansen, if I understand you correctly—"

"You do. Although the creature your cosmonauts found on the moon may be humanoid in appearance, it is definitely not related to *Homo sapiens*. It's not even mammalian. It is an intelligent *dinosaur*."

Frowning, Tereskevitch turned to the two military men accompanying him and spoke rapidly in Russian. Both their visitors knew that this was not mere translation, particularly when one man obviously disagreed with what Tereskevitch was saying to him.

That was encouraging. Unanimous opinion usually meant rejection. They were used to that, along with a lot of forced politeness. Lars Hansen's scientific credentials were too impressive for rudeness—at least to his face. Besides, Lars was a huge bear of a man who filled the cramped quarters Tereskevitch had picked for their meeting. His patience for lesser mortals was quite incongruous to his commanding presence.

Ellie Mercer, by contrast, had neither his bearing nor patience. She was short and stout—a decided advantage for field work but not in most social situations—and she had little tolerance for fools.

"All this is merely academic," said Tereskevitch to his guests, "since intelligent dinosaurs are a scientific impossibility."

"About as impossible," Ellie put in, "as what you found on the moon?"

Instantly, she was sorry. She'd promised herself to stay out of the discussions. Not to get riled up this time or lash back at their critics. But the smugness of the man was just too much.

Glancing apologetically at Lars, she was surprised how tickled he was by what she'd said.

Tereskevitch decidedly was not. "I regret I wasn't informed in advance of your coming. My people mentioned only your shuttle flight. They should stick to their own business and let me do mine."

Lars grinned sheepishly. "Well, since we *are* here . . ."

"But you come at a most inopportune time, Professor. We're in the midst of some, ah, delicate matters which require my immediate attention. So I'm afraid you're going to have to go back. At once."

"Dr. Tereskevitch—" Lars protested, rising to his full height—and promptly bumped his head against the upper bulkhead.

"Professor," said Tereskevitch. "Are you hurt?" There was genuine concern.

"No, no. It's nothing. *Nothing.* But surely you can't be serious? Leave now? When we just got here?"

The same Soviet official who disagreed with Tereskevitch before also objected. When Tereskevitch grew adamant, the other man became more insistant—and his Russian had the ring of authority to it.

"Well, Professor," said Tereskevitch, smiling without humor, "it seems that some of us would like to hear more about your, ah, rather amazing hypothesis—assuming that it won't take too long."

Visibly relieved, Lars said, "Perhaps if we had an opportunity to examine—"

"There's nothing for you to examine," declared Tereskevitch, "unless I say there is. Now, if you'll please proceed. My time here is extremely limited. Oh, and Professor, do try to restrain your enthusiasm. We'd like to keep these walls intact awhile longer."

Ellie bristled, but Lars didn't mind a bit. She knew that the only thing important to him was his—their—theory. All he had to do was present it and there would be immediate access to the *specimen*.

Ellie said nothing. But she thought she knew better.

For such occasions, Lars had two set speeches. The first, for the scientific community, was impressive in its technical detail. The second, for lay audiences, stressed the more sensational. As much as he professed distaste for such "pandering," it was this latter presentation that Lars found himself delivering far more often.

Ellie had no doubt which one he would give to their Russian hosts.

"Despite his name 'terrible lizard,' the dinosaur comprises a distinct branch of the reptilian family, unrelated to present-day lizards. It was during the 150-million-odd years of the Mesozoic that the dinosaur arose, flourished and then—very mysteriously—died out. Although other forms of reptiles then living—notably crocodiles and turtles—survive down to our own times, no member of the dinosaur branch lived beyond the end of the Mesozoic, approximately 65 million years ago.

"There simply is no adequate explanation for this mass extinction. Every theory so far proposed has its defects. But the most glaring is the assumption that the cause could only have been *natural*."

At this, even the seemingly disinterested Tereskevitch perked up.

"If you accept the fact that mammals have been the dominant life form on Earth for something less than 65 million years and evolved man in such a relatively short period, why couldn't a similar intelligent creature have emerged during the dinosaur age—a period at least twice as long?"

"A romantic notion," Tereskevitch interrupted, "except that the reptiles are lower on the evolutionary scale."

"Mammals are not so much a higher form of life," Lars replied, "as one more suitably adapted to an environment of rigorous temperature variations. Evolution, Doctor, is hardly a straight-line progression. During the Permian age more than 250 million years ago—a period of climatic extremes comparable to our own—a line of mammallike reptiles evolved with fatty layers under their skin and possibly even fur to keep themselves warm. Their line declined when the climate of the Mesozoic that followed warmed to one more compatible to conventional reptiles.

"And what splendid creatures evolved in the warm and even temperatures of the Mesozoic! The rich variety of specialization of the dinosaur rivals those of present-day mammals!"

Ellie knew what effort it took for the exuberant professor not to wave his arms wildly about in the narrow confines the way he did in class.

"Yes, yes, yes," growled Tereskevitch impatiently. "But still just brutes, for all of that. Nothing comparable to man."

Lars smiled. "Let me tell you something about revered *Homo sapiens*. He did not become what he is today by virtue of his brain alone. No, he required four additional physical attributes: walking upright to free the forelimbs for uses other than locomotion, hands that could grasp and hold tools, depth perception to utilize those tools, and a voicebox for speech and communication. Now this may surprise you, but in all evolution there's only one other class of creatures besides primates that possesses similar characteristics—the saurischian carnivorous dinosaur.

"Take one example I'm sure you're familiar with—the fearsome *Tyrannosaurus rex*. He walked upright. Had shortened forelimbs, very similar to the human arm, used to grasp and hold prey. His eye sockets were set more forward in his skull than to the side, giving him binocular vision. Of course, we don't know his internal physiology, since all we possess are fossilized skeletons. But he could have had some structure capable of emitting distinctive sounds. It needn't have been like our vocal cords. The modern parrot imitates the human voice quite neatly using the syrinx near the juncture of the trachea leading into its lungs."

"Professor, you have a knack for skipping over the most important points," said Tereskevitch. "You should have been a politician. But I would still like to know about the brain. If I remember rightly, all the dinosaurs were like the one with a brain no bigger than a walnut—the one with the plates on its back and the spiked tail. I forget its name—"

"*Stegosaurus*," supplied Lars. "Yes, I agreed with you that there were many dinosaurs like that. But we're not talking about the plant-eaters—the sheep and cattle of their day. We must look instead to the carnivores—and not the hulking monsters like *Tyrannosaurus* that didn't need intelligence to survive. But dinosaurs, like mammals, came in all sizes. It's the smaller, more agile ones that prove the most promising."

"Such as what?"

"Such as *Deinonychus*, with a nervous system so sophisticated that it had the coordination to stand on one leg while attacking its prey with the other. And *Dromaeosaurus*, with its greatly enlarged braincase. And *Stenonychosaurus*, which had a large brain, binocular vision, and opposable fingers. The fossil record supports the existence of these. There are more recent finds"—Lars glanced knowingly at Ellie—"which are still being bitterly disputed.

"Don't forget that man developed from the smaller, more intelligent primates. Just as we are not descended from the bison, Dr. Tereskevitch, don't look to *Stegosaurus* and his ilk for proof that intelligence could not have existed contemporaneously."

"What proof do you offer that it did?" asked the Russian.

Ellie caught Lars' questioning glance. She shook her head. Not yet. Tereskevitch still doubted too much.

"It, uh, would be very surprising if I had any at all," Lars hedged. "Paleontology depends on fossils. On land, the process which creates them is extremely rare. So rare, in fact, that out of the millions of individual members of some species, we possess only a couple of complete skeletons. Less than one-hundredth of the total species that lived in past eons—that's all we estimate that we know of."

Ellie's judgment was borne out by Tereskevitch's obvious incredulity.

"An example," said Lars, "out of my field, perhaps, but true nonetheless. All we know about certain types of ancient man comes from what, four or five specimens? That's because the number of individuals living at one time was always small. And the time span involved—only one to two million years compared to the tens of millions for most species of dinosaur—if there's any evolutionary parallel, the creature your cosmonauts found may not have existed long enough to leave a permanent geological record!"

"Interesting, your example of prehistoric man," said Tereskevitch, "only there's just one problem: today man numbers in the billions. Our presence at this stage would hardly go unnoticed by any curious future anthropologists."

"Maybe our intelligent dinosaurs were never very numerous. Remember how comparatively small human population was until recent centuries."

"What about their civilization itself? Their buildings, artifacts?"

"Gone. Vanished. All traces obliterated."

"That, I cannot accept."

"There are modern parallels. A hundred years ago, what did we know of Sumeria outside the Bible? Troy itself was just a legend. The Maya of Mexico—we knew nothing of abandoned cities *miles* long."

"But once discovered," said Tereskevitch, "there was a wealth of archeological finds."

"And much more that had been destroyed forever by the natural processes of nature. Doctor, we're not talking about hundreds or thousands of years. Nor just a million. Can you conceive of the result of *tens* of millions of years of erosion, decay, seas flooding dry land, mountains thrust up and worn down, the very continents torn apart and reshaped?"

"Surely something would remain," Tereskevitch said. "Tools of some kind—even if only like those found with primitive man?"

"Tools are barely distinguishable from the rocks in which they're found. It takes a trained eye to recognize them for what they are—something extremely unlikely if one has no reason to be looking for them."

There was a definite change in Tereskevitch. No longer was he openly skeptical. He was carefully considering everything Lars said.

"Even if I concede the possibility of such creatures—not to mention their entire civilization—escaping detection, one thing would not: their effect on the environment. Any civilization capable of putting one of its members on the moon—as you suggest—would require extensive use of coal or petroleum. Obviously, our present supplies have not been depleted by anyone other than ourselves."

Ellie might have pointed out that the era they were discussing was the source for today's oil. Coal, however, was formed in the Carboniferous, long before, so the point was probably well-taken.

But Lars didn't bother. "Why assume," he asked instead, "that they relied on fossil fuels, the way we've so foolishly done?"

"Now we're in *my* expertise, and I tell you that fire is essential to technology. Without it, man would still be living in caves."

"Ah, but what drove man into those caves in the first place? The Ice Age. Whatever else, fire became essential for survival against the cold. But there were no ice ages in the Mesozoic. With a warm and uniform climate, there wouldn't have been the overriding need for intelligent creatures to become dependent—fixated actually—upon fire."

"Maybe not in the primitive stages. But how could they possibly develop industry without fire to forge their metals?" Tereskevitch countered.

"I don't know," Lars admitted. "A substitute for the metals we know? A different source of power? You tell me. That's your field. Only I can't help wondering if you're letting your expertise blind you to different possibilities. Who says the way *we* did it is the only way? Cities, metals—all those things you find so essential—they've been around for only the last 5,000 years. Man became the master of Earth long before the rise of modern civilization. And there are cultures today—the Australian aborigines, for one—said to have societies more complex than our own, all without the trappings of so-called modern man. Could *that* be the model for our intelligent dinosaurs—rather than your country or mine?"

"Perhaps," said the Russian, "if we were talking about a body found in Australia. Maybe you can enlighten me, sir, on how an aborigine—without metals or other technological innovations—made it to the moon?"

"You mean, how could we do it the way we did it?"

"How else?"

"How else, indeed? Wouldn't it be wonderful to search for the answer here on Earth—rather than in some far-off and unknown solar system?"

Tereskevitch obviously agreed. "All this is very intriguing. A pity you have no evidence to support your theory."

"I never said that."

"What?"

"I've only tried to give you an idea how difficult it would be to find such evidence. Shall I go on, Doctor?"

Before Tereskevitch could say anything, a loudspeaker blared out his name.

The Russian words were indecipherable, but there was no mistaking the urgent tone.

"Excuse, please, Professor," Tereskevitch said quietly. "A brief moment. We'll be back as soon as possible."

As soon as the three had shut the hatch they passed through, Lars cried out happily, "By God, we've got them hooked, Ellie!"

Ellie wasn't so sure. Interested, yes. But so far it had all been one-sided. They'd listened to what Lars told them but promised nothing in return.

Poor Lars. So trusting. Never could understand that people could be mean or jealous because that's the way they are. Or that envy could be just as important in the rejection of their theory as honest skepticism.

"You ought to be the one to tell them about *Herman*," said Lars.

"Oh, no, Lars. I—I shouldn't say anything more. I almost blew it for us before."

"Not really. You've got to understand Tereskevitch. He'd have reacted the same no matter what either of us said. I was warned about him: part of the team that orbited Gagarin. Worked as hard as anyone to beat us to the moon. Really believed they would have if the politicians and bureaucrats had stayed out of it. Still thinks they should have. But he's a scientist. A damned good one. That's the side of him we've got to interest."

Lars grinned wickedly. "Besides, if you hadn't asked him that, I would have."

Still Ellie hesitated.

"After all, you discovered him," Lars pointed out. "And I can't help feeling I've monopolized the conversation long enough."

Ellie recalled every detail on the sun-baked plains of western Australia five years before. That, the skeptics could never take from her—the magical moment of discovery.

She had been a mere undergraduate, chosen by her favorite professor to accompany his fossil-hunting expedition during summer vacation (winter, fortunately, in the searing climes of the outback). What she lacked in confidence, she more than made up for in hard work. That was what originally brought her to Lars' attention and what qualified her for the expedition. It was also what led to her discovery.

It had been Ellie who put in the extra few minutes digging at dusk that uncovered the precious bones.

The new find had been unclassified. Its skeleton lay in a fetal position, with the shortened forelegs drawn up to the skull. Compared to the typical dinosaur death pose of head arched back due to postmortem tightening of the neck ligaments, this posture appeared extremely manlike.

Good-naturedly, Lars—then still "Professor Hansen"—suggested designating the new creature *Homosaurus mercer*.

Ellie preferred her own nickname for it: "Herman."

The more important discovery came the next morning. Ellie had awakened before dawn, long before any of the others, to be with *her* find. She had come a long way from a nondescript small town and the misery of being an unpopular and overweight girl in high school, who, to make matters worse, was smarter than any of her teachers. Now none of that mattered. How could anything human beings concerned themselves with compare to the 65 million years Herman had lain undisturbed?

As first light crept over the eastern hills, Ellie knelt in awe and pride before the partially exposed bones. Almost the entire left side of the specimen lay uncovered. As she watched, the shadows lifted in the morning sunlight from its small tail bones, then from the larger bones of the hips.

Frowning, Ellie looked more closely at one of the lower vertebrae. She bent over, whisking her tiny brush across the fossilized bone.

With a yelp, she leaped to her feet.

"Professor Hansen, Professor Hansen!"

Frantically, she raced back to camp.

Only the professor could confirm the impossible.

The Russians were all apologies when they returned. Perhaps Lars' intuition was correct. Ellie sensed renewed impatience, but it would have been much more difficult for them to be rude to her.

Any resentment she felt vanished as she described what it had been that so astonished the expedition, changing the course of Lars' and her lives. "The long rays of the morning sun made it stand out," she concluded. "An enormous swelling in the lower vertebrae. Even I—the greenest of all—could tell that the tiny lump that lodged there was not a bone fragment or anything similar. Most of it had broken off, but there was no mistaking what was still imbedded—the tip of a *spear* or *arrow*."

Ellie paused. Usually at this point came the denunciations.

She was especially sensitive about this since she had been alone for some period of time with the specimen and the implication was clear. One so-called expert even went so far as to accuse her of fabricating the point and sticking it into Herman herself.

Instead, Tereskevitch thoughtfully chewed his lip. "What sort of collaborative evidence did you find?"

"None," she had to say, "at least not at this site."

"But once the notion took hold that there might have been intelligent creatures predating man," said Lars, "we began to accumulate from all over the world items no one has been able to explain. This, for instance."

From his pocket, Lars removed a vial containing what appeared to be a piece of blackened eggshell. "This dinosaur egg came from Mongolia. Your people were quite helpful in supplying information about it. Apparently, this sat on the shelf unrecognized for years. Certainly, we in the West had no idea of its existence. Look at the markings on the outer surface."

One by one each of the Soviet officials viewed the object carefully.

"You are looking at what may be the egg of one of *their* young."

Tereskevitch looked up sharply from his examination.

Lars said, "Our theoretical creatures, being reptilian, probably laid eggs rather than bearing their young alive. This is no reason to believe they didn't lavish the same care and affection upon their children as we do. And I quite imagine that they would look upon an unprotected fetus carried for months in the womb with equal astonishment, if not outright disgust."

"These markings," Tereskevitch muttered, "could be natural."

"One straight line in nature," said Lars, "maybe even two could be explained. But six—interwoven to fit what could be a geometric pattern? If these eggs remained for any extended period unhatched, intelligent creatures might wish to designate and distinguish them. Perhaps what we're looking at represents the future child's name."

"You do have a tendency to humanize them, Professor. Forgive me if I say that I find this quite—quite disconcerting. Did you find any specimens of these creatures that had, ah, hatched?"

"No. And this leads to the most startling discovery of all."

Before Lars could go on, the third military man—the one who had not protested earlier when Tereskevitch wanted to end the discussion—whispered something to Tereskevitch. Irritated, Tereskevitch looked at his watch, then shook his head no.

"Forgive the interruption, Professor. Please continue."

"Generally reptile eggs are porous, permitting transfer of air from outside while retaining sufficient resilience to protect the developing individual inside. Detailed examination of the microstructure shows this particular eggshell lacks such properties. Whatever was inside could not have survived."

"So? A piece from a single egg?"

"Not just one egg," Ellie said. "Every single egg your people claim was found with this one was similarly affected."

"And all date from the same period," Lars added. "The late Cretaceous, the last period in the Mesozoic—the very end of the age of dinosaurs."

Tereskevitch frowned. "What are you trying to say?"

"There are certain things that could do this," Lars said. "Disease, for one. Some sort of chemical poison. Or radioactivity. Short, but intense. Such as in a major war."

"You—how do you say it?—jump to conclusions. Very unscientific, Professor."

"They had the ability to use weapons. That's the significance of Ellie's find. And we come back to the initial question: what single catastrophic event could have wiped out an entire line of creatures such as the dinosaurs? Do we ignore a possibility all too real in our own times?"

"Still you have no proof that these hypothetical creatures of yours possessed anywhere near a technology capable of such a thing."

"That's what I thought too," said Lars, "until your discovery on the moon. If the creature brought back turns out to be one of them, that would be such proof."

"How could you show any connection whatsoever?"

"If the skull has certain openings behind the eyes characteristic of the dinosaur branch of reptiles, we would know for sure."

Again the third Soviet officer touched Tereskevitch on the shoulder. This time Tereskevitch nodded his head.

The officer who had supported them before did nothing.

"What then, Professor?"

"We could tell the world."

"Why should we do that?" Tereskevitch's voice hardened.

"The knowledge it would bring—"

"There's no need to tell anyone at this time. *If* things were as you say, it could wait until confirmed by *our own* scientists."

Never had Ellie seen such dismay on Lars' face. "But this discovery belongs to all humanity."

"Assuming there was such a find," said Tereskevitch, "it

would still be within the province of *Soviet* scientists to release it. Don't you agree?"

Ellie knew it. It always amounted to the same thing. What made Lars think it would have been any different with Tereskevitch?

"I see," said Lars, the defeat so heavy in his voice that Ellie wanted to cry in anger. "But—how soon will you make the announcement? That much at least you'll tell us?"

"It has not been decided," said Tereskevitch, "when, *if at all*."

"What do you mean," exclaimed Lars, " 'if at all'?"

"I mean just that. How can there be an announcement if there is nothing to announce?"

"How can you say that? What have we been discussing all this time?"

"Your theory, Professor. And we've found it quite instructive. However, this interview now must end."

"Wait," Lars pleaded. "Let me prove it to you. Just a quick examination—"

"Examination of what? No body was found on the moon. If you must know, our cosmonauts did find some strange rocks. But, unfortunately, when they were brought on board and exposed to the air, *they crumbled into dust and are no more*."

The Soviet scientist smiled patronizingly. "So you may go back to Earth, secure in the knowledge that there's nothing for you—or any western scientist—to examine."

The shuttle orbiter backed off from *Gagaringrad*. Lars and Ellie sat in the two rear couches on the flight deck, still dressed in the pressure suits, minus helmets, required for the short EVA to and from the space station. It was much easier just to keep them on the short time it would take to return to Earth—particularly considering the effort it took to get the bulky professor into his in the first place.

They stared dejectedly at the slowly rotating dumbbell that seemed to shrink in the blackness as distance increased between them.

"I feel so—so used," said Ellie angrily. "We gave them everything. And then to tell us that they—they destroyed *him*—"

"Don't believe that for a moment," muttered Lars. "Someone else, maybe. Mistakes happen. Specimens get damaged or destroyed. But not Tereskevitch. He's too careful for that. No, he's got *Herman II* over there. Safe. But he intends to suppress any knowledge of his existence. That's what's so appalling."

It would be several minutes before they attained the point in orbit for firing their reentry rockets. Captain Bradley, command pilot of the orbiter, turned from his controls and asked, " 'Herman II,' sir?"

Despite everything, Lars had to smile. "Just our name for the Russian find. 'Herman I' was the fossil in Australia—the one Ellie thinks was killed in some form of intertribal warfare."

"Oh, I know you think he was just some animal being hunted," she retorted. "A more primitive stage in their evolution. But why couldn't the intelligent ones have retained their tails? They didn't have to be *exactly* like exalted *Homo sapiens*."

Ellie thought she detected the familiar twinkle in Lars' eye. Often he'd bring up points like this, delighting in drawing out the not-so-scientific basis for her insistence. He wanted her to learn to laugh more at things that bothered her. Was he doing that now—for both of them?

"Mind telling me one thing?" Bradley asked. "Just exactly what was it you think killed off the dinosaurs?"

Ellie cringed. That part of their theory Lars wished had never been raised. Sensationalism at its worse. Probably more than anything else the cause of most of the ridicule they'd received. She'd have ignored the question, told the captain to just go back to his controls, get them back to Earth as fast as possible.

But then, when could Lars *ever* give up an opportunity to lecture?

"Had to be a biological war," Lars told Bradley.

"You seem so positive," Bradley said.

Bradley was everything Ellie expected a shuttle pilot to be: stalwart, self-assured, moderately intelligent. He could have been her high school quarterback. She hadn't cared much for him either.

"Process of elimination," said Lars, "*if* you assume intelligent beings had anything to do with it at all. Nuclear weapons? No, they'd have destroyed indiscriminately all forms of life. Yet we find a continuity among the plants and animals other than dinosaurs. Chemical agents? Possibly. Except that the devastation was planetwide, affecting reptilian life in the seas as well as on land. The effect must have been multigenerational. This implies the ability to reproduce. So we come down to some type of living agent—a highly selective but worldwide plague."

"You make them sound a lot like us," Bradley said.

"I suppose so. A natural tendency for people who look upon the past as alive. You ought to see the pets Ellie's made of some of our specimens."

"Lots better," said Ellie, "than some of the things alive today."

"There is one way I hope they were like us," Lars said. "I keep wondering what we'd do if we'd survived the initial outbreak. Try to leave some sort of record—something to warn of the tragedy that befell us for whatever the future might bring. And someday we'll come across that—whatever their Rosetta Stone might be."

Bradley shook his head. "You've got me again, Professor."

Patiently, Lars explained, "In 1799 a piece of black basalt was found near the mouth of the Nile which bore inscriptions in an ancient Greek and Egyptian. Before its discovery, no one could interpret the hieroglyphics of ancient Egypt. The Rosetta Stone became literally the key to unlocking the secrets of a hitherto unknown world."

"And you think your intelligent dinosaurs left one of those?"

"I thought we had its equivalent over there." Lars gestured toward *Gagaringrad*, and Ellie saw the sigh—a small gesture that someone who did not know him well would have missed. "Well, whatever comes of that, Ellie and I will spend the rest of our lives looking for other traces that must be somewhere. Right, Ellie?"

So Lars had reconciled himself to the loss. And probably lost none of his faith in human nature. Ellie knew what he'd say about the way the Russians treated them: "They had their reasons"—as if that was enough. Damn it, why did he always have to be so generous? Hadn't he ever been kicked in the teeth? Big as he was, did he always have to be so far removed from ordinary human cussedness?

Difficult as it was, Ellie managed a fleeting smile.

"You know," Bradley went on in his obtuse fashion, "what you suggest sounds inefficient as hell. I mean, you'd think your dinosaurs would've tried something better than stone inscriptions to pass on their secrets."

"Well, I didn't mean that literally," Lars said.

"Yeah. Sure'd been interesting if they had some of the techniques NASA's been experimenting with."

"Such as?"

"Oh, things to cut down long-duration flight. Takes centuries to go even to the nearest stars with what we've got now. They're working with test animals. Freezing them. Dehydrating them. Trying to find some practical form of *suspended animation*."

"Aii—yeeeeeeeee!" Ellie's shriek cut through the cabin.

Lars was a half-step behind her. "The lifeless, eternal moon! No need to worry about the world changing about you! A landscape that's been the same for billions of years and would be for billions more!"

"Until intelligent life reestablishes itself on Earth," cried Ellie, "and finally develops the capability to get back to the moon and—and—and finds what's been left up there for them to find!"

"Oh, how close you were in naming him 'Herman'! Herman— *Hermes*—Hermes, the messenger of the gods!"

"What—what's got into you two?" said Bradley.

"Don't you see, man?" Lars said. "*That's* why they wouldn't let us see him. Not that they didn't find anything. Or destroyed what they found. No, they found more than they realized. All that activity, the impatience to be rid of us. They found out he's alive. And they didn't want any Americans around while they *revived* him!"

"The bastards!" Ellie exploded. "Leading us on like that! Laughing behind our backs! All the time knowing—"

"Wait, Ellie. The one thing we didn't have a chance to tell them—our theory about the plague. What if the specimen's *still* contagious?"

Lars told Bradley: "Contact the station! Immediately!"

"Professor, you can't be serious. A plague? Why, the thing over there's what, a reptile? You don't get disease from animals."

"Oh, you don't? Ever heard of anthrax, Captain? Bovine or poultry tuberculosis? Salmonella, that you catch from turtles? Or maybe you've forgotten that the carriers of the bubonic plague that wiped out a third of Europe were rats?"

"You've made your point," said Bradley. "But surely they've taken precautions. Decontamination procedures of some kind?"

"You mean like we did after the Apolo splashdowns?" said Ellie. "Scrubbing the capsule down by hand while it bobbed up and down in the middle of the most fertile natural medium in the whole damned world!"

"Captain, we don't know what the hell they're doing over there," Lars said. "Would you please just send a message?"

"All right," said the haggard shuttle commander.

Orbiter and space station continued in their joint orbit hundreds of meters apart. But the radio from *Gagaringrad* remained silent.

"They refuse to even acknowledge my signal," said Bradley.

"They must be going ahead with their experiment," Lars said.

"It is rather inhospitable," said Bradley grimly. "They can't know it's not an emergency over here."

"We can't wait any longer," Lars said. "Anybody got any ideas?"

Ellie did: "Ram them!"

"What!" Bradley protested.

"Well, that'd sure slow down whatever they're doing," she said.

"Captain, somebody's got to get on board before they have a chance to get into it. What about taking this ship close enough to let me try to sneak inside without being seen?"

"Professor, you're both talking crazy. Much as I wouldn't mind ramming this ship down those bastards' throats, that's obviously out of the question. In fact, *any* EVA's much too dangerous."

"We did it before," Lars said.

"Sure. On a line, with me guiding you at this end and a big smiling Russian on their side. Don't think there'll be too many of them smiling now."

Ellie watched Lars stare at the station so tantalizingly close. He was calculating the risks, and she thought she'd better start doing the same thing. One way or another, Lars was going across.

"Hell, let the Russians kill themselves," said Bradley, "if that's what they insist on doing."

"Don't you see the real danger?" Lars said. "Suppose the disease organism can't be controlled? We don't know how it's spread or whether it can be isolated to *Gagaringrad*—especially if the Russians refuse to believe us about the cause. And if they somehow manage to spread it to Earth . . ."

"Damn, you make sense even when you don't make sense," Bradley said. "Only *I'll* be the one to make the EVA. My copilot can take the ship in close. It'll be a bit tricky for one man, but I think—"

"But I'm already dressed for it," said Lars. "Besides, what would you tell the Russians once you got over? At least I can make a convincing case. You still only half believe it yourself."

"And you're the last person who should go, Professor. You don't know how to handle yourself in weightless space."

"Captain, as a paleontologist, I've climbed some places in my field work you wouldn't believe possible."

"It's a different ball game out here. You haven't the training. You'll just end up getting yourself killed."

"I have to go."

"We'll both go," Ellie declared.

Lars started to protest.

"Oh, don't be so impossibly noble," she told him. "You couldn't possibly make it by yourself—even with the fate of all mankind riding on those big broad shoulders."

That settled the matter.

Quickly Bradley helped Lars and Ellie put their helmets back on, and handed them safety lines. He gave what instructions he could, ending with an impassioned, "Most important of all, don't lose your heads. Especially you, Professor."

The two novices entered the tiny airlock to the rear of the flight deck. Lars managed to float down to the outer door without difficulty. But when Bradley fired the ship's main engines for a short burst, he banged against Ellie's space-suited figure.

Ellie knew this was insanity. Even if they did get across, why should the Russians listen to them? Didn't Lars learn anything about Tereskevitch before?

Still, they had to do something. And maybe this time they would gain access to the specimen.

They heard Bradley's voice through their suit radios: "Mayday! Mayday! This is Shuttle *Constitution*. We have a misfiring rocket."

"*Constitution*," came an alarmed Russian voice, "you are on a collision course. Turn or reverse power."

"Negative," said Bradley. "No other system functioning. Wait, I have powered down the malfunctioning engine."

Awkwardly with her gloved hands, Ellie had followed the instructions of Bradley in fashioning a wide noose in her safety line. It hung stiffly in the weightless space just beyond the open hatch. The idea was to somehow catch it on some projection from the space station.

Ellie was a lousy swimmer, but she could float in water indefinitely. She'd already decided that they would never make it across if she tried to "swim." But if she let the safety line do the work while she simply drifted with the motion of her body, there was a chance.

The hardest thing would be to ignore what was happening to Lars.

"Stand by," said Bradley to Lars and Ellie only. "I'm going to kill all forward velocity."

Gagaringrad's spin in space to provide artificial gravity was slow. Bradley had aimed toward the almost stable central hub to minimize the possibility of collision. "Get ready," he radioed, and Lars and Ellie braced themselves as best they could against the seal of the opened hatch.

The station's dull-gray hull filled the blackness ahead. Concentrating on the row of external hatches with their various extensions, Ellie grasped the line tightly. She couldn't throw it. She had to transfer to it the motion she would gain by kicking free from the orbiter, keep its loop wide, get close enough to the station to trail it across the hull.

She didn't want to think about the possibility that the Soviets' inhospitality included locked doors. Extremely unlikely, considering the intended use of the hatches, but still . . .

Through their suit radio, Ellie heard Lars mutter hopefully, "Maybe the near-miss itself will be enough."

Oh, Christ, Lars, she said in silent exasperation. *Do you want to go back now?*

No, she felt him crowding close to the hatchway. Come what may, he was going.

All right. Only please, if you don't do anything else, just stay out of my way until I can get us across.

The entire fabric of the orbiter shuddered as all forward reaction control engines ignited.

The deceptive gentleness of their approach must have deceived Lars. Unprepared, he found himself propelled out the open hatch by his own immense inertia.

Ellie couldn't stop him without being thrown out herself.

Ignoring his tumbling figure, Ellie kicked out as hard as she dared directly toward the slowly turning space station. So far so good. She remembered everything Bradley'd told her about keeping herself in line with her center of gravity. The noose was still wide, extended ahead of her toward the hull of *Gagaringrad.*

Damn, it was exhausting moving within her spacesuit! She began to puff. At least she was in good shape from her field work. And she didn't have to fight the direction she was coasting.

Keep floating, Ellie! she told herself. *Don't swim.*

Abruptly, her own motion stopped.

Even as she oriented herself, the snagged line brought her down to *Gagaringrad's* hull. And since her kicking had given her greater exit velocity, she had passed Lars on the way over. His slowly turning spacesuit, with its tangle of arms and legs, was coming her way.

Even the rotation of *Gagaringrad* was cooperating, bringing her toward him rather than away.

Ellie was not about to tempt luck any further. Before kicking off again, she resecured her line around the nearest support she could find.

As it was, she almost missed Lars as he drifted past in his desperate efforts to stop his tumbling, huffing and wheezing from the effort.

Her gloved hand just barely caught a thrashing foot and tugged.

"Lars, you big oaf, *relax*! Stop fighting me! You're too blasted strong! I'll pull us in. Just don't do anything!"

Like a caught fish, Lars let Ellie reel them both toward the hatch to which she had attached her line.

Within moments they were safely inside. Lars placed one gigantic gloved hand on Ellie's shoulder and, with a quick squeeze, said all that had to be said between them.

"Where now?" Ellie asked as they both caught their breath.

"Good question. Their labs must be located in the end opposite from where we met before. But damned if I can tell one from the other."

"Lars!"

Sounds of people approaching emanated from the central hub, which, because of the slight pull of centrifugal force at their present location, was "above" them.

"They just made up our minds," said Lars. " 'Down' we go."

The two Americans pushed themselves along a ladder, passing through a series of compartments with hatches that sealed each from the other. The farther down the passageway they traveled, the greater became their apparent weight, until they had to use the rungs of the ladder.

"Are we going the right way?" Ellie wondered.

"Fifty-fifty. But we haven't met anyone this way yet. Figures they wouldn't allow many people nearby when they started their experiment. They like to keep secrets, even from themselves."

The bottom compartment was much wider than those above. They had arrived at one of the two large personnel spheres located at each end of *Gagaringrad.*

Waiting for them were Tereskevitch and the same two as before.

"So, Professor Hansen, I suppose I should ask what the meaning of all this is."

The Russian scientist had his anger somewhat under control. The same could not be said for his two scowling comrades.

Ellie was first to remove her helmet. "You've got to stop what you're doing."

"Indeed? And just what, Miss Mercer, do you think that is?"

"You're going to revive Herm—the specimen. You can't do that."

"You *are* mad. I was just saying it before. But this. Do you have any idea the damage you almost caused this station? Or the repercussions?"

Finally Lars got his helmet off. "Doctor, please listen to us."

"They want to have you shot," said Tereskevitch. "They're quite serious. Fortunately—for you—we don't have an armory up here."

"Dr. Tereskevitch," Lars snapped, "while we stand here bickering, you may be destroying yourselves—and maybe the entire human race!"

"Huh?"

"You wouldn't listen to all our theory. How the dinosaurs destroyed themselves. We believe that the type of war they waged was biological. If the individual you found was placed in suspended animation after that conflict, every part of him— every organ, every cell—must have been preserved intact. *And every living thing that might have been inside his body.*"

Tereskevitch's jaw dropped.

Ellie reacted to the horror in Tereskevitch's face. "Oh, my God, Lars! We're too late!"

"No, no," stammered Tereskevitch. "Not yet. Maybe—"

He moved toward a sealed chamber. "Wait!" Lars said. "if that's where you've got him, you can't go in there now."

Resigned, the Russian turned back. "No, of course not. I wouldn't have anyway. The chamber's not supposed to be opened at all during the course of the experiment. My own orders . . ."

"When did it start?" Lars asked.

"We—activated the pumps only a few moments before we got the call about your ship. Now it's into the moisture cycle." Tereskevitch smiled ruefully. "You should've been more prompt, Professor."

Lars sighed. "The damage's already done. You'd better radio Earth and advise what's happened."

Tereskevitch hesitated. "I'd prefer, ah, not to have to contact anyone down there just yet. The creature's isolated in the vacuum chamber. Surely, there's no danger."

"We can't be sure. If it's the actual biological agent, we have to presume—if only from what it did before—that it's extremely virulent and easily spread. Perhaps even through the seal of that door."

"I'd still prefer to wait. Professor, please try to understand. The decision to proceed was—not unanimous."

"Further delay may be too late. What if we're unable to get word out because we've *already* been infected?"

Tereskevitch turned to his companions and again spoke in Russian.

"Tell them every second we delay may be crucial," Lars urged.

"How can we believe *you*?" spoke up the third officer, the one most opposed to their previous visit. "This is all some sort of capitalist plot to destroy us and our station. Just as your unauthorized boarding was in clear violation of our sovereignty and—"

Tereskevitch cringed at the man's words.

Lars did better. He voiced what must have been his Soviet counterpart's thoughts: "Oh, don't be an ideological ass! Anything happens up here, you think your leaders'll let any American spacecraft near? It'll be *your* cosmonauts transmitting the disease down to *your* country first."

Tereskevitch resumed arguing in Russian. The other man waivered, then rushed to the ladder and speedily clambered upward.

"He's going to the communications center," said Tereskevitch.

"But will he send the message?" said Lars.

"Dr. Tereskevitch," Ellie asked, "how did you discover that the specimen was actually alive?"

Grateful for the diversion, Tereskevitch said, "When our cosmonauts brought the body on board their craft, I sent specific instructions to keep it exposed to the vacuum. I was afraid of deterioration. Once they got it back here, we stored it in this vacuum chamber. Conducted all preliminary tests in the chamber. We placed tissue samples in a sealed air tank. Nothing happened. It was only a few days ago—we were interested in the dehydration—we added water. To our utter astonishment, the tissue not only absorbed the fluid but retained it, and—incredibly—began to *use* it. It gave all the appearance of cellular division, growth."

"But what precautions did you take during all this?" Lars insisted.

"Professor—we are not peasants sticking our boots in manure to hear them squish. Whatever you Americans think of our scientific methods, we took what we considered appropriate precautions. We were concerned about contamination. From us, of course, not from it. But it amounts to the same thing.

Everything was handled by remote instrumentation, the way we do radioactive materials. So even if you hadn't come thundering onto the scene like your beloved cavalry, there probably would've been no direct exposure anyway."

"Probably?"

"All right. Maybe we'd have sent someone inside eventually. Only not without proper testing first. I don't work that way, Professor. Nobody—and I mean not one person aboard this station, whatever his authority"—Tereskevitch glanced significantly at the man who earlier argued to hear Lars and Ellie out—"would dare enter that chamber without my direct permission and supervision. I don't care what's going on inside. And up to this point, nothing of note has."

"So far as you know. Since you commenced the tests on the tissue sample, has anyone returned to Earth?"

"No, Professor. I can assure you of that. In fact, your ship was the first to leave *Gagaringrad* since then."

"Which means *we* could have been the ones to spread the contagion!"

There was nothing Tereskevitch could say to that.

Instead, he took refuge in his explanation. "When we removed the water and air, the tissue sample stopped its activities. But it didn't die. Exposed to the vacuum, the only appreciable effect was to allow the fluid to exit without apparent damage to the cellular structure. So, becoming dormant, it resumed growing when again placed in air and water.

"Obviously, this was a process totally unknown to our science. The implications were staggering. After much deliberation up here—ground control knew as little as you did, Professor—we determined that there really was only one course for us to follow: place the entire creature in an environment that offered the best chance to revive it."

"Of course," added Lars, "you had no intention of sharing this experiment with anyone from the United States. Hence the secrecy, even from your own people."

The degree of bitterness shocked Ellie. How often had she tried to get Lars to see people as they truly were? Now she realized what a real loss that would be.

Tereskevitch sensed it too. "I could say that events dictated what we've done. We had no way of knowing what effect removing the body from its resting place would have. The fact that the experiment had to be conducted up here in a true vacuum. Time working against us . . ."

"But that wouldn't be the whole story, would it, Dr. Tereskevitch?"

"Why should we have shared this discovery with you?" Tereskevitch became increasingly defensive. "Would you Americans have been any more generous in our place? Besides—twenty years ago you had your chance on the moon. Now it's our turn."

Ellie couldn't stand this any longer. Besides, there was something much more important going on.

"Dr. Tereskevitch," she said, "is there some way to observe what's taking place inside the chamber?"

"We have television cameras inside. Over here's a monitor. I haven't yet been able to switch it on. Your untimely arrival—"

"Do so, man!" Lars cried, all resentment vanishing immediately.

The television screen waivered as Tereskevitch focused on a shape lying on a padded table. Then the camera dollied inward. Ellie's intake of breath was the only sound as Soviets and Americans crowded in front of the monitor.

At first it was difficult to observe. Clouds of steam filled the chamber, wreathed about the figure like the mists it may once have walked among 65 million years before on Earth.

It had wide saurischian hips, thick legs, and a full dinosaur tail—a victory for Ellie's position earlier—but the arms and shoulders were proportioned like those of a man. The one hand in view, though oversized, had no claws and one of the three fingers opposed the others. More they could not tell because of the wrinkled, dried-out appearance of the body. Yet as they watched, the contours began to fill out, the wrinkles slowly disappear, the body take on weight and color, changing from dead ash to living flesh.

"It seems to be rejuvinating itself from the moist air alone," said Lars.

"You see," Tereskevitch said to his companion, "your worries were all for nothing." To Lars and Ellie: "We're basing this procedure on numerous tests with the tissue samples. The air inside is saturated with as much humidity as possible. The body cells are refilling with water at a greatly accelerated, but not dangerous, rate. Total immersion in water would have been too much. Caused the cells to burst."

"Is it possible to focus for a close-up view?" Ellie requested.

"I'm not sure that we'll see with all that steam, but . . ." The Soviet scientist complied, and the upper body filled the screen. Most saurian characteristics were muted. The snout was greatly foreshortened, the mouth shrunk to less than twice the width of a human's. The large oval eyes—actually the eyesockets, the most prominent reptilian characteristic retained—were set close together in the center of the face, the enlarged cranium above promising a brain the equal to man's—if not greater.

"Despite everything, so much like us," Lars marveled. "He resembles his reptilian forebears as little as we do the ape."

"I wonder if he really is male," said Ellie.

When the Russians glanced at her, she declared, "Well, it's a logical question. Reptiles don't have external genitalia, male or female. And it certainly wouldn't have breasts. It's not mammalian, after all."

Tereskevitch became embarrassed.

Stifling a laugh, Lars said, "For now, he's officially—if tentatively—male. Don't want to complicate things too much."

"Dr. Tereskevitch!" the other Russian exclaimed.

Slowly the creature began to clench his fists.

"He seems to be stretching," said Lars. "Like awakening from a long sleep. Doctor, do you have an intercom into the chamber?"

"Of course. Stupid. How could I forget?"

Quickly Tereskevitch flicked a switch.

From inside the chamber came sounds of movement. The creature stirred, tried to rise, fell back. *Almost painfully*, thought Ellie.

Now, a kind of chirping. There was nothing else in the chamber that could be causing it. It had to be coming from the creature.

"Speech?" said Lars. "Listen how strained it sounds."

The creature stopped moving. But the same sound kept being repeated, growing louder, more insistent.

Lars turned to Ellie. The two paleontologists realized the same thing: "Something's wrong with him!"

"Not necessarily," said Tereskevitch. "We'll keep watching."

"No, dammit!" snapped Lars. "Look at him."

The face in the monitor. Tereskevitch hadn't worked with fossils, never reconstructed what they must have looked like. He couldn't see the agony that Lars and Ellie did.

"It must be water, Lars," said Ellie. "He's not getting enough from the air."

"There is some in the chamber?" Lars asked Tereskevitch.

"Of course. I'll get it to him."

Tereskevitch grasped two handles below the monitor. On the

screen, two mechanical arms appeared. One moved toward the creature on the table, a clear beaker clutched in its metal claw.

Both the creature's eyes snapped open. He saw the approaching arm through the clouds of steam, drew back feebly.

"He doesn't understand," Lars said.

"No, that can't be," said Tereskevitch. "He's intelligent. He's got to know we're only trying to help."

"But he doesn't," Lars said. "Maybe there's nothing in his experience anything like what you're putting him through."

Now the creature raised a three-fingered hand toward the beaker.

"There, you see," Tereskevitch started to say.

"No. Don't." Ellie cried.

He wasn't trying to reach for the container. He was trying to push it away.

Swearing, Tereskevitch grasped with both hands the left handle, trying to regain control of the mechanical arm and pull it back.

"We can't help him *this way*," said Lars.

It was the way he said it. Ellie turned toward him hoping she was wrong.

"Lars, you're not thinking of going inside there with him?"

"Somebody has to."

"But the disease—"

"That's why it has to be only one of us. The rest of you clear out. Seal off the entire area."

Tereskevitch protested, "I can't let you do that."

"Precautions be damned. You started this. Now that he's revived, we've got to do whatever we can to save him."

"I didn't mean that. *You*, Professor. I can't let you kill yourself."

Lars ignored him. "Ellie, use your suit radio to contact Bradley. Tell him what's happened. Have him relay it back to Earth."

"I can't just leave you," she said helplessly.

"You must. That message has got to get through. We don't know if their man sent anything. You're the only person I can trust to do it and make them understand. Now please go. *All of you!*"

Tereskevitch's associate slipped behind Ellie to the ladder. She couldn't make herself leave. All she could do was stare at big, clumsy generous Lars, who wouldn't even be there if it hadn't been for her.

Suddenly she was running to him, throwing her arms about him, the tears streaming down her cheeks.

Without any idea whether she made it to the ladder by herself or with Lars' help, Ellie began the long climb upwards. All she knew was that Lars was right. The message had to get out. Otherwise, she'd still be there with him.

Passing through the ceiling hatch, she saw that the first Russian had already reached the next compartment. How many more after that? Ten? Twelve?

As the hatch beneath slammed shut and locked, Ellie suddenly realized that Tereskevitch had not come up with either of them.

He was still down by the chamber with Lars.

Descending from the ladder, Tereskevtich asked, "Why are you doing this?"

Lars had been studying the complicated pump handle to the chamber door. "Get the hell out of here!" he said, without looking up.

"Not without knowing why you're so set on becoming a martyr," said Tereskevitch. "If you think your death will give your country some sort of claim to our find—? But no, it's not that with you, is it?"

"The door," said Lars, "how do I get it open the quickest way?"

"Personal glory then? Your name attached to what happens today? Your own life vindication for everything you've stood for?"

Lars straightened to his full height. Between the two men was the monitor, with the creature's tormented face a visage even Tereskevitch could now understand.

"Isn't that reason enough?"

Tereskevitch glanced at the monitor, then slowly nodded.

"And you," said Lars. "Why are you still here?"

"Because," said Tereskevitch, "it takes *two* people to get that damned door open in time."

Lars looked at him. "Who in blazes designed such a monstrosity?"

Tereskevitch shrugged. "A time and efficiency study committee. Who else?"

Lars began to laugh. Heartily, uproariously. And Tereskevitch, after only a moment's hesitation, joined in.

Both men were still laughing as they worked together to open the chamber door.

* * *

"There really wasn't any danger after all."

Lars and Ellie were relaxing in the small cabin assigned to them in their first moments alone after Lars' release from the chamber. The statement he'd just made was one of the few things he could say with any degree of certainty.

"But we were right about it being some sort of disease," said Ellie.

"Yes, even though the exact type of pathogen still hasn't been determined. But at least we have an idea how it worked. It didn't kill or cripple. Just attacked the sex cells, making it impossible for his species to reproduce."

"As well as any other species," added Ellie.

"Of dinosaur. That limitation's important. Not merely for the clue it provided us. But as an added safeguard. Whether it would affect mammals—particularly man—is an open question. One we'll never have to find out. Thank God."

"Can we really be sure?"

"Based on what we've learned, yes. We know that it thrived only on *living* gametes and that it had no dormant cycle. Once it completed its horrid work, there was nothing further to sustain it. So when our guest entered suspended animation, any residue in his body *had* to be dead."

Ellie could tell by the offhand manner he spoke that Lars was trying to minimize what he'd done. But she knew better. "You couldn't have known that *before* entering that chamber."

"No. But we should've guessed it. After all, precautions surely would have been taken to insure that the disease didn't spread any more after he was found and revived."

"Maybe," said Ellie, thinking of all those other species that vanished—the ones without intelligence.

"Anyway, the Soviet doctors went to great pains to make sure that there wasn't anything in our bloodstreams not easily identifiable before releasing Serge and me. *Our* pains, that is." Lars grinned, again making light of what took place for Ellie's benefit.

So now it's 'Serge,' thought Ellie. She'd come to doubt that Dr. Tereskevitch had a first name.

Despite the present atmosphere of camaraderie, she still didn't trust their Soviet hosts. All the Americans, Bradley and his copilot included, were temporarily quarantined aboard *Gagaringrad*. Ellie had insisted upon staying with Lars. Quite a few Russian eyebrows had been raised at this.

"With all their testing," said Ellie, "I just hope they don't forget one thing: *You* were the one who saved his life. Don't deny it, Lars. Dr. Tereskevitch never would have gone in there if it hadn't been for you. You know that's true."

"Oh, I'm not so sure about that," Lars disputed. "Serge's pretty hardheaded. But he did the right thing when it counted. And I think he'd have done it whether I was there or not. You ought to get to know him, Ellie. I think you two would get along just fine."

"Ugh! I'd rather spend my time with—Herman. I guess we can call him that—now that we know he's definitely male—until we find out his real name."

"That won't be for some time. Between the shock of revival and all he tried to do, he'll probably be sleeping for days. He tried to tell us so much. Tried to get across so much more we couldn't grasp."

"I still can't believe that you actually *talked* with him!"

"Don't credit us with that. It was entirely his doing. Learned enough of our language from the few words we were using to start conversing after just half an hour!" Lars shook his head in renewed amazement.

Lars had already related to Ellie how they managed to communicate. The "trilling" had originated from lower in the throat than the human voicebox. Lars' earlier analogy to the parrot's syrinx had been close. But the range of sounds produced surpassed even a human's. And they were spoken at a much faster rate.

It was the being who recognized this and adjusted his own speech patterns to the comparative slowness of the lower-pitched words spoken by Lars and Tereskevitch.

"W-a-a-a-ter-r-r-r," he had uttered, exaggerating the syllables with an underlying "hissing"—precisely the type of sound one would have associated with a reptile.

From this, he picked up human speech rapidly, never forgetting a word once he'd spoken it. Within minutes, he had acquired a sufficiently large vocabulary to assure his rescuers that they had nothing to fear from him.

"I suppose we shouldn't have been too surprised," said Lars to Ellie. "There are people with photographic memories. Math geniuses. Why shouldn't *he* have turned out to be some sort of language genius? After all, what would've been the purpose of sending a messenger if he couldn't communicate!"

He grinned wickedly. "Of course, Serge couldn't help being a bit miffed. We were speaking English, in deference to me, and *that's* the language he picked up on. I don't think he learned a single word of Russian the whole time!"

Ellie burst out laughing. She hadn't realized how much she needed to. And she didn't give a damn if it was picked up by any of the microphones she was certain the Russians had stashed about the cabin.

"Actually, I doubt if Serge cared all that much. He was really interested in one thing. Couldn't wait until there were enough words learned to ask him how he got to the moon. Herman—oh, that doesn't fit him, Ellie; *Hermes* is much more appropriate— Hermes couldn't answer at that point. Guess I'd have trouble too, if I'd only been speaking English for an hour!"

Ellie envied him—both of them—for those precious moments at the very beginning—when a new day for science had dawned and dark clouds not yet settled.

"The only way we could continue," Lars said, "was by explaining to him how we got there ourselves. Help him build up his vocabulary. Yet we couldn't get beyond the basics of rocketry. He kept on interrupting. Couldn't seem to understand why we'd ignored the greatest power source available—our own planet!"

"What could he have meant by that?"

"Serge's the engineer. He figures some sort of antigravity drive. Only Hermes didn't have the capability to supply a lot of detail. We're reasonably certain it wasn't done through any instrumentation we're familiar with. Throughout the discussion, he kept pointing to his head."

"Sounds like he just willed himself to go to the moon."

"No. That's not it either. Obviously, they needed protection from the vacuum of space, same as us. And they did use spacecraft of some type, although apparently quite different from what we have. It seems that their minds formed a vital component."

"Oh, Dr. Tereskevitch must have loved *that*."

"Actually, Serge was quite impressed. Don't forget, the Soviets have done much more in the fields of psychic energy, Kirlian photography, ESP, than we have. If there's a way, mentally, to tap the energy fields of Earth, you can be sure they wouldn't reject it out of hand. Not the way most Western scientists rejected our theory."

Lars hesitated. Obviously, there was a great need in him to go on. But also great reluctance. Usually Ellie would have resented such protectiveness. Now she wasn't so sure.

"You can see the difficulties we were getting into already.

The English language, Ellie, is such a marvelous tool. With just 150 words, you can make yourself understood in most common situations. Trouble is the intricacies after that point. What I've told you so far—however sketchy—at least there's little doubt what he was trying to get across. But the rest of it—well, you've got to bear in mind the handicap Hermes was working under, not being familiar with the wide variety of meanings that attach to words. And maybe a lot of it's merely Serge's or my interpretation. I don't know. In a way, I almost hope . . ."

Ellie understood. "The reason they destroyed themselves?"

Lars nodded. "Some of it makes sense. Much of it doesn't. The way they went about it: if you *are* going to eliminate someone, can you think of a more *benevolent* way of doing it? No death or destruction. Just stop all their births.

"But the destruction of other life forms—the *universality* of the tragedy—they couldn't have deliberately intended that. Not from what I've learned about them from Hermes."

Oh, sure, thought Ellie. *A little miscalculation. Happens all the time. Sorry.*

"Maybe that was the most horrifying thing of all to them," said Lars. "His people really were closely attuned to the natural processes of their world at one time. That comes out of almost everything he says. But gradually that changed. They turned away from what had previously sustained them. Began modifying their environment. Became more mechanical."

"In other words," said Ellie, "their civilization became more like ours?"

"I suppose so—although I wouldn't quite characterize it like that."

Ellie wasn't surprised. "And that, naturally enough, led to the war?"

"No. Not a war. At least, not the way we think of one. Something happened. Whether a single catastrophic event or a whole series of them, we're not sure. We know that the net result was so terrible that Hermes won't speak of it other than to acknowledge that it did occur. That led to the decision on their part. He wouldn't—perhaps couldn't—say who made it or how it was arrived at. But this much we do know: What they did was to commit *deliberate racial suicide*."

Ellie shuddered at his words.

"It would help if I could believe I misunderstood him," said Lars. "How can anyone come to the conclusion—as they apparently did—that all intelligence is an aberration? Maybe you can make sense out of that, Ellie. I can't," he said helplessly.

Ellie studied the cold metal walls about them. Very little made sense now. More questions than answers. Each new discovery more terrible in its implications. The dark clouds in this new day of science had indeed descended.

She knew that Lars had to find some way to reconcile this. He'd devote the rest of his life—in any event—helping and studying this being whose life he'd saved. But for Lars this—this anomaly could not stand.

For Ellie there was a much more vital concern.

"Why did Hermes survive? A messenger from their time? I can't believe that, Lars. Why would people who destroyed all intelligence—and almost their entire world as well—*care* about the future?"

"Maybe he was sent to guide us," suggested Lars. "Insure that we don't make the same mistakes they did."

Ellie expected Lars to say something like that. Why should he think the worse of anyone—or anything?

"What if it's more than that?" she said.

"What else could it be?"

"To *judge* us."

Lars looked at her. He had been closest to their Hermes. Closer probably than Tereskevitch. Ellie knew what was going through his mind. Why had he failed to detect that? Because of what he truly observed? Or because of the type of person he was?

"What do we do then, Lars? We don't know the full extent of the power he has. What he's capable of. He could destroy *us*, just like—"

"The answer's simple, Ellie. We'll just have to convince him that we are worthy. And maybe we've already made a big step in that direction, Serge and me."

The smile on Lars Hansen's face made Ellie almost forget her fears.

Almost.

PUSHBUTTON WAR

BY JOSEPH P. MARTINO

The hatch swung open, admitting a blast of arctic air and a man clad in a heavy, fur-lined parka. He quickly closed the hatch and turned to the man in the pilot's couch.

"O.K., Harry. I'll take over now. Anything to report?"

"The heading gyro in the autopilot is still drifting. Did you write it up for Maintenance?"

"Yeah. They said that to replace it they'd have to put the ship in the hangar, and it's full now with ships going through periodic inspection. I guess we'll have to wait. They can't just give us another ship, either. With the hangar full, we must be pretty close to the absolute minimum for ships on the line and ready to fly."

"O.K. Let me check out with the tower, and she'll be all yours." He thumbed the intercom button and spoke into the mike: "RI 276 to tower. Major Lightfoot going off watch."

When the tower acknowledged, he began to disconnect himself from the ship. With smooth, experienced motions, he disconnected the mike cable, oxygen hose, air pressure hose, cooling air hose, electrical heating cable, and dehumidifier hose which connected his flying suit to the ship. He donned the parka and gloves his relief had worn, and stepped through the hatch onto the gantry crane elevator. Even through the heavy parka, the cold air had a bite to it. As the elevator descended, he glanced to the south, knowing as he did so that there would be nothing to see. The sun had set on November 17th, and was not due up for three more weeks. At noon, there would be a faint glow on the southern horizon, as the sun gave a reminder of its existence, but now, at four in the morning, there was

63

nothing. As he stepped off the elevator, the ground crew prepared to roll the gantry crane away from the ship. He opened the door of the waiting personnel carrier and swung aboard. The inevitable cry of "close the door" greeted him as he entered. He brushed the parka hood back from his head, and sank into the first empty seat. The heater struggled valiantly with the arctic cold to keep the interior of the personnel carrier at a tolerable temperature, but it never seemed able to do much with the floor. He propped his feet on the footrest of the seat ahead of him, spoke to the other occupant of the seat.

"Hi, Mike."

"Hi, Harry. Say, what's your watch schedule now?"

"I've got four hours off, back on for four, then sixteen off. Why?"

"Well, a few of us are getting up a friendly little game before we go back on watch. I thought you might want to join us."

"Well, I—"

"Come on, now. What's your excuse this time for not playing cards?"

"To start with, I'm scheduled for a half hour in the simulator and another half hour in the procedural trainer. Then if I finish the exam in my corrrespondence course, I can get it on this week's mail plane. If I don't get it in the mail now, I'll have to wait until next week."

"All right, I'll let you off this time. How's the course coming?"

"This is the final exam. If I pass, I'll have only forty-two more credits to go before I have my degree in Animal Husbandry."

"What on earth do you want with a degree like that?"

"I keep telling you. When I retire, I'm going back to Oklahoma and raise horses. If I got into all the card games you try to organize, I'd retire with neither the knowledge to run a horse ranch, nor the money to start one."

"But why raise horses? Cabbages, I can see. Tomatoes, yes. But why horses?"

"Partly because there's always a market for them, so I'll have a fair amount of business to keep me eating regularly. But mostly because I like horses. I practically grew up in the saddle. By the time I was old enough to do much riding, Dad had his own ranch, and I helped earn my keep by working for him. Under those circumstances, I just naturally learned to like horses."

"Guess I never thought of it like that. I was a city boy

myself. The only horses I ever saw were the ones the cops rode. I didn't get much chance to become familiar with the beasts."

"Well, you don't know what you missed. It's just impossible to describe what it's like to use a high-spirited and well-trained horse in your daily work. The horse almost gets to sense what you want him to do next. You don't have to direct his every move. Just a word or two, and a touch with your heel or the pressure of your knee against his side, and he's got the idea. A well-trained horse is perfectly capable of cutting a particular cow out of a herd without any instructions beyond showing him which one you want."

"It's too bad the Army did away with the cavalry. Sounds like you belong there, not in the Air Force."

"No, because if there's anything I like better than riding a good horse, its flying a fast and responsive airplane. I've been flying fighters for almost seventeen years now, and I'll be quite happy to keep flying them as long as they'll let me. When I can't fly fighters anymore, then I'll go back to horses. And much as I like horses, I hope that's going to be a long time yet."

"You must hate this assignment, then. How come I never hear you complain about it?"

"The only reason I don't complain about this assignment is that I volunteered for it. And I've been kicking myself ever since. When I heard about the Rocket Interceptors, I was really excited. Imagine a plane fast enough to catch up with an invading ballistic missile and shoot it down. I decided this was for me, and jumped at the assignment. They sounded like the hot fighter planes to end all hot fighter planes. And what do I find? They're so expensive to fly that we don't get any training missions. I've been up in one just once, and that was my familiarization flight, when I got into this assignment last year. And then it was only a ride in the second seat of that two-seat version they use for checking out new pilots. I just lay there through the whole flight. And as far as I could see, the pilot didn't do much more. He just watched things while the autopilot did all the work."

"Well, don't take it too hard. You might get some flights."

"That's true. They do mistake a meteor for a missile now and then. But that happens only two or three times a year. That's not enough. I want some regular flying. I haven't got any flying time in for more than a year. The nearest I come to flying is my time in the procedural trainer, to teach me what buttons to push, and in the simulator, to give me the feel of what happens when I push the buttons."

"That's O.K. They still give you your flying pay."

"I know, but that's not what I'm after. I fly because I love flying. I use the flying pay just to keep up the extra premiums the insurance companies keep insisting on so long as I indulge my passion for fighter planes."

"I guess about the only way you could get any regular flying on this job would be for a war to come along."

"That's about it. We'd fly just as often as they could recover our ships and send us back up here for another launch. And that would go on until the economy on both sides broke down so far they couldn't make any more missiles for us to chase, or boosters to send us up after them. No thanks. I don't want to fly that badly. I like civilization."

"In the meantime, then, you ought to try to enjoy it here. Where else can you spend most of your working hours lying flat on your back on the most comfortable couch science can devise?"

"That's the trouble. Just lying there, where you can't read, write, talk, or listen. It might be O.K. for a hermit, but I'd rather fly fighter planes. Here's the trainer building. I've got to get out."

Seven o'clock. Harry Lightfoot licked the flap on the envelope, sealed it shut, stuck some stamps on the front, and scrawled "AIR MAIL" under the stamps. He dropped the letter into the "STATESIDE" slot. The exam hadn't been so bad. What did they think he was, anyway? A city slicker who had never seen a live cow in his life? He ambled into the off-duty pilots' lounge. He had an hour to kill before going on watch, and this was as good a place as any to kill it. The lounge was almost empty. Most of the pilots must have been asleep. They couldn't all be in Mike's game. He leaned over a low table in the center of the room and started sorting through the stack of magazines.

"'Looking for anything in particular, Harry?"

He turned to face the speaker. "No, just going through these fugitives from a dentist's office to see if there's anything I haven't read yet. I can't figure out where all the new magazines go. The ones in here always seem to be exactly two months old."

"Here's this month's *Western Stories*. I just finished it. It had some pretty good stories in it."

"No, thanks, the wrong side always wins in that one."

"The wrong . . . oh, I forgot. I guess they don't write stories where your side wins."

"It's not really a question of 'my side.' My tribe gave up the practice of tribal life and tribal customs over fifty years ago. I had the same education in a public school as any other American child. I read the same newspapers and watch the same TV shows as anyone else. My Apache ancestry means as little to me as the nationality of his immigrant ancestors means to the average American. I certainly don't consider myself to be part of a nation still at war with the 'palefaces.' "

"Then what's wrong with Western stories where the United States Cavalry wins?"

"That's a different thing entirely. Some of the earliest memories I have are of listening to my grandfather tell me about how he and his friends fought against the horse-soldiers when he was a young man. I imagine he put more romance than historical accuracy into his stories. After all, he was telling an eager kid about the adventures he'd had over fifty years before. But at any rate, he definitely fixed my emotions on the side of the Indians and against the United States Cavalry. And the fact that culturally I'm descended from the Cavalry rather than from the Apache Indians doesn't change my emotions any."

"I imagine that would have a strong effect on you. These stories are really cheering at the death of some of your grandfather's friends."

"Oh, it's worse than that. In a lot of hack-written stories, the Indians are just convenient targets for the hero to shoot at while the author gets on with the story. Those stories are bad enough. But the worst are the ones where the Indians are depicted as brutal savages with no redeeming virtues. My grandfather had an elaborate code of honor which governed his conduct in battle. It was different from the code of the people he fought, but it was at least as rigid, and deviations from it were punished severely. He'd never read Clausewitz. To him, war wasn't an 'Instrument of National Policy.' It was a chance for the individual warrior to demonstrate his skill and bravery. His code put a high premium on individual courage in combat, and the weakling or coward was crushed contemptuously. I don't even attempt to justify the Indian treatment of captured civilians and noncombatants, but nevertheless, I absorbed quite a few of my grandfather's ideals and views about war, and it's downright disgusting to see him so falsely represented by the authors of the run-of-the-mill Western story or movie."

"Well, those writers have to eat, too. And maybe they can't hold an honest job. Besides, you don't still look at war the way your grandfather did, do you? Civilization requires plenty of other virtues besides courage in combat, and we have plenty of better ways to display those virtues. And the real goal of the fighting man is to be alive after the war so he can go home to enjoy the things he was fighting for."

"No, I hadn't been in Korea long before I lost any notions I might have had of war as the glorious adventure my grandfather described it to be. It's nothing but a bloody business, and should be resorted to only if everything else fails. But I still think the individual fighter could do a lot worse than follow the code that my grandfather believed in."

"That's so, especially since the coward usually gets shot anyway; if not by the enemy, then by his own side. Hey, it's getting late! I've got some things to do before going on watch. Be seeing you."

"O.K. I'll try to find something else here I haven't read yet."

Eight o'clock. Still no sign of the sun. The stars didn't have the sky to themselves, however. Two or three times a minute a meteor would be visible, most of them appearing to come from a point about halfway between the Pole Star and the eastern horizon. Harry Lightfoot stopped the elevator, opened the hatch, and stepped in.

"She's all yours, Harry. I've already checked out with the tower."

"O.K. That gyro any worse?"

"No, it seems to have steadied a bit. Nothing else gone wrong, either."

"Looks like we're in luck for a change."

"Let me have the parka and I'll clear out. I'll think of you up here while I'm relaxing. Just imagine; a whole twenty-four hours off, and not even any training scheduled."

"Someone slipped up, I'll bet. By the way, be sure to look at the fireworks when you go out. They're better now than I've seen them at any time since they started."

"The meteor shower, you mean? Thanks. I'll have a look. I'll bet they're really cluttering up the radar screens. The Launch Control Officer must be going quietly nuts."

The Launch Control Officer wasn't going nuts. Anyone who went nuts under stress simply didn't pass the psychological tests required of prospective Launch Control Officers. However, he was decidedly unhappy. He sat in a dimly lighted room, facing three oscilloscope screens. On each of them a pie-wedge section was illuminated by a white line which swept back and forth like a windshield wiper. Unlike a windshield wiper, however, it put little white blobs on the screen, instead of removing them. Each blob represented something which had returned a radar echo. The center screen was his own radar. The outer two were televised images of the radar screens at the stations a hundred miles on either side of him, part of a chain of stations extending from Alaska to Greenland. In the room, behind him, and facing sets of screens similar to his, sat his assistants. They located the incoming objects on the screen and set automatic computers to determining velocity, trajectory, and probable impact point.

This information appeared as coded symbols beside the tracks on the center screen of the Launch Control Officer, as well as all duplicate screens. The Launch Control Officer, and he alone, had the responsibility to determine whether the parameters for a given track were compatible with an invading Intercontinental Ballistic Missile, or whether the track represented something harmless. If he failed to launch an interceptor at a track that turned out to be hostile, it meant the death of an American city. However, if he made a habit of launching interceptors at false targets, he would soon run out of interceptors. And only under the pressure of actual war would the incredible cost of shipping in more interceptors during the winter be paid without a second thought. Normally, no more could be shipped in until spring. That would mean a gap in the chain that could not be covered adequately by interceptors from the adjacent stations.

His screens were never completely clear. And to complicate things, the Quadrantids, which start every New Year's Day and last four days, were giving him additional trouble. Each track had to be analyzed, and the presence of the meteor shower greatly increased the number of tracks he had to worry about. However, the worst was past. One more day and they would be over. The clutter on his screens would drop back to normal.

Even under the best of circumstances, his problem was bad. He was hemmed in on one side by physics, and on the other by arithmetic. The most probable direction for an attack was from over the Pole. His radar beam bent only slightly to follow the curve of the earth. At great range, the lower edge of the beam was too far above the earth's surface to detect anything of military significance. On a minimum altitude trajectory, an ICBM aimed for North America would not be visible until it reached 83° North Latitude on the other side of the Pole. One of his interceptors took three hundred eighty-five seconds to match trajectories with such a missile, and the match occurred only two degrees of latitude south of the station. The invading missile traveled one degree of latitude in fourteen seconds. Thus he had to launch the interceptor when the missile was twenty-seven degrees from intercept. This turned out to be 85° North Latitude on the other side of the Pole. This left him at most thirty seconds to decide whether or not to intercept a track crossing the Pole. And if several tracks were present, he had to split that time among them. If too many tracks appeared, he would have to turn over portions of the sky to his assistants, and let them make the decisions about launching. This would happen only if he felt an attack was in progress, however.

Low-altitude satellites presented him with a serious problem, since there is not a whole lot of difference between the orbit of such a satellite and the trajectory of an ICBM. Fortunately most satellite orbits were catalogued and available for comparison with incoming tracks. However, once in a while an unannounced satellite was launched, and these could cause trouble. Only the previous week, at a station down the line, an interceptor had been launched at an unannounced satellite. Had the pilot not realized what he was chasing and held his fire, the international complications could have been serious. It was hard to imagine World War III being started by an erroneous interceptor launching, but the State Department would be hard put to soothe the feelings of some intensely nationalistic country whose expensive new satellite had been shot down. Such mistakes were bound to occur, but the Launch Control Officer preferred that they be made when someone else, not he, was on watch. For this reason he attempted to anticipate all known satellites, so they would be recognized as soon as they appeared.

According to the notes he had made before coming on watch, one of the UN's weather satellites was due over shortly. A blip appeared on the screen just beyond the 83° latitude line, across the Pole. He checked the time with the satellite ephemeris. If this was the satellite, it was ninety seconds early. That was too much error in the predicted orbit of a well-known satellite. Symbols sprang into existence beside the track. It was not quite high enough for the satellite, and the velocity was too low. As the white line swept across the screen again, more symbols appeared beside the track. Probable impact point was about 40° North Latitude. It certainly wasn't the satellite. Two more blips appeared on the screen, at velocities and altitudes similar to the first. Each swipe of the white line left more new tracks on the screen. And the screens for the adjacent stations were showing similar behavior. These couldn't be meteors.

The Launch Control Officer slapped his hand down on a red push button set into the arm of his chair, and spoke into this mike. "Red alert. Attack is in progress." Then switching to another channel, he spoke to his assistants: "Take your preassigned sectors. Launch one interceptor at each track identified as hostile." He hadn't enough interceptors to double up on an attack of this size, and a quick glance at the screens for the adjacent stations showed he could expect no help from them. They would have their hands full. In theory, one interceptor could handle a missile all by itself. But the theory had never been tried in combat. That lack was about to be supplied.

Harry Lightfoot heard the alarm over the intercom. He vaguely understood what would happen before his launch order came. As each track was identified as hostile, a computer would be assigned to it. It would compute the correct time of launch, select an interceptor, and order it off the ground at the correct time. During the climb to intercept, the computer would radio steering signals to the interceptor, to assure that the intercept took place in the most efficient fashion. He knew RI 276 had been selected when a green light on the instrument panel flashed on, and a clock dial started indicating the seconds until launch. Just as the clock reached zero, a relay closed behind the instrument panel. The solid-fuel booster ignited with a roar. He was squashed back into his couch under four gees' acceleration.

Gyroscopes and acceleration-measuring instruments determined the actual trajectory of the ship; the navigation computer compared the actual trajectory with the trajectory set in before takeoff; when a deviation from the preset trajectory occurred, the autopilot steered the ship back to the proper trajectory. As the computer on the ground obtained better velocity and position information about the missile from the ground radar, it sent course corrections to the ship, which were accepted in the computer as changes to the preset trajectory. The navigation computer hummed and buzzed; lights flickered on and off on the instrument panel; relays clicked behind the panel. The ship steered itself toward the correct intercept point. All this automatic operation was required because no merely human pilot had reflexes fast enough to carry out an intercept at twenty-six thousand feet per second. And even had his reflexes been fast enough, he could not have done the precise piloting required while being pummeled by this acceleration.

As it was, Major Harry Lightfoot, fighter pilot, lay motionless in his acceleration couch. His face was distorted by the acceleration. His breathing was labored. Compressed-air bladders in the legs of his gee-suit alternately expanded and contracted, squeezing him like the obscene embrace of some giant snake, as the gee-suit tried to keep his blood from pooling in his legs. Without the gee-suit, he would have blacked out, and eventually his brain would have been permanently damaged from the lack of blood to carry oxygen to it.

A red light on the instrument panel blicked balefully at him as it measured out the oxygen he required. Other instruments on the panel informed him of the amount of cooling air flowing through his suit to keep his temperature within the tolerable range, and the amount of moisture the dehumidifier had to carry away from him so that his suit didn't become a steambath. He was surrounded by hundreds of pounds of equipment which added nothing to the performance of the ship; which couldn't be counted as payload; which cut down on the speed and altitude the ship might have reached without them. Their sole purpose was to keep this magnificent high-performance, self-steering machine from killing its load of fragile human flesh.

At one hundred twenty-eight seconds after launch, the acceleration suddenly dropped to zero. He breathed deeply again, and swallowed repeatedly to get the salty taste out of his throat. His stomach was uneasy, but he wasn't spacesick. Had he been prone to spacesickness, he would never have been accepted as a Rocket Interceptor pilot. Rocket Interceptor pilots had to be capable of taking all the punishment their ships could dish out.

He knew there would be fifty seconds of free-fall before the rockets fired again. One solid-fuel stage had imparted to the ship a velocity which would carry it to the altitude of the missile it was to intercept. A second solid-fuel stage would match trajectories with the missile. Final corrections would be made with the liquid-fuel rockets in the third stage. The third stage would then become a glider which eventually would carry him back to Earth.

Before the second stage was fired, however, the ship had to be oriented properly. The autopilot consulted its gyros, took some star sights, and asked the navigation computer some questions. The answers came back in seconds, an interval which was several hours shorter than a human pilot would have required. Using the answers, the autopilot started to swing the ship about, using small compressed-gas jets for the purpose. Finally, satisfied with the ship's orientation, the autopilot rested. It patiently awaited the moment, precisely calculated by the computer on the ground, when it would fire the second stage.

Major Harry Lightfoot, fighter pilot, waited idly for the next move of his ship. He could only fume inwardly. This was no way for an Apache warrior to ride into battle. What would his grandfather think of a steed which directed itself into battle and which could kill its rider, not by accident, but in its normal operation? He should be actively hunting for that missile, instead of lying here, strapped into his couch so he wouldn't hurt himself, while the ship did all the work.

As for the missile, it was far to the north and slightly above the ship. Without purpose of its own, but obedient to the laws of Mr. Newton and to the wishes of its makers, it came on inexorably. It was a sleek aluminum cylinder, glinting in the sunlight it had just recently entered. On one end was a rocket motor, now silent but now still warm with the memory of flaming gas that had poured forth from it only minutes ago. On the other end was a sleek aerodynamic shape, the product of thousands of hours of design work. It was designed to enter the atmosphere at meteoric speed, but without burning up. It was intended to survive the passage through the air and convey its contents intact to the ground. The contents might have been virulent bacteria or toxic gas, according to the intentions of its makers. Among its brothers elsewhere in the sky this morning, there were such noxious loads. This one, however, was carrying the complex mechanism of a hydrogen bomb. Its destination was an American city; its object to replace that city with an expanding cloud of star-hot gas.

Suddenly the sleek cylinder disappeared in a puff of smoke, which quickly dissipated in the surrounding vacuum. What had been a precisely built rocket had been reduced, by carefully placed charges of explosive, to a collection of chunks of metal.

Some were plates from the skin and fuel tanks. Others were large lumps from the computer-banks, gyro platform, fuel pumps, and other more massive components. This was not wanton destruction, however. It was more careful planning by the same brains which had devised the missile itself. To a radar set on the ground near the target, each fragment was indistinguishable from the nose cone carrying the warhead. In fact, since the fragments were separating only very slowly, they never would appear as distinct objects. By the time the cloud of decoys entered the atmosphere, its more than two dozen members would appear to the finest radar available on the ground as a single echo twenty-five miles across. It would be a giant hay-stack in the sky, concealing the most deadly needle of all time. No ground-controlled intercept scheme had any hope of select-ing the warhead from among that deceptive cloud and destroy-ing it.

The cloud of fragments possessed the same trajectory as the missile originally had. At the rate it was overtaking RI 276, it would soon pass the ship by. The autopilot of RI 276 had no intention of letting this happen, of course. At the correct in-stant, stage two thundered into life, and Harry Lightfoot was again smashed back into his acceleration couch. Almost absent-mindedly, the ship continued to minister to his needs. Its atten-tion was focused on its mission. After a while, the ground computer sent some instructions to the ship. The navigation computer converted these into a direction, and pointed a radar antenna in that direction. The antenna sent forth a stream of questing pulses, which quickly returned, confirming the direc-tion and distance to the oncoming cloud of missile fragments. A little while later, fuel pumps began to whine somewhere in the tail of the ship. Then the acceleration dropped to zero as the second-stage thrust was terminated. There was a series of thumps as expolsive bolts released the second stage. The whine of the pumps dropped in pitch as fuel gushed through them, and acceleration returned in a rush. The acceleration lasted for a few seconds, tapered off quickly, and ended. A light winked on on the instrument panel as the ship announced its mission was accomplished.

Major Harry Lightfoot, fighter pilot, felt a glow of satisfac-tion as he saw the light come on. He might not have reflexes fast enough to pilot the ship up here; he might not be able to survive the climb to intercept without the help of a lot of fancy equipment; but he was still necessary. He saw still one step ahead of this complex robot which had carried him up here. It was his human judgment and his ability to react correctly in an unpredictable situation which were needed to locate the warhead from among the cluster of decoys and destroy it. This was a job no merely logical machine could do. When all was said and done, the only purpose for the existence of this magnificient machine was to put him where he was now; in the same trajectory as the missile, and slightly behind it.

Harry Lightfoot reached for a red-handled toggle switch at the top of the instrument panel, clicked it from AUTO to MANUAL, and changed his status from passenger to pilot. He had little enough time to work. He could not follow the missile down into the atmosphere; his ship would burn up. He must begin his pull-out at not less than two hundred miles altitude. That left him one hundred eighty-three seconds in which to locate and destroy the warhead. The screen in the center of his instrument panel could show a composite image of the space in front of his ship, based on data from a number of sensing elements and detectors. He switched on an infrared scanner. A collection of spots appeared on the screen, each spot indicating by its color the temperature of the object it represented. The infrared detector gave him no range information, of course. But if the autopilot had done its job well, the nearest fragment would be about ten miles away. Thus even if he set off the enemy warhead, he would be safe. At that range the ship would not suffer any structural damage from the heat, and he could be down on the ground and in a hospital before any radiation effects could become serious.

He reflected quickly on the possible temperature range of the missile components. The missile had been launched from Central Asia, at night, in January. There was no reason to suppose that the warhead had been temperature-controlled during the prelaunch countdown. Thus it probably was at the ambient temperature of the launch site. If it had been fired in the open, that might be as low as minus 70° F. Had it been fired from a shelter, that might be as high as 70° F. To leave a safety margin, he decided to reject only those objects outside the range plus or minus 100° F. There were two fragments at 500° F. He rejected these as probably fragments of the engine. Six more exhibited a temperature of near minus 320° F. These probably came from the liquid oxygen tanks. They could be rejected. That eliminated eight of the objects on the screen. He had nineteen to go. It would be a lot slower for the rest, too.

*   *   *

He switched on a radar transmitter. The screen blanked out almost completely. The missile had included a microwave transmitter, to act as a jammer. It must have been triggered on by his approach. It obviously hadn't been operating while the ship was maneuvering into position. Had it been transmitting then, the autopilot would simply have homed on it. He switched the radar to a different frequency. That didn't work. The screen was still blank, indicating that the jammer was sweeping in frequency. He next tried to synchronize his radar pulses with the jammer, in order to be looking when it was quiet. The enemy, anticipating him, had given the jammer a variable pulse repetition rate. He switched off the transmitter, and scanned the radar antenna manually. He slowly swung it back and forth, attempting to fix the direction of the jammer by finding the direction of maximum signal strength. He found that the enemy had anticipated him again, and the jammer's signal strength varied. However, he finally stopped the antenna, satisfied that he had it pointed at the jammer. The infrared detector confirmed that there was something in the direction the antenna pointed, but it appeared too small to be the warhead.

He then activated the manual piloting controls. He started the fuel pumps winding up, and swung the ship to point normal to the line-of-sight to the jammer. A quick blast from the rockets sent the image of the jammer moving sideways across the screen. But, of greater importance, two other objects moved across the screen faster than the jammer, indicating they were nearer the ship than was the jammer. He picked the one which appeared the nearest to him, and with a series of maneuvers and blasts from the rockets placed the object between himself and the jammer. He switched the radar on again. Some of the jammer signal was still leaking through, but the object, whatever it was, made an effective shield. The radar images were quite sharp and clear.

He glanced at the clock. Nullifying the jammer had cost him seventy-five seconds. He'd have to hurry, in order to make up for that time. The infrared detector showed two targets which the radar insisted weren't there. He shifted radar frequency. They still weren't there. He decided they were small fragments which didn't reflect much radar energy, and rejected them. He set the radar to a linearly polarized mode. Eight of the targets showed a definite amplitude modulation on the echo. That meant they were rotating slowly. He switched to circular polarization, to see if they presented a constant area to the radar beam. He compared the echoes for both modes of polarization. Five of the targets were skin fragments, spinning about an axis skewed with respect to the radar beam. These he rejected. Two more were structural spars. They couldn't conceal a warhead. He rejected them. After careful examination of the fine structure of the echo from the last object, he was able to classify it as a large irregular mass, probably a section of computer, waving some cables about. Its irregularity weighed against its containing the warhead. Even if it didn't burn up in the atmosphere, its trajectory would be too unpredictable.

He turned to the rest of the targets. Time was getting short. He extracted every conceivable bit of information out of what his detectors told him. He checked each fragment for resonant frequencies, getting an idea of the size and shape of each. He checked the radiated infrared spectrum. He checked the decrement of the reflected radar pulse. Each scrap of information was an indication about the identity of the fragments. With frequent glances at the clock, constantly reminding him of how rapidly his time was running out, he checked and cross-checked the data coming in to him. Fighting to keep his mind calm and his thoughts clear, he deduced, inferred, and decided. One fragment after another, he sorted, discarded, rejected, eliminated, excluded. Until the screen was empty.

Now what? Had the enemy camouflaged the warhead so that it looked like a section of the missile's skin? Not likely. Had he made a mistake in his identification of the fragments? Possibly, but there wasn't time to recheck every fragment. He decided that the most likely event was that the warhead was hidden by one of the other fragments. He swung the ship; headed it straight for the object shielding him from the jammer, which had turned out to be a section from the fuel tank. A short blast from the rockets sent him drifting toward the object. One image on the screen broadened; split in two. A hidden fragment emerged from behind one of the ones he had examined. He rejected it immediately. Its temperature was too low. He was almost upon the fragment shielding him from the jammer. If he turned to avoid it, the jammer would blank out his radar again. He thought back to his first look at the cloud of fragments. There had been nothing between his shield and the jammer. The only remaining possibility, then, was that the warhead was being hidden from him by the jammer itself. He would have to look on the other side of the jammer, using the ship itself as a shield.

He swung out from behind the shielding fragment, and saw his radar images blotted out. He switched off the radar, and aimed the ship slightly to one side of the infrared image of the jammer. Another blast from the rockets sent him towards the jammer. Without range information from the radar, he would have to guess its distance by noting the rate at which it swept across the screen. The image of the jammer started to expand as he approached it. Then it became dumbbell-shaped and split in two.

As he passed by the jammer, he switched the radar back on. That second image was something which had been hidden by the jammer. He looked around. No other new objects appeared on the screen. This had to be the warhead. He checked it anyway. Temperature was minus 40° F. A smile flickered on his lips as he caught the significance of the temperature. He hoped the launching crew had gotten their fingers frozen off while they were going through the countdown. The object showed no anomalous radar behavior. Beyond doubt, it was the warhead.

Then he noted the range. A mere thirteen hundred yards! His own missile carried a small atomic warhead. At that range it would present no danger to him. But what if it triggered the enemy warhead? He and the ship would be converted into vapor within microseconds. Even a partial, low-efficiency explosion might leave the ship so weakened that it could not stand the stresses of return through the atmosphere. Firing on the enemy warhead at this range was not much different from playing Russian Roulette with a fully loaded revolver.

Could he move out of range of the explosion and then fire? No. There were only twelve seconds left before he had to start the pull-out. It would take him longer than that to get to a safe range, get into position, and fire. He'd be dead anyway, as the ship plunged into the atmosphere and burned up. And to pull out without firing would be saving his own life at the cost of the lives he was under oath to defend. That would be sheer cowardice.

He hesitated briefly, shrugged his shoulders as well as he could inside his flying suit, and snapped a switch on the instrument panel. A set of cross hairs sprang into existence on the screen. He gripped a small lever which projected up from his right armrest; curled his thumb over the firing button on top of it. Moving the lever, he caused the cross hairs to center on the warhead. He flicked the firing button, to tell the fire control system that *this* was the target. A red light blinked on, informing him that the missile guidance system was tracking the indicated target.

He hesitated again. His body tautened against the straps holding it in the acceleration couch. His right arm became rigid; his fingers petrified. Then, with a convulsive twitch of his thumb, he closed the firing circuit. He stared at the screen, unable to tear his eyes from the streak of light that leaped away from his ship and toward the target. The missile reached the target, and there was a small flare of light. His radiation counter burped briefly. The target vanished from the radar, but the infrared detector insisted there was a nebulous fog of hot gas, shot through with a rain of molten droplets, where the target had been. That was all. He had destroyed the enemy warhead without setting it off. He stabbed the MISSION ACCOMPLISHED button, and flicked the red-handled toggle switch, resigning his status as pilot. Then he collapsed, nerveless, into the couch.

The autopilot returned to control. It signaled the Air Defense network that this hostile track was no longer dangerous. It received instructions about a safe corridor to return to the ground, where it would not be shot at. As soon as the air was thick enough for the control surfaces to bite, the autopilot steered into the safe corridor. It began the slow, tedious process of landing safely. The ground was still a long way down. The kinetic and potential energy of the ship, if instantly transformed into heat, was enough to flash the entire ship into vapor. This tremendous store of energy had to be dissipated without harm to the ship and its occupant.

Major Harry Lightfoot, fighter pilot, lay collapsed in his couch, exhibiting somewhat less ambition than a sack of meal. He relaxed to the gentle massage of his gee-suit. The oxygen control winked reassuringly at him as it maintained a steady flow. The cabin temperature soared, but he was aware of it only from a glance at a thermometer; the air conditioning in his suit automatically stepped up its pace to keep him comfortable. He reflected that this might not be so bad after all. Certainly none of his ancestors had ever had this comfortable a ride home from battle.

After a while, the ship had reduced its speed and altitude to reasonable values. The autopilot requested, and received, clearance to land at its preassigned base. It lined itself up with the runway, precisely followed the correct glide path, and flared out just over the end of the runway. The smoothness of the touchdown was broken only by the jerk of the drag parachute popping open. The ship came to a halt near the other end of the runway. Harry Lightfoot disconnected himself from the ship and opened the hatch. Carefully avoiding contact with the still-hot metal skin of the ship, he jumped the short distance to the ground. The low purr of a motor behind him announced the arrival of a tractor to tow the ship off the runway.

"You'll have to ride the tractor back with me, sir. We're a bit short of transportation now."

"O.K., sergeant. Be careful hooking up. She's still hot."

"How was the flight, sir?"

"No sweat. She flies herself most of the time."

THE LAST SHUTTLE

BY ISAAC ASIMOV

Virginia Ratner sighed. "There had to be a last time, I suppose."

Her eyes were troubled as she looked out over the sea, shimmering in the warm sunshine. "At least we have a nice day for it, though I suppose a sleet storm would match my mood better."

Robert Gill, who was there as senior officer of the Terrestrial Space Agency, regarded her without favor. "Please don't mope. You've said it yourself. There had to be a last time."

"But why with *me* as pilot?"

"Because you're the best pilot we have and we want this to be a snappy finish with nothing going wrong. Why am *I* the one who must dismantle the Agency? Happy ending!"

"*Happy* ending?" Virginia studied the busy loading of freight and the lineup of passengers. The last of both.

She had been piloting shuttles for twenty years, knowing all the time there would have to be a last time. You would think the knowledge would have aged her, but there was no gray in her hair, no lines in her face. Perhaps a life under constantly changing gravitational intensity had something to do with it.

She looked rebellious. "It seems to me that it would be dramatic irony—or maybe dramatic justice—if this last shuttle blew up on takeoff. A protest on the part of Earth itself."

Gill shook his head. "Strictly speaking, I should report that—but you're just suffering an acute attack of nostalgia."

"Well, report me. It would tab me as dangerously unstable and I would be disqualified as pilot. I can take my place as one of the six hundred sixteen last passengers and make it six hundred seventeen. Someone else can pilot the shuttle and enter the history books as the person who—"

"I have no intention of reporting you. For one thing, nothing will happen. Shuttle lift-offs are trouble-free."

"Not always." Virginia Ratner looked grim. "There was the case of Enterprise Sixty."

"Is that supposed to be a stop-news bulletin? That was a hundred seventy years ago and there hasn't been a space-related casualty since. Now, with antigravity assistance, we don't even have the chance of having an eardrum broken. The roar of the rocket takeoff is forever gone. —Listen, Ratner, you'd better go up into the observation deck. It's less than thirty minutes to lift-off."

"So? Surely you're going to inform me that lift-off's fully automated and that I'm not really needed."

"You know that without my telling you, but your presence on the bridge is a matter of regulations—and tradition."

"It seems to me that you're nostalgic now—for a time when a pilot made a difference and wasn't simply immortalized for doing nothing but presiding over the final dismantling of something that was so great."

Then she added, "But I'll go," and moved up the central tube as though she were a fluff of down rising in an updraft.

She remembered her salad days on the shuttle run when antigrav was experimental and required ground installations larger than the shuttle itself and when, even so, it usually worked jerkily or not at all, and space hands preferred the old-fashioned elevators.

Now the antigrav process had been miniaturized till each ship carried its own. It was never-fail and it was used for the passengers, who took it for granted, and for the inanimate cargo, which could then be moved into place with the help of friction-less air jets and magnetic levitation by crewmen who knew perfectly well how to manhandle large objects without weight but with full inertia.

No other vehicles ever built by human beings were as magnificent, as complex, as intricately computerized as the shuttles had been, for no other ships had ever had to fight Earth's gravity—except for those early ships which, without antigrav, had had to depend on chemical rockets for every last bit of power. Primitive dinosaurs!

As for the ship that dwelt in space alone, kicking off from a space settlement to a power station or from a factory to a food processor's—even from the Moon—they had little or no gravity to contend with, so they were simple, almost fragile, things.

She was in the pilot room now with its array of computerized instruments giving her the exact status of every functioning device on board, the site of each packing case, the number and disposition of every person among the crew and passengers. (Not one of those must be left behind. To leave one would be unthinkable!)

There was a three-hundred-sixty-degree television view of the panorama outside the ship, and she regarded it thoughtfully. She was viewing the place from which human entry into space had taken place in the old, heroic days. It was from here that people had hurtled upward to build the first space structures—power stations that limped—automated factories that required constant maintenance—space settlements that barely housed ten thousand people.

Now the vast, crowded technological center was gone. Bit by bit it had been pulled down until only the one installment remained for the departure of the last shuttle. That installment would remain standing, after the ship was gone, to rust and decay as a final sad memorial of all that had been.

How could the people of Earth so forget the past?

All she could see was land and sea—all deserted. There was no sign of human structure, no people. Just green vegetation, yellow sand, blue water.

It was time! Her practiced eye saw the ship was full, prepared, smoothly working. The countdown was ticking off the final minute, the navigational satellite overhead was signaling clear space and there was no need (she knew there would be none) to touch the manual control.

The ship lifted silently, smoothly, and all that had been worked for, over a period of two hundred years, was finally accomplished. Out in space, humanity waited on the Moon, on Mars, among the asteroids, in myriads of space settlements.

The last group of Earthpeople rose to join them. Three million years of hominid occupation of Earth was over; ten thousand years of Earthly civilization was done; four centuries of busy industrialization was ended.

Earth was returned to its wilderness and its wildlife by a humanity grateful to its mother planet and ready to retire it to the rest it deserved. It would remain forever as a monument to humanity's origin.

The last shuttle lifted through the wisps of the upper atmosphere and the Earth stretched below it and would now be shrinking as the shuttle receded.

It had been solemnly agreed by the fifteen billion residents of space that human feet would never stand on it again.

Earth was free! Free at last!

THE GETAWAY SPECIAL

BY JERRY OLTION

Allen Meisner didn't look like a mad scientist. He not only didn't look mad, with his blond hair neatly brushed to the side and his face set in a perpetual grin, but—at least in Judy Gallagher's opinion—he didn't look much like a scientist, either. He looked more like a beach bum.

But his business card read: "Allen T. Meisner, Mad Scientist," and he had the obligatory doctorate in physics to go with it. He also had a reputation as an outspoken member of INSANE, the politically active International Network of Scientists Against Nuclear Extermination, and he held patents on half a dozen futuristic gadgets, including the still-experimental positronic battery. He had all the qualifications, but he just didn't look the part.

That was all right with Judy. In her five years of flying the shuttle, most of the passengers she had taken up *had* looked like scientists, or worse: politicians. She enjoyed having a beach bum around for a change.

Right up to the time when he turned on his experiment and the Earth disappeared. She didn't enjoy that at all.

It started out as a routine satellite deployment and industrial retrieval mission, with two communicatons satellites going out to geostationary orbit and a month's supply of processed pharmaceuticals, optical fibers, and microcircuits coming back to Earth from the Manned Orbiting Laboratory. It was about as simple as a flight got, which was why NASA had sent a passenger along. Judy and the other two crewmembers would have time to look after him, and NASA could reduce by one more the backlog of civilians who had paid for trips into orbit.

Another reason they had sent him was the small size of his experiment. Since the shuttles had begun carrying payloads both ways there wasn't a whole lot of room for experiments, which meant that most scientists had to wait for a spacelab mission before they could go up. But Meisner had promised to fit everything he needed into a pair of getaway special canisters if NASA would send him on the next available flight. After all the bad publicity they'd gotten for carrying the laser antisatellite weapons into orbit, they'd been glad to do it. It would give the press something else to talk about for a while.

They had even stretched the rules a little in their effort to launch a scientific mission. Most getaway specials were allowed only a simple on/off switch, or at most two switches, but they had allowed Meisner an alphanumeric keypad and a small liquid crystal display for his. It had seemed like a reasonable request at the time. After all, he would be there to run it himself; none of the crewmembers needed to fool with it.

Officially his was a "Spacetime Anomaly Transfer Application Experiment." One of the two canisters was simply a high-powered radio transceiver, but the other was a mystery. It contained a bank of positronic batteries with enough combined power to run the entire shuttle for a month, plus enough circuitry to build a mainframe computer, all hooked to a single prototype integrated circuit chip the size of a deck of cards. That in turn was connected to a spherically radiating antenna mounted on top of the cannister. Rumor had it that someone in the vast structure of NASA's bureaucracy knew what it as supposed to do, but no one admitted to being that person. Still, it apparently held nothing that could interfere with the shuttle's operating systems, so they let it on board. It was Meisner's problem if it didn't work.

So on the second day of the flight, as mission specialist Carl Reinhardt finished inspecting the last of the return packages in the cargo bay with the camera in the remote manipulator arm, he said to Meisner, "Why don't you go ahead and warm up your experiment? I'm about done here, and you're next on the agenda."

Discovery, like all of the shuttles, had ten windows: six wrapping all the way around the flight controls in front, two facing back into the cargo bay, and two more overhead when you were looking out the back. Meisner was blocking the view out the overheads; he'd been watching over Judy's shoulders while she used the aft reaction controls to edge the shuttle slowly away from the orbital laboratory and into its normal flight attitude. He nodded to Reinhardt and pushed himself over to the payload controls, a distance of only a few feet. In the cramped quarters of the shuttle's flight deck nearly everything was within easy reach. It was possible—if you floated with your feet in between the pilot's and copilot's chairs and your head pointed toward the aft windows—to strand yourself without a handhold, but to manage it you had to be trying. Meisner had put himself in that position once earlier in the flight, and he'd gotten the worst case of five-second agoraphobia that Judy had ever seen before she could rescue him. After that he kept a handhold within easy reach all the time.

Judy finished maneuvering the shuttle into its parking orbit and watched the shadows in the cargo bay for a few more seconds to make sure that the shuttle was stable. She checked Reinhardt's progress as he latched down the manipulator arm, glanced upward through the overhead windows at the Earth, then turned to watch Meisner.

Here, in her opinion, was where the action was on this flight. For years NASA had promoted the image of the shuttle as a space truck, and that's what it had become, but for Judy the lure of space was in science, not industry. She wanted to explore, not drive a truck. But she was twenty years too late for Apollo, and by the looks of things at least twenty years too early for the planetary missions. Driving a space truck that occasionally did science projects was the best she could hope for.

She was looking over Meisner's shoulder now. His keypad took up a corner of one of the interchangeable panels that had been installed for controlling yesterday's satellite launches. Beside it was a simple toggle switch, which he flipped on. He looked at the display for a moment, then pushed a button labeled "Transmit/Time." The radio gave a loud beep, and the top line of the display began counting forward in seconds.

As he tapped instructions into the keyboard Judy saw a series of numbers flash on the display. They were in groups of three, but she could see no particular meaning to them.

"What are those numbers?" she asked.

"Coordinates," Meisner replied.

"Coordinates for what?"

Meisner smiled and pushed the *enter* button. "Us," he said. Reinhardt, who was still looking out the aft windows into the payload bay, shouted something like "Whaaa!" and leaped for the attitude controls.

Judy's flinch launched her headfirst into the instrument panel in front of her. She swore and pushed herself over beside Reinhardt. "What happened?"

He pointed through the overhead windows, but it took Judy a second to realize what he was pointing at, or rather what wasn't where he was pointing. In normal flight the shuttle flew upside down over the Earth, making for an excellent view of the planet overhead, but now there were only stars where it should have been. She pushed off to the front windows and looked to either side, but it wasn't there either.

Meisner said, "Don't worry, it's—"

"Not now," Judy cut him off. First thing in an emergency: shut the passengers up so you can think. Now, what had happened? She had a suspicion. Meisner's experiment had blown up. It had to have. She pulled herself up to the aft windows to get a look down into the cargo bay where the getaway special canisters were attached, next to the forward bulkhead. She couldn't see that close in, but there was no evidence of an explosion, nothing that could have jolted the shuttle enough to flip it over. Besides, she realized, nothing had. They would have felt the motion. The Earth had simply disappeared.

A long list of emergency procedures reeled through her mind. Fire control, blowout, toxic gases, medical emergencies—none of them applied here. There was nothing in the book about the Earth disappearing. But there was always one standing order that never changed. *In any emergency, communicate with the ground.*

"Don't use the jets," she said to Reinhardt, then, turning to the audio terminal she flipped it to transmit and said, "Control, this is *Discovery*, do you copy?"

Meisner cleared his throat and said, "I don't think you'll be able to raise them."

Judy shot him a look that shut him up and called again. "Control, this is *Discovery*. We've got a problem. Do you copy?"

After a couple of seconds she switched to another frequency and tried again, but still got no response. She was at the end of her checklist. What now?

Meisner had been trying to say something all along. She turned around to face him and said, "All right. What did you do?"

"I—ah, I moved us a little bit. Don't worry! It worked beautifully."

"You moved us. How?"

"Hyperdrive."

There was a moment of silence before Judy burst out laughing. She couldn't help it. *Hyperdrive?* But her laughter faded as the truth of the situation started to hit her.

Hyperdrive?

Behind her, Reinhardt began to moan.

As calmly as she could, Judy said, "Put us back."

Meisner looked hurt. He hadn't expected her to laugh. "I'm afraid I can't just yet," he said.

"Why not? You brought us here, wherever here is."

"We're somewhere between the orbits of Earth and Mars, and out of the plane of the ecliptic, but we could be off by as much as a few light-seconds from the distance I set. We shouldn't try to go near a planet until I take some distance measurements and calibrate—"

"Whoa! Slow down a minute. We're between Earth and Mars?" She felt a thrill rush through her as she asked the question. Could they really be? This was the sort of thing she had always dreamed of. Captain Gallagher of the Imperial Space Navy! Hopping from planet to planet at her merest whim, leading humanity outward from its cradle toward its ultimate destiny in space . . .

But right behind it came the thought, *I'm not in command of my ship.*

Meisner said, "If my initial calculations were correct we are. We'll know in a minute."

"How?"

"I sent a timing signal before we jumped. When it catches up with us I'll know exactly how far we moved. It should be coming in any time now."

Judy looked toward the radio speaker. It remained silent. Meisner began to look puzzled, then worried. He turned back to the keypad and began pushing buttons again.

"Stop!"

He looked up, surprised.

"Get away from there. Reinhardt, get between him and that panel."

Reinhardt nodded and pulled himself over beside Meisner.

"I'm just checking on the coordinates," Meisner said. "I must have miskeyed them."

After a moment's thought, Judy said, "Okay, go ahead, but

explain what you're doing as you go along. And don't even *think* of moving the ship again without my permission." She nodded to Reinhardt, who backed away again, then she suddenly had a thought. "Christ, go wake up Gerry. He'd shoot us if we didn't get him in on this too."

A minute later Gerry Vaughn, the copilot, shot up through the hatch from the mid-deck and grabbed the back of the command chair to slow down. He looked out the forward windows, then floated closer and looked overhead, then down. He turned and kicked off toward the aft windows, looked around in every direction, and finally backed away. Then, very quietly, he said, "Son of a bitch."

Meisner beamed.

"Where are we?"

He lost some of his smile. "I'm not sure," he admitted. "We're supposed to be two and a half light-minutes from Earth in the direction of Vega, but we either missed the signal or went too far."

"Signal?"

"Before we jumped, I transmitted a coded pulse. When the pulse catches up we'll know our distance. Next time we jump I'll send another pulse, and as long as we jump beyond the first one then we can triangulate our position when they arrive. That way I can calculate the aiming error as well as the distance error."

"Oh," Vaughn said. He looked out the windows again as if to assure himself that the Earth was really gone. Finally he said, "Look at the sun."

"What?"

"The sun."

Judy looked. It was shining in through the forward windows. She had to squint to keep it from burning her eyes, but not much, and now she could see what Vaughn was talking about. The solar disk was about a fourth the normal size.

Reinhardt had looked too. He made a strangling sound, looked over at Judy as if he was pleading for help, then his eyes rolled up and he went slack.

"Catch him!" Judy yelled, but it was hardly necessary. People don't fall when they faint in free-fall.

Neither do they faint. Blood doesn't rush away from the brain without gravity to pull it. So what had happened to him?

As she debated what to do, the answer came in a long, shuddering breath. "Oh," she said. "He forgot to breathe."

She laughed, but it came out wrong and she cut it off. She wasn't far from Reinhardt's condition herself.

Get it under control, she thought.

"Vaughn, help him down to his bunk."

When they had gone below, she said, "Well, Meisner, this is a pretty situation you've got yourself in."

"What do you mean?" he asked.

"I mean hijacking and piracy."

"What? You've got to be—" He stopped. She wasn't kidding. "All right, I can believe hijacking, but piracy?"

"We're carrying a full load of privately owned cargo, which you diverted without authority. That makes it piracy. You should have thought of that before you started pushing buttons."

Meisner looked at her without comprehension. "I don't get it," he said. "What's wrong with you people? I demonstrate a working hyperdrive engine and Reinhardt curls up into a ball, and now you start talking about piracy? Where's your sense of adventure? Don't you realize what this means? I've given us the key to the entire universe! We're not stuck on one planet anymore! I've ended the threat of nuclear extermination forever!"

Judy hadn't even thought of that angle. She'd been too busy trying to supress the hysterical giggles that kept threatening to bubble to the surface. Hyperdrive! But now she did think about it, and she didn't like what she came up with. "Ended the threat of nuclear extermination? You idiot! You've probably caused it! Do you have any idea what's going on at Mission Control right now? Full-scale panic, that's what. They've just lost an orbiter, gone, just like that, and it's not going to take long before somebody decides that the Soviets shot us down with an antisatellite weapon. I think you're smart enough to figure out what happens then."

She watched him think it through. He opened his mouth to speak, but he couldn't.

Judy said it for him: "We've got to get back within radio range and let them know we're okay, or all sorts of hell is going to break loose. So how do we do that?"

"I—without calibrating it we shouldn't—"

"I just want you to reverse the direction. Send us back the same distance we came. Can you do that?"

"Uh . . . yes, I suppose so. The error in distance should be the same both ways. But I don't think it's a good idea. We could be off in direction as well as distance. We could wind up in the wrong orbit, or underground for that matter."

Judy tried to weigh the chances of that against the chances of nuclear war. Since the Soviet Union had put missiles in Cuba again in response to American missiles in Europe, both sides were on a launch-on-warning status. If somebody decided they had already used their A-sat weapon . . . ?

She was starting to feel like a captain again. At least she felt the pressure of being the one in command. Four lives against five billion, hardly a choice except that she had to make it. She heard herself say, "It's a chance we'll have to take. Do it."

Seconds later she was convulsed in laughter. It was an involuntary reaction. The giggles had won.

Meisner stared at her for a moment before he ventured, "Are you all right?"

Judy fought for control, and eventually found it. She wiped fat globules of tears away from her eyes and sniffed. "Yeah," she said. "It just hit me." She pitched her voice in heroic tones and said, " 'I'll take that chance, Scotty! Give me warp speed!' God, if only the *Enterprise* had flown."

Meisner looked puzzled for a second before comprehension lit up his face. "The first shuttle. Okay." He laughed quietly and turned to his keypad. As he punched in the coordinates he said, "You know, I did try to buy the *Enterprise* for this, but I couldn't come up with the cash."

"I'm surprised you didn't build your own ship out of an old septic tank or something. Isn't that the way most mad scientists do it?"

"Don't laugh; I could have done it that way. But I didn't think a flying septic tank was the image I wanted. I thought a shuttle would be better for getting the world's attention."

"Well, you definitely did that. I just hope we can patch things back together before it's too late. Are you ready there?"

"Ready."

"Let's go then."

Meisner grinned. "Warp speed, Captain," he said, and pushed the button.

Earth suddenly filled the view again. It was at the wrong angle, but just having it there again made Judy sigh in relief. She tried the radio again.

"Control, this is *Discovery*. Do you copy?"

Response came immediately. "*Discovery*, this is Control. We copy. What is your status, over?"

"Green bird. Everything is fine. We've had a minor, uh, navigational problem, but we've got that taken care of. No cause for alarm. What is *your* status, over?" She realized she was babbling. There would be hell to pay when she got back on the ground, but she didn't care. Warp speed!

The ground controller wasn't much better off. "Everything is under control here too," he said. "Barely. What is the nature of your navigational problem? Over."

She suddenly realized that she had another big choice to make. Half the world must be listening in on her transmission; should she tell them the truth? Or should she do the military thing and keep it a secret? There were code words for just such a contingency as this.

It was a simple decision, even simpler than the one to return. She said, "Dr. Meisner has just demonstrated what he calls a hyperdrive engine. I believe his description of it to be accurate. We went—"

There was a violent lurch, followed by the beep of Meisner's radio pulse, and the Earth disappeared again.

"Damn it, I told you not to touch that until I gave the word! Get away from there!"

Meisner looked hurt. "I think I just saved our lives," he said. "Somebody shot at us." He pointed out the aft windows into the cargo bay, where a cherry-red stump still glowed where the vertical stabilizer had been. Hydraulic fluid bubbled out into vacuum from the severed lines.

Judy took it all in in less than a second, then whirled and kicked herself forward between the commander's and the pilot's chairs to look at the fuel pressure gauges. They remained steady, but the hydraulics and the auxiliary power units that drove them were both losing pressure fast. It hardly mattered, though; both systems were used only during launch and descent, and there could be no descent without a vertical stabilizer.

She shut off the alarms and clung to the command chair for support. "That was stupid," she said. "Of course the A-sat weapons would fire on something that suddenly pops into orbit where it doesn't belong. Damn it! Now there really is going to be a war." She turned around to face Meisner. "Take us back again, but this time put us short of the Earth. I don't want to go into orbit; I just want to be in radio range."

Meisner hesitated. "I—I don't think we should—"

"Do it! The end of the world is about fifteen minutes away. I don't care what it takes, just get us within radio range. And *outside* laser range."

Meisner nodded.

While he punched numbers on his keypad, Judy tried to compose what she was going to say. She wouldn't report the damage yet, not until she was sure everybody had his fingers off of the missile launch buttons. Ground control would know by their telemetry that something was wrong, but they wouldn't know how it happened, and the military would know that the Soviets had fired an A-sat weapon, but they wouldn't know at what. Or—she had a sudden thought. Who said it had to be a Soviet A-sat? It had to have been an automatic shot; that made it an even chance that it was an American beam.

It hardly mattered. Either way, it would mean war if she didn't explain what had happened.

Meisner looked over at her and said, "I've cut the radial distance by one percent. I don't know where that will put us, but it should at least be out of Earth orbit."

Judy nodded. "Okay. Do it." She turned to the radio.

The stars changed, but the Earth didn't fill the view. In fact it took Judy a moment to find it: a gibbous blob of white reminiscent of Venus seen through a cheap telescope. At least she supposed that was Earth. A bright point of light that might have shown a disk if she squinted had to be the Moon beside it. They were too close together, though, or so she thought until she remembered that the Moon could be between the ship and Earth, or on the other side of it, and the apparent distance would be shorter than it really was.

She shook her head. "Too far," she said. "We'd never make ourselves heard from this distance. You'll have to take us closer."

Meisner was starting to sweat. "Look," he said. "I can't keep moving us around without calibrating this thing. Every time we jump we're compounding our error, and we get farther and farther from knowing where we are."

"I know exactly where we are," Judy said. "We're too far for radio communications. Take us closer." She waited about two seconds while Meisner hesitated, then added, "Now."

"All right," he said. He tried to throw his hands up in a shrug, but he overbalanced and had to grab onto the overhead panel to steady himself. He pulled himself down again and began to work with the keyboard.

Judy heard the radio pulse and the view changed again. Earth was larger, about the size that it would be when seen from the Moon. She didn't see the Moon out the front windows, but when she looked back through the cargo bay windows she found it. It was bigger than the Earth. Much bigger. They couldn't have been more than a couple thousand miles from it. She watched the surface for a few seconds, trying to determine their relative motion. Was it getting closer? She couldn't tell.

All the same, as she plugged her headset into the radio she said, "Get ready to move us again." This time Meisner didn't argue.

"Control, this is *Discovery*, do you copy?"

She had forgotten about the time lag. She was about to call again when she heard, "Roger, *Discovery*, we copy, but your signal is weak and you have disappeared from our radar. What's happening up there?"

"We're not in orbit any longer. Doctor Meisner's experiment has moved us to the general vicinity of the Moon. I repeat, Doctor Meisner's experiment is responsible for our change in position. There is no cause for alarm. Do you copy?"

A pause. "We copy, *Discovery*. No cause for alarm. You bet. We'll tell the guys at NORAD and SAC to get their fingers off the buttons, then. Hold on a second—uh . . . we've just gotten word from the Pentagon that we're not to mention the nature of Doctor Meisner's experiment, over."

"Don't tell the world that we've got hyperdrive? You know where you can tell them to put it, control. Kindly remind the idiots at the Pentagon that I am a civilian pilot, and that my loyalty goes to humanity first, nation second. What they request is tantamount to suppressing knowledge of the wheel, so you can tell the Pentagon to stuff it deep, over."

Judy saw motion out of the corner of her eye and turned to see Meisner applauding silently. He said, "I have a—"

Judy held up her hand to quiet him as mission control responded. She could hear the cheering in the background. "Roger, *Discovery*. We copy and agree. Your, ah, hyperspace jump seems to have messed with the telemetry. We're getting low pressure readings in the hydraulics and APU's. Do you confirm, over?"

"Your readings are correct. We have sustained damage to the vertical stabilizer. We won't be able to reenter. Request you reserve space for us on the next flight down."

"Roger, *Discovery*. What kind of damage to the stabilizer?"

"It's been vaporized. Completely melted away. We assume it was either a particle beam or laser antisatellite weapon, automatically fired. We do not consider ourselves to have been attacked. Please be sure the Pentagon understands, over."

"Roger, *Discovery*. I'm sure they'll be glad to hear that."

Meisner butted in. "Uh, Commander?"

"I'll bet they will. Hold on a sec." She turned off the mike. "What, Allen?"

"I think we should get away from here. We're picking up velocity being this close to the Moon. It'll make it hard to put us back into orbit."

"Velocity? How?"

"Gravitation. We're falling toward the Moon. When we make our next hyperspace jump the velocity we gain will still be with us. We'll have to cancel it before we can go into Earth orbit."

"Oh. Right." Judy tried to visualize the situation in her mind. Too close to the Moon; well, "Can you put us on the other side of the Earth?"

"I don't want to fool around near the planets any more. I need to calibrate it. I think the danger of war is past, is it not?"

Judy nodded. "Okay. Give me a minute to explain what we're going to do, then you can take us wherever you want. Within reason," she amended quickly. She turned on the radio again and said, "Control, this is *Discovery*. Doctor Meisner says that the Moon's gravitation is causing us to build up unwanted velocity. We will have to make another hyperspace jump in order to leave the area, plus another series of jumps to calibrate the engine. We will be out of radio contact for a while. Promise you won't let them blow up the world while we're gone? Over."

"We'll do our best, *Discovery*. Things are a little hot down here."

"Just keep the lid on until we get back. Remind the President that this would be a really stupid time to go to war."

"We'll do that. Good luck, *Discovery*."

"Good luck to you. *Discovery* out." Judy switched off the radio, turned around, and screamed.

"Be calm," Vaughn said as he floated up through the hole between decks with the .45 from the emergency survival kit in his hand. "You may continue with your jump, Allen. Judy, you will please come away from the controls."

"What do you think you're doing?" she demanded.

"I am appropriating this vessel for the Soviet Union. You will not be harmed so long as you do as I say."

"Come off it, Gerry. You're not going to fire that thing in here. One stray shot and you'd lose all your air."

"There is that risk. I'd have preferred a less destructive weapon, but the survival kit doesn't carry a dart gun. I'll just have to be careful not to miss, won't I? Now come away. Slowly, that's it!" He reached out and stopped her in midair, leaving her floating where he could see her move long before she reached anything to push off against.

Vaughn glanced out the aft windows at the surface of the Moon and said, "Allen, you may move us any time now." The gun didn't quite point at him.

Meisner swallowed. "Right," he said. He turned to the keyboard and began keying in coordinates.

"Why are you doing this, Vaughn?" Judy asked. "You're not a Russian."

"That depends on your definition. I have been a sleeper agent since before I entered the space program. In any case, my nationality is not the issue. What matters is my belief that the Soviet Union should have this device."

Meisner cleared his throat. "I, uh, I was planning on giving it to everybody. You see, part of the reason I did things the way I did was to get everybody to listen, so I could transmit the plans by radio to the whole world."

Vaughn shook his head. "A noble thought. Unfortunately, the world is not ready for it. The Soviet Union must keep this idea secret until the rest of humanity is sufficiently civilized to handle something this dangerous."

"Bullshit," Judy said. "You can't believe—"

Vaughn waved the pistol toward her. "Be quiet. Allen, you will make the jump now."

Meisner turned back to his keyboard and pushed the button that sent the timing pulse, then after a few seconds pushed the transmit button.

Nothing happened.

"What—?" He looked out the window, pushed it again, and looked again. Still nothing changed.

"I must have miskeyed it," he said. He entered the coordinates again, canceled the timer and reset it, and hit "transmit" again.

Still nothing.

"Something's wrong."

"Meisner." Vaughn did have the gun pointed at him now.

"I'm not lying! It's not working! It's hardly surprising, with all the jumps we've been doing in a row. Something's probably overheated. It's still an experimental model, you know."

"Then you will find the problem and fix it." Vaughn glanced out the window and added, "I suggest you do it quickly."

Judy followed his glance. The surface was definitely closer now.

Meisner said, "You'll have to go out and get the canister."

"Not until you've exhausted the possibilities inside. The problem may be in the keyboard."

"It isn't. The signal is reaching the radio, and all the data uses one line. The problem is in the canister."

Vaughn thought it through and nodded. "All right, but Judy will go out and get it. I prefer to remain here where I can watch you."

The Moon was larger still by the time Judy stepped out into the cargo bay. She had cut the suiting-up time to its bare minimum, but it still took time breathing pure oxygen to wash the nitrogen out of her bloodstream, and even Vaughn with his pistol couldn't force her to go outside before she was sure she was safe from the bends. Once she was out she took time for one quick look—she could see their motion now—then unfastened the "mystery" canister and climbed back into the airlock with it under her arm. When she got back inside she handed it to Meisner and started to pull off her helmet.

"Leave it on," Vaughn said. Judy could hear the tension in his voice even through the intercom. She understood the reason for it, and for his order. She wouldn't have time to become uncomfortable in the suit. If Meisner found the problem she would have to take the canister back outside, and if he didn't they would crash into the Moon; either way she wouldn't have to worry about the suit for very long.

Meisner floated over to the wall of lockers in the mid-deck and opened the tool locker. Then he opened the canister and held it so the light shined down inside. It was a maze of wires and circuit boards. He looked for a minute, then reached in and pushed a few wires around. He let go of the canister and left it floating in front of him, looked up and said, "I think I've found it. Judy, could you help hold this a minute?"

She nodded and pushed off toward him.

"Here, around on this side," he said, pulling her around so he was between her and Vaughn. Reinhardt was still unconscious in his bunk beside them; evidently Vaughn had given him a sleeping pill when he had the chance. Meisner let himself drift forward far enough to make sure he was blocking Reinhardt too, handed the canister to Judy, then pulled a screwdriver out of the tool kit. He reached into the canister's open end with it, then looked at Vaughn.

"I've just taken over the ship," he said. "Gerry, float that gun over here, very gently."

Vaughn didn't look amused. "What are you talking about? Get busy and fix that before I—"

"Before you what? I give you ten seconds to surrender or I take this screwdriver and stir. Shoot me before I make the repairs and you get the same result. Maybe they'll name the crater after you."

Vaughn shifted the gun to point at Judy, and Meisner shifted his head to be the target again. "Won't work. You can't risk hitting me and you know it. Float the gun over. Five seconds." Meisner slowly threaded the screwdriver in between the wires until his hand was inside the canister, saying all the while, "Four seconds, three seconds, two seconds, one—very good, Gerry. Judy, catch that."

She let go of the canister and fielded the gun, holding it in between her gloved hands. She felt a moment of panic. "I can't get my finger in the trigger guard!"

"Trade me." Meisner let go of the canister and took the gun from her, then said, "Get in the bottom bunk, Gerry."

Wordlessly, Vaughn drifted over and slid into the bunk, and Meisner closed the panel after him. He hunted in the tool kit until he found a coil of what looked like bell wire and used that to tie the panel shut, then gave the gun back to Judy and took the canister. He began looking inside it again, poking and prodding around.

"What are you doing?" Judy asked.

"Looking for the problem."

"I thought you said you'd found it."

"I lied. I didn't figure there was much point in looking until we had Gerry safely out of the way."

"But what if—never mind. Just hurry. We don't have much time."

"It won't take long. If it isn't something simple I won't be able to fix it anyway. I don't have any test equipment. All I brought along was spare parts."

Judy propped herself against the lockers, her back against the wall and her feet out at an angle against the floor. She'd discovered the position on her first flight. It almost felt like gravity, at least to the legs, and it had the added advantage of holding her in place. She said, "I can't believe you. Do you have the slightest idea what this means to the human race?"

"I think I do, yes."

"Then why are you risking it like this? You should have made it public the moment you realized what you had. Good God, if the secret dies with us now, we—"

"It won't. I arranged a mailing to every member of INSANE the day before we launched. The plans should be arriving in the mail today, all over the world." Meisner raised his voice, though the intercoms made it unnecessary. "There are thirty-seven Russians in INSANE, Gerry. They each got the packet too. So you see, none of this really would have made much difference in the long run anyway. This was just a public demonstration so they wouldn't waste time trying to decide if it would really work. And I still intend to make a radio broadcast of the plans from orbit when we get back. I don't think any elite group should have a monopoly on space travel, not even INSANE." He paused, squinted inside the canister, and said, "I think I've found it. The heat blistered a ROM chip."

He opened his personal locker and got out a baggie full of electronics parts. He fished around until he found the one he needed, a black caterpillar of an I.C. chip about an inch long, and replaced the one in the canister with it. He put the lid back on and held it out. "Okay, you can put it back now."

Judy took the canister and pushed herself toward the airlock. Before she closed the door, she said, "Why don't I stay out there while you try it? It'll save time if we have to bring it in again."

"Good idea."

She closed the airlock door and began depressurizing it. It seemed to take forever to bleed the air out, but she knew that it only took three minutes. She could hear her own breathing inside her helmet, just the way she'd imagined she would when she was a little girl dreaming about space. The suit stiffened a little as the outside pressure dropped. When the gauge reached zero she opened the outer hatch and stepped out into the cargo bay.

The Moon was a flat gray wall of craters in front of her. She watched it for a moment, thinking, *This is what it looked like to the Apollo crews. And I thought I'd never get to see it.*

What sorts of other things would she be seeing that she had only dreamed of before? The other planets, almost certainly: Other stars? Why not? She knew she was going to be in trouble when she got back, but Meisner's invention practically assured her that the trouble wouldn't last. Space-trained pilots were going to be in very short supply before long. NASA couldn't afford to ground her now, but even if they did she knew she could get a job flying somebody else's ship. Or even her own, for that matter. She wasn't above flying a converted septic tank, if that's what it took to stay in space.

Judy heard a nervous voice over the intercom. "Having problems out there?"

She shook herself back to the present. The Moon was growing closer by the second. "No. Hang on." She fastened the getaway special canister back to the cargo bay wall and plugged in the data link to the ship. "How's that?"

"I'm getting power. Let me run the diagnostic check." A few seconds later, Meisner said, "Looks good. I'm keying in the coordinates."

"You sure you don't want to stay and admire the view?"

"Uh . . . some other time, maybe."

"Right." Judy reached out to steady herself against the airlock door. She looked up for one last look at the Moon, so near she almost felt she could touch it. Someday she would. Someday soon. She cleared her throat. "Whenever you're—"

But it had already disappeared.

BETWEEN A ROCK AND A HIGH PLACE

BY TIMOTHY ZAHN

"Ladies and gentlemen, shuttles one and two for United Flight 1103 are now ready for general boarding: Skyport service from Houston to Dallas–Ft. Worth, Los Angeles, and San Francisco."

Peter Whitney was ready; he'd been standing at the proper end of the waiting lounge for the past several minutes, as a matter of fact, eagerly awaiting the announcement. Picking up his carry-on bag, he stepped to the opening door, flashed his boarding pass for the attendant's inspection, and walked down the short tunnel to where the shuttle waited. The excitement within him seemed to increase with every step, a fact that embarrassed him a little—a twenty-eight-year-old computer specialist shouldn't be feeling like a kid on his first trip to Disney World, after all. But he refused to worry too much about it. Professional solemnity was still, for him, a recent acquisition, easily tucked out of the way.

The shuttle itself was unimpressive, of course: little more than a Boeing 727 with a heavily modified interior. Following the flight attendant's instructions he sat down in the front row, choosing the left-hand window seat. Pushing his bag into the compartment under his chair, he fastened his lap/shoulder belt and spent the next few minutes examining the ski-lift-style bars connecting his pair of seats to the conveyors behind the grooves in floor and ceiling. He'd seen specs and models for the system back in St. Louis, but had never given up being amazed that it worked as well as it did in actual practice.

His seatmate turned out to be a smartly suited business-woman type who promptly pulled out her *Wall Street Journal* and buried herself in it. A bored executive who flew in Skyports every week, obviously, and her indifference helped dispel Whitney's last twinges of guilt at having taken the window seat.

Within a very few minutes the shuttle was loaded and ready. The door was closed, the tunnel withdrawn, and soon they were at the edge of the runway, waiting permission to take off. Whitney kept an eye on his watch with some interest—Skyport logistics being what they were, a shuttle couldn't afford to be very late in getting off the ground. Even knowing that, he was impressed when the plane roared down the runway and into the sky only twelve seconds behind schedule.

They turned east, heading into the early-morning sun to meet the Skyport as it headed toward them from its New Orleans pickup. Whitney watched the city disappear behind them, and then shifted his gaze forward, wondering how far away something the size of a Skyport could be seen. Docking, he knew, would take place seventy to eighty miles out from Houston; assuming the shuttle was flying its normal four-ninety knots—five-sixty-odd miles an hour—meant an eight-to-nine minute trip. They'd covered seven of that already; surely they must be coming up on it by now. Unless . . .

With smooth abruptness, the horizon dropped below the level of his window, and Whitney knew he'd goofed. The Skyport was somewhere off to the shuttle's right, and the smaller craft was now circling around to get into docking position. Belatedly he realized he should have asked the flight attendant which was the scenic side when he first boarded.

The passengers on the other side of the aisle were beginning to take an interest in the view out their windows, and Whitney craned his neck in an effort to see. Nothing but ground and sky were visible from where he sat; but even as he settled back in mild disappointment the shuttle leveled out and began to climb . . . and suddenly, ahead and above them, the Skyport loomed into view.

No film clip, scale model, or blueprint, Whitney realized in that moment, could ever fully prepare one for the sheer impact of a Skyport's presence. A giant flying wing, the size of seven football fields laid end to end, the Skyport looked like nothing else in aviation history—looked like nothing, in fact, that had any business being up in the air in the first place. The fact that it also flew more efficiently than anything else in the sky seemed almost like a footnote in comparison, though it was of course the economic justification for the six Skyports now in service and McDonnell Douglas's main argument in their ongoing sales campaign. Staying aloft for weeks or months at a time, the

Skyports were designed for maximum efficiency at high altitudes and speeds, dispensing with the heavy landing gear, noise suppressors, and high-lift flaps required on normal jetliners. And with very little time spent on the ground amid contaminants like dust and insects, the Skyports had finally been able to take advantage of the well-known theories of laminar flow control, enabling the huge craft to fly with less than half the drag of planes with a fraction of their capacity. In Whitney's personal view, it was probably this incredible fuel efficiency that had finally convinced United and TWA to take a chance on the idea.

The shuttle was directly behind the Skyport now and closing swiftly. From his window Whitney could see five of the seven basically independent modules that made up the Skyport and, just barely, the two port engines of the sixth. That would be all right; since only the center module's engines fired during this part of the flight, docking one module in from the end was essentially equivalent in noise and turbulence to docking in the end section. Docking one module from center, on the other hand, was rumored to be a loud and rather unnerving experience. It was a theory he wasn't anxious to test.

A flash of sunlight off to the left caught his eye—the second Houston shuttle, making its approach toward the second-to-last module at the other end. He watched with interest as the distant plane nosed toward its docking bay, watched it until the portside engines of his own shuttle's target module blocked it from sight. The silvery trailing edge of the Skyport was very near now, and the slight vibration that had been building almost imperceptibly began to increase at a noticeable rate. Whitney was just trying to estimate the vibrational amplitude and to recall the docking bay's dimensional tolerances when a sound like a muffled bass drum came from the fuselage skin a meter in front of him and the vibration abruptly stopped. The docking collar, clamping solidly around them. With the noise of the Skyport's engines still filling the cabin, Whitney's straining ears had no chance of picking up the nosewheel's descent into the docking bay; but he *did* distinctly hear the *thump* as the bay's forward clamp locked onto the nosewheel's tow bar. Only then, with the shuttle firmly and officially docked, did he realize he'd been holding his breath. He let it out with a wry smile, feeling more than ever like a kid on a ride Disney had never dreamed of.

Another soft thump and hiss signaled that the pressurized tunnel was in place. A cool breeze wafted through the shuttle as the outer door was opened—and suddenly Whitney and his seatmate were moving, their ski-lift seats following the grooves in floor and ceiling as they were moved first into the aisle and then forward toward the exit. They turned left at the doorway, and Whitney caught just a glimpse of the shuttle's other seats in motion behind him. Then, with only the slightest jerk of not-quite-aligned grooves, they were out of the shuttle and into a flexible-walled corridor that looked for all the world like the inside of an accordion. The tunnel was short, leading to another airplane-type doorway. Straight ahead, stretching down a long corridor, Whitney could see a column of seats like his own, filled with passengers for the shuttle's trip back down to Houston. There didn't seem to be enough room beside the column for the emerging seats to pass by easily, but Whitney was given little time to wonder about it. Just beyond the doorway his seat took a ninety-degree turn to the right, and he found himself sidling alongside a wall toward what looked like a lounge. To his left he could see the rest of the shuttle's seats following like a disjointed snake. The airlines had balked at the ski-lift system, he remembered, complaining that it was unnecessarily complicated and expensive. But the time the shuttle spent in the docking bay translated into fuel for its return flight, and the essence of *that* was money . . . and the ski-lift system gave the shuttle a mere ten-minute turnaround.

It was indeed a sort of lounge the chairs were taking them into, a rectangular space done up with soft colors and a carpet designed to disguise the grooves in the floor. In the center was a large, four-sided computer display giving destinations and the corresponding modules in large letters. Whitney's seatmate retrieved her briefcase from under her chair and hopped off as the chair entered the room and began to sidle its way across the floor; glancing at the display, she strode out through one of the wide doorways in the far wall. Whitney obeyed the rules, himself, waiting until the seat had come to a complete stop before undoing his belt and standing up. He was in module six, the display informed him, and passengers for Los Angeles could sit anywhere in modules one, two, six, or seven. Since his boarding pass indicated he'd be disembarking from module six anyway, it made the most sense to just stay here, a decision most of the others also seemed to have reached. Picking up his carry-on, he joined the surge forward. A short corridor lined with lavatory doors lay ahead; passing through it, he entered—

Instant disorientation.

The room before him was *huge*, and was more a combination

theater-café-lounge than an airplane cabin. Directly in front of him was a section containing standard airline chairs, but arranged in patterns that varied from the traditional side-by-side to cozy circles around low tables. To either side were small cubicles partially isolated from the main floor by ceiling-length panels of translucent, gray-tinted plastic. Further on toward the front of the Skyport, partially separated from the lounge by more of the tinted plastic, was a section that was clearly a dining area, with tables of various sizes and shapes, about a third of them occupied despite the early hour. Beyond that, the last section seemed to be divided into three small movie/TV rooms.

It all seemed almost scandalously wasteful for a craft that, for all its size and majesty, still had to answer to the law of gravity; but even as Whitney walked in among the lounge chairs he realized the extravagance was largely illusory. Despite the varied seating, little floor space was actually wasted, and most of that would have been required for aisles, anyway. The smoked-plastic panels gave the illusion that the room was larger than it actually was, while at the same time added a sense of coziness to all the open space; and the careful use of color disguised the fact that the room's ceiling wasn't much higher than that of a normal jetliner.

For a few minutes Whitney wandered more or less aimlessly, absorbing the feel of the place. A rumble from his stomach reminded him that he'd had nothing yet that morning except coffee, though, and he cut short his exploration in favor of breakfast. Sitting down at one of the empty café tables, he scanned the menu card briefly and then pushed the call button in the table's center. Safety, he noted, had not been sacrificed to style; the table and chair were both fastened securely to the floor, and the metal buckle of a standard lap/shoulder belt poked diffidently at his ribs.

"Good morning, sir—may I help you?" a pleasant voice came from behind him. He turned as she came into view to his right: a short blonde, trim and athletic-looking in her flight attendant's uniform, pushing a steam cart before her. The cart surprised him a bit, but it was instantly obvious that true restaurant service for what could be as many as eight hundred passengers would be well-nigh impossible for the module's modest crew. Out of phase with the decor or not, precooked tray meals were the only way to serve such a crowd.

There were some illusions that even a Skyport couldn't handle.

"Yes. I'd like the eggs, sausage, and fruit meal—number two here," he told her, indicating it on the menu.

"Certainly." Opening a side door on her cart, she withdrew a steaming tray and placed it before him. The aroma rising with the steam made his stomach rumble again. "Coffee?" she added.

"Please. By the way, is there anything like a guided tour of the Skyport available? Upstairs, too, I mean?"

Her forehead wrinkled a bit as she picked up a mug and began to fill it. "The flight deck? I'm afraid not—FAA regulations forbid passengers up there."

"Oh. No exceptions, huh?"

"None that I know of." She set the mug down and placed a small cup of cream beside it. "Any special reason you'd like to go up there, or are you just curious?"

"Both, actually. I work for McDonnell Douglas, the company that built this plane. I've been doing computer simulations for them, and now they're transferring me to L.A. to do some stuff on their new navigational equipment. I thought that as long as they were flying me out on a Skyport anyway, it would give me a jump on my orientation if I could look around a bit."

The attendant looked duly impressed. "Sounds like interesting work—and about a million miles over my head. I can talk to the captain, see if we can break the rules for you, but I can't make any promises. Would you give me your name, please, and tell me where you'll be after breakfast?"

"Peter Whitney, and I'll probably be back in the lounge. And, look, don't go breaking any rules—this isn't important enough for anyone to get into trouble over."

She smiled. "Okay, but I'll see what I can do. Enjoy your meal, Mr. Whitney, and if you need anything else just use the caller." With another smile she turned her cart around and left.

Picking up his fork, Whitney cut off a bit of sausage and tasted it, and then sampled the eggs. Piping hot, all of it, but not too hot to eat—and it tasted as good as it smelled. Settling himself comfortably, he attacked his tray with vigor.

There was something magic about a Skyport flight deck.

Betsy Kyser had been flying on the giant planes for nearly eighteen months now—had been a wing captain, in charge of an entire hundred-meter-wide module, for four of them—and she still didn't understand exactly why this place always hit her so strongly. Perhaps it was the mixture of reality and fantasy; the view of blue sky through the tiny forward windows contrasting with the myriads of control lights and glowing computer readouts. Or perhaps it was the size of the flight deck itself, better than twice as large as that of a jumbo jet, that struck a chord within her, half awakening the dreams of huge spaceships she'd had as a child. Whatever the reason, she knew the feeling would wear off sooner or later . . . but until that happened, it was there for her to enjoy. Standing just inside the flight deck door, she drank her fill of the magic.

Slouched in the copilot's seat, Aaron Greenburg glanced back toward her, the gold wings on his royal-blue jumpsuit's shoulderboards winking at her with the motion. "Morning, Bets—thought I heard you come in," he greeted her.

"Morning, Aaron. Tom, Rick," she added as the pilot and flight engineer turned and nodded to her. "Any problems come up during the night?"

Tom Lewis, in the pilot's seat, raised his hands shoulder high in an expansive shrug. "What could go wrong?"

He had a point. Only the middle three wing sections ran their huge General Electric CF6-90C1 turbofan engines during normal flight, the outer two of those shutting down during the lower-speed shuttle pickups. Perched on the Skyport's starboard end, Wing Section Seven was essentially along for a free ride, with little to do but keep the passengers happy and make sure the fuel the shuttles brought up went down the internal pipeline to the sections that needed it. "You trying to tell me you get *bored* up here?" she asked in mock astonishment. "*Here*, aboard the greatest flying machine ever built by mankind?"

Before Lewis could answer, a voice spoke up from the intercom. "Wassamatta, Seven; isn't our company good enough for you? What do you want—home movies and pretzels?"

"We could let them have some of the navigational work," a new voice suggested.

"*Great* idea. Seven, why don't you hop outside and take a sun-sight?"

"I've got a better idea, Five," Lewis said, turning back to the intercom grille. "Why don't we do a Chinese fire drill and send One, Two, and Three around to hook up on the other side of us and let *us* drive for a while."

"Sounds like fun," a voice Betsy recognized as One's night-shift pilot broke in. "It'd confuse the passengers all to hell, though. Do we tell them, or see if they figure it out by themselves?"

"Oh, we could switch back before we got to L.A.," Lewis told him.

"I've got an even better idea, Seven," the rumbling voice of Skyport Captain Carl Young said from Four. "Why don't you all cut the chitchat and get ready to receive the Dallas shuttle."

Lewis grinned. "Yes, sir. Chitchat out, sir."

Betsy stepped forward. "All the way out, as a matter of fact. You can go on back, Tom; I'll take over here."

"I've still got over a half hour left on my shift, you know," he reminded her.

"That's okay—the quality of intercom banter this morning indicates *everyone* on this bird is suffering gobs of boredom fatigue. Go on, get some coffee and relax. And maybe work on your one-liners."

Lewis gave her an injured look. "Well-l-l . . . okay. If you insist." Pulling off his half-headset and draping it across the wheel, he slid out of his chair and stepped back from the instrument panel. "All yours, Cap'n," he added. "Try not to hit anything; I'll be taking a nap."

"Right," she said dryly, slipping into his vacated seat. "Aaron, Rick—you two want to flip a coin or something to see who goes on break first?"

There was a short pause. Then Greenburg glanced back over his shoulder. "Why don't you go ahead," he said to Rick Henson. "I'd like to stay for a bit."

Henson nodded and got up from his flight engineer's board. "Okay. Be back soon." Together he and Lewis left the flight deck.

Betsy looked curiously at Greenburg. "Never known anyone before who didn't jump at a mid-shift coffee break with all four feet," she said.

"Oh, don't worry—I'll take mine, all right. I just wanted to give you a word of warning about the shuttle coming in. Eric Rayburn's flying her."

Betsy felt a knot form directly over her breakfast. "Oh, hell. I sure have a great sense of timing, don't I."

"I can call Tom back in if you'd like," Greenburg offered. "You're not technically on duty for another half-hour."

She was sorely tempted. By eight o'clock Skyport time—seven Dallas time—the shuttle would have come and gone and be back on the ground again, and Eric Rayburn with it. She wouldn't have to talk to him, something she was pretty sure both of them would appreciate; and with her blood pressure and digestion intact she could go back to just flying her plane—

And to avoiding Eric.

"I can't avoid him forever, though, can I," she said, with a resigned sigh. "Thanks, but I'll stay here."

Greenburg's dark eyes probed her face. "If you're sure." He paused. "Shuttle's calling now," he informed her.

Nodding, she took the half-headset and put it on, guiding the single earphone to a comfortable spot in her left ear. Even before it was in place she heard Rayburn's clipped Boston accent. "—to Skyport Eleven-oh-three. Beginning approach; request docking instructions."

Besty pursed her lips and turned on her mike. "Dallas shuttle, this is Skyport Eleven-oh-three. You're cleared for docking in Seven; repeat, Seven." Her eyes ran over the instrument readouts as she spoke. "Skyport speed holding steady at two-sixty knots; guidance system radar has a positive track on you."

"Is that you, Liz? Son of a gun; I had no *idea* I was going to have the honor of docking with *your* own Skyport. This is *indeed* a privilege."

Betsy had been fully prepared for heavy sarcasm, but she still found her hands forming into tight knots of frustration at his words. *Liz*—early in their relationship he'd learned how much she despised that nickname, and his continual use of it these days was a biting echo of the pain she'd felt at their breakup. "Yes, this is Kyser," she acknowledged steadily. "Shuttle, you're coming in a bit fast. Do you want a relative-v confirmation check?"

"What for? I can fly my bird as well as you can fly yours, Liz."

"We're sure you can, Shuttle." Betsy's voice was still calm, but it was a losing battle and she knew it. "Dock whenever you're ready; we're here if you need any help." Without waiting for a response, she flipped off the mike and wrenched the half-headset off, cutting off anything else he might say.

For a moment she stared at the instruments without seeing any of them, slowly getting her temper back under control. Greenburg's quiet voice cut through the blackness. "You know, I'm always amazed—and a little bit jealous—whenever I come across someone with as much self-control as you've got."

She didn't look up at him, but could feel the internal tension ease a little. "Thanks. You're lying through your teeth, of course—I've never seen you even raise your voice at anyone— but thanks."

Her peripheral vision picked up his smile. "You give yourself too little credit, and me way too much. Inherent lack of temper isn't comparable with control of a violent one. *My* weaknesses are gin rummy and gin fizzes—usually together." He shook his head. "Eighteen months is a long time to carry a grudge."

"Yeah. I will never again let that old sexist cliché about a woman scorned go by unchallenged—some of you men are just as good at hell's fury as we are."

"If you'll pardon a personal question, is all this nonsense *really* just because you were chosen for Skyport duty and he was left back in the shuttle corps? I'd heard that was all it was, but it seems such a silly thing to base a vendetta on."

She was able to manage a faint smile now. "That shows you don't know Eric very well. He's a very opinionated man, and once he gets hold of an idea he will *not* let it go. He is thoroughly convinced United put me on the Skyport because of my looks, because they thought it would be good publicity, because they needed a token female—*any* reason except that I might have more of the qualities they were looking for than he did."

"One of his opinions is that women are inferior pilots to men?" Greenburg hazarded.

"Or at least we're inferior pilots to *him*. My flying skills were perfectly acceptable to him until United made the cut. In fact, he used to brag a lot about me to his other friends."

Unknotting her fists, she stretched her arms and fingers. "The irony of it is that he'd be climbing the walls here his first week on duty. He's a good pilot, but he can't stand being under anyone's authority once he's left the cockpit. Even the low-level discipline we have to maintain here around the clock would be more than he'd be willing to put up with."

"Maverick types we don't need here," Greenburg agreed. "Well, try not to let him get to you. In just over ten minutes he'll be nothing more than a bad taste in your memory."

"Until the next time our paths cross," Betsy sighed. "It's so hard when I remember what good friends we once were." A number on one of the readouts caught her eye, and she leaned forward with a frown. "I still read him coming in a shade too fast. Aaron, give me a double-check—what's the computer showing on his relative-v?"

Greenburg turned to check. As he did so, Betsy felt the Skyport dip slightly, and her eyes automatically sought out the weather radar. Nothing in particular was visible; the bump must have been a bit of clear air turbulence. No problem; with a plane the size of Skyport normal turbulence was normally not even noticed by the passengers—

Without warning, her seat suddenly slammed up underneath

her as the flight deck jerked violently. Simultaneously, there was a strangely indistinct sound of tortured metal . . . and, as if from a great distance, a scream of agony.

Betsy would remember the next few seconds as a period of frantic activity in which her mind, seemingly divorced from her body by shock, was less a participant than a silent observer. With a detached sort of numbness she watched her hands snatch up her half-headset—realizing only then that that was where the distant scream had come from—and jam it into place on her head. A dozen red lights were flashing on the instrument panel; and she watched herself join Greenburg in slapping at the proper controls and shutoffs, turning off shorting circuits and leaking hydraulics in the orderly fashion their training had long since drummed into them. And all the time she wondered what had gone wrong, and wondered what she was going to do. . . .

The slamming-open of the door behind her broke the spell, jolting her mind back into phase with reality. "What the hell was *that?*" Henson called as he charged full-tilt through the doorway and dropped into his flight engineer's chair. Lewis was right behind him, skidding to a stop behind Greenburg.

"Shuttle crash," Betsy snapped. Emergency procedures finished, she now had her first chance to study the other telltales and try to figure out the exact situation. "Looks bad. The shuttle seems to have gone in crooked, angling upwards and starboard. Captain Rayburn, can you hear me? Captain Rayburn, report please."

For a moment she could hear nothing through her earphone but a faint, raspy breathing. "This is—this is Rayburn." The voice was stunned, weak, sounding nothing like the man Betsy had once known.

"Captain, what's the situation down there?" she asked through the sudden tightness in her throat. "Are you hurt?"

"I don't know." His voice was stronger now; he must have just been momentarily stunned. "My right wrist hurts some. John . . . oh, God! *John!*"

"Rayburn?" Betsy snapped.

"My copilot—John Meredith—the whole side of the cockpit's caved in on him. He's—oh, God—I think he's dead."

Betsy's left hand curled into a fist in front of her. "Rayburn, snap out of it! Turn on your intercom and find out if your passengers are all right. Then see if there's a doctor on board to see to Meredith. If he's alive every second could count. And use your oxygen mask—you've probably been holed and the bay's not pressurized."

Rayburn drew a long, shuddering breath, and when he spoke again he sounded almost normal. "Right. I'll let you know what I find."

A click signified the shuttle's intercom had been switched on. Listening to him with half an ear, Betsy pushed the mike away from her mouth and turned back to Greenburg. "Have you got a picture yet?" she asked.

The copilot was fiddling with the bay TV monitor controls. "Yeah, but the quality's pretty bad. He took out the starboard fisheye when he hit, and a lot of the overhead floods, too."

Betsy peered at the screen. "Port side looks okay. I wish we could see what he's done to his starboard nose. Top of the fuselage looks like it's taken some damage—up there, that shadow."

"Yeah. A little hard—"

"Betsy!" Henson broke in. "Take a look at the collar stress readouts. We've got big trouble."

She located the proper screen, scanned the numbers. There were six of them, one for each of the supports securing the docking collar to the edge of the bay. Four of the six indicated no stresses at all, while the other two were dangerously overloaded; and it took a half second for the significance of the zero readings to register. "Oh, great," she muttered, pulling the mike back to her lips. "Rayburn?"

"Passengers are okay except for some bruises and maybe sprains." Rayburn's voice was muffled, indicating he'd put his oxygen mask on. "We've got a doctor coming to look at John."

"Good. Now listen carefully. You're holding onto the Skyport by the skin of your teeth—four of the collar supports have been snapped, and the drag on you is straining the last two. Start firing your engines at about—" She paused, suddenly realizing she had no idea how much power he'd have to use to relieve the strain on the clamps. "Just start your engines and run them up slowly. We'll tell you when you're at the right level."

"Got you. Here goes."

It took nearly a minute for the stresses to drop to what Betsy considered the maximum acceptable levels. "All right, hold at that level until further notice," she told him. "Is the doctor in the cockpit yet?"

"He's just coming in now."

"When he's finished his examination give him a headset and let him talk to one of us here."

"Yeah, okay."

Pulling off her half-headset, Betsy draped it around her neck and looked over at Greenburg. "Stay with him, will you? I need to talk to Carl."

Greenburg nodded, and Betsy leaned over the intercom. "Carl? This is Kyser on Seven."

"We've been listening, Betsy," the Skyport captain's calm voice came immediately. "What's the situation?"

"Bad. We've got a damaged—possibly wrecked—shuttle with a probably dead first officer aboard. A doctor's with him. Somehow the crash managed to tear out four of the docking collar supports, too, and if the other two go we'll lose her completely."

"The emergency collar?"

"Hasn't engaged. I don't know why yet; the sensors in that area got jarred pretty badly and they aren't all working."

"The front clamp didn't make it to the nosewheel, I take it?"

"No, sir." Betsy studied the TV screen. "Looks like it's at least a meter short, maybe more."

"Those clamp arms aren't supposed to run short, no matter where in the bay the shuttle winds up," someone spoke up from one of the other wing sections. "Maybe it's just hung up on something, and in that case you should be able to connect it up manually from inside the bay."

"There isn't supposed to be anything in there for the arm to hang up *on*," Greenburg muttered, half to himself.

Young heard him anyway. "Unless the crash jarred something loose," he pointed out. "Checking on that should be our first priority."

"Excuse me, Carl, but it's not," Betsy said. "Our first priority is to figure out whether something aboard Seven caused the crash."

"A board of inquiry—"

"Will be too late. All our fuel comes up via these shuttles. If a flaw's developed in Seven's electronics or computer guidance programming we've got to find out what it is and make sure none of the other wing sections has it. Because if something *is* going bad, it has to be fixed before we can allow any more dockings. Otherwise we could wind up with *two* smashed shuttles."

Behind her, she heard Lewis swear under his breath and head over toward the flight deck's seldom-used computer terminal. "You're right," Young admitted. "I hadn't thought that far. Can you run the check, or shall I send someone over to help?"

"Tom's starting on it now, but I'm not sure what it'll prove. The computer's supposed to continually run its own checks and let us know if there's any problem. If there's a flaw the machine missed, a standard check isn't likely to find it, either."

"Then we'll go to the source. I'll put a call through to McDonnell Douglas and see if they can either run a deeper check by remote control or tell us how to do one."

Betsy glanced at her watch. Six-forty St. Louis time; two hours earlier in Los Angeles. They'd have to get the experts out of bed, a time-consuming process. She was just about to mention that fact when Paul Marinos, Six's captain, spoke up. "Wait a second. There's a guy aboard who works for McDonnell Douglas—Erin told me he'd asked her about a tour of the flight deck."

"Does he know anything about our electronics?" Young asked.

"I don't know, but she said he does *something* with computers for them."

Betsy turned around to look at Lewis, who shrugged and nodded assent. "Close enough," she told the Skyport captain. "Can you get him up here right away?"

"I'll go get him myself," Marinos volunteered. "I'll be there in a couple of minutes."

"All right. Let's get back to the shuttle itself, then," Young said. "Betsy you said the collar supports were broken. Any idea how that happened?"

"I can only speculate that the collar had established a partial grip before the shuttle did its sideways veer into the bay wall."

"In that case, the crash may have left both the outer shuttle door and the exit tunnel intact. Any chance of getting the two connected and getting the passengers out of there?"

"I don't know." Betsy peered at the screen, made a slight adjustment in the contrast. "They're out of line, for sure. I don't know if the tunnel will stretch far enough to make up the difference."

"Even if it does, we'd need portable oxygen masks for all the passengers," Henson pointed out from behind her. "They have to be using the shuttle's air masks, and they can't travel with those."

"That's not going to be a problem," Young said. "I've already invoked emergency regulations; we're bringing her down to fifteen thousand feet."

"Well, there's nothing more I can tell from here." Betsy

shook her head. "Someone's going to have to go down and take a look. Who aboard this bird knows the most about docking bay equipment?"

There was a pause. "I don't know whether I know the *most*," Greenburg spoke up diffidently at Betsy's right, "but I've seen the blueprints, and I worked summers as a mechanic's assistant for Boeing when I was in college."

"Anyone able to top that?" Young asked. "No? All right, Greenburg, get going."

Betsy put her half-headset back on as Greenburg removed his and stood up. "A set of the relevant blueprints would be helpful," he said, looking back at Lewis.

"I'm having the computer print them," the other told him. "If you want to go down and get the oxygen gear together, I'll come down and give you a hand."

Greenburg glanced questioningly at Betsy. "Can you do without both of us that long?"

She hesitated, then nodded. "Sure. But make it a fast looksee. You're not going down there to do any major repair work."

"Right." Greenburg started for the door. "Meet you by the port-aft cargo access hatch, Tom."

Lewis waved an acknowledgment, his eyes on the computer screen, as Greenburg exited. Betsy turned back to face forward, and as she did so Rayburn's voice crackled in her ear. "Skyport, this is Rayburn. The doctor says John's alive!"

A small part of the tightness across Betsy's chest seemed to disappear. "Thank God! Is the doctor still there? I want to speak with him."

"Just a second." There was a moment of silence punctuated by assorted clicks, and then a new voice came tentatively on the line. "Hello? This is Dr. Emerson."

"Doctor, this is Wing Captain Elizabeth Kyser. What sort of shape is First Officer Meredith in?"

"Not a good one, I'm afraid," Emerson admitted. "He seems to have one or more cracked ribs and possibly a broken collarbone as well. The way the fuselage has bent inward and pinned him makes it hard to examine him. I could try pulling him out, but that might exacerbate any internal injuries, or even drive bits of glass into him from the broken windows. He's unconscious, but his vital signs are stable, at least for the moment. I'm afraid I can't tell you much more."

"Just knowing he's alive is good news enough," Betsy assured him. She thought for a moment. "What if we could cut the whole chair loose? Is there enough room behind him to move the chair back and get him out that way?"

"Uh . . . I think so, yes. But I don't know what we would do after that. I heard the flight attendant say the door was jammed."

Betsy frowned. Rayburn hadn't mentioned that to her. "We might be able to force it open anyway and get it connected to the rest of the Skyport. Are the rest of the passengers all right?"

"A few minor injuries, mostly bruises due to the safety belts. We've been very lucky."

So far. "Yeah. Thank you, Doctor. Please let us know immediately if there's any change."

"Got the prints, Betsy," Lewis called as she turned off the mike. "I'm heading down."

He was gone before she could do more than nod assent, leaving her and Henson alone. For some reason the empty seats bothered her, and she briefly considered calling in some of Seven's off-duty crewmen. But as long as they were stuck in this virtual holding pattern, extra help on the flight deck would be pretty superfluous. Turning back to the instrument panel, she felt a wave of frustration wash over her. So many unanswered questions, most of them crucial to the safety of one or more groups of people aboard the Skyport—and she was temporarily at a loss to handle any of them. For the moment there was nothing she could do but try and line up the problems in some sort of logical order: if A is true then B must be done, and D cannot precede either B or C. But it was like juggling or playing chess in her head; there were just too many contingencies that had to be taken into account every step of the way.

Behind her the door opened, and she turned to see two men walk in. One she knew: Paul Marinos, captain of Wing Section Six. The other, a thirtyish young man in a three-piece suit, she'd never seen before. But she knew instantly who he was.

"Betsy," Marinos said, "this is Peter Whitney, of McDonnell Douglas."

Whitney had been daydreaming in his lounge chair, enjoying the unique Skyport atmosphere, when the violent bump jerked him back to full alertness. He shot a rapid glance around the room, half expecting to see the walls caving in around him. But everything looked normal. Up ahead, he could hear muttered curses from the dining room—prompted, no doubt, by spilled coffee and the like—while from the lounge itself came a heightened buzz of conversation. Whitney closed his ears to it all as best he could, straining instead to listen for some clue as to what had happened. An explosive misfire in one of the engines was his first gut-level guess; but the dull background rumble seemed unchanged. A hydraulic or fuel line that had broken with that much force might still be leaking audibly; again, he could hear nothing that sounded like that. Had there been that bogey of the '70s and early '80s, a midair collision? But even small planes these days were supposed to be equipped with the Bendix-Honeywell transponder system—and how could any pilot fail to see the Skyport in the first place?

The minutes dragged by, and conversational levels gradually returned to normal as the other passengers apparently decided that nothing serious had happened. Whitney suspected differently, and to him the loudspeaker's silence was increasingly ominous. Something serious *had* happened, and the captain was either afraid to tell the passengers what it was or the crew was just too damn busy fighting the problem to talk. Neither possibility was a pleasant one.

A flash of royal blue caught the corner of his eye, and he turned to see a chunky man in a Skyport-crew jumpsuit step from the dining area into the lounge. The flight attendant who'd served Whitney's breakfast was with him, and Whitney watched curiously as her gaze swept the room. It wasn't until she pointed in his direction and the two started toward him that it occurred to Whitney that they might be looking for *him*. Even then uncertainty kept him in his seat until there was no doubt as to their target, and he had barely enough time to stand up before they reached him.

"Mr. Whitney?" the jumpsuited man asked. His expression was worried, his tone was politeness laminated on urgency. The girl looked worried, too.

Whitney nodded, noticing for the first time the gold wings-in-a-circle pins on his chest and shoulderboards. A wing captain, not just a random crew member. Whitney's first hopeful thought, that this was somehow related to the tour he'd asked for, vanished like tax money in Washington.

"I'm Captain Paul Marinos," the other introduced himself. "We have a problem, Mr. Whitney, that we hope you can help us with. Is it true that you work with computer systems for McDonnell Douglas?"

Whitney nodded, feeling strangely tongue-tied, but finally getting his brain into gear. They were almost certainly not interested in just general computer knowledge; his nodded affirmative needed a qualifier added to it. "I know only a little about current Skyport programming, though," he told them. "I mostly work with second-generation research."

Marinos's expression didn't change, but his next words were almost a whisper. "What we need is a malfunction check on our shuttle approach and guidance equipment. Can you do that?"

The pieces clicked almost audibly into place in Whitney's mind. It *had* been a crash, and one that all the Bendix-Honeywell collision-proofing in the world couldn't prevent. "I don't know, but I can try. Where do I find a terminal?"

"On Seven," was the cryptic response. "Come with me, please."

Marinos led the way across the lounge and back into the dining room. A door in the right-hand wall brought them into one of the module's food preparation and storage areas. The blond flight attendant left them at that point; moving forward through the galley, Marinos and Whitney arrived at an elevator. One deck up was a somewhat cramped hallway lined with doors—crew quarters, Whitney assumed. In the opposite direction a heavy, positive-sealing door stood across their path. Marinos unlocked it and swung it open; and to Whitney's mild surprise an identical door, hung the opposite way, faced them. The captain opened this one, too, and gestured Whitney through, sealing both doors again behind them. "We're on Wing Section Seven now," he told Whitney, leading the way down a hall that mirror-imaged the one they'd just left. "The wing captain here is Betsy Kyser. You'll be working with her and her crew."

Beyond the hallway was a small lounge; passing through it, they entered what appeared to be a ready-room sort of place with a half-dozen jumpsuited men and women listening intently to an intercom speaker; and finally, they reached the flight deck.

"We appreciate your coming up here," Captain Kyser said as Marinos concluded the introductions. "I hope you can help us."

"So do I," Whitney said. "Anything at all you can tell me about your malfunction? It might help my search."

"All we know is that it's somewhere in the equipment or programming that guides shuttles into the docking bay." In a few terse sentences she told him what was known about the shuttle crash, including the craft's current orientation in the bay. "My indicator said its approach velocity was too high, if that's significant," she concluded. "But I don't know it that was just my indicator or if the whole system was confused."

"The shuttle's radar is independent of your equipment, though, isn't it? Maybe the pilot can corroborate your readings."

"Maybe—but if he'd seen anything wrong he'd almost certainly have yelled. But I'll ask him. First, though, I want to get you started. Paul, will you monitor the shuttle?"

Marinos, who had already quietly seated himself in the copilot's seat, nodded and put on a headset. Kyser removed her own and led Whitney to a console built snugly into the flight deck's left rear corner. Motioning him into the chair in front of it, she leaned over him and tapped at the keys. "Here's the sign-on . . . access code . . . and program file." A series of names and numbers appeared on the screen. "Any of those look familiar?"

"Quite a few, if the programming division's keeping its nomenclature consistent." Whitney scanned the list, experimentally keyed in a number.

"That's the standard equipment-check program," Kyser told him. "We've already run that one and come up dry."

"No errors? Then the problem probably isn't in the computer system."

She shook her head. " 'Probably' isn't good enough. Aren't there more complete test programs that can be run?"

"You're talking about the full-blown diagnostic monsters that ground maintenance uses." Whitney hesitated, trying to remember what little he knew about such programs. "It seems to me that the program should be stored somewhere in your system, probably on one of the duplicate-copy disks. The catch is that the thing takes up almost all of your accessible memory space, so anything that normally uses that space will have to be temporarily shut down while it's running."

Kyser looked over at the flight engineer. "Rick?"

"Jibes with what I've heard," he agreed. "Most of the programs that take a lot of space are connected with navigation, radar monitoring, and mechanical flight systems and cargo deck stuff. We're not using any of those at the moment, anyway, so that's no problem. I can also switch a lot of the passenger-deck functions from automatic to manual control." He craned his neck to look at Whitney, sitting directly behind him. "Will that free up enough memory?"

"I don't know—I don't know how much room it'll need. But there's another problem, Captain. Since it *is* such a big program, there'll almost undoubtedly be safeguards to keep someone from accidentally loading it and losing everything else in the memory."

"A password?"

"Of some kind." Whitney had been searching the program

list and had already checked the descriptions of two or three of the entries. Another of them caught his eye and he keyed it in. "You may need to check with ground control to even find the name . . . hold it. Never mind, I've found it. DCHECK. Let's see. . . ." He advanced the description another page, skimmed it. "Here it is. We need something called the Sasquatch-3L package to load it."

"Will Dallas ground control have it?" Henson asked.

"I would think so—if not, they can probably get it by phone from one of the Skyport maintenance areas." Whitney hesitated. "But it's not clear whether or not that'll do you any good."

"Why not?"

"Well, remember that the whole reason you don't have the loading code in the first place is that they don't want you accidentally plugging in the program and wiping out something the autopilot's doing. So they may not legally be able to release the code to a Skyport crew, especially one that's in flight."

"That's stupid!"

"That's bureaucratic thinking," Captain Kyser corrected—or agreed; Whitney couldn't figure out which. Leaning over Whitney's shoulder again, she spoke toward a small grille next to the display screen. "Carl? Did you get all that?"

"Yes," the intercom answered, "and I suspect Mr. Whitney's basically right. But there have to be emergency procedures for something like this—else why have the program stored aboard in the first place? It should simply be a matter of getting an adequately prominent official to give an okay. I'll get the tower on it right away."

"And hope your prominent official can move his tail this early in the morning," she muttered under her breath.

Whitney had been thinking along a separate track. "There's one other thing we can try," he said. "Can you patch me into the regular phone system from up here?"

"Trivially. Why?"

"I'd like to call my former supervisor back in Houston. He might be able to get the package, either from his own office or from someone in L.A."

"You just said it was illegal to release the code," Henson objected.

"To you, yes; but maybe not to me. I *work* for the company, after all."

Henson started to growl something vituperative, but Kyser cut him off. "We'll complain to the FAA later. For now, let's take whatever loopholes we can get our hands on. Put on that half-headset, Mr. Whitney, and I'll fix you up with Ma Bell."

The call, once the connection was finally made, was a remarkably short one. Dr. Mills, seldom at his best in the early morning, nevertheless came fully awake as Whitney gave him a thumbnail sketch of the crisis. He took down the names of both the diagnostic program and the loading code, extracted from Captain Kyser—via Whitney—the instructions for placing a return call to the Skyport, and promised to have the package for him in fifteen minutes.

"Well, that's it, I guess," Whitney remarked after signing off. "Nothing to do now but wait."

"Yeah. Damn."

Whitney looked up at her as she stared through the computer console, concentration drawing her eyebrows together. She had been something of a surprise to him, and he still found it hard to believe a Skyport wing captain could be so young. Marinos, he estimated, was in his early fifties, and Henson wasn't much younger. But if Betsy Kyser was anything past her early forties she was the best-preserved woman he'd ever seen. Which meant either United was hard up for Skyport personnel or Captain Kyser was one very fine pilot. He fixed the thought firmly in his mind; it was one of the few things about all this that was even remotely comforting. "Uh . . . Captain?" he spoke up.

She focused on him, the frown lingering for a second before she seemed to notice it and eased it a bit. "Call me Betsy," she told him. "This isn't much of a place for formalities."

"I'm Peter, then. May I ask why you need to know about the electronics right *now?* I would think the shuttle's safety would be the thing you need to concentrate on."

"It is, but we can't do anything about that until we're sure more shuttles can dock safely." He must have looked blank, because the corner of her mouth twitched and she continued, "Look. Whatever we wind up doing to the shuttle, odds are we don't already have the necessary equipment on board. That means—"

"That means you'll have to bring it up via shuttle," Whitney nodded, catching on at last. "So you need to find the glitch in your docking program and make sure it hasn't also affected the other modules' equipment."

"Right. After that the next job'll be to either get the passengers out or secure the shuttle into the bay, whichever is faster and safer."

Whitney nodded again. In his mind's eye he could see the

damaged shuttle hanging precariously out the back of the Skyport, holding on by the barest of threads. The picture reawakened the half-forgotten vertigo of his first—and last—roller-coaster ride twenty years ago, and he discovered he was gripping the arms of his chair a shade more tightly than necessary. Firmly he forced his emotions down out of the way. "There's going to be a fair amount of drag on the shuttle from the Skyport's slip-stream," he commented, thinking aloud as a further distraction from discomfiting images. "That means a lot of stress on the docking collar. Would it help any if the shuttle dumped its fuel, to make itself lighter?"

"Just the opposite; the eng—" She paused, a strange look flickering across her face. Behind her, Whitney saw peripher-ally, Marinos had swiveled around, his attention presumably attracted by Betsy's abrupt silence. "Paul," she said without turning, "run a calculation for me. At its present rate of burn, how much fuel has the shuttle got left?"

"What diff—?" Marinos stopped, too, the same look settling onto his own features. Turning back, he began punching calcu-lator buttons.

"Right," Betsy muttered tartly. "We've gotten too used to the easy transfer of fuel between shuttle and Skyport . . . or I have, anyway." Whitney had figured out what was going on, but Betsy spelled it out for him anyway. "You see, Peter, the shuttle's currently firing its engines, at about medium power, to counteract the drag you mentioned. I guess I was subcon-sciously assuming we could feed it all the fuel it needed from the Skyport's reserves."

"But the connections are out of line?"

"Almost certainly. The fuel line's on the starboard side, too, which means there's not likely to be enough room to even get in and connect them manually. Probably no access panels close enough, either, but I guess we'll have to check on that." She grimaced. "Something else to do. I hope someone's keeping a list."

"Got it, Betsy," Marinos said, looking up once more. "At current usage, he'll run dry in a little over seven hours."

"Seven hours." She pursed her lips. "And that assumes nei-ther of his main pumps was rattled loose by the impact. Carl?"

"I heard, Betsy," the intercom grille said. "That's not a lot of time."

"No kidding. How much fuel has the whole Skyport got; for our own flying, I mean?"

"At our current speed, a good ten hours. All the tanks are pretty full."

"Okay. Thanks."

"Still no word from ground control on your program," he added. "They're trying to look up the regs and track down the guy who's got the actual package, and doing both of them badly."

"Betsy?" Marinos again. "Sorry to interrupt, but it's Eric Rayburn on the shuttle. He wants to talk to you."

Whitney started to reach for the earphone he was wearing, but Betsy shook her head, stepping back to her chair and picking up her own set. "This is Kyser," she said into the slender mike.

"Liz, what the hell's going on up there?" a harsh voice said into Whitney's left ear.

With the kind of crisis they were all facing up here, Whitney wouldn't have believed the tension on the flight deck could possibly increase. But it did. He could feel it in the uncomfortable shifting of Henson in his chair, and in Marinos's furtive glance sideways, and in Betsy's tightly controlled response. "We're trying to figure out how to get you and your passengers out of there alive," she said.

"Well, it's taking a damn sight too long. Or have you forgotten that John's in bad shape?"

"No, we haven't forgotten. If you've got any suggestions let's hear them."

"Sure. Just open this damn collar and let me fly my plane back to Dallas."

Betsy and Marinos exchanged glances; Whitney couldn't see Betsy's face, but Marinos's looked flabbergasted. "That's out of the question. You don't even know if the shuttle will fly anymore."

"Sure it will! I've still got control of the engines and control surfaces. What else do I need?"

"How about electronics, for starters? You apparently don't even have enough nav equipment left to know where you are. For your information, you wouldn't be flying 'back' to Dallas, because we haven't left—we're circling the area at fifteen thousand feet and about two-seventy knots."

"All the better. I won't need any directional gear to find the airport."

Betsy's snort was a brief snake's hiss in Whitney's ear. "Eric, did you turn your oxygen off or something? Neither you nor the shuttle is in any shape to fly. Period." Rayburn started to object, but she raised her voice and cut him off. "We know you're worried about your first officer, but once we make sure it's safe to dock again we can have doctors and emergency medical equipment brought aboard to take care of him."

"And then what? Try to land with me still hanging out your rear? Don't be absurd. Like it or not, you're eventually going to have to let me go. Let's do it now and get it over with."

"No," Betsy said, and Whitney could hear a tightness in her voice. "There are a minimum number of tests we'll have to run before we can even consider the idea. You can help by starting a standard preflight check on your instruments and systems and figuring out what's still working. Other than that, you'll just have to sit back and wait like the rest of us."

"Wait!" He made the word an obscenity.

"Skyport out." Betsy reached over and flipped a switch, then pushed her mike off to one side. Whitney couldn't see much more than the back of her head, but it was very obvious that she was angry. He shifted uncomfortably in his chair, wishing he were somewhere else. There'd been elements about the whole exchange that had felt like a private feud, and he felt obscurely embarrassed that he'd been listening in.

"Don't let him get to you, Betsy," Henson advised quietly. "He's not worth getting upset about."

"Thanks." Already she seemed to be getting her composure back. "Unfortunately, he *did* hit one problem very squarely on the head."

"The landing problem?" Marinos asked.

Betsy nodded. "I don't know how we're going to handle that one."

"I don't understand," Whitney spoke up hesitantly. "You would just be separating off this module and landing it with the shuttle, wouldn't you?" A horrible thought struck him. "I mean you *aren't* thinking about landing the whole Skyport . . . are you?"

Betsy did something to her chair and swiveled halfway around to look at him. "No, of course not. There isn't a runway in the world that could take an entire Skyport, although the space shuttle landing area at Rogers Dry Lake might be possible in a real emergency."

"Then what's the problem? The modules are supposed to be able to land on an eighteen-thousand-foot runway, and Dallas has to have at least one that's that long."

"The eighteen thousand is for a wing section by itself, Peter," Marinos said patiently. He held up a hand and began ticking off fingers. "First: with the extra weight and—more important—the extra drag, we'd have to put down at something above our listed one-sixty-five-knot landing speed. That'll add runway distance right off the bat. Second: one of the weight savings on the wing sections is not having thrust reversers on our engines to help us slow down. We rely on landing wheel brakes and drogue chutes that pop out the back. With the shuttle adding weight out the back—and its gear will be at least a couple of feet off the ground when ours touches down, so there'll be a *lot* of weight—our balance will change. That means a little less weight on the front landing gear, which means a little less braking ability for those six sets of wheels. Maybe significantly less, maybe not; I don't know. And third, and probably most important: the drogue chutes come out the center and ends of our trailing edge—and we won't be able to use any of the center ones while the shuttle's in the way." He shook his head. "I wouldn't even attempt to land on anything shorter than twenty-five thousand under conditions like this."

"I'd hold out for thirty, myself," Betsy agreed grimly. "We just don't *know* how much extra room we'd need. And don't bother suggesting we put down on a cotton field or straddling both lanes of Interstate 20. One of the other ways you save weight on a Skyport is in the landing gear, and landing on something too soft would tear it to shreds."

An idea was taking shape in the back of Whitney's mind . . . but he wanted to think about it before saying anything to the others. "So that leaves, what, the Skyport maintenance facility outside L.A.?" he asked instead.

"Or the one in New Jersey," Betsy said. "L.A.'s closer." She looked at her watch—the fourth time, by Whitney's count, that she had done so in the last ten minutes. "Damn it all, what's holding up ground control?"

As if in answer, the intercom suddenly crackled. "Bets, this is Aaron," a voice said. "We're ready here to start on down."

"Roger, Aaron; keep your line open," Betsy's voice said, too loudly, in Greenburg's ear. He resisted the impulse to turn down the volume on his portable half-headset; in a moment there would be another aluminum-alloy deck between them that should take care of the problem.

"Right. We're opening the access hatch now." As Lewis looked on, Greenburg undid the three clasps securing the surprisingly light disk and levered it up, making sure it locked solidly into its wall latch. Feeling around the underside of the hatch rim, he located the light switch and turned it on. The blackness below blazed with light, and with a quick glance to make sure he wouldn't be landing on unstable footing he grasped the rungs welded to the hatch and started down the narrow metal ladder, tool belt banging against his thigh.

The lowest of the Skyport's three decks was devoted to passenger luggage and general cargo and to the equipment necessary to move it from shuttle to Skyport, between wing sections where necessary, and back to shuttle again. The hatch the two men had chosen led to one edge of the cargo area, and most of the equipment in Greenburg's immediate area seemed to be motors and electronic overseers for the intricate network of conveyor belts and electric trams that sorted incoming luggage by destination and carted it to the proper storage area. All without human supervision, of course—and, despite that, it generally worked pretty well.

"The bay is straight back that way." Lewis had appeared beside him, clutching a sheaf of computer paper. "I think around that pillar thing would be the best approach."

They set off. Greenburg had been on a Skyport cargo deck only once, back in his training days, and was vaguely surprised at the amount of dirt and grease around the machinery they passed. Within a dozen steps his blue jumpsuit had collected a number of greasy smears and he found himself wishing he'd had the extra minute it would have taken to change into something more appropriate for this job. But even a minute could make a lot of difference . . . and Bets was counting on them.

They reached the curved wall that was the lower half of the docking bay within a few minutes, arriving just forward of a wide ring bristling with hydraulic struts that Greenburg knew marked the position of the emergency docking collar. He glanced back at it as they headed forward under the wall's curve, wondering why the backup system hadn't worked. It should have kicked in as soon as the main collar's supports gave way.

"Watch your step," Lewis said sharply, and Greenburg paused in midstep, focusing for the first time on the dark-red puddle edging onto the path in front of him. Peering along the base of the wall, he could see more of the liquid, more or less collected in a narrow trough there. He squatted, touched it tentatively with a fingertip. It felt thick and oily. "Hydraulic fluid?" Lewis asked.

"Yeah. From the emergency collar, probably." Greenburg straightened and, with only a slight hesitation, rubbed the fluid off on his jumpsuit. Stepping carefully around the puddle in his path, he continued on.

The panel they'd decided on was precisely where the blueprints had said it would be: some two meters around the port wall from the heavy forward clamp machinery at the docking bay's forward tip. About forty centimeters by seventy, the panel sat chest-high in the wall and was, for a wonder, not even partially blocked by any of the conveyor equipment. Selecting a wrench from his belt, Greenburg began loosening the nuts.

"I hope there's nothing in here that can't take low air pressure," Lewis remarked as he untangled the two oxygen sets he was carrying and clipped one of the tanks onto the back of Greenburg's belt. "You want me to put the mask on you?"

"I'll put it on when I get this open," Greenburg grunted as he strained against a particularly well-tightened nut. "I don't like stuff hanging from my face while I'm working. Distracts me."

"Put it on before you lose pressure in there, Aaron," Betsy's voice came in his ear.

"Aw, come on—Bets," he said, the last word a burst of air as the nut finally yielded. "We're only a thousand feet or so higher than Pikes Peak, and I've been climbing around up there since I was ten. I'm not going to black out up here for lack of air."

"Well . . . all right. But I want it on you as soon as you've finished with the panel."

"Sure."

It took only a couple of minutes to loosen all the nuts and, with Lewis's help, remove them and force the panel out of its rubber seating. For a minute there was a minor gale at their backs as the pressure inside the cargo deck equalized with that in the bay, and Greenburg realized belatedly he'd forgotten to check whether or not Lewis had remembered to close the hatch behind him. If he hadn't, this windstorm was going to keep going for quite a while . . . but even as he finished adjusting his oxygen mask over his nose and mouth the rush of air began to subside and finally stilled completely. "Here goes," Greenburg muttered as, stooping slightly, he eased his head through the opening, blinking as a cold breeze swept his face.

It was an impressive sight. Even twisted too far toward the bay's starboard wall, the shuttle's nose still seemed almost close enough for him to touch as it loomed over him, vibrating noticeably in the incomplete grip the broken collar provided. To his left and only slightly below him, he could see that the shuttle's front landing gear had descended just as it was supposed to, and was hanging tantalizingly close to the extended forward clamp. Moving his mike right up against his oxygen mask—it was noiser in the bay than he'd expected—he said, "Okay. First of all, I can't see anything that could be interfering with the clamp or arm. Rick, do the telltales read the arm as fully extended?"

A short pause, then Henson's voice. "Sure do. It's still got lateral and vertical play, though. Want me to swing it around any?"

"Waste of time, as long as it's too short. Someone's going to have to go down there and take a look at it, I guess."

"That's not your job, though," Betsy spoke up. "Carl's lining up a mechanical crew to come up from the airport as soon as it's safe. They can do all the work that's needed in the bay."

"I'm sure they'll be thrilled at the prospect—and don't worry, I wasn't volunteering." Greenburg twisted his head around the other direction. "Now, as to the shuttle door . . . hell. I can't be certain, but it looks like the edge of the collar is overlapping it—the shuttle must have slid back and then shot forward and starboard as the collar was engaging. What the hell kind of guidance system error could have caused *that?*"

"We should know in ten or fifteen minutes," an unfamiliar voice put in.

"Who's that?" Greenburg asked.

"Sorry—maybe I shouldn't have butted in. I'm Peter Whitney; I'm helping to run the diagnostic program that will hopefully locate the problem."

Peter Whitney?—ah, the McDonnell Douglas computer expert Paul Marinos had said he was bringing in. "Have you got the program running yet?"

"Yes; a friend just radioed us the loading code."

"Well ahead of ground control's efforts, I might add," Betsy said. "We'll let you know when we identify the glitch. For now, let's get back to the shuttle door, okay? We think the sensors indicate hydraulic pressure problems in the emergency collar. Is there any chance we could fix that and get it to lock onto the shuttle? Then we could release the main collar and get the shuttle door open."

Greenburg shifted position again and peered at the top of the shuttle, wishing all the floodlights hadn't gone when the craft hit. "I don't think there's any chance at all," he said slowly. "As a matter of fact, it looks very much like the emergency collar's responsible for most of the cockpit damage. It seems to have come out of the wall just in time for the shuttle to ram into it. If that kind of impact didn't do anything more than rupture a hydraulic line or two, I'll be very much surprised."

Betsy said something under her breath that Greenburg didn't catch. "You sure about that?" she asked. "I can't see any of that on the monitor."

"As sure as I can be on this side of the bay. I can go to the starboard side if you'd like and check through the panel there. Probably have to go over there to find out exactly where this fluid came from, anyway."

"Maybe later. Any other good news for us from there, first?"

"Actually, this *is* good news. Somehow, while the shuttle was rattling around the bay, it completely missed the Skyport passenger and cargo tunnels. If we can get everybody *out* of the shuttle, we can get them *into* the Skyport."

"Well, that's something. Any suggestions on how we go about carrying out that first step?"

Greenburg frowned. Something about the shuttle was stroking the warning bells in his brain . . . but he couldn't seem to put his finger on the problem.

"Aaron?"

"Uh . . . yes." His eyes still probing the vibrating fuselage, Greenburg replayed his mental tape of Betsy's last question. "The, uh, side window of the cockpit seems undamaged. It should be big enough for most of the passengers to squeeze through. Of course, it's a four-meter drop or thereabouts, so we'd need to rig up some way to either get them down and then back up to the tunnel door or else to get across to it directly. Maybe rig something up to the ski-lift mechanism in the tunnel . . ."

His voice trailed off as the warning bells abruptly went off full force. *The nosewheel was slightly closer to him!*

"Bets, the shuttle's sliding backwards!" he shouted into the mike. "The collar must be slipping!"

For a few seconds all he could hear was the muffled, indistinct sound of frantic conversation. Eyes still glued to the slowly moving nosewheel, he jammed his earphone tighter against his ear. "Bets, did you copy? I said—"

"We copied," Paul Marinos's voice told him. "Betsy's getting the shuttle to boost its thrust. Stand by, okay?"

Pursing his lips tightly under his oxygen mask, Greenburg shifted his gaze back along the shuttle to its main passenger door. If the collar was slipping he should be able to see the door slowly sliding further and further beneath the huge ring. . . .

He still hadn't decided if it was moving when Betsy's voice made him start.

"Aaron? Is the shuttle still moving?"

"Uh . . . I'm not sure. I don't think so, but all the vibration makes it hard to tell."

"Yeah." A short pause. "Aaron, Tom, you've both done some shuttle flying, haven't you? What are the chances Rayburn could bring this one down safely, damaged as it is?"

Something very cold slid down the center of Greenburg's back. Betsy knew the answer to that one already—they all did. The fact that she was asking at all implied things he wasn't sure he liked. Surely things weren't desperate enough yet to be grasping at *that* kind of straw . . . were they?

Lewis, after a short pause, gave the only answer there was. "Chances are poor to nonexistent—you know that, Betsy. He'd have to leave here at a speed of at least a hundred sixty-five knots, and with one or more windows gone in the cockpit he'd have an instant hurricane in there. He sure as hell won't be able to fly in that, and I personally wouldn't trust any autopilot that's gone through what his has."

"You can't slow down past a hundred sixty-five knots?" Whitney, the computer man, asked.

"That's our minimum flight speed," Lewis told him shortly.

"I know that. What I meant was whether you could try something like a stall or some other fancy maneuver that would pull your speed temporarily lower."

"Wouldn't gain us enough, I'm afraid," Betsy said, sounding thoughtful. "Besides which, wing sections aren't designed for fancy maneuvers." She seemed to sigh. "We've got a new problem, folks. The shuttle's backwards drift, Aaron, was *not* the collar slipping. It was the last two supports *bending*, apparently under slightly unequal thrusts from the shuttle's engines."

Lewis growled an obscenity Greenburg had never heard him use. "What happens if they break? Does the collar fall off the shuttle?"

"The book says yes—but exactly *when* it goes depends on how fast the hydraulic fluid drains out. My guess is it would hold on long enough to turn the shuttle nose down before dropping off and crashing somewhere in the greater Fort Worth area."

"Followed immediately by the shuttle," Greenburg growled. His next task was clear—too clear. "All right, say no more. Tom, there should be a supply locker just forward of here. See if there's any rope or cable in it, would you?"

"What do you want that for?" Betsy asked, her tone edging toward suspicious.

"A safety harness. I'm going to go inside the bay and see if there's any way to get that forward clamp connected. Tom?"

"Yeah, there's some rope here. Just a second—I have to untangle it."

"Hold it, Tom," Betsy said. "Aaron, you're not going in there. You're a pilot, not a mechanic, remember? We'll wait for some professionals from the ground to handle this."

"Wait how long?" he shot back, apprehension putting snap into his tone. "Rayburn can't keep firing his engines all day; and even if he could you have no guarantee the thrusts from all three turbofans would stay properly balanced. Do you?"

There was a short silence, during which Greenburg was startled by something snaking abruptly across his chest. It was Lewis, perhaps sensing the outcome of the argument, starting to tie Greenburg's safety line around him. "No," Betsy finally answered his question. "Rayburn's on-board can't give us those numbers any more, and the support stress indicators aren't really sensitive enough."

"Which means chances are good the shuttle's going to continue putting stresses on the clamps—variable stresses, yet. They're bound to fatigue eventually under that kind of treatment."

"Mr. Greenburg—Aaron—look, the program's almost finished running." Whitney, putting in his two cents again. "Once it's done we can have people up here in fifteen minutes—"

"No; only once we've found the problem *and made sure the other wing sections don't have it*. Who knows how long *that'll* take?" A tug on the rope coming off the chest of the makeshift harness Lewis had tied around him and a slap on the back told him it was time. Gripping the edges of the opening, he raised a foot, seeking purchase on the curved wall. Lewis's cupped hands caught the foot, steadied it. Greenburg started to shift his weight . . . and paused. He was still, after all, under Betsy's authority. "Bets? Do I have permission to go?"

"All right. But listen: you've got *one* shot at the clamp, and whether it reaches or not you're coming straight out afterward. Understand? No one's ever been in a docking bay during flight before, and you're not equipped for unexpected problems."

"Gotcha. Here goes."

Greenburg had spent the past couple of minutes studying the curving bay wall, planning just how he was going to do this maneuver. Now, as he shifted his weight and pushed off of

Lewis's hands, he discovered he hadn't planned things quite well enough. Pushing himself more or less vertically through the narrow opening, he twisted his body around as his torso cleared, coming down in a sitting position with his back to the shuttle. But he'd forgotten about the oxygen tank on the back of his belt, and the extra weight was enough to ruin his precarious balance and to send him sliding gracelessly down the curving metal on his butt.

He didn't slide far; Lewis, belaying the line, made sure of that. Getting his legs back around underneath him, Greenburg checked his footing and nodded back toward the opening. "Okay, I'm essentially down. Let me have some slack." Moving carefully, he stepped down into the teardrop-shaped well under the shuttle and walked to the nosewheel.

The forward clamp was designed to slide out of the wall as the landing gear was lowered, locating the tow bar by means of two short-range transponders installed in the gear. Earlier, up on the flight deck, Greenburg had confirmed the clamp operation had been begun but not completed; now, on closer study, the problem looked like it might be obvious.

"The shuttle's not only angled into the bay wrong, but it's also rotated a few degrees on its axis," he reported to the others. "I think maybe that the clamp's wrist rotated as far as it could to try and match, and when it couldn't get lined up apparently decided to quit and wait for instructions."

"The telltales say it *is* fully extended, though," Henson insisted.

"Well . . . maybe it's the sensors that got scrambled."

"Assume you're right," Betsy said. "Any way to fix it?"

"I don't know." Greenburg studied the clamp and landing gear, acutely aware of the vibrating shuttle above him—and of the vast distances beyond it. *But even if the shuttle fell out and my rope broke I'd be all right*, he told himself firmly. Standing in the cutout well that gave the shuttle's nosewheel room to descend, he was a good two meters below the rim of the bay's outer opening. There was a fair amount of eddy-generated wind turbulence plucking at his jumpsuit and adding a wind-chill to the frigid air—but it would take a *lot* of turbulence to force him up that slope and out. At least, he thought so. . . . "Why don't you try backing the clamp arm up and letting it take another run at the tow bar?"

"We'll have to wait for Peter's program to finish," Henson said. "The computer handles that."

"Oh . . . right." Greenburg hadn't thought of that. "How much longer?"

"It's almost—it's done," Whitney said.

"Where's the problem?" Betsy asked. Even with the turbo-fan engines droning in his ears Greenburg could hear the twin emotions of anticipation and dread in her voice.

"There doesn't seem to be one."

"That's ridiculous," Greenburg said. "*Something* made the shuttle crash."

"Well, the program can't find it. Look, it seems to me I felt the Skyport bounce a little just before the crash—"

"Clear-air turbulence," Betsy said. "That shouldn't have been a problem; the guidance program is supposed to be able to handle small perturbations like that."

"Let's forget about the 'how' of it for now," a new voice broke in—Carl Young's, Greenburg tentatively identified it through the noise. "The point is that we can start bringing shuttles back up again. Greenburg, is there anything you can suggest we bring up from the ground to secure the shuttle with?"

"Uh . . . hell, I don't know. Something to use to get the passengers off would certainly be handy. And if this clamp arm won't rotate any further we might need an interfacing of some kind—maybe an extra clamp-and-wrist piece to extend our clamp's rotational range."

"I've already ordered some spare ski-lift track from the ground—it should be coming up aboard the first shuttle, along with men to handle it. The clamp-and-wrist section we may be able to remove from one of the other bays; other people will be coming up to try that. What I meant was, can you see anything from there that we didn't already know about?"

"Not really." Greenburg was starting to feel a little foolish as his brave descent into the bay began to look more and more unnecessary. With the guidance system coming up clean, shuttleloads of experts would be here in minutes. *So much for the value of impulsive heroics*, he thought acridly; but at least it hadn't wasted too much time. He'd always been much better as a team player, anyway. "Hold on tight, Tom; I'm coming up," he called, getting a grip on his safety line.

"Just a second, Aaron," Henson said. "I've got the computer back now. Why don't you stay put while I try the clamp again like you suggested."

"All right. But make it snappy—it's freezing in here."

There was a heavy click, and the clamp arm telescoped smoothly back into itself, rotating to the horizontal as it did so. It paused for a second when fully retracted and then reversed direction, angling toward the landing gear like some rigid metallic snake attacking its prey in slow motion. It stopped, again a meter short, and with a sinking feeling Greenburg saw his mistake. "It's not just the angle the nosewheel's at," he informed the others. "The clamp rotates a little as each segment telescopes out, not all at once at the end of the extension. It's not quitting because it doesn't know how to proceed—it's quitting because it's run out of length."

"That's impossible," Betsy retorted. "I've checked the stats— the arm's *got* to be long enough to reach."

"Then it's been damaged somehow," Greenburg said irritably. If they had to replace the whole arm, and not just the clamp . . . He shivered as a newly sharpened sense of the shuttle's vulnerability hit him like a wet rag.

For a moment the drone of the turbofans was all he could hear. Then Carl Young said, "We'll have the ground people check it out when they get here. Greenburg, you might as well come out of there. You'll need to put the access panel back in place temporarily so we can repressurize the deck."

"Understood." Turning back to the curving wall, his hands numb with cold, Greenburg began to climb.

"The shuttle will dock in Six in about four minutes," the Skyport captain's voice came over the intercom.

"Okay, Carl," Betsy said. "Six, do you have someone at the bay to meet it?"

"Not yet," was the response. "We wanted to have all the stations up here manned during docking, to watch for any trouble. We could call in somebody off-duty, if you want."

"Don't bother," Paul Marinos said, unbuckling his seat belt and getting to his feet. "I'll go down and meet the shuttle. You won't need me before Tom gets back, will you?" he added, looking at Betsy.

She shook her head. "Go ahead. As a matter of fact, you can probably escort Mr. Whitney back down on your way. Mr. Whitney, we very much appreciate your help here this morning."

"Uh, yeah. Your welcome."

Unlocking her chair, Betsy swiveled around. Whitney was hunched forward in his own seat, frowning intently at the computer display screen. "Anything wrong?" she asked, her mouth beginning to feel dry again. That shuttle would be trying to dock in a half-handful of minutes. . . .

Whitney shook his head slowly, his eyes never leaving the screen. "I'm just rechecking the readout, trying to see if there's anything that looks funny but somehow didn't register as a problem." He keyed for the next page; only then did he look up. "If it's not too much trouble, though, I'd really like to stay up here for a while. I can be an extra hand with the computer, and there's another project I want to discuss with you."

"Passengers usually aren't permitted up here at all," Marinos said with a frown.

Whitney shrugged. "On the other hand, I *am* already here."

"All right," Betsy said, making a quick decision. Even if Whitney's primary motivation was nothing more than simple curiosity, he'd already been a big help to them. It was an inexpensive way to pay back the favor. "But you'll have to stay out from underfoot. For starters"—she pointed at the display— "you'll need to finish that up quickly, because Tom Lewis's on his way up to make some more blueprints."

"Yes, I know. I'll be finished." He turned back to the console. Nodding to her, Marinos left the flight deck.

Swiveling back forward, Betsy squeezed her eyes shut briefly and took a long, deep breath. The tension was beginning to get to her. She could feel her strength of will slowly leaking away; could feel her decision-making center seizing up—and this only some eighty minutes into the crisis.

The strength of her reaction was more than a little disturbing. True, the lives of a hundred sixty people were hanging precariously in the balance back there . . . but she'd been holding people's lives in her hands since her first flight for the Navy back in 1980. She'd had her share of crises, too, probably the worst of them being the 747 that had lost power in all four engines halfway from Seattle to Honolulu. She'd had to put the monster into a five-thousand-foot dive to get the balky turbofans restarted—and she hadn't felt anything like the nervousness she was feeling now. Was it just the *length* of this crisis that was getting to her, the pumping of adrenaline for more than five minutes at a time? If so, she was going to be a wreck by the time this whole thing was resolved. Or—

Or was it the people—*be honest, Betsy; the* person—involved? Could being forced to deal with Eric Rayburn again really hit her this hard?

"Excuse me, Captain; is it all right if I sit here?"

She opened her eyes to see Whitney standing beside her, indicating the copilot's seat. Craning her neck, she saw that Lewis had returned and had taken over the computer terminal again. "Yeah, sure," she told Whitney, thankful for the interruption. "Just don't touch anything. Tom, you need any help?"

"No, thanks; just getting the schematics for the clamp arm mechanism, the emergency collar, and whatever I can find on the Skyport door and tunnel." Paper was beginning to come from the printer slot; Lewis glanced at it and then looked at Betsy. "Anything new from the shuttle?"

"Rayburn's still checking out his instruments. So far the altimeter, Collins nav system, and at least one of the vertical gyros seem to be out; the compass and collision-proofing are intact; the autopilot is a big question mark."

"I met Paul Marinos on the way up here. He said it was Rayburn who came up with that half-assed idea of letting the shuttle fly home alone."

"That's right," Betsy confirmed. "He's still making noises in that direction, too."

"Good. Aaron and I thought *you'd* thought it up, and we were getting a little worried."

She snorted. "Thanks for your confidence. You staying with Aaron after you deliver the schematics?"

"Depends on whether they need me or not," he said, pulling the last sheet from the printer slot and flipping the "off" switch. "Talk to you later."

He got up and left, and as he did so the intercom crackled. "This is Marinos. The shuttle has docked. Textbook-smooth, I might add."

Betsy turned to the intercom grille, feeling a minor bit of the weight lift from her shoulders. "Aaron, you copy that? Prepare for company down there."

"Got it. Paul, let me know when you're all down, so I can start taking this panel off again."

"Will do."

The intercom fell silent, and Betsy leaned back in her seat again. Staring out the window at the blue sky, she tried to organize her thoughts.

"Captain? Are you all right?"

She glanced at Whitney, favoring him with a half smile. "I thought I told you we all went informal up here," she chided mildly. "My name's Betsy."

"Oh . . . well . . . you called me 'Mr. Whitney' a while back, so I thought maybe that had changed." He looked a little embarrassed.

"Force of habit, I guess. Anyone wearing a three-piece suit

looks like management to me. And as to your question, yes, I'm fine."

"You look tired. How long have you been flying?"

A chuckle made it halfway up her throat. "About twenty-six years, all told. This session, though, less than an hour and a half. I came on duty just before the shuttle crashed."

"Oh." His tone said he wasn't thoroughly convinced.

She looked at him again. "Really," she insisted. "What you're calling tiredness is just tension, pure and simple."

The corner of his mouth quirked. "Okay. I always *was* a lousy detective." The quirk vanished and he sobered. "What do you think their chances are? Honestly."

"It all depends on how fast we can get the shuttle secured—or how fast we find out we *can't* do it."

Whitney frowned. "I don't follow. Are you talking about the"—he glanced at his watch—"six hours of fuel the shuttle's got left?"

"Basically—except that it's only about five and a half now; we nudged his thrust up a notch in two of his engines a while ago." She turned to face forward again, lips compressing into a thin line. "We're in a very neat box here, Peter. You know the Skyport clockwise circuit, don't you?"

"Sure: Boston, New York, Philadelphia, Washington, Atlanta, New Orleans, Houston, Dallas, L.A., San Francisco, Denver, Kansas City, Chicago, Detroit, Cleveland, Pittsburg, Washington, then back up the pike to Boston." He rattled off the names easily, as someone who'd learned them without deliberate effort. "A twelve-hour run, all told."

"Right. Now note that once we secure the shuttle, there are exactly two places we can land with it: the Skyport maintenance facilities at Mirage Lake, nar L.A., and the Keansburg Extension of New Jersey; and L.A.'s probably a half hour closer. *But*"—she paused for emphasis—"between here and L.A. there are no Skyport cities. Which means no shuttles. Which means any equipment we want to bring aboard to work with has to come from here. Which means we have to *stay* here until we're sure we've got everything we're going to need."

"Wumph." Whitney's breath came out in a rush, and for a moment he was silent. "But couldn't you head toward L.A. right away, circling there until you have the clamp fixed? Oh, never mind; you'll probably need the transit time to work. But wait a second—you could head back *east* now, toward New Jersey. Any extra stuff you needed could be brought up from

Atlanta, or even Washington; you'd pass close enough to both cities on the way."

She'd had the same brilliant idea nearly twenty minutes ago, and had been just as excited by it as he was. It was a shame to have to pop his bubble. "The fly in that particular soup is John Meredith, the injured shuttle copilot. If we stay here and then manage to get him and the other passengers out within an hour, say, we can get him to a hospital a lot faster than if we had to wait till we reached Atlanta. That time could be life or death for him—and it's the uncertain nature of his injuries, by the way, that gives our box its other walls. Besides," she added grimly, "if we wind up losing the shuttle completely, I'd rather try and find an empty spot in Arizona than in Pennsylvania to drop it into."

"Damn," he muttered. "You've thought through the whole thing, haven't you?"

"I hope not," she countered fervently. "Things don't look too good in my analysis. If I haven't missed something we're probably going to lose either an expensive shuttle or at least one irreplaceable life." She snorted. "Damn the FAA, anyway. We've been on their tail for least two years now to push for a few more wing-section-sized runways scattered among the major airports."

"Yeah, I've always thought it was a bad idea to leave thrust reversers off Skyport engines. The way things are now, you could lift a module off from a ridiculous number of runways that you couldn't put it down on in the first place."

"It's called economy. No one wants to build extra-big runways until they're sure the Skyports are going to catch on." She shook her head. "Enough self-pity. What's this project you mentioned?"

"Right. You said earlier that no one knew what sort of landing distance a wing-section/shuttle combo would require. Well, I've done some figuring, and if I can use the combined computer facilities of two modules I think I can get you a rough estimate."

She blinked in surprise. "How?"

"My work for McDonnell Douglas has been on computer simulations for second-generation Skyport design. Most of it involves adjusting profile, mass, and laminar flow parameters and then testing for lift and drag and so on. I remember the equations I'd need and enough about module and shuttle shapes to get by. And it's not *that* complicated a program."

"What about the brakes and drogue chutes?" she asked doubtfully.

"I can put them in as extra drag effects."

Betsy frowned, thinking. There was no way the runways at Dallas would be long enough—of that she was certain. But . . . the figures would be nice to have. "Okay, if we can get two of the other wing sections to agree. You can't use Seven's computer; we'll need to leave it clear for the work down below."

"That's okay—I can link to the other systems and run everything from here."

Betsy turned toward the intercom. "Carl? What do you think?"

"It's worth trying. Two, Three—you've just volunteered your computers to Mr. Whitney's use."

It took Betsy a few minutes to show Whitney how to set up the two-system link, but once he got started he did seem to know what he was doing. She watched over his shoulder for a minute before returning to her seat. It was indeed a good idea, but she had to wonder why he hadn't simply called back his friend in Houston and had him run the program. With the—undoubtedly—larger machine there and the proper program already in place, they could surely have had the answer faster than Whitney could get it here. It was looking very much like he did indeed want an excuse to stay on the flight deck and observe the proceedings. She grimaced. The report he was presumably going to be making to McDonnell Douglas wasn't likely to be a flattering one.

She shook her head to clear away the cobwebs. There were plenty of unpleasant thoughts to occupy her; she didn't need to generate any extra ones. And, speaking of unpleasantries . . . Steeling herself, she pulled her half-headset mike to her lips and switched it on. "Skyport to Shuttle. Status report, please."

"Oh, there's nothing much new here, Liz—just sitting around watching my copilot dying."

She'd been unprepared for the sheer virulence of Rayburn's tone, and the words hit her with almost physical force. Unclenching her jaw with a conscious effort, she asked, "Is he getting worse? Dr. Emerson?"

"He sure as hell isn't getting any better," Rayburn snapped before the doctor could answer.

Betsy held her ground. "Doctor?" she repeated.

"It's hard to tell," Dr. Emerson spoke up hesitantly. "He's still unconscious and his breathing is starting to become labored, but his pulse is still good."

"Well, we should at least have him out from under all that

metal soon," Betsy told him. "The ground crew's aboard now, and they'll be bringing a torch aboard to cut the chair free."

"Yeah, I can see them climbing in down there," Rayburn said. "How do they expect to get up here?"

"Through your side window; I presume they brought a rope ladder or something with them. You'd better open up and be ready to catch the end when they toss it up."

"Hell of a lot of good it's going to do," the shuttle pilot growled. "How're they going to get him back out—tie a rope around him and lower him like a sack of grass seed?"

"If he's not too badly injured, yes," Betsy said, feeling her patience beginning to bend dangerously. "If not, we'll figure out something else. We're going to try and rig up a ski-lift track from your window to the Skyport door to get the passengers out; maybe we can bring Meredith out that way on some kind of stretcher."

"A *ski-lift track*? Oh, for—Liz, that's the dumbest idea I've ever heard. It could take *hours* to put something like that together!"

The tension that had been building up again within Betsy suddenly broke free. "You have a better idea, spit it out!" she barked.

"You've already heard it," he snapped back. "Let me take this damn bird down *now*, and to hell with ski tracks and nosewheel clamps. All you're doing is wasting time."

"You really think you can fly a plane with its nose smashed in, do you?" she said acidly. "What're you going to use for altimeter, autopilot, and gyros?"

"Skill. I've flown planes in worse shape than this one."

"Maybe. But not with a sprained wrist, and not with a hundred sixty passengers aboard. And *not* while under my command."

"Oh, right, I forgot—Liz Kyser's the big boss here." Rayburn's voice dripped with sarcasm. "Well, let me just remind you, Your *Highness*, that I don't *need* your permission to leave your flying kingdom. All it would take is a simple push on the throttle."

Betsy's anger vanished in a single heartbeat. "Eric, what are you saying?" she asked cautiously.

"Don't go into your dumb-blonde act—you know what I'm talking about. All I have to do is cut power and snap those last two collar supports and you can yell about authority all you want."

"Yes—and you'll either fall nose-down with the collar still

around you or drop it onto someone on the ground." Betsy forced her voice to remain quiet and reasonable. "You can't risk innocent people's lives like that, Eric."

"Oh, relax—I'm not going to do anything that crazy unless I absolutely have to. I'm just pointing out that you don't have absolute veto power over me. Keep that in mind while you figure out how to get John to a hospital."

"Don't worry. We want him safe as much as you do." *Especially now.* "We'll keep you posted." Reaching over, Betsy turned off the mike.

For a moment she just sat there, her mind spinning like wheels on an icy runway. The flight deck suddenly felt cold, and she noticed with curious detachment that the hands resting on the edge of her control board were trembling slightly. Rayburn's threat, and the implied state of mind accompanying it, had shocked her clear down to the marrow. He'd always been loyal to the crews he flew with—it had been one of the qualities that had first attracted her to him—but this was bordering on monomania. Bleakly, she wondered if the accident had damaged more than Rayburn's wrist.

There was a footstep beside her. Whitney, looking sand-bagged. "Betsy, is he—uh—?" He ran out of words, and just pointed mutely toward her half-headset.

"You heard, huh?" She felt a flash of embarrassed annoyance that he, an outsider, had listened in on private Skyport trouble.

Whitney, apparently too shaken to be bothered by his action, nodded. "Is he all right back there? I mean, he sounds . . . overwrought."

"He does indeed," she acknowledged grimly. "He's under a lot of pressure—we all are."

"Yeah, but you're not threatening to do something criminally stupid." He gestured at the intercom. "And why didn't Captain Young at least back you up?"

"He probably wasn't listening in—the radio doesn't feed directly into the intercom." She took another look at his expression and forced a smile she didn't feel. "Hey, relax. Eric hasn't gone off the deep end; he was just blowing off some steam."

"Hmm." He seemed unconvinced. "And how about *you?*"

The question caught her unprepared, and Betsy could feel the blood coloring her face. "I got a little loud there myself, didn't I?" she admitted. "I guess I'm not used to this kind of protracted crisis. Usual airplane emergencies last only as long as it takes you to find the nearest stretch of flat ground and put down on it."

"I suppose so. Anything I can do?"

"Yes—you can haul yourself back to the computer and finish that program."

Surprisingly, something in her tone seemed to relieve whatever fears he had about her, because the frown lines left his forehead and he even smiled slightly. "Aye, aye, Captain," he said and headed aft again.

Well, that's convinced him. Now if only she could persuade *herself* as to Rayburn's self-control. Pushing the half-headset mike away almost savagely, she leaned toward the intercom. "Aaron, Paul—what's holding things up down there?"

The rolled-up end of thin rope smacked against the top of the window as it came in through the opening. Startled a bit by the sudden noise, Dr. Emerson turned his head—the only part of his body he could conveniently turn in the cramped cockpit—in time to see Captain Rayburn field the rope and begin pulling it in. Tied to the other end, its rungs clanking against the side of the shuttle, was a collapsible ladder, of the sort Emerson made his kids keep under their bunk bed at their Grand Prairie condo. He watched as Rayburn set the outsized hooks over the lower edge of the window and then turned back to his patient with a silent sigh of relief. At least the waiting was over. Now all he had to do was worry that Meredith was healthy enough to satisfy Rayburn—and *that*, he reflected darkly, was definitely a major worry. Rayburn's last stormy conversation with the Skyport had completely shattered Emerson's comfortable and long-held stereotype of the unflappable airline pilot and had left him with a good deal of concern. Searching the unconscious copilot's half-hidden face, Emerson wondered what it was about this man that had caused Rayburn to react so violently. Was he a good friend? Or was it something more subtle—did he remind Rayburn of a deceased brother, for instance? Emerson didn't know, and so far he hadn't had the nerve to ask.

"Okay, Doc, here they come." Rayburn, who'd been leaning his head partly out the window, began unsnapping his safety harness. "Let's get out of here and give them room to come in."

Emerson rose from his crouch, grimacing as his legs registered their complaint. Trying to look all directions at once, he backed carefully out of the tiny space, and made it out the cockpit door without collecting any new bruises. Rayburn was out of his seat already, standing in the spot Emerson had just vacated, shouting instructions toward the window. "Okay—easy—just keep it away from the instruments—okay, I've got it." Two small gas tanks, wrapped together by metal bands and festooned with hoses, appeared in his hands and were immediately tucked under his right arm. The second package was, for Emerson, far more recognizable: the big red cross on the suitcase-sized box was hard to miss. A moment later he had to take a long step toward the shuttle's exit door as Rayburn backed out of the cockpit. "Watch the controls!" he shouted once more as he set down his burden and reached back with a helping hand.

It took only a few minutes for them to all come aboard. There were three: two mechanic-types who set to work immediately turning the gas tank apparatus into an acetylene torch; and an older man who caught Emerson's eye through the small crowd and headed back toward the passenger section. Emerson took the cue and followed.

"I'm Dr. Forrest Campbell," the newcomer introduced himself when the two men reached the pocket of relative quiet at the forward end of the passenger compartment.

"Larry Emerson. Glad to have you here. You work for the airline?"

"Temporarily coopted only—and as the man said, if it weren't for the honor I'd rather walk." He nodded down the rows of ski lift seats. "First things first. Are the passengers in need of anything?"

"Nothing immediate. There are some bruises and one or two possible sprains. Mostly, everyone's just scared and cold."

"I can believe that," Campbell agreed, shivering. "I'm told the Skyport's come down to eight thousand feet, but it still feels like winter in here. I hope the next shuttle up thinks to bring some blankets. All right, now let's hear the bad news. How's the copilot?"

"Not good." Emerson gave all the facts he had on Meredith's condition, plus a few tentative conclusions he hadn't wanted to mention in Rayburn's earshot. "We'll have to wait for a more thorough examination, of course, but I'm pretty sure we're *not* going to be able to risk lowering him out that window at the end of a rope."

"Yes . . . and I doubt that a stretcher would really fit. Well, if we can get him stable enough he can stay here until the shuttle can be landed again."

"I guess he'll have to." A sharp *pop* came from the cockpit, and looking past Campbell he saw the room aglow with blue light. "I hope they're not going to fry him just getting him out," he muttered uneasily.

"They'll have attached a Vahldiek conductor cable between the part of the chair stem they're cutting and the fuselage, to drain off the heat," Campbell assured him. "Let's go back in; this shouldn't take long."

It didn't. They had barely reentered the exit door area—now noticeably warmer—and opened the big medical kit when the torch's hiss cut off. Rayburn stepped back from the doorway, muttering cautionary instructions as the unconscious copilot, still strapped into his seat, was carried carefully out of the cockpit.

"For now, just leave him in the chair," Campbell said as they set down the seat and disconnected the thin high-conduction line. Stethoscope at the ready, he knelt down and got to work.

Emerson stepped over to Rayburn. "Shouldn't you be getting back to the cockpit, Captain?" he suggested quietly.

Rayburn took a deep breath. "Yeah. Take care of him, Doc, and tell me as soon as you know anything."

"We will."

Stepping carefully around the figures on the floor, Rayburn went forward, and Emerson breathed a sigh of relief. At least the shuttle had a pilot again, should something go wrong with what was left of the docking collar. Now if only that pilot could be persuaded not to do anything hasty. . . . He shivered, wondering if Rayburn would really rip the shuttle from its unstable perch . . . wondering if the Skyport's holding pattern was taking them over Grand Prairie and his family.

Pushing such thoughts back into the corners of his mind, he squatted down next to Dr. Campbell and prepared to assist.

"All right, let it out again—real easy," the gravelly voice of Al Carson said in Greenburg's ear. Mentally crossing his fingers, Greenburg kept his full attention on the clamp arm as, up on the flight deck, Henson gave it the command to extend.

But neither Greenburg's wishes nor Carson's quarter-hour of work had made any appreciable change in the arm's behavior. As near as Greenburg could tell from his viewpoint by the access panel, the arm followed exactly the same path he'd seen it take earlier. It certainly came up just as short.

Carson swore under his breath. Once again he took the sheaf of blueprints from his assistant, and once again Greenburg gritted his teeth in frustration. Neither Carson nor the rest of his crew were experts on Skyport equipment—such experts were currently located only on the east and west coasts—but even so they'd identified the basic problem in short order: one of the four telescoping segments of the arm apparently was not working. That much Carson had learned almost immediately from the blueprints (and Greenburg still felt a hot chagrin that he hadn't caught it himself); but all the lubricating, hammering, and other mechanical cajolery since then had failed to unfreeze it. And they were running low on time.

"Hey, you—Greenburg." Carson gestured up at him. "C'mere and give us a hand, will you?"

"Sure." Gripping the line coming from his safety harness—a *real* safety harness; the ground crew had brought along some spares—he stepped up on the box they'd placed beneath the opening and wriggled his way through. He was most of the way into the bay before he remembered to check the space above him for falling debris, but Lady Luck was kind: none of the rest of the crew was working directly overhead. He gave their operation a quick once-over as the motorized safety line lowered him smoothly down the bay wall, and was impressed in spite of himself. The Skyport tunnel had been run out as far to the side as possible and locked in place pointing toward the open cockpit window, and already the first part of the ski-lift framework had been welded between the tunnel and shuttle fuselage. A second brace was being set in place; two more, and the track itself could be laid down. It wouldn't take long; six men—fully half the group that had come up—were working on that part of the project alone. In Greenburg's own opinion more emphasis should have been placed on getting the clamp attached, but he knew it would be futile to argue the point. The crew took their orders from the airline, and the airline clearly had its own priorities.

He reached bottom and, squeezing the manual release to generate some slack in his line, ducked under the shuttle and headed over to where Carson and his assistant waited. "All right," the boss said, indicating a place on the clamp arm. "Greenburg, you and Frank are going to pull here this time. Henson? Back it up about halfway."

The arm slid back. Greenburg and Frank gripped the metal and braced themselves as Carson armed himself with a large screwdriver and hammer. On his signal Henson started the arm out again, and as the other two pulled, Carson set the tip of the screwdriver at the edge of the segment and rapped it smartly with the hammer.

It didn't work. "Damn," Carson growled. "Well, okay, if it

was the catch that was sticking that should have taken care of it. The electrical connections seem okay—the control lines aren't shorted. That leaves the hydraulics." He picked up the blueprints and started leafing through them. "Okay. We got separate lines for each segment, but they all run off the same reservoir. So it's gotta be in the line. You got any pressure indicators on these things up there?"

"We're supposed to," Henson replied. "But we seem to have lost them when the emergency collar went—"

"Wait a second," Greenburg cut in as his brain suddenly made a connection. "The hydraulic lines for the arm run by the emergency collar?"

"Yeah, I think so," Carson said. "Why?"

Lewis, listening from outside the bay, swore abruptly. "The broken hydraulic line!"

"Broken lines?" Carson asked sharply. "Where?"

"Back there, by the emergency collar." Even as he said it Greenburg remembered that the ground crew had been brought into the cargo deck further forward, that they hadn't seen the pool of hydraulic fluid that he and Lewis had had to step over earlier. "There's leakage on both sides of the bay. Most of it's from the collar itself, we think, but some of it could be from the line that handles this segment. Couldn't it?"

"Sure could." Carson didn't look very happy as he found the schematic he wanted and glared silently at it for a moment. "Yeah. All the arm segment lines run separately all the way to the reservoir, it looks like, so that if one gives you've still got all the rest. They all run along the starboard side of the bay, right where the shuttle hit. Ten'll get you a hundred that's the trouble."

"Rick? How about it?" Greenburg called.

"Probably." Henson sounded disgusted. "I think the sensors are located in the same general area. You could probably track the line back visually and confirm it's broken."

"For the moment don't bother; it's not worth the effort," Betsy's voice came in for the first time in many minutes. "Mr. Carson, can it be fixed or will we have to replace the whole arm?"

"I don't know. Frankly, I'm not sure either one can be done outside a hangar. Leastwise, not by me."

"I see." There was a pause—an ominously long pause, to Greenburg's way of thinking. "I'd like you to look at the arm, anyway, if you would, and see how much work replacing it

would take. Aaron, would you come to the flight deck, please?
We need to have a consultation."

"Sure, Bets." He made the words sound as casual as possible, even as his stomach curled into a little knot inside him.
Whatever she wanted to discuss, it was something she didn't
want the whole intercom net to hear . . . and that could only be
bad news.

Moving as quickly as he dared, he headed back under the
access panel and, kicking in his harness's motor, began to climb
the wall.

It was, to the best of Betsy's knowledge, the first time the
closed intercom system had ever been used aboard a Skyport,
and she found her finger hesitating slightly as it pressed the
button that would cut Seven's flight deck off from everyone
except Carl Young on Four. But she both understood and
agreed with the Skyport captain's insistence that this discussion
be held privately. "All set here, Carl," she said into the grille.

"All right," the other's voice came back. "I'm sure I don't
have to remind either of you what time it's getting to be."

"No, sir." The instrument panel clock directly in front of her
read 10:02:35 EST, with the seconds ticking off like footsteps
toward an unavoidable crossroads. "At just about fourteen
twenty-five the shuttle runs out of fuel. If we're going to reach
Mirage Lake before that happens, we've got to leave Dallas
right now."

"Or in twenty minutes, if we wind up running right to the
wire," Greenburg muttered from the copilot's chair. A shiver
ran visibly through his body; but whether it was an aftereffect
of the cold air down below or a reaction to the same horrible
image that was intruding in Betsy's own mind's eye, she had no
way of knowing.

"True; but we don't dare cut things that fine," Young said.
"We don't know how long those two collar supports will hold
under a full strain. How is the forward clamp?"

"It's shot," Greenburg said succinctly. "One of the segments
has a broken hydraulic line, we think."

"Replaceable?"

Greenburg hesitated. "I don't know. The ground crew boss
doesn't think so."

"What about the escape system for getting the passengers
off?"

"Proceeding pretty well. If no new problems crop up I'd say
they'll be ready with the thing in half an hour or so."

"Well, that's something, anyway. Betsy, what's the latest on Meredith's condition?"

Betsy took a deep breath. "It's not good, I'm afraid. The doctors say he's got at least a couple of broken ribs, a possible mild concussion, and slow but definite internal bleeding. They've got him laid out on cushions in the shuttle's aisle and have asked for some whole blood to be sent up. I've already radioed the ground; it'll be brought by the next shuttle up."

Greenburg gave a low whistle. "That doesn't sound good at all."

"It's not," she admitted. "There's also evidence that some of the blood may be getting into one of his lungs. Even if it's not, putting new blood into him's a temporary solution at best."

"How long before he has to get to a hospital?" Greenburg asked bluntly, his eyes boring into Betsy's.

"The doctors don't know. At the moment he's relatively stable. But if the bleeding increases—" She left the sentence unfinished.

"Four hours to L.A. at this speed. That's a long time between hospital facilities," Young mused, and Betsy felt a stab of envy at the control in his voice. Ultimately, it was really Carl, not her, who was supposed to be responsible for the safety of the Skyport and its passengers. What right did he have to be so calm when she was sweating buckets over this thing?

"Wait a second," Greenburg spoke up suddenly. "It doesn't have to be an all-or-nothing proposition. We could dock a shuttle in, say, Six and carry it with us to L.A. Then if Meredith got worse we could land him at any of the airports along the way.'"

"You're missing the point," Betsy snapped. The sharpness of her tone startled her almost as much as it did Greenburg, judging from his expression, and she felt a rush of shame at lashing out at him. "The problem," she said in a more subdued voice, "is that stuffing Meredith out that cockpit window and into a ski-lift chair could kill him before we could get him down and to a hospital. The doctors didn't actually come out and *say* that they wouldn't allow it, but that was the impression I got. Given Rayburn's state of mind, I didn't want to press the point with him on the circuit."

"So what you're saying is that Meredith is stuck on the shuttle until it can be landed," Young said.

"Yeah, I guess that's basically what it boils down to," Besty admitted. "Unless he takes a turn for the worse, in which case we'll probably have to go ahead and take the chance."

"Uh-huh." Young was silent for a moment. "All right, here's how things look from where I sit. I've been in contact with United, and they have absolutely insisted that getting the passengers out of the shuttle be our top priority—higher even than Meredith's life, if it should come to that. A second crew will be coming up with that shuttle you mentioned to help with the off-loading. The airline chiefs say they want—and I quote— 'everyone safely aboard the Skyport with complimentary cocktails in their fists' within an hour." For the first time, Young's voice strayed from the purely professional as a note of bitterness edged in. Somehow, it made Betsy feel a little better. "What happens to Meredith and the shuttle is apparently *our* problem until then, when presumably they'll be willing to lend more of a hand."

"So what do we do?" Greenburg asked after a short pause. "Get everything aboard that we'll need for the ski-lift track and hightail it for L.A.?"

"We also need to fasten the shuttle more securely before we go," Betsy said. "Rayburn wants Meredith in a hospital immediately if not sooner, and if we try telling him he's going to have to wait another four hours he may try taking Meredith's safety into his own hands."

Greenburg frowned at her. "What do you mean?"

"Oh, that's right—you didn't hear that little gem of a conversation." In a half-dozen sentences Betsy summarized Rayburn's earlier outburst. Greenburg's eyes were wide with shocked disbelief by the time she finished. "Carl, we've got to get him out of that cockpit before he flips completely," he said, his left hand tracing restless patterns on the armrest.

"On what grounds? He hasn't actually tried to *do* anything dangerous. He could claim he was just blowing off steam."

"But—"

"No buts." The Skyport captain was firm. "We can't justify it—and besides, how do you think he'd react to an order like that?"

Greenburg clamped his lips together, and Betsy thought she saw some of the color go out of his face. "That's a little unfair," she said. "We don't *know* that he'd react irrationally." It felt strange to be defending Rayburn; quickly, she changed the subject. "Anyway, we're getting off the point. The immediate issue here is whether or not we head west in the next fifteen minutes. Carl, I guess this is your basic command decision."

Young's sigh was clearly audible. "I'm afraid I don't see any real alternative. We're just going to have to gamble with Mr.

Meredith's life. All of the ski-lift track and auxiliary equipment we're using only exists at fields that handle Skyport shuttles. If the crew putting the escape system together runs short of anything halfway to L.A. they'll have no way to get extra material quickly. We have to stay here at least until all of that's completed."

Betsy nodded; she'd more or less expected that would be the way the decision would break. The airline was clearly going to keep up the pressure, and the ski-lift-track system was the only way to get that many passengers off with anything like the speed and safety United would be demanding.

"And after they're off?" Greenburg asked quietly.

"We'll head toward L.A. and hope we've either secured the shuttle by then or that the last two collar supports are stronger than they look."

"Yeah." Shaking his head, Greenburg got to his feet. "I hope to hell we're doing the right thing, Carl. I'm not convinced, myself."

"Me, neither," Young acknowledged frankly. "But I don't see what else we can do. If we should somehow lose the shuttle with the passengers still aboard . . . it's not something I want to think about."

Greenburg nodded, shifted his gaze to Betsy. "I'm going back down and lend a hand, unless you need me here."

"No, go ahead. And Aaron—sorry I snapped at you earlier."

"Forget it. We're all tense." His hand touched her shoulder briefly and then he was gone.

"Betsy?" a tentative voice asked from behind her as she switched the intercom back to normal and the buzz of low-level conversation abruptly came back.

"Yes, Peter, what is it?" she asked, turning her head.

"I've got the first results of my program now, if you're interested."

She'd almost forgotten about Whitney; he'd been so quiet back there. "Sure. Let's hear the bad news."

"Well . . . it could be off ten percent or so either way, understand; but the number I get is seven point eight kilometers."

She did a rough conversion in her head, nodded heavily. "About twenty-five four hundred feet."

"Close enough," he agreed. "I can probably get a more refined version to run before the shuttle passengers are off."

She shook her head. "Not worth it. The longest runway at Dallas is twenty thousand feet, and even if your numbers are fifteen percent high we still would never make it."

"Yeah." Whitney hesitated, a half-dozen expressions flickering across his face. "You know, Betsy, this really isn't any of my business . . . but I get the impression you're upset with yourself for not being—oh, as cool and calm as maybe you think you should be. Is that true?"

Betsy's first and immediate reaction was one of annoyance that he should bring up such a personal subject. Her second was that he was absolutely right, which annoyed her all the more. "How I feel about myself is irrelevant," she said, a bit tartly. "I'm in command here; that requires me to be competent at what I do. Pressure like this isn't new to me, you know—I've been in crisis situations before."

"But they haven't been like this one, I'll bet, because you're *not* really in command here—not entirely, anyway. That's where the trouble is." There was an odd earnestness in his face, as if it were very important for some reason that he get his point across to her. "You see, if you were flying a normal airplane, you *would* be in complete control—I mean as far as human control ever goes—because all the buttons and switches would be under your hands alone. But *here*—" he gestured aft, toward the shuttle—"here, even though you're still claiming all the responsibility for what happens, half of the control is back there, with Captain Rayburn. He's got a mind and will of his own; you can't force him to do what you want, like you can your engines or ailerons. Of *course* you're going to be under extra pressure—you've never had to *persuade* part of your plane to cooperate with you before! It's *normal*, Betsy—you can't let it throw you." He stopped abruptly, as if suddenly embarrassed by the vehemence of his unsolicited counsel. "I'll shut up now," he muttered. "But think about it, okay?" Without another word he slipped back to the computer console.

Betsy leaned back in her seat, her thoughts doing a sort of slow-motion tumble. The last thing in the world she had time for right now was introspection . . . but the more she thought about Whitney's words, the more sense they made. Certainly Rayburn was only nominally under her control—his threats had made that abundantly clear—while it was equally certain that diplomacy and persuasive powers had never been among her major talents. Was this *really* the underlying source of her tension, the fact that she wasn't properly equipped for that aspect of the crisis?

Oddly enough, the idea made her feel better. She wasn't, in fact, getting old or losing her nerve. She was simply facing a brand-new problem—and new problems were *supposed* to be stressful.

For the first time since the shuttle crash, Betsy felt the tightness in her stomach vanish completely as all her unnamed fears, now robbed of their anonymity, scurried back into the darkness. If controlling Rayburn was what was required, then that was what she would do, pure and simple. All it took was strength and self-confidence—and both were already returning to her. She would have to thank Whitney later for his well-timed brashness. Right now, however, she had work to do. "Greenburg?" she called into the intercom grille. "I've got a couple of suggestions on how you might fix that clamp."

Seen through the distorted view of a fisheye camera, the escape system apparatus resembled nothing more dignified than a jury-rigged carnival ride—but it worked, and it worked well, and that was what counted. Even as Betsy returned her attention to the monitor, a pair of legs poked out the cockpit window and, above them, a line and hook were handed up to the man leaning vertically along the windshield. Eye-level to him was the newly built ski-lift track; into it he dropped the end of the hook. The hook immediately moved toward the passenger tunnel, and as the line tightened, the dangling legs bounced forward and out and became a business-suited man seated securely in a breeches-buoy type of sling. Even as he traveled toward the tunnel, an empty sling passed him going the other direction, and another set of legs poked tentatively out the cockpit window. Total elapsed time per passenger: about fifteen seconds. For all one hundred sixty of them . . . Betsy glanced at the clock and did the calculation. Maybe three or four left aboard now. And once they were off, a new confrontation with Rayburn was practically inevitable. Her throat ached with new tension as she tried to plan what she would say to him.

All too soon, the familiar voice crackled in her ear. "This is Rayburn. Everyone's off now except John and the two doctors. What's next?"

His harsh, clipped tone made the words a challenge, and Betsy felt the self-confidence of ninety minutes ago drain completely away. "We're leaving for L.A. in a few more minutes," she told him. "With the cable on your tow bar and the extra support of the escape system framework, the docking collar should hang on even after you run out of fuel."

"Who are you trying to kid, Liz?" The bitterly patronizing

tone struck her like a slap in the face, and she felt her back stiffen in reaction. He continued, "I saw that so-called cable when they brought it in—it wouldn't hold for two minutes. And you're drunk if you think a little spot-welding along the fuselage is going to do any good at all."

Betsy opened her mouth, but no words came out. In smaller quantities, she shared his own doubts about the cable looped around the nosewheel and the end of the clamp; they'd done the best they could, but the clamp simply wasn't designed to handle a line of any real diameter. Heavier cables were available, but there weren't any good places to attach them, either on the shuttle or the inner bay wall. "There are other things we can try on the way," she said, getting her voice working at last. "A stronger line, perhaps run through the access panels we've been using." Though where the ends would be anchored she had no idea.

But Rayburn didn't even bother to raise that point. "Swell. And what about John—or don't you care if he bleeds into his gut for another four hours? What're you going to do, just keep pumping blood into him and hope the leaks don't get worse? Or maybe you're going to stuff an operating room in through the window?"

"And what do you think the shock of landing will do to him?" Betsy countered.

"He's got to land *some*time. Better now than later, when he'll probably be weaker." Rayburn paused, as if waiting for an argument. But Betsy remained silent. "So okay, I'm going to take him down. I'll give you fifteen minutes to get rid of that cable and junk pile by my window; otherwise I'll just have to pull them out when I leave."

Betsy swallowed. She had no doubt that he could indeed tear off the cable if he really worked at it—and the chances were excellent he'd damage his front landing gear in the process. And that would essentially be signing his death warrant, because even if he somehow managed to keep the crippled plane from diving nose-first into the ground, there was no chance whatsoever that he could control it accurately enough to safely belly-land on a crash-foamed runway. He had to know that; he couldn't be *that* far gone. But she didn't have the nerve to call his bluff. "Eric, if you disobey orders like this you'll never fly again for any airline," she pointed out, trying to keep her voice reasonable. "You know that, don't you?"

"I don't give a damn about the airlines or your tin-god

orders—you should know me better than that by now. All I care about anymore is John's life. Fifteen minutes, Liz."

Stall, was all she could think of. "We have to get Dr. Emerson off the shuttle first," she told him. "You can't risk his life on this."

Rayburn snorted impatience. "All *right*. Doc! No, you—Doc Emerson. You're to get your things and leave; Skyport orders. Sorry, no . . . but, look, thanks for everything."

The earphone went silent. Betsy pushed the mike away from her with a trembling hand. Whitney's earlier words echoed through her mind—but it did no good to recognize on an intellectual level that once Rayburn defied her instructions she was absolved from all responsibility for the shuttle's safety. Emotionally, she still felt the crushing weight of failure poised above her shoulders.

Because, down deep, she finally knew what the real problem was. Not theoretical concepts like command and responsibility; not even Rayburn's open rebellion.

The problem was her. *Leadership is what command is all about*, she thought, a sour taste seeping into her mouth. *A captain needs to* act; *but all I can do with Eric is react*. She should have seen it long ago, and recognized it as the one remaining legacy of their long-since-broken relationship. Then, for reasons that had seemed adequate at the time, she had allowed his overpowering personality to take charge, submitting to his lead in all things, until in its subtle and leisurely way a pattern had been set for all their future interactions. He acted, she reacted; a simple, straightforward, and unbreakable rule . . . and men would probably die today because of it And even as she contemplated that consequence of her failure, a second, more brutally personal one drove itself into her consciousness like a thorn under a fingernail: for a year and a half Rayburn's name, face, and voice had been instant triggers of guilt-tinged pain to her . . . and if he died now, under these circumstances, he would haunt her from his grave for the rest of her life. "No!" she hissed aloud, beating gently on the edge of her instrument panel with a tightly curled fist. The pattern could be broken; *had* to be broken. She couldn't afford to accept his assumption that no alternative solutions existed. Their lives, and her future sanity, could depend on her proving him wrong.

Gritting her teeth tightly together, she stared at the monitor screen, her eyes dancing over the broken shuttle, the inside of the bay, the inadequate cable. Somewhere in all of that there was an answer. . . . Dr. Emerson's legs appeared through the cockpit window, his hand groping upward with the hook until the man on the windshield took it from him and set it in place. The line tightened and the doctor popped out of the window, flailing somewhat with his carry-on bag as he swung in midair.

And Betsy had the answer. Maybe.

"Peter!" she called, spinning around in her chair. "Did you finish that second landing-distance analysis yet?"

Whitney looked up at her. "Yes—it came out a little better this time: about seven point seven one kilometers, plus or minus five percent, maybe."

"How much worse would it be on a foamed runway?"

He blinked. "Uh, I really don't know—"

"Never mind. Warm up the machine again; I need some fast numbers from you." She flicked on her mike again. "Eric? Hold the ceremonies; I've got an idea."

"Save your breath. Whatever you've come up with, I'm going anyway."

"I know," she said, smiling coldly to herself. "But you're not going alone. We're going to hand-deliver you."

The sky had been a perfectly cloudless blue when the Skyport first approached Dallas earlier that morning. Now, five hours later, it looked exactly the same, giving Betsy a momentary feeling of déjà vu. But the sensation faded quickly. The airport that was just coming into view through the flight deck windows was to the north of them this time, instead of to the west, and even at this distance the heavily foamed runway was clearly visible in the noonday sun. And the throbbing roar of the engines behind her was a powerful reminder that this time the silver giant that was Wing Section Seven was fully awake.

"Range, twenty miles," Greenburg said from the copilot's seat. "Sky's clear for at least five miles around us."

She nodded receipt of the information, her eyes tracing a circuit between the windows, the computerized approach monitor, and the engine and other instrument readings. They were barely six minutes from touchdown now, and the pressure was beginning to mount. For a moment she wished she'd accepted Lewis's offer to do the actual landing, which would have left her with Henson's task of coordinating operations with the shuttle. But Lewis had already put in a full shift when the accident occurred, and whether he would admit it or not he was bound to be getting tired. Besides, this gamble was Betsy's idea alone. If something went wrong, she didn't want anyone else to share in the blame. Or in the physical danger, for that matter—

but there she'd met with somewhat less success. Ordering Lewis and the rest of Seven's off-duty flight crews to join the passengers in moving across to Five and Six had resulted in a quiet but firm mutiny. They'd helped the flight attendants get the passengers moved out, but had then returned en masse to the lounge, where most of them had spent the rest of the morning anyway, out of the way of the on-duty crew but close by if needed. Betsy had groused some about it, but not too loudly; though she couldn't imagine what help they could possible be, their presence was somehow reassuring.

And reassurance was definitely something she could use more of. "Eric, we're about four minutes away. Are you ready?"

"As ready as I'm going to be." Even half buried in the rumble of Seven's engines, Rayburn's voice sounded nervous, and Betsy felt a flash of sympathy for him. The shoe that had been pinching her all morning was now squarely on *his* foot. Not only was his plane going to be brought down by someone else while he himself had to sit passively by, but he was going to be essentially blind during the entire operation. "You just be sure to hold a nice steady deceleration once we hit the runway."

"Don't worry." Betsy stole a quick glance at the bay monitor. The escape system had been dismantled before Seven broke off from the rest of the Skyport, and the passenger tunnel retracted into the bay wall; the front landing gear, freed from the tethering cable, had been similarly retracted into its well. Betsy's jaw tightened and she winced at the thought of the shuttle hitting that foamed runway belly-first at a hundred twenty knots. Rayburn would have a massive job on his hands at that point, trying to maintain control of his skid while bringing the shuttle to a stop. But there was no way around it—the shuttle couldn't leave the docking bay with its nosewheel extended, and with less than a six-foot drop from its docked position to the ground there would be nowhere near enough time to get the landing gear in position once the shuttle was out. She hoped to hell the airport people had been generous with the foam.

"Seven miles to go," Greenburg murmured. "Final clearance has been given. Seven at one-seven-five."

One hundred seventy-five knots—one statute mile every eighteen seconds; a good fifty knots higher than the shuttle's own landing speed—and even at that Seven was barely staying aloft. Betsy's mouth felt dry as she made a slight correction in their approach path. Not only did she need to put Seven down on the very end of the runway if they were going to have any chance of pulling this off, but the runway itself was only two hundred feet wide, barely thirty feet wider than Seven's wheel track. She needed to hit it dead center, and stay there . . . and all of its markings were hidden by the foam.

"Betsy!" Henson's voice crackled with urgency. "Rayburn's lowered his main landing gear!"

"What?" Both her hands were busy, but Greenburg was already leaning over to switch the TV to Seven's outside monitor . . . and Henson was right. "Rayburn!" she all but bellowed into her mike. "What in hell's name do you think you're doing?"

"Trying to make this landing a little easier," he said, his voice taut.

"How?—by skidding into Dallas on your nose?"

"No—listen—all I have to do is control my exit from the bay so that my nosewheel is clear before I'm completely out."

"And then what—dangle by your nose until the wheel is down?" Betsy snorted. "Forget it. If you don't make it you could go completely out of control when you hit. Retract that gear, now."

"I can *do* it, Betsy—really. Please let me try."

For Betsy it was the final irony of the whole crisis; that Rayburn, having resisted her authority all morning, should be reduced to wheedling to get his way, even to the point of discarding the use of her hated nickname. But she felt no satisfaction or sense of triumph—only contempt that he would stoop to such shabby tactics, and bitter disappointment that he thought her fool enough to fall for something that transparent. And with sudden clarity she realized the reason for his new submissiveness: with Seven flying at such a low altitude Rayburn couldn't risk the unilateral action he'd hinted at earlier, because there was no way to guess whether or not the collar, once torn loose, would fall off fast enough for him to regain flying trim.

But it wasn't going to work. She was finally in command here, and nothing he could say or do was going to change that. If he didn't retract his gear as ordered she would simply pull out of her approach and circle the field until he did. This would be done her way or not at all.

Beside her, Greenburg shifted in his seat. "It's your decision, Betsy," he murmured, just loud enough for her to hear over the engines. "What do you think?"

She opened her mouth to repeat her order to Rayburn . . . and suddenly realized what she was doing.

She was still *reacting* to him.

It's your decision, Betsy. For the first time in years she really paused to consider what the words *decision* and *command* required of her. Among other things, they required that she dispassionately consider Rayburn's idea on its own merits, that she weigh his known piloting skill higher than his abrasive personality. And for perhaps the first time ever, she realized that accepting a good suggestion from him was not a sign of weakness. Perhaps even the opposite. . . .

The airport filled the entire window, the foamed runway pointing at her like a sawed-off spear less than a mile away. "All right," she said into her mike. "But you damn well better pull this off, Eric. And do *not* jump the gun."

"Got it. And . . . thanks."

The individual undulations in the foam were visible now as the edges of the runway disappeared from her field of view. Betsy eased back on the throttle, remembering to compensate for the fact that the shuttle's extra length limited the attack angle she could use to kill airspeed just before touching down. The leading edge of the foam flashed past—and with a jolt the wing section was down.

"Chutes!" she snapped at Greenburg, tightening her grip on the wheel as she braced for the shock. A moment later it came, throwing her roughly against her shoulder straps as the two drogue chutes on each end of the wing burst from their pods and bit into the air. Grimly, she held on, riding out the transient as she fought to keep Seven's wheels on the slippery runway. Within seconds the shaking had subsided from dangerous to merely uncomfortable, and Betsy could risk splitting her attention long enough to ease in the brakes. The straps dug a little deeper into her skin as the wheels found some traction. But it wasn't nearly enough, and she knew at that moment that Whitney's numbers had indeed been right: there was no possible way for Seven to stop on this runway. She could only hope the other numbers he'd worked out for her were equally accurate.

Through the vibrational din she could hear Greenburg shouting into his mike: "One-sixty . . . one-fifty-five . . . one-fifty . . ." Seven's speed, decreasing much too slowly. Betsy gritted her teeth and concentrated on her steering, trying to ignore the trick of perspective that made the end of the runway look closer than it really was. There were no shortcuts that could be taken here; if Seven was moving faster than a hundred twenty knots when they released the shuttle, the smaller aircraft would become airborne, with the disastrous results she was risking Seven's crew precisely to avoid.

". . . one-forty . . . one-thirty-five—get ready—"

A sudden thought occurred to Betsy. "Eric!" she shouted, interrupting Greenburg's countdown. "Just before we release the collar we'll cut all braking here—that'll give you a constant speed to work against instead of a deceleration. You copy that, too, Rick?"

"Roger. Cue me, will you?"

"Right. Aaron, drop the chutes at one-twenty exactly."

"Roger. One-twenty-five . . . three, two, one, *mark!*"

There was no jerk this time, just a sudden drop in shoulder-strap pressure as one of the discarded drogues flashed briefly across the outside monitor screen. Simultaneously, Betsy released the brakes, and Seven was once again rolling free. "One-nineteen," Greenburg sang out.

"Collar!" Betsy snapped to Henson—and for the first time since touchdown gave her full visual attention to the monitor screen.

It was probably the finest display of engine and brake control that she had ever witnessed. Released abruptly from all constraints, the shuttle's tail dropped the short distance to the runway, landing on its main gear with a bump and splash of foam that made Betsy wince. At the same time the shuttle slid backward across the screen, as the extra air drag on its less aerodynamic shape tried to pull it out of the bay. But almost before the sliding began it was abruptly halted as Rayburn, with a touch even more skillful than Betsy had expected, nudged his engines up just exactly enough to compensate. She watched, fascinated, as the shuttle drifted back another few feet and again halted. There it sat, balanced precariously by its battered nose on the docking bay rim, its wheels and engines kicking up foam like mad, while its nosewheel—finally clear of the bay's confines—descended and locked in place.

And then, with one final lurch, the shuttle vanished from the screen.

"He's free!" Henson shouted unnecessarily. A tower controller, his voice a bare whisper in Betsy's ear, confirmed it, adding something about the shuttle being under good control as it braked . . . but Betsy wasn't really listening to him. Ahead, barely a mile of runway was left to them—just thirty seconds away at their current speed . . . and there was no way on Earth for them to stop before they reached it.

But Betsy had no intention of stopping. Instead, she opened the throttle all the way, and with a thunderous roar that drowned out even the rumble of landing gear on tarmac, the giant plane

leaped forward, pushing Betsy deeply back into the cushions of
her seat. Beside her, Greenburg would be calling off the speed
increments; but she couldn't hear him, and she didn't dare take
her eyes from the window to check the numbers for herself. She
could see the end of the runway rushing toward her, and
unconsciously she braced herself for the terrible crash that
would signify that her gamble had failed. The edge of the foam
swung at her like a guillotine blade—passed beneath her—

And the crash didn't come. Instead, the barren ground at the
end of the runway flashed by, visibly receding below.

They'd done it!

Betsy let Lewis and Greenburg handle the routine business of
flying Seven back to link up again with the rest of the Skyport.
The two had insisted, and Betsy's hands were shaking so much
from delayed reaction that doing it herself would have been
difficult. Besides, a sort of celebration had erupted spontane-
ously in Seven's crew lounge, at which the wing captain's presence was being demanded.

What with the flurry of congratulatory hugs and handshakes
and the general babble of tension-releasing conversation, Betsy
missed the exact moment when the link-up occurred; her first
real indication that Seven was back with the Skyport was the
two grinning figures that strode unexpectedly into the lounge.

"Hey, Carl!" the first person to spot them shouted, waving a
dangerously full glass. "Join the celebration!"

"Sorry—I can't spare the time," the Skyport captain said,
speaking just loudly enough to penetrate the racket. "I just
came by to congratulate Betsy in person. Mr. Whitney seems
to think he's earned the right to do likewise."

"Thanks," Besty called, handing her glass of fruit juice—she
was on duty, after all—to the nearest bystander and making her
way through the crowd. "Hang on a second—I want to talk to
both of you."

She led them out into the hallway, where normal conversational levels would be possible. Once outside the din she turned
to Young; but he'd already anticipated her first question. "I
just talked to the tower," he said, "which had been in contact
with the hospital. The landing did some extra damage to Meredith's internal bleeding problems, but with the ambulance and
emergency room personnel standing by they think they got him
in time. I'm also told, though very unofficially, that he probably
wouldn't have made it if we'd tried to take him to L.A. instead."

Betsy let out a breath she hadn't realized she'd been holding.

They really *had* done it; they'd gambled Seven, the shuttle, and a lot of lives, and had won back all of it.

Young was still talking. "We're moving your passengers back in for the moment, though of course they'll have to leave again before we reach L.A. I've talked to McDonnell Douglas and United, and they'll have another wing section ready to replace you when we arrive. This one was due to go in for routine maintenance next month, anyway; you'll just be a little early." He harrumphed. "The United man I talked to seemed a bit concerned that you'd be landing with your corner drogues missing. I told him that anyone who can do a touch-and-go with a flying football field wasn't someone he needed to worry about."

She smiled. "That's for sure. After today, landing at Mirage Lake will feel like aiming to hit Utah. No problem."

"Well, at least you've got your confidence back," Young said, smiling in return. "I had been wondering about that earlier."

"Me, too," she admitted. "Which reminds me . . . Peter, I owe you a vote of thanks for that pep talk on command and responsibility you gave me a few hours ago. I don't know if it really made sense to me at the time, but it was just what I needed to break up the gloom and panic I was digging myself into."

Whitney actually blushed. "Yeah, well . . . I felt a little strange playing psychiatrist but . . . well, I had to say *something*. I was getting pretty worried about Captain Rayburn, and, frankly, I was scared to death you were going to go off the same end of the pool—no offense."

"No offense," Betsy assured him. "I can't honestly say that I wasn't a little worried about it myself." She shook her head, turning serious. "I still can't believe Eric went so badly to pieces. I know he was worried about Meredith's safety, but he was getting practically obsessive about it. He'll be *very* lucky if United doesn't boot him out for insubordination."

Young cleared his throat self-consciously. "Actually, Betsy, I suspect his flying career is over anyway. I haven't got any proof yet, of course, but I'll wager any sum of money that when the shuttle's flight recorder is played back it'll show that Rayburn had his automatic approach system off and was flying manually when the crash occurred. He's docked like that before, I'm pretty sure, and if we hadn't hit that patch of turbulence he might have gotten away with it this time, too."

Betsy felt her eyes widen in disbelief . . . but even as she opened her mouth to argue, all the puzzling parts of the incident suddenly made sense, and she knew he was right.

"But isn't that dangerous, not to mention illegal?" Whitney asked.

"Highly," Young told him, answering both parts of the question. "Even with an empty shuttle, which is how I gather he usually does it. Whatever possessed him to try it with a full passenger load I'll never know."

Betsy's lip curled, ever so slightly; but she held her peace. A figurative rape, perhaps? Or just an overwhelming desire to prove in her presence that he was a superior pilot? It didn't really matter; either way, it told her something about Eric Rayburn that she had never suspected.

"Anyway, as long as that's just my unsupported opinion, I'd appreciate it if you'd both keep it to yourselves," Young was saying. "Betsy, I've got to get below now, help ease any ruffled feathers among the passengers. Congratulations again on your fine job here." With a nod to Whitney, the Skyport captain headed off down the hall.

Betsy watched him go, but without really seeing him. *So it comes full circle,* she thought bemusedly. *I fight to quit reacting to Eric, and find out he's been reacting just as blindly and irrationally to me.* She shook her head minutely. *Puppets, all of us—even all the ones who think they're mavericks. Puppets pulling on each other's strings.*

"I suppose I should go back down, too," Whitney said, breaking into her thoughts. "It was really a privilege to watch you in action, Betsy—thanks for letting me be part of it."

"Just a minute, Peter," she said as he turned to go, pushing the growing bitterness determinedly from her mind. After all, she was only forty-five—far too young to become a cynic. "I seem to recall you were interested earlier in a tour of the Skyport topdeck. That still true?"

"Uh, yes," he said, an uncertain smile playing around his lips. "If it's not too much trouble."

"No trouble at all." And besides, reacting with cynicism would just be giving Rayburn one final victory over her. "Come on, we'll start with the crew lounge. Drinks are on the house—and I understand the fruit juice is excellent today."

TO GRAB POWER

BY HAYDEN HOWARD

On the next downtrip, while the short-winged shuttle skimmed through the man-made atmosphere high above the instaplanet's rain-filled meteoritic craters, someone fell out.

Or so it appeared on the luminescent screen in the dark stone hut—like a falling spark, falling like a shriek. The young bodyguard stared at it with surprise which plunged through horror to excitement.

Falling below the shuttle's radar blip, the spark seemed big to be a man. It was as if his arms and legs were spread in the thickening air and he were resisting the inevitable.

"Is he conscious?" cried the old man's voice in the hut.

"Maybe if he had time to close his helmet—"

The bodyguard's boyish face became wide-eyed as he imagined himself falling toward the instaplanet. Its meteor-pocked surface would be glittering with thousands of crater-ponds like new coins. Airdrops had planted fish in them. But for some reason all of the villages still crowded around this vast polluted lake, where the little volcanic island muddied the clouds with smoke. The spark was approaching the island.

"He's falling through the air too fast, getting too hot" —the bodyguard's snub nose and broad forehead wrinkled—"unless he's in an escape bag with an ablative foot-cone."

From the bottom of the screen rose the volcano's image. The bodyguard's heart pounded. One of his greatest desires was to enter its smoldering crater and search for the forbidden weapons rumored to be hidden there.

"No parachute has opened," he breathed as the spark faded into the radar-confusing smoke, "so I guess he wasn't in an escape bag. But whatever he was in made an awful big blip on the screen." His youthful gestures were lightning-quick. "Look, now the shuttle is following its usual landing spiral back toward our end of the lake, so it couldn't have been the pilot who fell out."

Another gust of rain lashed through the crevices in the crude stone hut.

"It must have been Henrydavid," the old man moaned, leaning forward until his jagged face was silhouetted against the screen. His bodyguard looked away in embarrassment at the rough stone wall that was weeping rain.

The bodyguard fidgeted. To him the old man had long seemed a source of power. It was power too unsubstantial to be grasped.

"The world turns—" the old man murmured. "Do you think this is another attempt by those unforgiving Centralist exiles?"

"More likely an accident in the shuttle," his bodyguard said. "But you'd better go back to the village." The young man took a deep breath. "I'll paddle out to meet the shuttle."

"No," the old man said uncertainly. "No—"

Without replying, the bodyguard darted out under the smoky sunlight-edged clouds. He was uncomfortably short, but no one taunted him anymore. He had wide shoulders. After his strange battle on that volcanic island, he'd been asked by the old man to be his bodyguard. And he had agreed because he was restless, born restless. He wanted to be near power. As a small boy he had dreamed of becoming so big he filled the universe with his power.

Now, as he looked up at the rainbow-arched sky, he felt tall. He imagined Henrydavid, not falling through the air but standing lithely again inside the shuttle while it clung to a synchronously orbiting freighter. Aluminum-shelled supply containers as big as caskets were being shoved in through the flexible iris that was its hatch. Henrydavid's job as customs inspector was to open them immediately.

With mixed emotions, the bodyguard frowned. These old men were still trying to prevent Centralist propaganda from reaching the instaplanet via the shuttle. The certain young men here . . .

"We'll both go out to meet it," the old man said, lifting the other end of the heavy greenish canoe.

The bodyguard had shaped it by hand-pressing layers of filamentous algae over the hull of an earlier canoe. When it had firmed, he had smeared it with fish oil and dutifully baked it in the sunlight. Then he had cheated a little and also baked it in his village's hydrogen-fusion-powered electric oven.

The wooden paddles were imported from Earth. While the crude canoe sloshed out on the immense lake the water became lively with raindrops and minnows. He had been taught that the lake and the countless crater-ponds had been filled by the Great Rain ten years before he was born here. Before that the supersaturated air for this instaplanet had been produced by remolecularizing the rocks from both poles. After the air became sweet and the rains diminished, the planet had been planted with life. The old man and his followers were delivered to it as an experiment. Economic or philosophic? The bodyguard wondered what kind of world it would become.

Now the greenish lake was swirling with great fish devouring each other in richly putrefying jungles of algae. But the land had remained barren rock, as clean and simple as the Decentralist ideal.

In the bow of the canoe the old man's slender back and arms moved his paddle with quiet grace. In the stern the young bodyguard paddled with driving force and steered as the huge shuttle taxied toward them, pushing a mustache of foam.

For the bodyguard the shuttle carried the exciting power of Earth, where he wanted to go. Its heat-stained hull contained beautiful steel tools, bright mirrors, colorful beads. He had heard fabulous tales of Earth weapons with wonderful thunder-and-lightning power which could be held in a boy's hand. He had decided the shuttle to the freighters was the one contact with Earth which must never be broken, no matter what the old man preached.

"Now it's killed someone," the old man blurted as the shuttle's scarred hull surged threateningly close to the canoe.

But his bodyguard smiled with excitement. The shuttle contained power that could be grasped. Already concealed in his kirtle of woven algae was his most wonderful possession, a steel dagger smuggled from Earth. If the old man had known he would have told him to throw it overboard, because it was a *weapon*, as was any knife more than three inches long.

The old man would have said, "Weapons lead to uncontrollable power, to Centralism. Beware."

The bodyguard scowled at the straight old back as the canoe drifted alongside the shuttle. Respectful people in the villages still addressed the old man as Mr. Decentralist and some had shortened this to Mr. Decent. But restless young men laughed bitterly. It was their fathers who had brought Decentralism to this instaplanet. The young men paced the barren rocks and looked out at the volcanic island, remembering Big Village before its fall. They stared at the forbidden island, dreaming of another central city, and cursed the old man behind his back.

The bodyguard laid down his paddle and picked up his trident fish spear. His clumsy algal canoe bumped the marvelously complex shuttle. Without its usual hiss of equalizing air pressure, the shuttle's hatch opened like a camera eye. Its inner iris looked rubbery.

The pilot's oddly blank face protruded.

"It wasn't my fault." The shiny arm of his metalized suit flew up. "Your customs inspector was blown out like that! The valve popped off our emergency air tank and air pressure did the rest. I always said that valve was dangerous. It was poorly designed."

Or sabotaged, the bodyguard thought as he scrambled into the shuttle. This downtrip there seemed to be no unannounced passengers. He eyed the rows of long aluminum supply containers, which they received from Earth in exchange for their little bottles of fish-gland extracts. Whenever he had entered the shuttle, it had had this fishy smell.

"So the air pressure shot up in here," the pilot kept explaining.

His jowls quivered and the young bodyguard remembered Mr. Decentralist's warning that such stocky or obese men were apt to be unfaithful to Decentralist ideals. It was true that the most dedicated Decentralists, who lived with austerity and simplicity, had naturally narrow physiques like Mr. Decent's. The bodyguard's wide-cheeked face grimaced, then scowled again. He didn't trust the pilot.

The pilot blustered: "I always said this loading iris is too flexible. All that pressure bulged it out, blew him out."

"Did Henrydavid have time," Mr. Decentralist murmured hopelessly, "to close his helmet visor?"

"Don't know. I had to hang on to the control panel." The pilot shifted his gaze from the old man's jagged face to the bodyguard's blunt expression of disbelief.

"Why," the bodyguard challenged, "weren't any of these containers blown out with him?"

"Because he'd already inspected them and strapped them down again," the pilot answered, "for landing as usual. Anyway, they're too streamlined to be sucked out."

The bodyguard felt outsmarted. He quibbled. "This one isn't strapped tight."

He knew the customs inspector had been a conscientious man who would have tightened the strap if he'd had time. He deliberately pointed his fish spear, which was defined as a tool, not a weapon, toward the pilot's abdomen. "Did Henrydavid have time to open all the containers?"

"Yes, he always does—open them," the pilot blurted and looked to Mr. Decent. "I feel bad about this."

"I think we'd better inspect them again," the bodyguard said.

"Not now," replied Mr. Decent. "We've got to search for Henrydavid."

The bodyguard blinked with surprise.

The pilot also stared at Mr. Decent.

"We wouldn't be able to find anything," the pilot explained. "The shuttle was moving so fast when he was blown out, his descent speed was so great that his body was burned in the atmosphere."

The bodyguard looked at the emergency rack's twelve cubicles where the glittering, heat-reflective escape bags lay. Their "feet" were ablative cones for casting off flame as they penetrated the atmosphere. Their "heads" were two-stage parachutes. All twelve were still in the rack. No bags were missing. The bodyguard scowled, feeling baffled.

"He wasn't falling that fast," he argued. "In his safety suit like yours his body wouldn't—burn—very much."

"You don't understand anything," the pilot retorted, "about atmospheric entry speed. It would have burned him—to a crisp."

"You're the expert," Mr. Decent murmured to the pilot, "but I know we must recover his body."

"It was burned to ashes," the pilot insisted and added too gently: "He often said he'd want to go this way, with his ashes scattered over the lake he loved so well. There's no use searching for his ashes. He would have wanted it this way."

Enough lies, the bodyguard thought, now convinced that the shuttle's speed had been reduced by the time Henrydavid was "blown out." The body couldn't have burned to ashes. But he didn't want to look for it either. He wondered if this "accident" were a decoy or a trap.

But he was so angry he said, "I know his suit will have preserved most of his body. We should start searching near the island."

"Near Big Village?" the pilot protested. "For his ashes?"

"Yes, in the water around the volcano," the bodyguard replied, observing the pilot's unhappy face. "Did you know we were watching the radar screen when it happened?"

The pilot glanced at Mr. Decent. "It would be too dangerous for you—for anyone—to go over there in a canoe."

"Too slow," the old man said enigmatically. And then his voice broke: "Henrydavid may be alive—floating—drowning—"

"He means rush us over there in this shuttle," the bodyguard said.

The pilot began to protest: "Using a space shuttle like a canoe—"

The bodyguard snorted. "That's what we've always used it for when no freighters have been in orbit. Push the REFUEL button."

Gurgling, the shuttle refilled its water tanks. It was frequently employed to distribute supplies to other villages along the lake shore.

"Now pull the FUSION lever only to the first mark." The bodyguard had ridden in the craft several times and knew it merely needed steam now, not disassociated hydrogen and oxygen flaring and hurling the shuttle into space, where he'd only been as far as the freighter orbit. "We're only going around Volcano Island."

A humming sound came from the shuttle's bowels, where the magnetic bottle, containing its hydrogen fusion, produced heat. There was hissing as the water turned to steam and a roar from the dual-purpose thruster as the shuttle surged across the wide lake, steam billowing behind its high-finned tail.

"Look at that little canoe over there," the bodyguard shouted, surprised and suspicious because it seemed to be headed toward the forbidden island. Its paddlers noticed the shuttle's course and, as if they had guilty consciences, turned back to the mainland.

The volcanic cone squatted on the contorted rim of a half-drowned meteoric crater. The bodyguard knew this lone volcano had burst from a crack while the planet was being distorted by the remolecularization of rock from its poles. The crater had cooled while he had been a little boy. But smoke rose from a recent split in its flank.

The main reason people with Centralist tendencies had established a village beside the cone, upon the meteoric rim which enclosed the harbor, was to tap the volcano's heat for use in illegal manufacturing. They had begun making metal forks and spoons—and sharper things that the bodyguard secretly wished he could own. Daggers. Ever more powerful weapons.

Centralists were never satisfied, he thought, and now their village was deserted. Wonderful things had been thrown into the lake. His visualization of those beautiful lost weapons made his heart pound with desire. He wanted again, on this errand, to search the crater for unfinished weapons but the old man was along. The bodyguard glared toward the mainland.

"There's another canoe," the bodyguard shouted harshly. "See from that new village—a long dark canoe?"

And it didn't seem intimidated by the shuttle. The bodyguard thought it might be headed for the island—or its dozen paddlers might simply be loyal Decentralists going fishing. He remembered that some of the Centralists had been dispersed along the shore adjacent to the new village after Mr. Decent had ordered the volcanic island evacuated.

While the shuttle cruised around it, the bodyguard watched for telltale gulls, but there was no sign of the customs inspector's body.

"Go into the harbor," Mr. Decentralist said unexpectedly.

The bodyguard's heart thudded as they entered the harbor's rocky jaws. Big Village clung to the cliffs, deathly silent, its empty-eyed stone huts staring at him. He felt both guilt and pride and clutched his fish spear as if it were—a weapon. It was here he had shown he was a—man.

A gull fluttered from the water, but it had been feeding on a big dead fish. The bodyguard knew the volcanic cone above Big Village had polluted its harbor even more than its air. He winced and felt nostalgia, remembering Big Village that final day when it had been alive with runaway girls singing and illegal forges clanging.

He had been a youth in the angry armada of paddlers from the little villages who had cautiously approached this Centralist stronghold. He had felt awe and envy when he had seen how rich and populous Big Village had become. There were more than two hundred huts. Centralists had crowded the stone dock. His heart had leaped when he had seen they had already manufactured three of the Supreme Weapons. All three had glinted in the sunlight.

Now he scowled, peering down at the dark, deep water of the harbor.

But Mr. Decent's voice was crying: "Look up there."

A blade of sunlight illuminated a tiny red stain on the volcano's flank, high above the dead village and the old man was moaning: "Henry, Henry—"

The bodyguard realized this was where their falling customs inspector had struck the planet like a meteorite. His gaze rose to the lip of the crater and he tried to suppress his desire to enter it. This wasn't a good time, although the rim was only a few minutes climb above the red splash of Henrydavid.

"I've got to go up," Mr. Decent bleated. "Henry, oh, Henry—"

The bodyguard began to argue that it was forbidden to land on the island. "You made the rule. Anyway this may be a trap."

But the distraught old man ordered the pilot to bring the shuttle alongside the algae-shrouded stone dock.

"That canoe may get here soon," the bodyguard warned. "They may be coming because they saw him fall."

But there was no use arguing with the old man, and unless the wind changed so that the paddlers could open their sailing umbrellas, the bodyguard knew the canoe couldn't get here for at least an hour. He started to follow the old man on to the dock. His own desire rose.

He slipped. Algae had grown where there had been blood, he realized, and he recovered his natural alertness. He jumped back aboard the shuttle before it could escape. His fish spear backed the pilot toward one of the aluminum containers.

"Open it. Now dump out those pamphlets. Pamphlets? Anyway, get in. You won't smother. The lid doesn't fit that well." He tightened the straps. "Don't go away," he said, clambering out on the shuttle's deck. He made it fast to a stone cleat on the dock.

He ran after the old man, through the crumbling village of memories. When the armada had approached it Big Village had illegally contained at least a thousand people, although the maximum permissible size for a community on this instaplanet was a hundred. It was a fabulous place, and young runaways had flocked to it. He remembered smiling with excitement rather than fear, even when he had seen its three supreme weapons gleaming.

Mr. Decent had boldly landed on the dock to negotiate or accuse.

"You've already taken away the nuc-boxes from five villages, depriving them of electricity."

"You old hypocrite," the mayor of the Big Village had retorted. "You complain about us taking their electricity, but you've been urging them to decentralize into tens—or families to live without electricity. Look, we have so many people here who need it, we ought to have ten electric-boxes, not five. Listen, Earth sends a box to this planet for each hundred people, so we have the right to proportional allocation of electric power. We ought to have ten boxes."

"No. You're rebuilding all the confusion and greed we tried to leave behind on Earth," the old man had shouted. "You're even manufacturing inhuman weapons."

All three glinted sharply in the sunlight.

Mr. Decentralist had rashly grabbed at one. When he had fallen down during the scuffle, his shrill Decentralists had begun scrambling from their canoes to the dock, thrusting out their fishing spears like weapons.

"Defense," the major had yelled over his shoulder, and the three holders of the supreme weapons had waddled forward, deflecting fish-spears with their aluminum shields and raising their beautiful steel weapons.

As their blades flashed in the sunlight the future bodyguard's heart had pounded with desire instead of fear even as the Centralists attacked.

They struck off hands and arms and heads in a frantic display of power. Instead of fleeing, he had circled. A Centralist had slipped on the flood and fallen, his supreme weapon clanging against the stones.

The future bodyguard had rushed forward and wrested away the sword.

Now it's mine, he had thought excitedly, gripping its hilt.

The second swordsman had waddled toward him. He had dodged the thrust. These three supreme weapons were so valuable that they had been carried by three of the most important men in Big Village, fat, middle-aged men.

With youthful quickness the bodyguard-to-be had swung his great blade back and forth. It had struck his opponent's neck. Now that he had the knack of it the bodyguard-to-be had rushed at the third middle-aged man. Around him the excited Decentralists had attacked with their fish spears. Blood sprayed.

The Big Villagers had scattered, ending the strangely abrupt battle and beginning the problem of what to do with so many defeated people who were still Centralists at heart.

Now, as the bodyguard ran upward through the empty village after the old man, he thought the wind might be changing. The long canoe could be approaching rapidly. It might be filled with Centralist renegades, returning.

On the side of the volcano he saw Mr. Decent kneel in the great red splash. The old man seemed to be murmuring to a fragment of Henrydavid's safetysuit. He was picking it up.

The bodyguard climbed past, hurrying to reach the top to spot the canoe over there—and for another reason.

From the rim of the volcano he looked out over the immense wind-wrinkled lake and the lonely land beyond, glittering with countless crater-ponds, where the old man wanted people to spread out in smaller groups in an ever simpler way of life.

The bodyguard smiled and shook his head. The long dark canoe was still a long way off. Whether it contained faithful Decentralist fishermen or unrepentant Centralist rebels, they were still paddling against the wind. His heart leaped. He might have time to search the crater.

He peered down into the darkly jumbled funnel and his heart pounded as it had when he had seized the sword in the Battle of Big Village. The greatest disappointment of his life had come after the fighting, when the old man had honored him by choosing him as his new bodyguard and then told him to throw all three swords into the lake.

The bodyguard had secretly returned later and dredged for them, cursing and crying because he had stupidly thrown away their power.

No unfinished swords had been found in Big Village, and he thought the illegal weapons forge might have been concealed in this crater. As he descended, his snub nose wrinkled at the sulphurous stench. He searched under lava ledges for even an unfinished sword, which could give him power to—

His eyes widened. At the bottom, beside a vertical split where steaming rainwater drained out of the crater, he saw something white and rumpled. He clutched his fish spear like a weapon and clambered down, sending rocks rattling.

His eyes widened. The whiteness was a folded parachute partially covering an escape bag. Except for its ablative foot cone, the bag lay flat. It was a different model from the twelve in the shuttle. He could see it was empty. No one was on the nearby rocks. The bag was open. He thought the inspector must have fallen out—but why would he have been in an escape bag descending into the crater?

Anyone peering through the bag's periscope could have steered its chute toward the volcano. Any man could have been breathing from its oxygen tank. The bodyguard didn't think Henrydavid would have had a reason to ride down in an escape bag.

He clutched his spear and looked around quickly, but no one was crouching in ambush among the rocks.

"Don't move," a hoarse voice said, and the parachute cloth

squirmed. A swollen-faced, middle-aged man had been lying motionless underneath it. A gleaming metal rod with a round hole in its end was pointing out at the bodyguard. The man sat up. "Throw away your spear—that's right."

The bodyguard's heart was again drumming with excitement rather than fear as he stared at this absolutely ultimate weapon which could change life on his instaplanet. Its barrel and folding stock were gleaming with the promise of power. One of the man's hands gripped its long bullet clip. The other enclosed its trigger mechanism. The bodyguard shivered with desire because he wanted the weapon more than anything in the universe.

"Stop smiling," the man's voice shrilled as if he were in great pain. "Who are you?"

"A fisherman," the bodyguard finally answered, surprised the man hadn't recognized him from the Battle of Big Village or its aftermath. "I just climbed here to—"

"Don't move. I'll shoot." The parachutist's blotchy face grimaced, smiled, then looked disappointed. "Don't you know who I am?"

"No," the bodyguard lied, his thoughts racing between the future and the past.

He began to glimpse the brilliant scheme by which this exiled mayor of Big Village had hoped to reenter the instaplanet undetected. The falling spark on the radar screen—anyone familiar with the operation of the shuttle would have reasoned it to be the customs inspector falling all alone because of some accident. But Henrydavid had not fallen alone.

The pilot had been part of the conspiracy, the fat-faced pilot. The bodyguard imagined the scene inside the shuttle, among the containers from the freighter. The pilot must have struck Henrydavid on the head. Then this blotchy-faced man had emerged from a container and dragged out his special escape bag from another. He would have tied Henrydavid's body to the outside of this bag, using one of its parachute control lines and a slip-knot. After arranging the bag against the hatch iris the Centralist ex-mayor must have sealed himself inside it and waited.

The bodyguard's eyes widened in admiration. When the shuttle had approached the smoke from the volcanic island the pilot must have knocked the valve off the reserve air tank. The sudden increase in air pressure had blown the flexible iris outward and the escape bag had hurtled into space, falling diagonally toward the island and appearing on their radar screen as a single spark. No wonder it had seemed surprisingly large to represent one man.

The bodyguard smiled at this fabulous ex-mayor who must have yanked the extra control line at the last moment, freeing himself from the weight of Henrydavid's body as the escape bag vanished into the radar-confusing smoke. He had deployed the drogue chute. After his main chute opened, he had skillfully steered it to his island, disappearing into the volcanic crater.

The bodyguard's smile became a grin because, in landing down here, the man seemed to have broken his leg.

"Let me help you—to climb out of here."

"Keep away."

The gun barrel rose. The Centralist's thick body shifted and his face contorted in pain. His left leg had an unusual bend in it.

The bodyguard nodded obediently, waiting his chance. His gaze devoured the beautiful gun, the first he had ever seen except in smuggled pictures.

"Is it called a submachine gun?"

"You don't even know who I am," the middle-aged man exclaimed angrily. "You don't know what to do."

The bodyguard considered the dagger concealed in his kirtle and said, "Let me help or you'll die down here."

He thought whipping out his dagger would take too long. He'd better grab at the gun.

"Look, there's blood leaking where you opened that leg-zip on your suit. A compound fracture?"

"Stay back," the man rasped. "I don't need you. Others are coming to this island to meet me."

"In canoes?" The bodyguard feigned surprise. He doubted the man could have seen that long canoe through his periscope while his bag was descending. "There aren't any canoes out there—except mine. So you need my help. I've always wanted the good things they have on Earth. I wish I'd been born there—with all the autocars and television boxes, and great cities—"

While he tried to sound like a Centralist, his voice grew so convincing that what he said became true. He realized how much he wanted what the Centralists wanted, and he watched that beautiful gun barrel lowering as the parachutist's arms relaxed. In a little while he would have an opportunity to grab this wonderful submachine gun, the ultimate weapon on the instaplanet.

Rocks rattled behind him. He whirled. Up there a half-naked, scrawny figure was clambering down from the rim.

"Who's that?" the parachutist hissed.

"Another fisherman," the bodyguard lied hopelessly.

"Wave to him to come down." Evidently the Centralist thought he might need two to carry him up.

"He already is coming," the bodyguard gritted, wishing that old man would see the gun and run. Mr. Decent had upset his plan before he could execute it. He had intended to hide the submachine gun after taking care of the parachutist—and to return for it later. But Mr. Decent must see the gun by now and eventually he would tell his bodyguard to drop it into the lake. The bodyguard scowled.

The old man was scrambling down clutching a bloody scrap of cloth as if it were all that was left of Henrydavid.

"You!"

"You! Don't come any closer." The parachutist's aim shifted between the bodyguard and the old Decentralist. "I'll shoot you, you old hypocrite."

"You agreed not to return," Mr. Decent wheezed as the wind wailed above the crater. "Why are you here?"

High above the old man's jagged face volcanic smoke writhed across the sky and the bodyguard realized the wind had changed. In their long canoe the fishermen who might be Centralists would be opening their sailing umbrellas. Their dark canoe would be surging toward the island. The bodyguard's young, wide, muscular body felt as if it were swelling. He couldn't wait much longer. While he watched for a chance to leap at the gun, he felt as strong and quick as when he had dodged those sword thrusts. He supposed a bullet wouldn't be much faster than a sword, and it was such a little thing. The round eye of the gun muzzle stared at him.

"Move back," the parachutist hissed. "Closer to Mr.—Decentralist."

The bodyguard smiled and didn't move, silently willing Mr. Decent not to remark that a long canoe was coming. The parachutist would assume it carried the Centralist activists who were supposed to meet him. He would feel free to squeeze the trigger, shooting the old man. But the bodyguard couldn't conceive of himself being killed and leaned toward the Centralist leader, waiting for his opportunity.

"You can't become mayor of an empty village," Mr. Decent's voice bargained. "I let you go before. I'll let you go back to Earth again."

"Hypocrite!" the ex-mayor cried. "You talked of peace and individual freedom but led the attack on Big Village. It would have been kinder if you'd executed me then. This is my island. Where are my people now?"

"Dispersed," the old man retorted. "Enjoying pure and simple lives again."

"He's a fanatic," the Centralist hissed frantically to the bodyguard, "a fanatic old man. He thinks a hundred people are too many for a village. He wants to disperse families, one to a pond—and after that what?"

"Transcendent freedom," the old man replied "to contemplate."

"Freedom to isolate yourself beside a pond," the Centralist cried, "on a bare planet, and think about what? You hypocrite, already in your little villages there's no freedom for young people to do what they want to do, which is to get together and—"

"They're growing up unspoiled." Mr. Decent looked to his young bodyguard, who realized that both of them, the old man and the middle-aged man, the Decentralist and the Centralist, were speaking to him rather than to each other.

"This old man is trying to be a mental jailer for you young people. Listen!" The parachutist obviously wanted his help and allegiance. "Listen—"

Each seemed to be trying to win him, to use him, as if he represented all of the young people on the planet, its future.

The Centralist insisted: "It's this old man's fault your instaplanet is tied to an unfair economic plan. That damned plan for economic decentralization was written by bureaucrats on Earth for the benefit of Earth. That's why we weren't allowed to manufacture anything. That's why villages were limited to a hundred people. In that inhuman plan all we're supposed to do is catch fish and send their glandular extracts to Earth. Listen, unless we centralize, our instaplanets' unfavorable balance of trade will keep us poor colonial slaves."

"Who needs trade?" the old man retorted. "Good Decentralists are learning to do without Earth's corrupting products. We have fish and health-giving algae. We can weave kirtles and build stone shelters. We can become free of Earth trash. We don't need that accursed shuttle anymore. We don't have to rely on Earth.

"That's right," the Centralist interrupted and smiled at the young man. "When we have a great industrial city we won't have to rely as much on Earth. We can enjoy—"

"—polluting our lives!" the Decentralist shouted. "We came here to escape evil and noise and greed. That's why we had to accept that Economic Plan, so Earth would pay our transportation here."

The parachutist nodded and stared at the young man. "Yes, after the Bureau of Colonization created air and water on this planet it wrote our unfairly limited Economic Plan so we'd always be dependent on them." He grimaced and hissed, with pain, trying to move his leg. "It contradicted our Constitution," he added bitterly.

"You signed the Plan though," the old man said.

"So did you—and I was younger than you and innocent then," the middle-aged parachutist retorted. "You hypocrite! You signed the Economic Plan—but in your own way you're trying to be free of it, too. You've been telling villagers to forget their material needs, to stop sending fish extracts to Earth. You claim we'll be free of Earth your way if we'll scatter from this lake to isolated ponds. To philosophic idiocy. But most of us want the freedom to build a great city. We'll have our own independent industries. That's the way to be free of Earth."

The Centralist looked hopefully at the young man, who was smiling at the submachine gun.

The bodyguard wished the Decentralists and Centralists could agree beyond the need for independence from Earth. He wished each group would simply follow its own desires. What he wanted was the gun.

"Keep back," rasped the parachutist, aiming between them.

"Give up," the old man demanded. "Give up the gun."

"Hypocrite!" the Centralist cried. "It was you who used force against us. First you old hypocrites tore out the last page of our Constitution, so you could feel free to attack us. You tore out the right to assemble, to choose a way of life, to build a city. All that was in our Constitution until you old men became so terrified you tore it out. You stole freedom from our young people." He looked at the young man. "Our Constitution was written on Earth by experts and was above the Economic Plan. Ask him what happened to its last page."

The young bodyguard had been vaguely aware that there was a weathered copy of the Constitution on display in his village, but he had never gotten around to reading it. He shrugged.

"The majority of our elders in all the villages voted to remove the last page," Mr. Decent wheezed, "because it was necessary to defend our villages from you—"

"Hypocrite! That wasn't the reason," the Centralist gasped.

"It was," Mr. Decent retorted. "We can't permit violations of Decentralism which would seduce our young people. We can't permit corruptions such as Big Village if our way of life is to survive. You criminal, you murderer" —the old man pointed a finger red with the blood of his customs inspector—"you murdered Henrydavid, didn't you?"

The old man began to shiver violently with scrawny rage. The bodyguard expected him to leap at the Centralist. Now he hoped the parachutist would shoot Mr. Decent—that instant would be his opportunity to grab the gun, all its power!

The young bodyguard's face hardened. The parachutist raised the gun.

"Give it to me." The old man stepped toward the ex-mayor and reached out his hand for the submachine gun as if he were simply dealing with another young Decentralist villager. "I say, give it to me!"

As the gunman's own tendons tightened, the bodyguard saw he was going to shoot. He was going to kill Mr. Decentralist. The act was no longer in his imagination—it was going to be real. The bodyguard lunged faster than thought in a conditioned reflex called duty and his hand grabbed the submachine gun's barrel, yanking it aside as it roared. It was hammering and burning, slapping his chest so hard he fell backward and the rocks seemed soft.

He hadn't expected this. He had wanted the old man—the old order—to die. But he had saved Mr. Decent's life.

He clung to the gun, to its warmly quiet smoothness. As he sat up he was amazed at how much his chest hurt when he coughed. Blood was splattering all over the gleaming mechanism. Frantically he tried to wipe it off. He wanted to say something.

"You've shot him," Mr. Decent's distant voice was yelling at someone. "He's dying."

The bodyguard couldn't remember having shot anyone. He clung to the gun, knowing he hadn't fired it yet, but to do so was what he wanted more than anything in the world. His hand searched along its slipperiness for the trigger. He wanted to feel its power blasting—to release all his strength. He had the ultimate weapon.

In the dizzily fluctuating light and darkness he became aware that the Centralist was crawling toward him, dragging a broken leg, reaching out to retrieve the gun.

"Shoot, shoot," the old man's voice was shouting.

The bodyguard needed to pull the trigger, but as his numbed fingers groped for it he saw Mr. Decentralist's angular shadow hurl itself upon the Centralist. They were struggling on the rocks. Decentralist and Centralist indistinguishable in this crazy darkness in his head. As if he were going blind, the bodyguard peered out, trying to see which of his enemies was on top.

If he shot the Centralist, he knew Mr. Decent would thank him then and later tell him to drop this wonderful submachine gun into the lake where the swords had been lost.

The bodyguard's mind rebelled dimly while they thrashed about in the crater. If he shot Mr. Decent instead—he wondered if the grateful parachutist would let him keep the gun. Not for long. In his veins he felt the dark canoe approaching. Even if he joined them, he knew the Centralists would seize the gun because it was the ultimate power.

"Shoot, shoot—" a strange, hoarse voice was shouting.

In his darkness he felt his power swelling with realization that he could shoot both of them while they struggled, entwined. His finger began to curl around the trigger while his imagination hurried to strip off the parachutist's safety suit. Its smoothly metallized cloth became a perfect fit for him, shiny and unsullied by the bullet holes in his body. He pushed the Centralist's bloody, bullet-riddled body under a ledge and it vanished as if from a dream.

In that overlapping instant all the men from the dark canoe stood around the volcano's rim like teeth and he was gurgling: "Come down. We will build a great city." They became towers around his harbor. He led them to the mainland, covering the whole instaplanet with his city of power. "That's not all I want—"

His finger was squeezing the slippery metal hull of the shuttle and it roared deafeningly, capturing the freighters in orbit. When his glittering armada landed on Earth, he gripped the hot steel microphone and gurgled sensuously. His great fleet was rising from all over his Earth. With his finger rigidly contracted on the vibrant trigger, he sprayed his power outward through the darkness of the Universe.

The old man kneeled in perplexed horror beside his bodyguard. The canoemen clambered down from the rim. Their thick faces glanced from the corpse of the parachutist, whose forehead had been crushed, as if by a brutal caveman, by Mr.

Decentralist's jagged rocks—to the young bodyguard, who lay on his back, clutching the submachine gun.

His chest had been riddled by bullets during that Pavlovian instant when he had yanked the gun away from the parachutist by its barrel and saved the old man. He had fallen backward with it, coughing and writhing, splattering the rocks with his blood, while his numbing hands searched its slippery steel. His forefinger still gripped the trigger of the emptied submachine gun. His eyes—

The most massive of fishermen wrenched the gun away, grunting excitedly. "We seen a parachute come down," he told Mr. Decent. "We come. We broke your rule again, but we landed on this island. Good thing. This is a—gun!"

The old man looked up along the fisherman's bulky torso to his greedily grinning face. Plainly this was not a thoughtful man who would be satisfied with the solitude and austerity of his own Walden Pond.

"Where are the rest of the bullets?" the big fisherman croaked while the other thick-bodied men crowded around.

The old man looked down past his own thin fingers, stained with blood, to the splay feet and heavy legs of these fishermen, who still must consider themselves Decentralists. But he felt a hot wind whirling in the crater, as if from the future, heard their hoarse voices arguing as they struggled for the gun.

"Where are the bullets?"

In the hot crater Mr. Decentralist felt his lifelong beliefs shriveling. He became terrified that this barren instaplanet had defeated his ideals and dreams. A hoarse-voiced generation of greedy Centralists seemed as close as his death.

The unexplainable bullet wound in his side bled. After this—whom could he trust?

Bending over his young bodyguard's inscrutably dead face, the old man wept.

He felt his power draining away.

COMING OF AGE IN HENSON'S TUBE

BY WILLIAM JON WATKINS

Lobber ran in shouting like it was already too late. "Keri's gone Skyfalling! Keri's gone Skyfalling!" He was the kind of kid you naturally ignore, so he had to shout *every*thing. I ignored him. Moody didn't. It made no difference. Lobber went right on shouting. "I saw him going up the Endcap with his wings!"

Moody shouted right back. "Why didn't you stop him?!"

"Who?! Me?!! Nobody can stop Keri when he wants to do something. He's crazy!" Lobber was right, of course. Keri *was* crazy; always putting himself in danger for the fun of it, always coming out in one piece. You couldn't stop him. Even Moody couldn't, and Moody was his older brother.

Moody grabbed a pair of Close-ups and started for the door. "He better *not* be Skyfalling! He's too young!"

That almost made me laugh really, because we were *all* too young. But Moody had done it two years ago without getting caught, and I had done it last year. Lobber would never do it. I guess that was why he shouted so much. If you even mentioned it to him, he'd say, "Are you crazy?! You could get killed doing that!"

And he was right about that too. Every couple years, somebody would wait too long to open their wings, or open them too often, and that would be it. Even the lower gravity of Henson's Tube doesn't let you make a mistake like that more than once. My father says he saw his best friend get killed opening up too late, and I remember how Keri started crying when Moody came plummeting down out of the air and we thought he'd never open his wings and glide.

Still, when you get to be a certain age in Henson's Tube, you go up the Endcap to the station and hitch a ride on the catchrails of the Shuttle. And when it gets to the middle of the cable, you jump off. It's not all that dangerous really if you open your wings at the right times. The way gravity works in Henson's Tube, or any of the other orbiting space colonies for that matter, makes it a lot less dangerous than doing the same thing on Earth.

The difference in gravity comes from the way Henson's Tube is shaped. It's like a test tube, sealed at both ends. The people all live on the inside walls of the tube, and the tube is spun, like an axle in place, to give it gravity. If you look with a pair of Close-ups, you can see land overhead above the clouds, but the other side of the Tube is five kilometers away, and that's a long way when it's straight up.

If you were born in the Tube like we all were, it doesn't seem unnatural to you to be spun around continually in two-minute circles, and even tourists find it just like Earth, all rocks and trees and stuff, until they look up. Of course, the one half gravity at "ground level" makes them a little nervous, but the real difference in gravity is at the center of the Tube. There's a sort of invisible axle running down the center of the tube lengthwise, where there's no gravity. That's where the Shuttle runs on its cable from one Endcap to the other. And that's where you start your Fall.

You step off the Shuttle halfway along its ride, and you drift very slowly toward one side of the Tube. But pretty soon the ground rotates away, under you, and the wind begins to push you around the center cable too. Only you don't just go around it in a circle, because going around starts giving you some gravity, so you come spiraling down toward the ground, rotating always a bit slower than the Tube itself.

The closer you get to the sides, the faster the Tube—the ground—spins on past you. The gravity depends on how much you've caught up with the rotating of the Tube. If you didn't have wings, you'd hit hard enough to get killed for sure, partly from falling and partly because the ground would be going past so fast when you hit. If you do have wings, then they slow down your falling okay, but then they catch the wind more, so you're rotating almost as fast as the Tube is. Only then, because you're going around faster, the gravity is stronger and you have to really use the wings to keep from landing too hard. Only by then you're probably halfway around the Tube from where you wanted to land, and it's a long walk home.

Usually, you just step off the Shuttle and drop with your

wings folded until you get scared enough to open your arms. When you do, your wings begin to slow your fall. If you don't wait too long, that is. If you *do* wait too long, when you throw your arms open, they get snapped up and back like an umbrella blowing inside out, and there's nothing left to stop you. Most of the people who get hurt Skyfalling get scared and open their wings too soon or too often. Most of the ones who get killed open their wings too late. Nobody had ever seen Keri get scared.

That was probably what Moody was thinking about as he ran for the door. I know it was what I was thinking about as I grabbed a pair of Close-ups that must have been Keri's and ran after him. Lobber ran after both of us, shouting. By the time we got outside, the silver, bullet-shaped car of the Shuttle was about a third of the way along its cable, and there was nothing to do but wait until it got almost directly above us.

At first, we couldn't see Keri and we thought he must have missed the Shuttle, but then we saw him, sitting on the long catchrail on the underside of the Shuttle with his feet over the side. Lobber kept trying to grab my Close-ups, shouting, "Let me look! Let me look!" I ignored him and said, "Shut up, Lobber, just shut up!" Lobber looked like he was going to start shouting about being told to shut up, but the Shuttle was almost directly overhead by then, so he did shut up and watched.

When the Shuttle got where he wanted it, Keri stood up, stopped for a second to pick out his landmarks and then just stepped off. He fell slowly at first, almost directly above us. But soon he began to slide back and away from us in wider and wider spirals as the Tube revolved. For a second, he looked like he was just standing there watching the Shuttle go on down the Tube and us slide away beneath him.

But in a couple of seconds he went from being as big as my thumb to being as big as the palm of my hand. We could tell he was riding down the pull of gravity at a good speed and getting faster all the time. He had his head into the wind and his body out behind him to cut down his resistance, so the wind wasn't rotating him with it too much, and his speed was going up and up and we knew he'd have to do something to cut it down.

When he was half a mile above us, he still hadn't opened his wings. Moody lowered his Close-ups and shook his head like he was sure Keri would never make it. When he looked up again, Keri was a lot closer to the ground, and his blue wings were still folded across his chest. It's hard to tell from the ground how far you can fall before you pass the point where it's too late to

open your wings, but it looked to us like Keri had already
passed it. And he still hadn't spread his wings.

"Open up!" Moody shouted. "Open up!" And for a little
while Keri did just that, until he began to slide back around the
curve of the Tube. But long before he should have, he pulled
his arms back in and started that long dive again. All Lobber
could see was a small fluttering fall of blue against the checker-
board of the far side of the Tube. "He's out of control!"
Lobber shouted.

He was wrong, of course. For some crazy reason of his own,
Keri had done it on purpose, but when I went to tell Lobber to
shut up, I found that my mouth was too dry to talk. It didn't
matter, because Lobber went suddenly quiet. Moody stood
looking up through his Close-ups and muttering, "Open up,
Keri! Open up!"

It seemed like an hour before Keri finally did. You could
almost hear the flap of the blue fabric as he threw his arms
open. His arms snapped back, and for a minute, I thought he
was going to lose it, but he fought them forward and held them
out steady.

But it still looked like he had waited too long. He was sliding
back a little, but he was still falling, and falling fast. I could see
him straining against the force of his fall, trying to overcome it,
but I didn't think he was going to make it.

I didn't want to follow him in that long fall all the way into
the ground. I thought about how my father said his friend had
looked after he hit, and I knew I didn't want to see Keri like
that. But just before I looked away, Keri did the craziest thing I
ever saw. Falling head down with his arms out, he suddenly
jackknifed himself forward, held it for a second, then snapped
his head up and spread-eagled himself. His wings popped like a
billowbag opening up.

Moody gave a little gasp and I felt my own breath suck in.
But it turned out that Keri knew more about Skyfalling than
either of us ever would and when he threw his arms back, he
had almost matched ground speed and the maneuver had put
him into a stall so close to the ground that I still don't believe it
was possible.

Of course, Keri being Keri, he held his wings out just a
fraction too long, and he went up, and over before he could
snap his arms down completely and came down backward. You
could almost hear the crunch when he hit. I swear he bounced
and flipped over backwards and then bounced and rolled over
four more times before he stopped. For a second we just stood

there, too stunned to move, and then we were suddenly all running toward him, with Moody in the lead.

When we got to Keri, he was sitting up, unsnapping his wings and rubbing his shoulders. His arms were a mess, all scraped and scratched, but not broken. Even though he had a helmet on, one eye was swollen shut. But he was smiling.

Moody got to him first and helped him up. "You're crazy, Keri! You know that?! You could have got yourself killed! You know that?! You know that?!" I don't think I ever remembered Moody being that mad. He sounded like his father. "Look at you! You're lucky you didn't get killed!"

But Keri just kept grinning and the louder Moody got, the wider Keri grinned until Moody just turned away in disgust. Nobody said anything for a while, not even Lobber. Finally Keri said, "C'mon, Moody, I didn't act like that when *you* came down."

Moody turned around and looked at his brother like he knew Keri was right, but he wasn't ready yet to forgive him for scaring us like that. "Yeah, but I didn't wait until I almost hit the ground before I opened up! I didn't scare anybody half to death thinking I was going to get myself killed!"

Keri looked at him and chuckled. "Didn't you?"

"That wasn't the same!" Moody said. But you could tell he knew it was. Finally, he grabbed Keri's wings. "Here, give me those before you tear them."

Keri laughed and handed him the wings. He gave me a wink with his good eye. "Not easy being on the ground. Is it?" I shook my head. Moody just snorted and folded the wings. I kept waiting for Lobber to start shouting again, but he didn't. He just looked up at where the Shuttle had passed, and when he spoke, his voice was wistful and quiet like he knew Skyfalling was something he would never be able to do, no matter how much he might want to. "What does it feel like, Keri?" he said.

Keri shrugged, and I knew it was because there is something in the Fall, something about the way it gets faster and faster, and the ground rushes up at you like certain death, that he couldn't explain. I could see the freedom of it still sparkling in his eyes. "It feels like being alive."

DEBORAH'S CHILDREN

BY GRANT D. CALLIN

The second ring on the phone got them both half awake.

"Your turn, Dal."

"Prove it."

"Last Thursday. We were in the bathtub." She turned over and buried her head under a pillow.

"How come you're always right?" He reached over and picked up the receiver. "This is Draper . . . say that again . . . Jesus. Is this a joke? Stan, is that you? So help me I'm gonna . . . What? . . . Yes, she's here. I'll tell her. Where do we . . . okay. We'll be there soon."

He hung up and turned back around; her head was still buried. He raised the pillow and kissed a silken cheek. "Debs. It's a Red 47. For both of us."

"Tell 'em I'll come in the morning."

"Hey, sweetheart, shuttle pilots aren't supposed to pout."

"I pout, you whine. Nobody else knows. Us against the world." She sat up and rubbed his rump affectionately. "We haven't had a practice alert in two years. And why in the middle of the night?"

"It's not a practice, Debbie. Bring clothes for a week. We're going to the Cape."

"What in the world for?"

"Beats me. The duty officer acted like he was doing me a favor telling me we were going to Kennedy."

At the Johnson airstrip they were met by a guard who checked their faces carefully against their IDs, then crossed their names off a short list and gestured to an old T-39 two hundred yards downstrip; it was lit up and the ground generator was purring.

"Tail number 802. You're the last ones; they're waitin' for you to take off."

The woman looked at him irritably. "Isn't there something we can use to wheel our luggage with? This stuff weighs a ton."

The guard said: "Sorry, Ms. Champion. They sprung this on us all of a sudden. Duty officer says: 'Minimum personnel and material involvement—and don't even tell your wife about it!' " He grinned apologetically. "Hell, I don't even know where you're goin'."

As they labored toward the aircraft, Dallas broke the silence with three words: "Curiouser and curiouser."

"Yeah, maybe it'll be something to tell our grandchildren about."

"Grandchildren? We've got to have children first. And before that, we ought to get married. Better hurry; you're not getting any younger."

"Dallas, you are an old-fashioned gentleman and I love you very much. Seven more flights and I'm eligible for pension."

"Is that a proposition?"

They had arrived at the plane. She put her luggage down and looked at him. "I think so." Before he could reply she turned and began to climb the boarding ramp. Over her shoulder she said: "You get to stow the bags. I'm going to flirt with our fellow passengers before I get too old."

Dallas whistled to himself as he helped the ground crew with the luggage.

Aboard the aircraft were three other Orbiter pilots and two of Draper's fellow encrypted voice communicators. One of the latter spoke first: "Hello, Chief. Guess the party can start now."

"Hello, Mike; hi, Stan. Anybody know what this is all about?"

One of the pilots said: "Hell, no. We were hoping one of you EVCOMs could tell us; you're the ones with the hairy clearances."

For the first part of the flight there was wild speculation among the seven passengers; then the late hour and the filtered white noise of the jets overcame them one by one. They slept as southern cities sparkled underneath the wings.

"Ladies and gentlemen, the information I'm about to impart carries the highest possible security classification . . ."

During the stir that followed, Dallas leaned over and spoke in Deborah's ear: "Listen, Deb; this whole charade has the smell of a volunteer mission. Do me a favor and remember your contract. You can refuse any mission without prejudice if it entails a higher than normal—"

She shushed him as the speaker resumed.

"—ree weeks ago, in response to a cryptic call, the Deuxième searched an abandoned house in a Paris suburb. In it they found a horrible thing: a very large nuclear device containing a very stubborn computer. It was planted by an unknown—at least it was unknown at the time—French-Italian terrorist organization.

"They left a complicated set of instructions and demands. Among them was a requirement for the delivery of the equivalent of $800 billion gold bullion . . ."

The CIA agent waited patiently for the audience to quiet down, then continued: "The terrorists seemed to have every expectation that the major industrial nations would pool their resources to meet this demand. You see, part of the package they left contained detailed plans and specifications of the device. These, together with X-rays and radiation measurements, lead us to believe that it is the largest nuclear weapon ever assembled—somewhere between 400 and 700 metatons. . . ."

There were gasps and exclamations from the crowd. The agent continued in a louder voice to make himself heard: "The effects of detonating such a device in the center of Europe are so terrible they defy description. The loss of land, industrial base, and technical skills would run into the trillions in Europe alone. The loss of life—well, a lot would depend on atmospheric conditions during the first years after the formation of the mushroom; but I assure you that no nation in the northern hemisphere would be unaffected. We calculated somewhere between 300 and 800 million lives—"

The noise in the room rose to a roar, forcing him to stop again. Draper looked over and met Deborah's eyes; he was surprised to find them dripping tears. She spoke in a broken voice: "Oh, Dallas, we didn't make it!"

He reached over and gently rubbed the tears into her cheeks. "What do you mean, sweetheart?"

"When I was in college in the early '80s and found out what a mess the world was really in, I made kind of a bet with myself: if we could hang on until the year 2000, if we could just keep the technology and space exploration and science chugging along till then without any major wars or disasters to set them back, we'd make it."

She sniffed, looking very young in the dim auditorium lighting. "And we were doing it, Dal. All the good stuff is getting started—smart computers, and fusion, and genetic engineering, and plans for high colonies. But now they're going to blow it all. And we still have three years to go!" She sniffed again and half-smiled. "Oh, shit, Dal, I know there's nothing magic about the year 2000. But somehow . . ."

He leaned over and kissed her ear, handed her a handkerchief. "Here. Let's listen; he's starting again. Maybe it isn't as bad as all that."

"—also left a schematic of the computer logic and communications setup. They gave us ten days to arrange a global communications network involving four geosynch satellites and dedicated frequencies—duplex channels from all four to the device, and also channels for voice communications.

"We were ready in seven days, and broadcast a prearranged signal two days later. Immediately information began flowing to and from the device; the communications are dual-key encrypted, of course. There's no way to crack the code in the forseeable future."

He paused again while the listeners quieted down. It didn't take long; most of them seemed to be in shock.

"We're reasonably certain the information coming from the computer inside the device consists only of temperature and pressure readings from monitoring transducers. We presume, of course, that any attempt to break into the device or to disrupt communications will result in its detonation."

A voice from the back of the room interrupted: "Why are you telling us all this? I'm getting a sinking feeling in the pit of my stomach."

The speaker allowed himself a slight smile. "Sir, that sinking feeling is something we have been living with for some time. I'll answer your question by saying that every major nation is cooperating in this affair. There are thousands of agents involved, even though most of them don't know the exact nature of the danger. And we have unlimited funds, of course. The United States, for its part, has contributed dollars, electronics and computer experts—and," he looked out over the audience, "we have tentatively agreed to use NASA facilities to attempt to place the device in Earth orbit."

"What the hell—!"

"How can you—"

"You can't just—!"

The agent let chaos reign for a moment, then raised both hands to quiet the group. "Please, ladies and gentlemen! I said

tentatively! We will not do this without your voluntary cooperation. We—"

"Just a second!" This was a stentorian voice from one of the
VPF crewchiefs. "How do you know you can even move the
bomb without setting it off?"

The CIA man smiled tightly. "Research with unlimited funds.
We know now that this terrorist group is a front for the dictator
of a North African country. He has invested his entire private
fortune in this venture—and he must protect that investment.
Accelerometer triggers are too risky; there are only pressure
and temperature sensors. No, they employed a very conservative technique to be sure the device wasn't moved: they simply
established watchers in nearby buildings. We found them, of
course; five of them. It was easy to buy them off—we just
showed them the truth. There might be more at long range, but
we circumvented that problem by moving the device on a very
dark night and keeping away from street lights. Our—"

"My God!" This was from a woman who worked in Mission
Control. "You mean to tell us that you took even the slightest
chance with something that monstrous?"

The speaker pursed his lips. "Madam, we were very scared,
believe me. But by then, we'd found out something even scar-
ier: you see, we quickly penetrated their headquarters elec-
tronically—please don't ask how—and now have a deep surveillance team listening in. We know with certainty that they intend to detonate the device anyway, after they get the bullion . . ."

A roar was growing in the audience, and the agent had to
shout to finish: "You see, with Europe in chaos, and other
nations mobilizing to protect themselves from fallout, they believe they can use the bullion to gain economic control of the
world!"

Pandemonium reigned.

After a while, one of the audience stood: it was the NASA
Chief Astronaut. As the members of the group recognized him,
quiet spread once again. His words dropped into silence:

"Could you please tell us where the device is now?"

The agent looked at him. "Certainly. It's in the Shuttle
Payload Integration Facility. The SPIF, I believe you call it."

The SPIF was on the Canaveral side of the Banana River—
about three miles from where they were sitting. Dallas Draper's
immediate reaction was identical to that of many others in the
room: he started up from his seat without thinking. The impulse
he followed was universal—to get a thousand miles away from

there as fast as he could. Then he checked himself and looked at Debbie, who had remained in her seat. He sat back down and said ruefully: "You didn't even blink. I guess that's what they mean by 'the right stuff.' "

She pointed to the Chief Astronaut, who was surveying the room with his eyes. "That's what Steve is checking out. I think he knew the answer already, and just wanted to see the reactions of his pilots. You can bet he's already eliminated a few of the nervous nellies."

Draper's face clouded up. "Deborah—"

"Shhh, Dal; he's started again."

"—been here for three days, in fact. Volunteer groundcrews are modifying it to fly in the shuttle. When it's ready to—"

An impatient question was shouted from the floor: "Why orbit the thing? Why not put it in Siberia, or Antarctica, or a mineshaft?"

The agent answered patiently: "It turns out, to the best of our ability to calculate, that there is literally no safe place on Earth to put it. We might be able to prepare such a place, but that would take longer than we have. We're delivering the bullion as slowly as possible; but when enough of it is in their hands, we think they won't hesitate to detonate the device at the least suspicion of further delay."

The speaker looked at his watch as the murmur from the crowd died down. "Now, ladies and gentlemen, I must return to Washington, so I'll turn this meeting over to your Mission Director. Thank you for your attention."

The agent stepped offstage to be replaced by the familiar portly figure of Frederick Fishbein. He smiled apologetically.

"Please excuse our abrupt handling of your affairs this morning—but I think you can appreciate the necessity. Now once you leave this room it is imperative that you speak with no one about this, unless you know that person is aware, and you are in a most secure area.

"Those going back to Houston, we'll get you back right away. You'll be pretending this was a Red 47. Those staying— primarily some of the Orbiter pilots—will have cover stories prepared on an individual basis. All unusual activity here will be covered by a routine DOD-sensitive Mission Change Notice."

Fishbein looked over his notes before continuing. "You will all be briefed in detail; for now I'll give an overview so you'll know generally what the others will be doing.

"The device is being externally modified to mate with an IUS Airborne Support Equipment cradle; that means we'll be flying essentially an IUS mission. All components of the IUS will be replaced with breakout boxes, except those needed for the functioning of the ASE and Super Zip.

"Furthermore," he looked at the Chief of Range Safety, "all launch decision criteria will be liberalized to the maximum. We'll use redundancy management to the fullest extent possible.

"The role of the EVCOM will be especially important." Now it was Dallas's turn for a hard look. "As far as the world will know, the four crew members originally scheduled for the upcoming mission will be aboard. In fact, they're making tapes right now for playback during ascent and the first two orbits. Actually, only one pilot will be aboard, and all communications will be through Houston EVCOM."

Dallas felt Deborah stir, and looked over, her face was unreadable. Uneasily, he gave his attention back to Fishbein.

"—so it'll be your show, Dal. John Falkes will be talking off a script to the playback tapes out front, but the real situation will be tracked from your shop."

Draper nodded, unable to speak. There was a knot growing in his stomach.

The Mission Director continued: "Okay, a final word. The CIA agent said this job would be contingent on our voluntary cooperation. In truth, it's our only choice; madmen have forced this on us, whether we like it or not. So now we're simply two groups of people: those of us who know, and those who don't. The latter are the lucky ones, of course."

He smiled thinly. "Good luck, and now I'm going to turn you over to Steve Shannon. I'll see you at your debriefing." He exited the stage as the veteran astronaut strode from the audience to take his place at the podium.

Shannon was in his early fifties, barely grizzled. He'd flown thirty-seven missions before retiring and accepting the post of Chief Astronaut. His professionalism and honesty were held in wide respect. As he began to speak, all side conversations stopped.

"All right, we've had the bad news and the pep talk: we're going to do this because we have to, like it or not.

"In a minute I'm going to call for volunteers, and here's what I'll be looking for: unmarried pilots with IUS experience, and with plenty of simulator time on fly-alone missions. That means you newer pilots will be low on the totem pole for consideration."

As Shannon spoke, Dallas's chest tightened. He knew Debbie qualified in all three categories mentioned by her chief. Almost in a panic, he leaned over and whispered to her: "Listen, Debs, you've got to—"

"Hush, Dal; Steve's still talking." She put a hand on his arm. "I want to hear what he's saying."

"—kay, so here's the drill: I'm going to ask everyone but volunteers to leave the room. There will be no stigma—repeat *no stigma*—attached to nonvolunteers. Furthermore I will not consider anyone who isn't well qualified to fly this mission—so please don't stay just to impress me or your fellows; you'll only be wasting my time and yours.

"All right, everyone but volunteers please leave. Go to room 348 for your debriefing by Fred Fishbein and the security team. Thanks for your attention."

Dallas took Deborah by the hand and stood up to go. "C'mon, Glibs."

She stood and looked at him. "I'm going to stick around for a while. You go ahead."

He held her hand tightly. "Deborah, you know damn well you're a prime candidate, and you know further damn well I don't want you to go. What I want is for you to come with me on a sudden vacation to New Zealand."

She looked to the front of the auditorium; Dallas followed her gaze to see the Chief Astronaut looking at them. Shannon raised his eyebrows. Deborah nodded with a movement so slight as to be almost imperceptible.

The interchange wasn't lost on Dallas. "Dammit, Deb, for the last time . . ."

"Please, Dal. Steve's waiting. Don't try to change what I am."

He released her hand. She kissed him on the chin and said: "I'll see you later, sweetheart." Then she was off down the aisle. By the time Draper got to the door, she was already in earnest conversation with Shannon; the six other volunteers stood back, listening.

"Dal, you've got to pay attention: there won't be any written instructions."

"Sorry, Freddie; my mind was wandering."

"Listen Chum: You know and I know that Debbie's probably going to fly that mission. And if I didn't need you so badly in Houston I'd just lock you in a padded cell for the next eight days. But dammit, man, can't you see that you'll give her the best chance by doing your own job right? We've got to have airtight links into the back room at Johnson."

Draper took a breath, let it out. "I know, Freddie." He rubbed his eyes with tired hands. "Okay, go over it again, then I'll get the hell out of here."

The last time he saw her was outside the Headquarters building. False dawn was a ghost of brightness over the Atlantic to the east; a staff car waited impatiently to take him to the airstrip.

"Thanks for sticking, Dallas. It would have hurt bad if I didn't get to see you again."

"Come with me, Glibs. There's lots of pilots, but only one of you."

"I can't, Dal. I'm Steve's first choice. Jake's the backup, and he's got less than half my simulator solo time."

"Then I'll stay, too."

"Come on, Dal; you know they need you—*I* need you—to give us an airtight EVCOM. You're acting like a kid."

"I whine, you pout. Us against the world. Deb, listen. I love you, and I want you to come back. Get that sucker in orbit and retroburn your butt back here."

She smiled. "I'll see what I can do." Rising on tiptoes, she leaned into him with a short, hard kiss. "My love. Go catch your plane, and I'll see you in nine days."

The next week was one of the busiest in Draper's life. He set up and coordinated secure links with Paris, New York, Moscow, and Washington. There was a permanent sick feeling in his stomach. He wasn't allowed to phone Deborah.

As the communications links were established one by one, the EVCOM Center became a beehive of agents. He overheard quiet conversations that made him increasingly uneasy. The gold shipments were being deliberately slowed by the European powers; negotiations and excuses became increasingly elaborate as the terrorists grew more impatient and suspicious. Dallas slept little, ate less.

The night before launch Stan Michaels approached him and spoke earnestly: "Dal, I've had a talk with Fred Fishbein. He says to tell you that you've done a hell of a job, and he wants you to take the day off tomorrow and sleep. I'll handle the EVCOM for the flight."

"Stan, in the first place if Debbie climbs into that Orbiter tomorrow and doesn't hear my voice, she's going to think something's wrong no matter what you tell her; in the second place, if Fishbein wants me off that mike while Debbie's flying, he'll have to shoot me. So go tell Freddie to blow it out his ear."

MAIN ENGINES AT NINETY PERCENT . . . THREE . . . TWO . . . ONE . . . SRB IGNITION . . . LIFTOFF . . . TOWER CLEARED . . . PITCHOVER . . .

"Turn that damned thing off!" The annoyed command came from Fred Fishbein as the voice from Mission Control blared over the wall speaker in the EVCOM Center. The voice was for the benefit of the listening public out front. The real action was centered around Dallas Draper's EVCOM post; here were huddled Fishbein, Steve Shannon, and the Chief of CIA Operations. Flight data were read and interpreted by computer; in case of problems, seven top engineers were at standby consoles. Debbie herself would be only medium busy; but if the flight monitoring software hiccupped, she'd have to do the jobs of two crewmembers.

Tension was high. During the next minutes the bomb would be put to a severe test. Vibration and noise levels well over 120 db existed in the cargo bay during atmospheric flight; such levels could shake circuit boards loose, and even back screws out of their sockets. The bomb had been sealed in an airtight cowling, and cushioned heavily; but there had been no time for tests, no guarantees. Even the construction of the device, and fitting it to the IUS ASE cradle, had been a miracle of sweat and ingenuity. Dallas tried to keep the tension from his voice as he activated the communicator.

"Champion, Houston. Encrypted voice check. How's the ride, over?"

"Houston, Champion. Copy you five by. The ride's rough and noisy as usual, Dallas. How's our friend in the bay, over?"

Draper glanced up to a large wall display where the digital readouts of communications to and from the bomb were shown in real time on a split screen. Since its installation the screen had never been idle; there had been messages continuously from one side or the other. At the moment traffic was from the bomb; the ones and zeroes flashed across its half of the screen in unbroken rhythm.

"Ticking away like clockwork, Champion. And we're showing max Q in twenty seconds. Strap down your false teeth, Granny."

This was one of the worst times of all. But as the Orbiter punched through the aerodynamic barrier the digital readout from the bomb continued without a falter. Finally Dallas was able to report with great relief:

"Champion, Houston. Through max Q. Main engine throttle-up. You're now at seven nautical miles altitude and four downrange. And according to the experts here, you're probably high enough so that very little ocean water would be sucked into the radioactive fireball. You have just saved an indeterminate but large number of millions of lives Congratulations."

"Houston, Champion. Goodie for us. Now showing fifty-five seconds to booster sep—"

"Stand by, Champion. We're getting traffic from the terrorists." A receiver at the other end of the room had come alive and was blaring in an unfamiliar language; the harsh tones made Draper's skin crawl. When the voice stopped, the agents began speaking among themselves in low, urgent tones. The CIA Chief had left Draper's post and was talking on the Washington link; Dallas thought he recognized the voice of the Secretary of State coming over the speaker. After a moment he broke away and hurried back to speak to Fishbein: "Fred, the Secretary wants to know how much longer until the shuttle ejects the device and moves to a safe distance."

The Mission Director frowned. "Well, our schedule calls for the escape OMS burn about two hours from now. But we—"

"Thanks, Fred. Just a second." The agent hurried back to the Washington link and spoke briefly to the Secretary. Soon the latter's voice issued from another speaker, simultaneously translated into the terrorists' language.

Just then Deborah's voice came over the EVCOM speaker.

"Houston, Champion. I have booster separation. Hey, what's going on down there, over?" Her voice was cheerful, with tense overtones which Dallas doubted anyone else recognized. He activated his mike.

"Champion, Houston. Two minutes, thirty seconds. Altitude thirty nautical miles, forty-three downrange. Six minutes to MECO. No news yet on the message. The Secretary of State is just finishing his reply. No doubt they'll tell us working peasants when they get good and ready." He looked up and saw the agent approaching again. "Stand by one, Glibs. I think we're about to get the news. Back in a moment, clear."

The agent looked worried, and Draper's stomach knotted even before he began to speak. "Fred, the Secretary would like to know when is the soonest the device will be in a safe orbit."

"What do you mean, 'safe orbit'?" Steve Shannon snapped.

The agent looked at him. "So there's no chance that it will

ever detonate in the atmosphere—no matter what happens to the shuttle."

Steel showed in Shannon's eyes as he answered: "That would be at the end of the second OMS burn, about thirty-five minutes from now."

"Thank you." The agent left.

Fishbein hurried after him. "Just a minute . . ." His voice faded as both men approached the CIA group.

"Champion, Houston. L plus give minutes . . . mark. Three minutes, thirty seconds to MECO."

"Houston, Champion. That was a pretty long moment, Draper. What's the news, over?" The worry in her voice was now evident.

"Fishbein's over at the Washington link talking to the Secretary of State, Deb. I'm just as much in the dark as you. Keep the pedal to the metal, over."

"Roger that, Houston."

"Champion, Houston. MECO at my mark . . . three . . . two . . . one . . . mark. MECO at eight minutes, thirty-seven seconds; fifty-five nautical miles altitude, 770 downrange. E-T separation in five seconds . . . three . . . two . . . one . . . mark."

"Houston, Champion. Confirm E-T sep. Where's Freddie now, Dallas?"

Draper glanced over his shoulder. Fishbein was in earnest conversation with the mission sequencer, the IUS expert and the Chief Astronaut.

"He's gabbing with Bert Congdon, Shelly, and Steve. If he doesn't get over here by the end of the OMS burn, I'm personally going to drag him back to the mike. Hang tight, Glibs."

"Champion hanging and clear."

"Champion, Houston. Confirm OMS-1 termination. We have an orbit of 35 × 132 nautical miles. You're go for OMS-2 in twenty-six minutes . . . Mark."

"Copy go for OMS-2, Houston. What's happening in the rest of the world, over?"

"No word yet, Debbie, but I think we're about to find out. I've got a whole gaggle of people moving this way. Stand by."

"Champion, Houston. Deborah, this is Steve Shannon. Here's the situation: the CIA now thinks there *were* some accelerometers aboard the bomb—simple one-shots that trip only when acceleration exceeds a certain value. Anyway, during ascent we got a message from the terrorists; they wanted the gold shipments stepped up right away, and also wanted to know why we were moving the bomb. The Secretary gave them a cock-and-bull story abut trying to put it in a shockproof mounting in Paris, and it slipping off the hoist. The terrorists said if it happens again, they'll detonate it. In the meantime the shipments are being stepped up a little."

"Copy, Houston. What's the prognosis, over?"

Fishbein took the mike. "Champion, this is Fishbein. I'm afraid it's not good. We've already delivered about 400 billion, and the deep surveillance team says the terrorists are talking seriously about setting the thing off. They also think we're lying, but aren't sure. Deborah, as of now the device is too high to do more than token damage. I want you to know that whatever happens, we'll be in your debt for—"

Draper reached over to grab the mike, but Shannon beat him to it. "Can that crap, Freddie. Debbie, listen to me. Starting now, we're throwing the book away. I've got Bert and Shelley here, and we've worked out an accelerated mission sequence. We'll open the bay doors before OMS-2; then as soon as the burn terminates, we'll raise and separate the bomb. We'll initiate an emergency OMS burn about thirty seconds after the Super Zip, with the bay doors still open. After the OMS we'll close up shop and let the computers figure out what we did. You copy, Champion?"

"Copy manual mission. Steve, I'm going to need a little help; I've got a lot of buttons to push and I don't want to screw it up, over."

Bert Congdon was already taking the mike. "Champion, this is Congdon. We've worked out the sequencing down here, so put away your T-O and take my direction." He glanced at a sheet of notepaper in his hand. "In the order in which I give them to you, open the following safety interlocks . . ."

Draper took the Mission Director by the arm and led him to one side. "Listen, Freddie, is it really as bad as you said?"

Fishbein looked at the floor. "It may be even worse. I think it's a toss-up between the terrorists' greed and fear. They're right on the edge; they could blow the thing anytime."

"Jesus," said Draper, "why couldn't the Secretary—"

They were interrupted by one of the agents. "Excuse me, but we have some bad news: we've lost contact with our deep surveillance team. We must presume they've been found out and captured or killed."

Dallas groaned with a dry throat. "Oh, God. Now we've had it."

"Not necessarily," the agent said. "This might give them pause to think. They know we have the location of their headquarters, and that they assure their own destruction if they detonate the device."

"On the other hand," Fishbein said sourly, "they might just blow the thing out of spite if they figure the game is up." He looked over to the mission clock. "Fifteen minutes to OMS-2."

"Champion, Houston. On my mark, five seconds to OMS ignition. Mark . . . four . . . three . . . two . . . one . . . ignition at thirty-seven minutes, forty-five seconds."

"Houston, Champion. Confirm; we're burning. It's good to hear your voice, Draper. Where you been, over?"

"Twiddling my thumbs while you threw switches and pushed buttons. You know what you're going to do after cutoff, over?"

"Roger, Dal. I'm going to hoist my fanny aft and throw more switches and push more buttons."

". . . two . . . one . . . OMS termination. Orbit 132 × 136 nautical miles. Unstrap and go, Champion. And I'm turning the mike over to Segal."

"Houston, Champion. Confirm OMS term. Unstrapped and heading aft. Let's have the drill, Shelley. Over."

Segal had already pushed Draper aside. "Okay, Champion, first give us lights and TV from the forward bay camera."

After a ten-second wait: *"Camera on, confirm?"*

Five pairs of eyes went to the video monitor; after a moment the picture formed in sharp relief. They were looking at the forward ASE, which was normally used to cradle the front end of an IUS vehicle. It looked much like the fork of the Palomar telescope: half-circle, open at the top. It enveloped an ugly, unfinished-looking metal cylinder about nine feet in diameter—the hastily constructed shell surrounding the bomb. They saw it head-on; communications antennas jutting out along its length were in profile. As Dallas stared, a shiver crawled across the back of his neck; he was sitting in the middle of civilization, looking at chaos.

Suddenly there was movement at each side of the bomb; he stared, then realized that the latches holding the device to the forward ASE had been activated.

"PRLAs open, Houston."

Draper had missed some of the conversation. Now Segal was talking again:

"Confirm, Champion. Now switch on the AFT." The Aft

Frame Tilt Actuator was the screw-driven piston which would pivot the aft ASE and bomb upward through a fifty-eight-degree angle.

"Roger, Houston." For five seconds, only the sound of Deborah's breathing came over the speaker, then: *"AFTA activated. Confirm, Houston."*

This time Dallas was ready for movement on the monitor—but there was none. Segal spoke while taking the mike over to the IUS console: "The damn thing isn't elevating. Standing by one, Champion." He looked carefully at the readouts. Suddenly he said: "Champion, switch off immediately! We've got stall current on the AFT motor."

"AFT off, Shelley. Shall I go to backup, over?"

"Affirmative, Champion. But be ready to deactivate immediately; we've probably overheated the primary already."

"Roger, Houston. Activating backup AFTA on my mark, ready . . . mark."

"Turn it off, Champion!"

"Backup off, Houston. Suggestions, over?"

Segal's face was a study in concentration. "Deborah, it's got to be the keel pin. That's the only place it could be stuck. You know what a kludge that payload is—and we sure as hell didn't have time to figure twist and sway forces during ascent. What you're probably got is a lateral pressure freezing the keel pin in the ASE guide slot."

"Sounds like a crowbar job, over." The crowbar had found its way informally into the Orbiter's on-board inventory back in the '80s. It was used on about one mission in five—never by design.

"Roger that, Champion." Segal was still frowning in thought. "But give me control of the Power Control Panel before you go EVA. We'll save time if we work it together, over."

"Copy, Shelley. Switching control . . . okay, you've got it. Heading for the airlock to suit up. Stand by five, clear."

During the wait that followed, the Chief Astronaut approached Draper. "Dal, once she's back inside you'll have her again. The emergency OMS maneuver has already been punched in; all she'll have to do is an attitude correction, then burn. I want her to stay suited. It'll save time, and"—he looked hard at the pilot's lover—"it will be an extra bit of protection in case that thing goes off a little too—"

Suddenly the terrorist link came to life again. Dallas's hackles rose; the knot in his stomach tightened. The message was short. Almost as soon as it was over, he heard the Secretary's voice over the closed link into the EVCOM Center. Shortly an agent almost ran over to Fishbein and began to speak. Draper moved up to listen in.

"—sking why the temperature of the bomb is dropping. They're threatening immediate detonation if the situation continues."

They all looked at the TV monitor. The Orbiter had been in Earth shadow since the beginning of the second OMS burn, and would not emerge for another half hour. The cargo bay lights illuminated the scene coldly.

Draper had never felt so helpless. He growled inaudibly, then reached out and grabbed the agent's arm. "Listen," he said, "that temperature's going to be dropping for another forty-five minutes and there's not a damned thing we can do about it. So you go back and tell the Secretary to buy us some time. An hour. Even half an hour. But goddammit, tell him to get us some time!"

The agent looked at Fishbein; the Mission Director nodded. The agent hurried back to the CIA group, spoke briefly. Soon the Secretary's message to the terrorists was on its way. Their reply was short, then their link went silent. The agent turned to Draper and shrugged, palms up.

"Houston, Champion. Suit check, over."

"Champion. Houston. Five by. Commence EVA at your discretion."

"Copy, Houston. Airlock cycling."

Soon the monitor picked up Deborah's figure as she made her way into the cargo bay, umbilical trailing, crowbar in hand. Her movements were clumsy; as a pilot, she'd had very little EVA time.

She worked her way carefully back to the cargo and examined the keel pin. It jutted down from the bottom front of the makeshift bomb cover, to fit into a matching hole in the forward ASE. The pin was inserted just a few inches into the cradle; it was for alignment purposes only.

"Shelley, you there, over?"

"Affirmative, Champion. Ready to activate AFTA on your mark, over."

"Stand by."

She moved back to the ASE and, holding onto it with one hand, reached down and inserted the crowbar into the narrow gap between the bomb casing and the cradle near the pin. Her feet tumbled upward; almost immediately her breathing became labored.

"Shelley . . . it's stuck, all right . . . gotta get better leverage . . . stand by."

Slowly she worked both legs down until she could hook her boots between the ASE and the floor of the cargo bay. By this time she was panting.

"Okay, gonna give it . . . a try . . . unnnh! . . . it gave . . . a little . . . one more try . . . unnh—ahhh! . . . that's got it!"

She was gasping for breath, but now the casing was free and bounding slightly between the fork arms of the forward ASE. She removed her feet and backed cautiously from the device.

"Try the AFTA, Shelley . . . I'm going . . . to stay out here . . . until we're sure . . . everything works okay . . . over."

Segal started to reply but Draper cut him off. "Negative, Champion. Throw that crowbar away and get inside fast. We're on a tight timeline."

Nevertheless, she hesitated a moment until the device actually began to rise.

"Champion, Houston." Segal was speaking again. "Backup AFTA functioning on specs. Suggest you follow Draper's advice. If the Zip doesn't go, we're dead in the water anyway, over."

"Roger, Houston. Heading for the airlock. Keep me posted, clear."

"Champion, this is Draper. Keep your suit on through the OMS burn; Shannon's idea, and I concur—we'll save a few minutes, over."

"Copy, but I think both you guys have a mother complex. Shelley, how's it going, over?"

Draper watched the monitor as Segal spoke: "Payload at fifty-eight degrees and locked. Activating Super Zip on my mark. . . ." With the bomb case tilted to its full extension Dallas could see the underside along the whole length of the structure. The device was mated to the aft ASE by a hardened aluminum ring about three inches wide. In the middle of the ring, around its entire circumference, was a groove—a deliberate weakening of the metal. Detonation of an explosive cord sealed within the ring would cause a clean separation precisely at the groove.

". . . mark!" Segal looked from his console up to the monitor. "Bomb's away!" Without so much as a puff of smoke the device separated, pushed off by the eight powerful springs in the aft ASE. Ponderously it rose up, until finally it was out of the field of the monitor.

"Jesus Christ!" Fred Fishbein's exclamation turned their stares.

He was pointing to the screen monitoring signals to and from the bomb. It was blank on both sides. "The terrorists were transmitting, then stopped, and the bomb didn't answer. It was like they cut off in the middle of a sequence."

Suddenly a signal came from the bomb; the ones and zeroes flashed on the screen for a second, then stopped. No reply came from the other side. After about five seconds the bomb again initiated a short transmission; again there was no reply. Another five seconds, then the sequence was repeated.

Draper's heart was in his throat. He jumped at the sound of Steve Shannon's voice from behind his shoulder: "So there's a built-in delay. Question is, how long?"

"Attitude tracking."

"Copy, Champion, and you're go for OMS. Get the hell out of there."

"Okay, Houston, punching in OMS burn at L plus fifty-nine minutes, thirty seconds. Ignition on my mark plus ten seconds . . . mark."

"Copy that, Champion. OMS at L plus 59.30."

"Four seconds . . . three . . . two . . . one . . . ignition. Whew. It's good to be moving away from that thing." Her voice then became tentative. *"You know, Draper. I've been thinking . . ."*

"Don't strain yourself, Glibs."

"Seriously, Dallas. About children. After this week that pension doesn't look so inviting any more. So why don't we—"

Static.

"Champion, Houston, over."

"Champion, this is Houston, over."

Draper felt a hand on his shoulder, and turned his head; the Chief Astronaut was there. "Dallas, look at the monitors."

The video screen showed only static. The screen monitoring bomb communications was blank, and stayed that way.

The engineers were all talking to Fishbein; he broke away and approached with a worried look. "All telemetry from the Orbiter has stopped." He started to add something else, then saw the look in Draper's eyes and changed his mind. "I'm sorry, Dal."

The Washington link had come to life; the agents were all listening. One of them left and hurried over to the three men at Draper's post: "Sir, Washington just got a report from Darwin. There was a brilliant light in the sky—brighter than the sun, they said. It lit up the entire western half of Australia. The Secretary wants to know if the Shuttle is safe."

In a flat voice Shannon said: "The Orbiter was only a few hundred feet from the bomb when it detonated. There's nothing left of it."

The agent said: "Sir, we all wish to express our deepest—"

"Thank you," said Shannon. "Please go away."

Draper stared at the floor for a long time. When he finally raised his head he saw that the Chief Astronaut was looking at him.

"Steve, Deborah's gone."

"Yes."

Draper got up and walked over to the mission clock. The digital display flashed the seconds mockingly: 00:01: 06:46 . . . 00:01:06:47 . . . 00:01:06:48 . . . He reached up and pressed the reset button, then buried his head in his hands.

". . . *estimated that her funeral rites were seen by more than three billion people. Yes, Deborah Champion is truly the heroine of the millenium. But more than saving millions of lives and preserving our civilization, her act of heroism and sacrifice set an example that the leaders of nations are finding impossible to ignore. As of this morning, with France finally signing the Global Nuclear control Treaty, every nation on Earth with nuclear technology has now placed itself under the strictest international control agency ever formed.*

"And the U.S. is also using its renewed world prestige to good advantage. Under this nation's leadership Russia, China, France, India, Pakistan, Israel, Saudi Arabia, Kenya, Brazil, Japan, Argentina, Great Britain, Mexico, Australia, and Canada have convened in the World Conference to Restrict Nuclear Arms Deployment on Earth and in Space. Thus we can predict with some certainty that the reverberations of Deborah Champion's act will echo for many years in the—"

Draper shut off the HV with a savage motion, then collapsed back in his chair as if the act had drained him of all energy. He spoke in a whisper to Steve Shannon:

"You know, she was scared the whole time."

"I know, Dal. She took all our fears up with her."

"Now you sound like the holo commentators. Dammit, Steve, she was a vibrant woman, full of love and life. We were going to have children. . . ." He blinked hard, tried to swallow the lump in his throat.

Shannon reached over and put a hand on Draper's shoulder. "Dallas, I'm not going to ask you to put away your grief, but

I'd like you to think about something. For the past hundred years our technology has been running way ahead of our human rules of conduct. We've been dealing with dangerous problems nation by nation, one at a time. The world needed a hard kick in the ass; the only problem was, that kick was likely to destroy us.

"So now it's come. And thanks to Debbie, we're all still here. Now I think we'll grow instead of dying—and don't kid yourself; those were the only two choices."

Dallas spoke with a cracked voice: "But just a few more minutes, and she could have come home safe. . . ."

Shannon was shaking his head. "No, Dal. That would have made her just another risk-taker. Thousands of us did that, and we only got passing mention. Her sacrifice was important; we needed that ultimate act of altruism. Yes, she could have made it home, and eventually had children. But grandchildren? I don't know."

"It just doesn't help, Steve. I loved her so much. I'll always love her."

"And so will I, Dal. Because now *I'm* one of her children. One of billions. . . ."

THE BOOK OF BARABOO

BY BARRY B. LONGYEAR

BALLYHOO

Officer Horth Shimsiv closed his weary, green-lidded eyes and brought his scaled head up from the handwritten book as his right fist came down hard upon the rude wooden table. "By the tail of the Mighty Gonzor! Is there no simple way to obtain a simple answer from a human?" He sensed a presence to his right, looked in that direction, then came to a stiff parade position of attention. "My . . . my apologies, Major Smith. An unthinking outburst." He swallowed and held out his hand toward the half-read tome before him. "It's just that . . . that . . ."

The major, clad in the red blouse and black trousers of the Ninth Quadrant Admiralty Office, relaxed a frown and then nodded his head. "No apologies are necessary, Lieutenant. I often feel the same way." Major Smith waved a hand toward the stool upon which Shimsiv had been sitting. "Relax, Lieutenant. Please."

Officer Shimsiv swallowed again, then resumed his seat on the painfully short stool. "Thank you, sir." Smith was less of a disciplinarian than most of the humans Shimsiv served under in the Admiralty Office; but with the scaleless bipeds in control of the Quadrant Assembly, it never hurt to spread it on thick, humans being the touchy sort they were. "And, sir, again I ask you, please excuse my outburst—"

"Never mind that, Shimsiv. Consider the incident closed." Smith moved until he was standing on the opposite side of the wooden table. He tapped the book with the forefinger of his right hand. "Have you managed to glean any information from that yet?"

Shimsiv returned his gaze to the yellowed pages and sighed. His eyes were tired and he felt the beginnings of a tension cramp in the middle of his tail. "Well, sir, not much. It confirms the Admiralty records on Earth, insofar as the starship *City of Baraboo* being constructed by the old Arnhein & Boon shipyard is concerned. It also confirms the purchase of the ship by one John J. O'Hara, owner of O'Hara's Greater Shows, fifty-six standard years ago; but . . ."

"But what?"

"The account here is in considerable variance with the Admiralty Office Investigation Division's report that was filed back then."

Major Smith nodded. "Situation normal . . ."

Shimsiv frowned. "Sir?"

"The beginning of an expression." Major Smith rubbed his chin, and looked down at the book. "Is there anything else related to our investigation?"

Shimsiv shook his head. "Thus far, Major, it is just an accounting of O'Hara's circus's beginnings on Earth and its performances on a number of Ninth Quadrant planets—"

"Back to work, then, Lieutenant. I need some answers and I need them fast."

Shimsiv studied the expression on the human's face. "Is something wrong, sir?"

Major Smith nodded. "O'Hara's was the first starshow circus; therefore, our activities have drawn the attention of all the human populated planets—particularly Earth. The Quadrant Assembly appears to be turning this into a political issue, and now there's some question as to our jurisdiction in the matter at all. . . ." Smith rubbed the back of his neck. "That's why I dropped by, Lieutenant."

"Sir?"

"I have to take the shuttle upstairs to the ship. General Kagiv—he wants to chew on me in person—the General has laid down the law. He wants the books closed on this one and out from under the Office's responsibility before this thing grows out of all proportion and gets thrown in front of the United Quadrants."

Shimsiv nodded. "I see, sir."

Major Smith leaned on the book with his left hand and poked Shimsiv in the lieutenant's chest with the extended forefinger of his right hand. "With Kagiv involved, that means that everyone in the chain of command will be involved, and tail-chewing as if their pensions depended on how deep they can bite. Understand?"

Shimsiv swallowed and nodded. "Yessir."

Major Smith stood up. "Good. Just remember that your own tail is the grand prize in this mastication contest."

Shimsiv closed his eyes as he felt himself becoming slightly dizzy. Yes, that tension cramp in his tail was definitely approaching reality. He opened his eyes. "Yessir. I understand, sir."

Smith nodded and walked to the open door of the white-washed adobe building. He talked as he left the room. "I'll send the shuttle back as soon as I'm on board. When you find out something, get it to me fast."

The major was out through the door before Shimsiv could perform the courtesy of coming to attention. "Yessir," said the lieutenant to the empty doorway. Shimsiv scratched his head with the claws of his right hand as he flexed his tail to work out the cramp. He heard Smith's voice in the distance muttering something about wishing he'd never set foot in the damned place and so forth. Shimsiv was about to extend his uncommunicated sympathies to the major having to face General Kagiv. Nuumiians were mean little bastards by nature, but General Kagiv—bless his blue-hided four-fingered self—was the meanest pick of an above-average litter. But, as he recalled Major Smith's comment regarding just whose tail was closest to the grinder, Lieutenant Shimsiv reserved his sympathies for him who was most in need and resumed his task with restored vigor. He turned to the gaudily decorated page beginning the book's next section, and continued reading.

WORKING THE ROUTE BOOK

ONE

It was the beginning of the 2144 season (Earth Time) and O'Hara's Greater Shows' third season in the circus starship *City of Baraboo*. Never had Divver-Sehin Tho had a passing thought of being employed by humans, and a circus was beyond his experience. He was a reasonably secure language clerk in the Bureau of Regret in Aargow, capital of the planet Pendiia. The Democratists had been in office less than three years, replacing a monarchy that had been in place for twelve centuries. Divver had fought in the revolution on the Democratists' side, but as the wheels of reform reduced the Bureau of Regret to a loosely supervised chaos, he found himself half wishing for the return of the monarchy.

It was in such a frame of mind, aided by a hysterical division supervisor who the day before had been attempting to maintain his prerevolutionary position by creating endless work, that Divver found himself at odd moments reading the help-wanted ads in the news chips. It was not that he was thinking seriously about leaving his position; he simply wanted to assure himself that the choice was still his. It was on the first day of his vacation, and he was occupied with the want ads, when one listing caught his eye:

Call! Call! Call! Where are you Billy Pratt? Jowles McGee, stay where you are. State lowest salary in first letter. Need one to work the route book. Must read, write English, experience in history useful. Apply in person to O'Hara's Greater Shows, Westhoven.

Divver frowned. The human entertainment company had put down on Pendiia some months before, but he had never seen the show. Since he was familiar with the Earth tongue called English and had a smattering of history and an overwhelming curiosity, he decided to journey to the manicipality of Westhoven and see what could be seen.

As he put up the rented scooter and came on the lot at Westhoven, the number of humans on the lot began making him nervous. Earth had supported the old monarchy in the revolution until the Ninth Quadrant forces intervened to let the Pendiians settle their own politics.

In the center of the lot was spread a huge canvas structure supported by poles and tied down by endless lengths of rope. Human painters were touching up the red paint and gold leaf on numerous wagons with brightly colored, spoked wheels. Performers practiced between several smaller canvas structures—a juggler, a woman who appeared to be tying herself into a knot, a few tumblers—when a human mountain clad in rough workalls and a sloped-front hat stood up from untangling some rope and turned in Divver's direction. "Help you?"

"Why, yes." Divver looked at the note he had made from the news chip. "Where do I apply for a position?"

The big man's eyebrows went up, then he shifted the stub of a cigar from one side of his mouth to the other. Lowering his brows again, he pointed with his thumb over his shoulder. "Back in the treasury wagon."

Divver looked in the indicated direction and saw a forest of brightly painted wagons. "Which would be the treasury wagon?"

The big man rubbed his chin, squinted, raised one eyebrow, then poked the Pendiian in the ribs with a finger shaped much like a knockwurst. "You wouldn't be that shakedown artist with the sweet tooth, would you?"

Divver backed away, rubbing his ribs. "I'm certain I have no idea to what you are referring!"

The big man rubbed his chin some more, then nodded. "You speak that stuff pretty good." He held out a hand the size of a soup plate. "I'm called Duckfoot. Boss Canvasman."

Divver had seen the curious human ritual before. He lifted his arm and placed his hand against the human's. In a moment, the Pendiian's hand disappeared as it underwent a friendly mangle. "My name is . . . ah! . . . . Divver-Sehin Tho."

Duckfoot nodded as the Pendiian counted, then flexed his fingers. "Divver-Sayheen . . . well, that won't last long. Are you going to work the route book?"

"I'm looking into the position."

Duckfoot cocked his head back toward the wagons. "Come on, I'll take you to see the Governor." The pair crossed the lot until they stood before a white-and-gold wagon with a caged window set into the side. Duckfoot mounted the stairs leading to the door and opened it. "Mr. John. First of May out here."

The door opened all the way exposing a rotund, but very tall, human dressed in loud-checkered coat and trousers. He was hairless on top, but sported white, well-trimmed facial hair. He looked down at Divver, then motioned with his hand toward the interior of the wagon. "Come in and find a spot to squat. Be with you in a minute." He turned and went into the wagon.

Divver nodded at the Boss Canvasman as the large man came down the stairs. "Thank you." Duckfoot waved a hand and moved off toward his pile of rope. Divver swallowed, walked up the stairs and entered the wagon. Four desks crammed the interior along with cabinets and tape files. Every portion of wall space not taken up with furniture, bulletins, or windows was hung with brightly colored paintings of fierce animals, strangely painted humans, and a white and gold spaceship decorated with strange patterns. In the rear of the wagon, the white-bearded man was seated in a comfortable chair facing a tall, thin human dressed in a black suit. Divver found a chair and sat down.

The bearded human nodded at the thin one. "Go ahead, Patch."

"Well, Mr. John, I appreciate the offer, but I'm getting a little old for the road. On the *Baraboo* between planets isn't bad, but trouping on the surface is wearing me down."

Mr. John shook his head. "Hate to lose you. You're the best fixer in the business."

"Was, Mr. John, was." The thin man shook his head. "I hate to go off and leave you with Arnheim & Boon on the warpath, but retirement is the only thing left in the cards for me."

"Are you certain everything is worked out?"

The Patch nodded. "Easiest fix I ever put in." He shrugged and held out his hands. "These guys are real punks."

Mr. John clasped his hands over his belly and smiled. "Sure you won't miss the show?"

"I'll miss it, but I think the work will be interesting. It's no circus, but there's plenty need for a fixer."

O'Hara stood and held out his hand. "Good luck, and send a note along when you can."

The thin man shook Mr. John's hand, then he turned and left the wagon. Divver stood up and approached the bearded man's desk. "My name is Divver-Sehin Tho. I've come about the advertisement."

The Governor looked off into the distance for a moment, then turned his eyes in Divver's direction. His eyes were bright blue under shaggy, white brows. "Divver-Sehin Tho. Well, that won't last long. Know English, do you?"

"Yes . . ." The Pendiian looked toward the door, then back at the Governor. "If you don't mind my asking, just what is a fixer?"

"Legal adjuster. Keeps us out from under permits, coppers, local politicos. I don't know if I'll ever be able to replace him." He leaned forward and stroked his short-cropped white beard. "Know anything about the law, how to spread sugar where it does the most good?"

The Pendiian shrugged. "Not a thing. I came about the advertisement. You wanted someone who could read, write, and speak English. This is my function in the Bureau of Regret."

"Hmmm." The Governor leaned back in his chair. "What's your name again?"

"Divver-Sehin Tho."

"Ummm." The Governor stroked his beard again. "See here, Divver, what I had in mind was a . . . man. A human."

"That seems pretty narrow-minded. A goodly number of the creatures I saw out there on the lot hardly look human!"

O'Hara laughed, then nodded. "We do come in a variety of sizes and shapes."

"I had a particular reference to the one with two heads."

"Oh, Na-Na is with the kid show. All the same, she's human." The Governor leaned forward. "What I need is someone to keep the route book for the show. O'Hara's Greater Shows was the first circus to take to the star road. Now, even though that was only two years ago, there must be thirty companies flying around right now calling themselves circuses. Most of them come from non-Earth planets, but even the ones from Earth are nothing but flying gadget shows." The Governor stabbed a finger in Divver's direction. "I don't ever want *this* company to forget what a real circus is."

Divver held out his hands. "What has this to do with your route book?"

The Governor leaned back in his chair, spread open his coat, and stuck his thumbs behind thick, yellow suspenders. "Now, Spivvy, a route book is a show's log of the season. It works just like a ship's log. It has daily entries that tell where we are, what's happening, and what kind of shape we're in." O'Hara pulled one of his thumbs out from under a suspender and used the forefinger on the same hand to point at Divver. "But, I want more out of my route-book man . . . or creature. I want to keep the book just like a running history. I need someone to write the history that this show will **make**. How does that sound?"

Divver rubbed his bumpy chin. "I'm curious to know what happened to the former occupant of this position."

"Killed. In a clem on Masstone at the end of last season." O'Hara frowned. "I've been keeping it since, but I'm not doing the job the way I want." He studied the Pendiian, then nodded. "You Pendiians have good eyesight, I hear."

Divver frowned, lowered his voice, and leaned forward. "I must tell you that I have grave doubts about this position."

"What kind of doubts?"

"Among others, I fought against humans during the Revolution. Would I be placed in a position where I might be subjected to hostility?"

The Governor laughed and shook his head. "No. Place your mind at rest, Skivver. The purpose of a show is to entertain, not be political. See, we have to appeal to everyone, and so we stay out of politics." O'Hara snapped his yellow suspenders.

"That's one principle that's set in concrete." He grabbed a coat lapel with each hand and looked through his shaggy brows at the ceiling. "An alien working the route book—" He nodded. "That just might be the ticket." The Governor looked at Divver. "You'd be putting down the kind of detail a trouper would take for granted, and that's just the kind of stuff I don't want to lose—"

The door opened and the Boss Canvasman stuck in his head. "Mr. John, my gang is back from the polls. I'm putting them on the spool wagons for the rest of the day."

"All the repairs on the old rag completed? I don't want anything to hold up tomorrow's opening."

"All done. Is the road clear yet?"

O'Hara shook his head. "See that fellow with the sweet tooth on the lot?"

"Yeah. He's been rubbering around the lot for the past few minutes." Duckfoot turned his head and looked over his shoulder. "Here he comes now." The Boss Canvasman stood in the doorway until a voice spoke up with a thick Pendiian accent.

"I am here to see the owner."

Duckfoot stepped aside and held out a hand in O'Hara's direction. "There is himself." Duckfoot left laughing, as the Pendiian climbed the steps and walked inside.

The Pendiian looked at Divver, frowned, then performed the shallow quarter-bow indicating the greeting of a superior to an inferior. Divver barely cocked his head in return. The newcomer studied Divver a moment longer. "I am Mizan-Nie Crav, code enforcement officer for the Municipality of Westhoven."

"Divver-Sehin Tho."

Crav turned to O'Hara, then looked back at Divver. "Might I ask why you are here?"

"You might." Divver's steam was up. A haze over the subject of sugar and Crav's sweet tooth began lifting. Crav was holding up the show's permits until credits exchanged hands. Divver suspected that Crav was wondering whether the Pendiian in O'Hara's wagon was an investigator.

"Then, why are you here?"

"It is none of your concern."

O'Hara chuckled. "Now, now, Skivvy, that's no way to talk to a high municipal official." The Governor turned and faced Crav. "Skivvy here is applying for a job. What's on your mind, Crab?"

"That's *Crav*, Mister O'Hara." The officer folded his arms and looked down his lumpy nose at the Governor. "I see by the posters and banners stuck and hung all over the town that you intend to conduct your parade and opening show as scheduled."

O'Hara nodded. "True. Very observant." The Governor turned to Divver. "I always said you Pendiians have sharp eyes." He looked back at Crav.

"Mister O'Hara, I thought we had an understanding."

O'Hara held out his hands and shrugged. "What can I do, Crav? Those tackspitters and bannermen are just plain thick. I've explained bribes, crooks, and such to them time and again; but they just don't seem to get it."

Crav squinted. "As I said before, O'Hara: There will be no parade and no show unless . . . certain conditions are met." The officer turned, marched to the door, then faced the Governor. "Set one foot on a Westhoven street or let one customer into your tent, and I'll arrest the lot of you!"

As Crav left, O'Hara chuckled and turned toward Divver. "Now, where were we?"

Divver turned his head from the door, frowning. "That creature! He is demanding money! He should be reported to the Bureau of Regret—"

The Governor held up his hands. "Hold your horses. Crav is being handled. We were saying . . . ?"

Divver shrugged. "You were explaining the nonpolitical nature of the circus when the Duckfoot fellow interrupted to inform you that his crew had just returned from the polls. Are humans voting in the municipal election?"

O'Hara raised his brows and pursed his lips. "They've been here long enough to establish residency. Shouldn't they?"

"What you said about the show being nonpolitical—"

"Oh, *that*. Well, I can't stop my people from voting, can I?" O'Hara shrugged. "Besides, all three of Westhoven's candidates were out here offering handsome prices for troupers' votes."

Divver stood. "*Buying* votes! That's . . . disgraceful! To suffer a revolution to—"

O'Hara held up his hands. "Calm down, Skivvy. Calm down. It's nothing to get upset over." Divver resumed his seat. "If you troupe with this show, you'll see worse things out of politicos than that."

Divver folded his arms and snorted. "Do you know whose credits will buy the election?"

"Why, let's see. Each candidate promised five credits for showing up and voting. That's fifteen, and an easier fifteen is hard to come by. So they pick up their fifteen, then take advantage of the secret ballot."

Divver stood again, clasped his hands behind his back, and began pacing before the Governor's desk. "An outrage, that's what it is. The revolution less than three years old, and corruption run rampant! Bribes, vote buying . . ." He stopped and faced O'Hara. "I *must* report this! All of this—"

The Governor shook his head. "No. We take care of shakedown artists in our own way. We never call copper." O'Hara shrugged. "Besides it would take forever to square things away through the coppers; it's faster to let Patch handle it."

Divver sat down. "What can he do? I don't see—"

"It's like when we put into orbit around Masstone last season. Now, our nut's pretty heavy, and—"

"Nut?"

O'Hara shook his head and raised his brows. "My, but aren't you a First of May? The nut is our daily cost of operation. See, what with paying off the *Baraboo*—that's our ship—fuel for the shuttles, wages, supplies, permit fees, taxes, maintenance, property, and so on, it figures out to forty-nine thousand credits a day. That's our nut."

"I see."

"Well, once we put into orbit and put down the show planetside, you can see why we have to start playing to two straw houses right off."

"Full houses?"

"That's what I said. Anyway, once we put down on Masstone, the shakedown artists dropped on us and wouldn't let us open unless we spread the sugar." O'Hara leaned forward and pointed a thick finger. "Now, I can see helping an underpaid civil servant make ends meet now and again; but shakedowns are a different matter. We don't give in to 'em. It's the principle of the thing."

Divver decided that the Governor was a man of principles. "What did you do?"

"Patch caught up with our advertising shuttle and had the lithographers make up some new paper." O'Hara pulled his beard, shook his head and chuckled. "See, we'd been advertising the show on Masstone for weeks, and the gillies were looking forward to seeing us. Patch sent out the brigade loaded with hods of posters all over the big towns and had the mediagents work the papers and stations with readers—press releases. Well, all they said was that there would be no show because of permit difficulties." The Governor slapped his knee. "In the space of a week, Masstone almost had a revolution on its hands and the authorities were begging us to put on the show, and no charges for the permits. Well, we sat back and thought about it, know what I mean?"

"I'm not sure. You didn't take the permits?"

O'Hara nodded. "We took 'em, after they paid us two hundred thousand credits to take 'em."

"You mean . . ."

"We shook *them* down."

The Governor studied the Pendiian, waiting for his reaction. All Divver could do was nod. "I see why you will miss Mister Patch."

O'Hara nodded. "Oh, I could tell you a thousand stories about Patch. I have the call out for another fixer—Billy Pratt—but I don't know if I can get him."

The wagon door opened, and in walked a dapper fellow dressed in a red coat with black collar, black trousers tucked into shiny black boots. "Governor, I've brought the rest of the performers back from the polls. Are you finished with the parade order?"

O'Hara pushed some papers around on his desk, then pulled one out and handed it to the man, then turned toward Divver. "This is Sarasota Sam, the Circus Equestrian Director. Sam, meet Skivvy-Seein Toe."

He stood and let Sarasota Sam crush his fingers. "My name is Divver-Sehin Tho."

Sam smiled. "Well, that won't last long."

"Skivvy's taking the route book."

"I'm considering it."

Sam held up the paper and turned toward O'Hara. "I'd better get together with the property man about this."

O'Hara nodded and Sam left the wagon. Divver faced the Governor. "If I did take the position, what would I be paid?"

"Eighty a week—that's seven Earth days—bed and board. Holdback is ten a week and you get it at the end of the season if you can cut it."

By the time the Pendiian had returned to his living unit, had put in a night's sleep, and had thought about it, the entire prospect of wandering around the Quadrant like a nomad with a collection of peculiar beings seemed foolish. This feeling was underlined by the pay, which was half of his take at the Bureau. Divver could imagine himself in the Patch's position—old, worn-out, and cast adrift on a strange planet when he couldn't "cut it" anymore. In addition, it appeared that the "English" the Governor wanted hadn't been covered in Divver's education.

Despite the meaninglessness of his position at the Bureau and the tarnish gathering on the glory of the revolution, Divver had made up his mind to expect less from life and return to the Bureau at the end of his vacation. He chanced then to read his morning news chips. When the Pendiian had stopped laughing and had recovered enough to rise from his prone position on the floor, he had made up his mind to take the route book. Divver-Sehin Tho would follow the red wagons on their route to strange, unpredictable worlds.

The news story was a simple account of the Westhoven municipal election. The three candidates on the ballot had been defeated by a surprise write-in campaign. The picture next to the story showed the aging winner dressed in black coat and trousers, his large watery eyes looking back at the reader. The circus would get its permit; Westhoven would get its parade; and the fixer, Patch, had found something to occupy his retirement years—being mayor of Westhoven. As the Patch had said, it isn't the circus but there's plenty need for a fixer.

TWO

At the conclusion of his third night with O'Hara's Greater Shows, Divver-Sehin Tho pulled himself into the office wagon while it was being loaded on the shuttle to be moved to the next stand. He sat at his desk, located across the aisle from the treasurer's workplace, heaved a tired sigh, then lifted his pen and began his work.

ROUTE BOOK, O'HARA'S GREATER SHOWS
2 MAY 2144.

The Governor insists that the route book use Earth time designations, which means having to ask the date, since no one has provided me with a date table. I asked why Earth time, when every other institution in the Quadrant uses Galactic Standard. He says that if we don't use Earth time, we won't know when to layup at the off season. I offered to keep track in Galactic, but he thinks calling a "First of May"—a first-season trouper—a 12-point-04 shreds the designation of meaning and romance.

It distresses me to see myself falling so easily into the lingo—circus talk. Climbing ropes are "tapes," the lot entrance is the "Front Door," or "8th Avenue Side"; performers are "kinkers" of "spangle pratts." Perhaps the last refers to the location of costume sequins—perhaps not.

Much of the language appears designed to bunk the customers, while at the same time maintaining a peculiar brand of integrity among the circus people. To the patrons (rubes, gillies, guys, towners) Zelda's establishment is "Madam Zelda, Fortune Teller extraordinary, palm reader and medium, will probe the past and the future using the vast array of Dark Powers at her command." To the show people, it's called a "mittjoint." The "Emporium of Pink Lemonade" is the "juice joint"; and after witnessing the beverage's manufacture, I have sworn to shrivel up and blow away in the heat before letting a drop pass my lips. Nonetheless, the gillies imbibe it by the vat. Weasel, the fellow who has the juice joint privilege, explained that the slices of lemon on top of the evil brew are called "floaters"; and he boasted that his property lemon would last through the entire season.

Thus far we have been keeping up with our paper (we're on schedule) and we've had one blow-down (wind storm) and two cleans (fights with towners). The horse piano (calliope, pronounced CA-LY-O-PEE by all English-speaking peoples, but CAL-EE-OPE by show people) has been repaired, and our ears are once again assaulted by the horrible strains of Doctor Weems' steam music. The Governor wants everything in perfect order when we put in to Vistunya after our Wallabee tour. Thus spake John J. O'Hara:

"You have to understand, Warts (my new name), the circus has to appeal to all sexes, all ages, all races, all brands of religion, morality, and politics. Those folks on Vistunya are upset about dirt—they think it's perverse, dirty, depraved. We could run the entire company around the hippodrome stark naked; and as long as they were clean, no one would be offended. But dirt? Never. We have to keep those things in mind when we're picking our route."

"Do you pick the route?"

"No. Rat Man Jack Savage is our route man. He's about a year ahead of us. He keeps in touch through the general agent and he tells us what to watch out for as far as local taboos. So, remember: if the gillies consider it politics, smut, racism, or religion, we don't do it. It's the principle of thing. That's how we're keeping the traditions of the old circus alive, Warts: principles."

"Governor, it seems to me that my people back on Pendiia

would consider Patch's fix in Westhoven to be politics. What about that?"

O'Hara raised one white eyebrow at me, pursed his lips, shrugged and held out his hands. "Well, Warts . . . you gotta be flexible."

Circus names, although terribly uncomplimentary, never are occasions for offense. The names derive from a physical peculiarity, former association, or incident. My own name of Warts is due to the usual bumps found on a Pendiian. Duckfoot Tarzak has a distinctive walk; while Quack Quack, the mediagent, has a distinctive voice. Goofy Joe's name was attached for obscure reasons, since I found the canvasman to be at least as intelligent as the show's run of roughnecks. In any event, it was Goofy Joe who related the tale of how Stretch got his name.

Goofy Joe Tells His Tale

I couldn't say this if we was back with the main top. This is one story that Duckfoot doesn't go out of his way to hear. First, there's something you have to know about the Boss Canvasman. Duckfoot Tarzak's people come from Poland. That's why the center poles on the big top have those funny names: Paddyowski, Wassakooski, and such. When we have the bulls hooked to the block and tackles pulling the baling rings up those sixty-foot sticks. Duckfoot calls out "Go ahead on Paddyowski . . . hold Paddy . . . go ahead on Wassakooski . . . hold Kooski . . ." until all six rings are peaked, raising the old rag. But, see, you have to be on the lot awhile to learn those names; and Stretch didn't know them.

I guess it was our third or fourth stand on Occham, and there was cherry pie all around. The reason we were shorthanded was a blow-down that splintered two of the center poles on the main top and busted up a few of the sports on the guying-out gang. Duckfoot was taking on some new roughnecks, and Stretch was one of the ones he hired. If you look at Stretch, you know why the Boss Canvasman took him on. Big, strapping, good-looking fellow, and as green a First of May as you ever saw.

Stretch—or Ansel as he was called then—he was put in Fatty Bugg's crew: and even though Fatty was a bit in his cups, everything was going fine. The poles were up, the canvas spread and laced, and side poles were up. Fatty took Ansel, a bull, and an elephant man under and hooked onto Cho-pan; that's the number-three pole. With a crew on each stick, Duckfoot hollers out, "Go ahead on Paddyowski," and the bull on number-one stick pulls up the baling ring fifteen feet. "Hold Paddy . . . go ahead on Wassakooski . . . hold Kooski." About then, Fatty Buggs slapped Ansel on the shoulder and told him to take over. Then Fatty stumbles away from the stick a few feet and goes to sleep.

"Go ahead on Cho-pan!" calls Duckfoot, but nothing happens. "Cho-pan, go ahead," he calls again, but nothing happens. Duckfoot sticks his head under the edge and in the dark sees the bull hooked to the number-three stick. He points at it and yells, "Wake up, and go ahead!" Ansel gives the elephant man the high sign, and the bull moves out. Up goes the baling ring about fifteen feet, and Duckfoot calls out, "Hold Cho-pan!" But the ring keeps going up, and he calls out again, "Hold Cho-pan!"

Well, the ring is about thirty feet up Cho-pan, and Duckfoot runs under the rag and tells Ansel's elephant man to hold up, then he turns to Ansel. "You deaf? I called hold on this stick! Where's Fatty?"

"There." Ansel pointed.

Duckfoot stomps over, kicks Fatty in the leg. "Hit the treasury wagon, Fatty, and collect your pay." Then he goes to the sidepoles and calls for Blue Pete to take over Ansel's bull. "What about me?" asks Ansel and Duckfoot turns and rubs his chin as he studied the boy.

"The quarter poles go up next and we have the wrong size. You go find the Boss Hostler and get the pole stretcher." Ansel runs off. Duckfoot shakes his head, then goes back to calling up the rings.

Well, the Boss Hostler sent Ansel to the Boss Porter, who sent him to the loading runs, where one of the razorbacks sent him off to the property man. Just about then, I guess, Ansel realized that the only thing that was getting stretched was his leg.

Well, Duckfoot had about half the quarter poles up when Ansel drives up in a cat pulling a flatbed wagon. On the wagon is this huge crate, and lettered on its side it says "Little Eureka Pole Stretcher." Duckfoot comes up as Ansel's getting down from the cat and points at the crate.

"Here's the pole stretcher, Duckfoot. Had a devil of a time finding it."

Duckfoot frowns, then walks up to the crate. Just then howls and screams come from inside and the whole thing starts to rock and shake. Out of the top the crate comes this huge, black, hairy hand, each finger tipped with a knife-sized claw. It grabs around a bit, then goes back inside. Duckfoot turns to Ansel and says "What's that?"

"That's your pole stretcher, Duckfoot. Go ahead and open it up and you'll see a pole get stretched good and proper."

Well, Duckfoot taps his foot on the lot, folds his arms and glowers at the kid for a while, then he nods. "Good job, but . . . seems like all the poles around here are just the size I want them. Take it back."

Ansel hops back on the cat, and off he goes. Ever since then, he's been called Stretch. Go over to the Boss Animal Man sometime and ask him to show you a picture of that four-ton clawbeast the show picked up on Hessif's Planet. The thing was too vicious and had to be destroyed, but while it was in the menagerie, its name was "Little Eureka." No one ever did figure out how Stretch got it in that crate.

2 MAY 2144.

Tonight we tore down the show at Vortnagg on Pendiia, loaded and made ship for the next stand, which will be the fourth planet in the Gurav system, called Wallabee. The Governor had me leave with the last shuttle to permit my observation of the tear-down process. I confess I was not quick enough on my toes to see the entire operation. I felt safe in thinking that I would be able to enjoy the finish of the performance, but that was not to be. Before half the customers were out of the main top—being hustled through the entrance by impatient ushers—the elephants and the roughnecks began piling through the performer's entrance.

I was hustled out with the rest and was stunned to see the animal top—containing the menagerie—the cockhouse, dressing top, sideshow, all gone. By the time I made it back into the main top, the customers were gone and three hundred canvasmen, propmen, ring makers, side-wall men, electricians, and rigging men were stripping the inside. The folding plank platforms that serve as seats were being hydraulically collapsed into the backs of waiting vans, while the performers' rigging and stages were being detached, pulled apart, and digested by more wagons. Lights began going off as the electricians removed the heavy light arrays. Meanwhile the elephants—bulls—were being directed to unseat the quarter poles supporting the middle of the top between the peak and the side-walls. Before they were finished, it was black inside, and I moved out fast, having no desire to be trampled underfoot.

I stood to one side of the former main entrance, after the last of the wagons and bulls had exited, and heard the Boss Canvasman say, "Let 'er go!" A blast of air mixed with all the smells of the circus rushed from under the tent, almost carrying the six men who ran from beneath the collapsing fabric. Even before the huge sea of canvas had settled to the lot, canvasmen jumped on it and began unlacing the sections. In moments, the huge sections were folded, rolled, and stored upon the spool wagons. The six sticks—center poles—of the main top were lowered, while countless stakes were pulled up by a tractor and loaded into more wagons.

It seemed that a city had vanished; and as I stood in the empty lot watching scraps of paper being pushed by the gentle breeze, I felt a hand on my shoulder. I turned and saw a rugged, black face. "I bet that's the first time for you, isn't it?"

I nodded. "I've never seen anything like it—"

He held up a hand, then pointed it at the departing wagons. "You better get going. Those wagons will be loaded and the shuttle gone in another twenty minutes."

"Aren't you coming?"

He shook his head. "I'm Tick Tock, the twenty-four-hour man. I have to stay behind to clean up the lot and make sure the city is happy with the way we leave the place."

I looked at the wagons. "But how will you get to the ship?"

"I don't. I jump ahead of the ship to prepare the next lot. Been with Mr. John nine years, now; and I've never seen the show." He pointed again at the wagons, and I ran. I made the Number Ten shuttle just as the sixty-foot center pole wagon was being pulled inside.

I had no time to gawk at the *City of Baraboo*. No sooner had the shuttle docked and made fast to the exterior of the hull than I was hustled off and directed to report to Mr. John's quarters. I was carried by the stream of traffic, and by chance managed to make it. The door was open, and I entered. My entrance was acknowledged by the Governor raising one eyebrow, giving me a quick glance, then returning his gaze to the papers on his desk. Two men were in the compartment, standing next to the desk; and when Duckfoot and another man pushed in behind me, the six of us appeared to crowd the tiny room.

The Governor sat up and nodded at Duckfoot. "Close the door. Fill the Boss Hostler and Boss Porter in after we talk." Duckfoot turned, pressed a switch, and faced O'Hara as the door hissed shut.

"What's up, Mr. John?"

The Governor looked at me. "Warts, this is Rat Man Jack, our route man, and Stretch Dirak. Stretch manages the advance car." He indicated the two men standing next to his desk. "You know Duckfoot; the fellow who came in with him is Bald Willy, pilot and Boss Crewman of the *Baraboo*." He pointed at me. "This is Warts." I nodded at the others. The Governor nodded at Rat Man. "Tell them."

Rat Man Jack faced the rest of us. "Two things: there's a civil war brewing on Wallabee and the Abe Show is going to try running day-and-date with us there to try and split the circus crowd."

Duckfoot issued a low whistle, then shook his head. "Rat Man, is there any chance that the civil war will begin shooting while we're on the skin?"

Rat Man shrugged. "No one can be certain, but things are pretty tense." He turned to O'Hara. "What about the Abe Show? If Arnheim & Boon knew about the political situation, maybe they'd call off the duel to another time."

The Governor smiled and closed his eyes. "They know." His eyes opened again. "They get their information from the same places that we get ours. I think that Arnheim knew first about the possible rebellion, and then decided that it might be to his advantage in his war with us."

The Rat Man held out his hands. "Well, do we blow the planet and find greener grass, or do we slug it out?"

The Governor bowed his head for an instant, then came up with fire in his eye. "We play Wallabee, as scheduled. The route, contracts, advertising—everything—is already done. We'd have to delay for a month or more to alter the route now, and that would give Karl Arnheim just what he wants, *and* without bruising one knuckle." He turned to the Boss Canvasman. "Duckfoot, can you peel off a couple dozen of your roughnecks and give them to Stretch? I want to beef up the advance's opposition brigade."

Duckfoot nodded. "There'll be cherry pie all around, but we can handle it."

"Good." Mr. John faced me. "Warts, I want you to go with the advance."

"Me?"

"Yes, you. A good bit of the action will be on the advertising car, and I want you go get it all down. I'll take notes on the show so you won't fall behind." He turned to Bald Willy. "The *City of Baraboo* has to be protected at all costs. I don't put it past Arnheim to try and pull something on board."

Bald Willy nodded. "Don't worry, Mr. John. No one knows this tub better than I do."

The Governor nodded, then raised his eyebrows. "And don't *you* forget that this ship was built by Arnhein & Boon Conglomerated Enterprises." He turned back to his papers. "That's it."

As we left the compartment, the one called Stretch, a huge, powerful looking man, grabbed my arm and began pulling me along in his wake. "Wait, I have to pick up my things!"

"No time, Warts. No time. In the advance that's all you have time for: no time."

THREE

The advance is the advertising arm of the show. It is housed, between planets, in a quad-shuttle commando raider named the *Blitzkrieg*. The shuttles are named *Cannon Ball, Thunderbird, Battle Bolt*, and *War Eagle*, I am told, after the advertising cars used by the now-extinct RB&BB Show. The belligerence of the names might lead one to conclude that the advance's role is of a combative nature. In such a case, one would be right.

Before the *City of Baraboo* had left orbit, the *Blitz*'s last shuttle, *War Eagle*, was up from the surface of Pendiia with Tick Tock, the twenty-four hour man. No sooner had Number Four docked, than the *Blitz* streaked out ahead of the *Baraboo* toward Wallabee. What happened next might be called an executive meeting or strategy session in an advertising firm, but on the *Blitz* we gathered for a Council of War.

In the tiny wardroom, there was Stretch Dirak; the four "car" managers; Fisty Bill Ris, the boss of the opposition brigade; and myself. Stretch greeted everyone, and sat down behind the wardroom table. We all took our seats around the table, then Stretch began. "The Abe Show intends to pull day-and-date with us on Wallabee, so you all know what that means for us. There'll be overbilling of our paper, opposition; and depending on how far ahead of us their advance is, the squarers might have difficulty in securing poster space, banner permits—"

Cross-eyes Oscar, manager of the *Cannon Ball*, held up a hand, then dropped it on the table. "Stretch, are we going to run the order the way we did on Masstone?"

"For you it'll be the same. I hate to leave you naked, Cross-eyes, but I figure the Abe Show opposition to hit the last three cars. That's where the paper is." He turned to Fisty Bill.

"Fisty, I want twenty roughnecks in *Thunderbird*, twenty in *Battle Bolt*, and the remaining sixty in *War Eagle*."

The manager of the *Thunderbird* shook his head. "Stretch, you know they're going to be waiting for us, and when we start putting up our paper—or overbilling theirs—we're going to get opposition. Twenty isn't going to be enough. With my crew and billposters, tack-spitters, that leaves me with less than eighty men."

Stretch nodded. "I'm going to use *War Eagle* as a flying attack and reserve brigade." He turned to Six Chins Ivan, manager of the *War Eagle*. "In addition to the brigade, you'll still handle the checkers-up and the twenty-four-hour man; but most of the time you'll be in the air looking for trouble. If you don't find it, start it." He looked around the table. "I'll be moving between all four cars, and remember to keep the radio net complete at all times. The Governor wants clean victory with each opposition, and I don't ever want the Abe Show to forget that they tangled with us."

Later, Stretch and I worked the *Blitz*'s research files on Wallabee. Unfortunately, they were pretty skimpy, it being a new stand for the show. The Nithads, the dominant race on the planet, are stooped-over, vaguely egg-shaped. Their backs are armored with a thick, segmented shell; but they do have bipedal locomotion. Their arms and hands extend from under the shell. There are two arms per Nithad, and two opposing fingers per hand.

Since Wallabee is the nearest habitable planet to Pendiia, the history of the planet had been touched on during my education; and I had been following several trends in the interplanetary section of the news chips. The race had a written history over twenty thousand of their years long; and during that period, no wars, revolutions, or even riots had been recorded, leading to such expressions as "having the heart of a Nithad" to denote a peaceful, nonviolent person, and "having the courage of a Nithad" to denote a coward.

Nevertheless, the ruling class of the Nithads had followed a pattern as old as life itself: thought itself threatened, then proceeded to eliminate the opposition by a variety of oppressive measures, including the confinement of political prisoners, elimination of local elections (even though the ruling class had the only qualified candidates), and the total elimination of communications freedom. Following the pattern, the ruling class was outnumbered, and the Wallabee Liberation Front grew into a powerful force almost overnight. Organized rebellion so far had only involved boycotts of ruling-class merchants and compulsory ceremonies, but it had been reported to the Ninth Quadrant Commission on Interplanetary Political Stability (9QCIPS) that the rebels had obtained a quantity of weapons from the Nuumiian Empire. Open hostilities were considered only a matter of time. It was in this atmosphere that O'Hara's Greater Shows and the Abe Show planned to wage their own war.

FOUR

7 MAY 2144.

The *Blitzkrieg* makes orbit around Wallabee. Stretch assigns me to the Number Two car, the *Thunderbird*, managed by Razor Red Stampo. The *Thunderbird* follows the *Cannon Ball* by four days. This enables the mediagents (press agents) and squarers to prepare the way. *Cannon Ball* makes certain readers are issued to the mass media, and that permission for space to put up paper and banners is obtained. Cross-eyes Oscar reports back to the *Blitz* that, although the Abe Show already has paper up, there has been no trouble in obtaining permission for our own displays. Stretch decided to go down to the first stand with the *Thunderbird*.

11 MAY 2144.

Garatha, on Wallabee. When the *Thunderbird* arrived this morning, we found the city papered with the Abe Show's bills. Razor loads down the billposters with hods of newly printed paper and sends them out to cover the enemy paper. Stretch has been walking through the city and has come back with a puzzled expression on his face.

"The Abe Show's paper is the only advertising I've seen in Garatha. The enemy's hits on buildings is impressive but I don't see where the Nithads advertise. Have to think on it."

Opposition in Garatha. The billposters covering up Abe Show paper on Viula Street have called in for help. A force of ten Abe Show roughnecks has cornered three of our men. Stretch and Razor mount up the twenty-man opposition brigade on cycles and head for the spot. By the time we arrive, half our paper has been re-covered. Razor sends out the brigade, and it wades into the Abe Show's opposition. Duckfoot's toothpicks, the four-foot tent stakes, make short work of the Abe Show toughs; and they retire.

While Razor re-covers the Abe Show paper, Stretch watches the Nithads that had gathered to watch the fight. None of them are looking at either the Abe-Show paper or ours. Instead, after watching the fight, they leaned forward and wandered off. Stretch examined the buildings around us, looking back at the few Nithad that remained, then hopped on a cycle and sped off toward the *Thunderbird*. When I arrived an hour later, Stretch was deep in conversation with the *Thunderbird*'s lithographer. They were bending over a layout of a poster, and when I peeked around Stretch's arm, I saw that it was our usual poster, except all the type was reversed. Instead of reading the posters from the top down, they had to be read from the bottom up. I could tell that, even though the posters were printed in the Nithad language.

In two hours we had the new posters, and Stretch called in the billposters, and issued new paper and instructions. We were not to cover the Abe Show's paper on the buildings. Let them have the vertical surfaces, he told them. *Our* posters were to be pasted onto the sidewalks. The Nithad habitually looks down because of his armored back and stooped over position. Hence, the place they will see the most is the sidewalk. The billposters gathered up their hods of paper and vanished into the city. I, myself, saw an elderly Nithad come to a poster, examine it carefully as he traversed its surface, then rush on to the next poster, all the time ignoring the Abe-Show paper covering the wall of the building to the fellow's left.

15 MAY 2144.

The Governor has reported back to us that opening night was a sellout, while the Abe Show performed at barely a quarter of its capacity. Almost at the same moment, the Abe Show opposition began contesting our domination of the sidewalks. The *War Eagle* kept busy. There was hardly a town, large or small, that did not see a battle between opposition brigades. Paper covered paper, then was itself re-covered, then overbilled again. Gangs of stake-swinging roughnecks prowled the cities being billed, and it was a rare stand that did not leave a half a dozen or more men laid up in the local hospital with mashed faces, broken limbs, or cracked skulls.

19 MAY 2144.

We have gotten word that the Quadrant Commission (9QCIPS) has warned both O'Hara and the Abe Show to knock off the war. The Commission fears that our performances will trigger an uprising on Wallabee. Since the layers of posters on some of the sidewalks were thick enough to impede traffic, the Commission's warning appeared to have little effect. At Stutladop, for reasons unknown, the Abe Show offered no opposition, but jumped ahead to the next stand.

FIVE

24 MAY 2144.

I was with the *Battle Bolt*, the Number Three car, covering over the paper the Abe Show had overbilled which was put down by the *Thunderbird*. The news from the grapevine was encouraging. The Abe Show was finding day-and-date with the Old One (that's what we called O'Hara's Show) an economic disaster. The Nithads may have been oppressed and preoccupied with their plans for revolution, but they could still tell the difference between a real circus and a traveling gadget-show.

When the *Battle Bolt*'s crew reached Hymnicon, we found our paper on the sidewalks untouched, and assumed that the Abe Show had either given up or had jumped ahead as before. Both turned out to be in error.

At night, midway through the show, the *Battle Bolt* got word that the Abe Show was sending their opposition brigade against the show itself. Of course we were fighting mad, since it ran against circus ethics to fight at the stand, unless the combatants happened to be towners. One show does not attack another show at the stand, because there is the possibility of customers getting hurt. Nevertheless, the word came in, and the *War Eagle* picked up on our opposition brigade after picking up the brigade from the *Thunderbird*.

The full brigade streaked back toward the stand; and by the time we circled the area, we could see the Irish Brigade tangling with the Abe Show's opposition. In between and scattered all around were Nithads scurrying out of the show. We put down on the edge of the lot, grabbed our stakes, then piled out of the doors and joined the battle. We could see several of the Abe Show people heading for the main top and menagerie with torches. The canvas itself was inflammable; and between the seats in the main top and the straw in the animal top, there was reason enough to trample the Nithads that got in the way to get at the firebugs.

Opposition brigade ethics authorize only that amount of force necessary to make one's side victorious. Therefore, when the fists and stakes start swinging, there is a degree of restraint involved. Sending the opposition to the hospital is acceptable, whereas sending them to the morgue is not. At the battle of Garatha, there were no such restraints. Circus people do not sabotage one another, particularly if it might endanger the patrons. Since the Abe Show had thrown the rule book out of the window, we did the same.

Bodies dropped as blood-soaked stakes whipped through the night, landing upon skulls and breakable legs. The baggage horse top erupted in flame; and as the animal men led the Perches and rosinbacks out through the fire, the rest of us threw ourselves against the Abe Show's roughnecks. In seconds, performers, office workers—the Governor himself—were on the lot busting skulls. Here and there a Nithad would be caught by a backswing or kicked out of the way by someone anxious to get into the thick of the brawl. Eventually, all the egg-shaped creatures were huddled under their armor, looking like so many loaves of bread on the lot.

I had just finished thumping an obnoxious character when an Abe Show toothpick caught me between the eyes. When I woke up to the sound of my own bells, the opposition had retired and the Nithad patrons were coming out of their shells and scurrying off the lot. I saw the Governor being helped to his wagon by two canvasmen, and would have helped, except that I passed out again.

25 MAY 2144.

About to return to the advance, head bandaged nicely, when the grapevine reports that we've been kicked off the planet! The Abe Show has already left, but the Quadrant Commission insists that we are a poor influence on a people trying to avoid open rebellion. The show is torn down, loaded and sent upstairs to the *City of Baraboo.*

27 MAY 2144.

I was feeling pretty glum as I walked past the Governor's quarters. I heard laughter coming from within; and being in such a condition that I could stand a good laugh, I knocked on O'Hara's door.

"Come in! Come in!"

I pressed the door panel, it hissed open, I stepped in, and it hissed shut behind me. Stretch Dirak was seated across from the Governor at his desk, and both of them were drying their eyes. "What's so funny?"

The Governor handed me a flimsy upon which was printed a radio message. I read it and was instantly confused. The Nithad—both ruling class and liberation front—had called off the revolution and had vowed to resort to peaceful means in the resolution of the issues that divided them. It appeared that the Nithad's total lack of war for the proceeding twenty thousand years had not prepared them for the kind of conflict they had witnessed between the two shows. After that sight, both sides had decided that there *had* to be a better way, and immediate negotiations had begun. The flimsy was from the Ninth Quadrant Commission, and it concluded by calling the Abe Show and O'Hara's Greater Shows "Agents of reason and peace."

I looked at the Governor. "Does this mean that we'll be able to finish off our stands on Wallabee?"

"No." He laughed, then handed me another flimsy. "I went directly to the Wallabee Ruling Council and asked. This is their reply."

I took the sheet of paper and read it. It read in part: ". . . we must refuse. There is only so much of your 'peace and reason' that a planet such as ours can take."

THE SLICK GENTLEMEN

SIX

The secretary pushed open the door to the dark office. Entering, she closed the door behind her. In a moment the black mass before the sparkle of the city lights resolved into Karl Arnheim. "Mr. Arnheim?"

The black mass didn't move. The secretary stepped a little to one side and could see the lights from the streets below reflected in Karl Arnheim's unblinking eyes. "Mr. Arnheim?"

The eyes blinked, but remained fixed in their direction. "Yes, Janice?"

"Mr. Arnheim, I'm going home now. Do you want me to call for your car?"

"No."

Janice fidgeted uncomfortably in the dark for a moment, then put her hand on the door latch. "I've arranged for your annual physical for ten tomorrow—"

"Cancel it."

"But, Mr. Arnheim, this is the third year in—"

"I said cancel it." The mass turned. She could not see his face, but could feel his eyes burning into her. "Did you transfer those funds to Ahngar as I directed?"

"Yes, Mr. Arnheim. And I prepared those papers for the

board meeting tomorrow. The proxies look pretty close. A lot of the stockholders are with Milton Stone about—"

"About what?" Silence hung heavy for a moment, then came the sound of a fist hitting a hardwood surface. "Stone, that two-bit accountant! What can he do, except sharpen his pencils? I'll run this corporation the way I always have, and if I choose to use every asset of this enterprise to drive John J. O'Hara into the dirt, I'll do it! What's more, no one can stop me!"

Janice clasped her hands in front of her, looking for an opening to bid her employer good night. "Sir, I—"

"Janice, by the end of this season, O'Hara will be ruined. He's on the rocks now, and he has to take that offer. He just has to!"

"Yessir."

The black mass turned, and Janice could again see the city lights reflected from Arnheim's unblinking eyes. "In a few months, O'Hara's name won't be worth the spit it takes to say it."

Janice saw the black mass's head nod, then become still. "Good night, Mr. Arnheim." She waited for an answer, and when none came, she turned, opened the door and left the office. As she closed the door behind her, she nodded at a mousy fellow clad in gray-and-black plaids. "It's no use, Mr. Stone."

Milton Stone nodded, then smiled. "That's it, then. The board can't stop the current stunt he's pulling in his personal vendetta, but we can certainly cut off his water after tomorrow." He nodded again, then left.

Janice looked at Arnheim's door and wondered if she should extinguish the lights to the outer office. Karl Arnheim always used to storm over every needless expenditure, although of late he seemed obsessed with other things. But he'd need the light to find his way to the elevators if he went home. Janice shrugged. Karl Arnheim hadn't gone home for three days. She turned off the lights and left.

SEVEN

ROUTE BOOK, O'HARA'S GREATER SHOWS
6 JUNE 2144.

After getting kicked off of Wallabee for our little tiff with the Abe Show, O'Hara's Greater Shows was decidedly between a mineral mass and an unyielding location. It was not only that interrupting the show's schedule interfered with the Governor's payments on the *City of Baraboo*, although this weighed heavily upon O'Hara's mind. Erker IV, the Monarch of Ahngar, had come through with eighty million credits when nothing less would save the ship; and the Governor felt a special obligation to make good the loan. If the 2144 season had gone as well as had been expected, the loan would have been paid off by laying-up time. But after having a third of our scheduled stands blown by being evicted from Wallabee, O'Hara had doubts about meeting the payroll.

We had made orbit around Ahngar to replace the equipment and people lost in the contest with the Abe Show; and the Governor was working with the route man, Rat Man Jack, trying to piece together a makeshift route to fill out the season. There were only three planets within an economical distance of Vistunya and Groleth—our two remaining scheduled planets— and none of the three had even been played by O'Hara's, or any other show. Deciding upon a new planet is very complicated, involving a great deal of investigation. Visiting one of the three untried planets, if the stand was unsuccessful, would ruin us. The Governor had gone over the information that he had on the planets and had just about decided to run out the first third of the season on Ahngar. It was too recent to play the larger cities again, but he figured there were probably enough smaller towns remaining that we could keep losses down and break even for the season.

Rat Man and I were in the *Baraboo*'s wardroom cutting up jackpots and becoming very depressed about the season, when Fish Face Frank, the side show director, came by and told us that we were wanted in the Governor's office. Fish Face went with us, and when we arrived, the Governor nodded and introduced us to a very dapper fellow, striped trousers and maroon frocked coat with rings on six of his fingers and a big shiner stuck in his pearl colored cravat. He had one of those skinny, straight mustaches, and black hair greased back against his head.

The Governor pointed at us in turn. "This is Fish Face Frank Gillis, director of the kid show. He'll be giving the orders." The man nodded, held out a hand and smiled as he shook hands with Fish Face. "Rat Man Jack Savage, our route man, and Warts Tho. Warts keeps the route book." Nods and hand shaking. "Boys, this is Boston Beau Dancer."

The three of us could have been pitched off our pins by a feather. Everyone had heard of the notorious Boston Beau,

King of the Grifters; but we had never expected to see him trouping with our show. Everyone knew what the Governor thought of grifters. We mumbled a few appropriate responses, then sat down on chairs around the Governor's desk.

O'Hara rubbed his chin, cleared his throat, then leaned back in his chair. "Boys, you know what kind of trouble we're in. Boston Beau has made me an offer that I can't bring myself to turn down. In exchange for the usual privileges, he will pay enough to guarantee the remainder of the debt on the *Baraboo* and to assure us a profit for the first third of the season. This means—"

"Grifters?" Fish Face went red. "I don't get it, Mr. John! O'Hara's has never had grifters before. What about our reputation?"

O'Hara shrugged. "I can't see any other way out, Fish Face. I hope you'll see—"

"I won't see nothing! I quit!" Fish Face stood, turned and stormed out of the compartment.

The Governor turned back to Boston Beau. "I apologize, but it'll take some time for Fish Face to get used to the idea."

Boston Beau smiled, displaying two gold teeth among his otherwise immaculate collection. "A man in my profession cannot afford to take offense, Mr. O'Hara." He drew a small lace cloth from his sleeve, sniffed at it, then tucked it back in the sleeve. "To make certain we have our terms straight, in exchange for my payment to you of twenty-two million credits, my boys will take over the ticket windows, run the games, and we will keep all that we make. Also, I must fix my own towns and keep my people separated from the rest of the show."

"That's for the first planet. If we are both satisfied at the conclusion of the first third of the season, you have an option to renew your offer, Boston Beau." The Governor nodded at me. "Also, there is the thing I discussed with you."

Boston Beau looked at me, then smiled. "That's hardly a condition. I would be honored."

The Governor nodded. "Good."

Boston Beau turned to Rat Man, then back to O'Hara. "I know there will be ripe pickings whenever you put down the show, but I am curious to know where it will be."

O'Hara looked at Rat Man. "Read Boston the figures on Chyteew, Rat Man."

Rat Man Jack pulled a pad from his pocket, opened it, then smiled. "Yes, Mr. John. The population is concentrated into urban production and commercial centers. No circus has performed on Chyteew before, but there are entertainments, and they are supported. The gross product of the planet for the year 2143 was ninety-one trillion credits, with first-quarter figures for this year showing a sixteen percent increase—"

Boston Beau held up his hand. "That's all I need to know." He stood, bent over Mr. John's desk, and shook his head. "I'll have my people and the money together and up here in ten hours." He turned toward me. "Come along, Warts. You're to stick to me like a second skin."

I turned toward O'Hara. "Mr. John?"

The Governor nodded. "Boston Beau and his people represent a distasteful, but historically valid, part of the circus. I've arranged with him to have you accompany him during his stay with us, and he has promised to talk your ear off about his operations."

Boston Beau bowed as the door opened, then held out his hand. "After you, Warts."

I shrugged, stood, and walked through the door.

EIGHT

7 JUNE 2144.

I was distressed, as was the rest of the company, at turning *The* Circus into a grift show. Despite this, I quickly found myself caught up in the strange world of the "lucky boys." Boston Beau and I took a shuttle down planetside, then hopped around to several different cities, each time picking up one or two of Boston's associates. "A grifter can always make a living on his own, Warts, but to make the real coin, you have to be tied in with a show. A circus is the natural habitat of the *Trimabulis Suckerus*; therefore, that is where a true scientist should observe and pluck them."

"Scientist?"

Boston Beau grinned, flashing his two golden teeth. "We are not gamblers, my lumpy friend. Gamblers take chances." He pointed at one of the passengers in the shuttle, an overweight fellow wearing a brown-and-tan suit. He was slouched in his couch and had his cap, a flat straw affair, pulled over his eyes. "That's Jack Jack, one of our most eminent scientists. He operates a Three Card Monte game—"

"He's a card shark."

Boston Beau shrugged. "Now, there is a bigoted reference if I ever heard one. Not only is Jack Jack a scientist, he is an artist as well."

I rubbed my chin and nodded. Three Card Monte had been described to me, and it sounded simple. Three cards are placed, on a flat surface. One card is picked by the "sucker," then placed face down along with the other two. The card shark then moves the cards around, stops, then invites the customer to turn over his card. I smiled, because Pendiians have very sharp eyes, and I prided myself on my ability to detect sleight-of-hand maneuvers. I turned to Boston. "I'd like to see a little of this so-called science."

Boston motioned with his hand and we both stood and went over to the couches facing the slumbering Jack Jack. We sat down, Boston next to the window and I directly across from the obese card mechanic. Boston leaned forward and said quietly, "Jack Jack, I have a seeker of wisdom for you."

Jack Jack animated one arm and pushed the straw hat back on his head with a single finger. The tiny, dull eyes looked at me for an instant. "So, my boy, you have come to learn, eh?"

I sneered and raised my brows. "I'd like to see a little of this Three Card Monte. It doesn't sound too difficult."

Jack Jack's face remained impassive as he reached into his coat. "Ah, yes. A lesson of great value hovers above your bumpy head; and when that lesson settles about your shoulders, you shall understand science."

Boston Beau pulled the folding table out from the bulkhead and locked it in place. "Jack Jack, it is part of my arrangement with the Governor that we do not trim the other members of the company."

Jack Jack shrugged. "Scientific research must be funded, Boston Beau. If this fellow—what's his name?"

"This is Warts Tho, from Pendiia. He works the route book, and Mr. John has him doing a little history of us."

Jack Jack nodded as he pulled a deck of cards from his pocket. The deck was sealed. "A Pendiian, eh?"

I nodded. "That's right."

"Pendiians are quick with their eyes, aren't they?"

I smiled, detecting a crack in Jack Jack's façade of confidence. "Very quick."

Jack Jack broke the seal on the deck, opened the box and pulled out the cards. He spread them on the table, face up, and pulled two Jacks out. He looked up at me. "You have a favorite card?"

I shrugged, then reached forward and pulled out the ace of hearts. "That one."

Jack Jack gathered up the remaining cards, placed them in

the box, and returned the box to his pocket. As he placed the three cards face up in a row, he talked to Boston Beau. "As I was saying, scientific research must be funded. I have expenses to meet, equipment to keep up. Why, have you seen the price of cards lately? This fellow will be learning something that will always be of use to him, and surely that is worth a small investment."

Boston Beau looked at me and I turned to Jack Jack. "What kind of investments are you talking about?"

The corners of Jack Jack's mouth turned down. "Oh, my boy, just enough to satisfy custom. A friendly sum—say, one credit?"

Boston Beau poked me in the arm as I nodded at Jack Jack. "Please remember to tell Mr. John that I tried to discourage this transaction. Agreed?"

"Agreed." I pulled a credit note from my pocket, placed it on the table, and it was soon joined with a note Jack Jack peeled from an enormous wad of bills. He returned the wad to his pocket, then arranged the cards, ace in the middle. "Now, my boy, what I will do is to turn these cards over, rearrange them, and then you must find the ace."

"I understand."

I watched closely as Jack Jack flipped over each card with a snap, then straightened out the row. I could see a small bend in the corner of the center card, a bend that only a Pendiian could see. Jack Jack moved the cards around slowly, and it was easy to follow the ace. He stopped, looked at me, and smiled. "And now, seeker of truth, can you find the ace?"

I turned over the card to my right and placed it face up. It was the ace. "There."

Jack Jack's eyebrows went up. "Well, my boy, you do have fast eyes. Would you care to try another game?" He pulled the wad from his pocket.

I pointed at the two credit notes on the table. "Very well. I'll bet two."

Jack Jack peeled off two credits, added them to mine, then arranged the cards again, ace in the middle. He turned them over with a snap each time, then moved them around. But this time the cards moved with such speed and complexity of motion that I lost track. He stopped the cards, arranged them in a row, then grinned. "And, now, my boy, the ace."

I looked at the cards feeling a little foolish, until I saw that the card on the left had the slight bend in it that I recognized. I pointed at it. "That one?"

Jack Jack reached out his hand. "Let's see—ah! The ace! My, but don't you have fast eyes?" He frowned. "You wouldn't consider trying it one more time, would you?"

The space between my ears was filled with visions of Jack Jack's roll of credits. I reached into my pocket, pulled out the forty-three credits that remained from my week's pay and added them to the four credits already on the table. Jack Jack pursed his lips, frowned, then pulled out his roll. "Warts, my boy, you appear pretty sure of yourself."

I nodded, and he peeled off forty-seven credits and added them to the pile. He arranged the cards, ace in the middle, then flipped them over, each one with a snap. "And now, my boy, the lesson."

The cards moved so fast that I couldn't follow the ace, but I didn't try. I waited for the cards to stop, then looked for the card with the bend. All three cards had identical bends. "Ah . . ."

"Pick out the ace, my quick-eyed friend."

I reached out my hand, hovered it over the left card, then moved it and picked up the middle card. It was a Jack. As Jack Jack gathered up the credit notes he made a disgusting slurping sound with his mouth. Boston Beau folded up the table, then stood, pulling me to my feet. "Thank you, Jack Jack. I'm certain that Warts found the demonstration very enlightening."

I was feeling pretty hot. "But . . ."

Boston Beau steered me back to our couches, then plunked me down in mine and resumed sitting in his own. "As I said, Warts, a science." He turned toward me and flashed his dental bullion. "Notice how he got you to rely upon that bend in the card?"

I frowned. "You could see it?"

Boston Beau shook his head. "No, but I knew it was there. You're a Pendiian, and Jack Jack bent the card accordingly. Since you thought you had won twice on the basis of an unfair edge, a bend you could see and that the dealer could not, you could hardly protest when all three cards came up with the same bend."

I glowered at the back of the couch in front of me. "What was that sound he made?"

Boston Beau frowned, then smiled. "Oh, that. Didn't you ever wonder where the term 'sucker' comes from?" He frowned and rubbed his chin. "Come to think of it, though, considering the direction in which the money went, I guess that would make

Jack Jack the sucker." He smiled at me. "That would make you the suckee."

I looked back at Jack Jack. He was again slouched in his couch, hands clasped over his belly, hat over his eyes.

NINE

12 JUNE 2144.

After a few days with this slick gentlemen, I was convinced that the population of Chyteew would be plucked naked by the time the show moved on to Vistunya. "Science" is such a poor word to describe the method of these fast-fingered fellows. Boston Beau Dancer began his career back on Earth as a "dip"—a pickpocket. When I expressed disbelief that anyone could put hands into my pockets without my being aware of the event, Boston Beau handed me back my billfold, pocket knife, and small change, and then explained the difference between a street scene and a show scene when dipping for leathers.

"Warts, a street dip works with at least one other person, sometimes two. The ideal in such circumstances is to have number one attract the touch's attention, while number two— the dip—lifts the leather, then palms it off to number three to get rid of the evidence. A terrible waste of manpower. Working the push at a circus is different—it's mass production. The dips spread out in the crowd, then I'll get up on a stand and call attention to myself. Once everyone is watching, I will explain to the touches that it has been reported that there are pickpockets working the show, and that everyone should keep a close watch on their belongings, and thank you kindly."

"You warn them?"

Boston Beau nodded. "As soon as they are warned, the first thing they do is grab for wherever it is that they keep their coin. The dips in the crowd note the locations, then the only limit on leathers is how much you can carry."

Working for the benefit of all, the steerers would wander the streets of the large city nearest the show, looking for high rollers who could be coaxed onto the lot to investigate the games. There they would witness a happy customer or two win a few games of Leary Belt, Three Card Monte, Innocent Strap, Shell-and-Pea, or whatever, thereby becoming convinced that the game could be beaten. These happy "customers," known as "cappers," were associates of Boston Beau. "Science" is such a feeble word with which to describe the methods the slick gentlemen used to part the sucker from his credits. And as my faith in my nimble Pendiian eyes diminished, my respect for the grifters increased. It takes no small amount of courage—no matter how corrupted—to sit behind a flimsy table by yourself and steal a hard rock miner's money under his nose with no one nearby except the hulking brute's friends and relatives. I suppose my respect for the lucky boys could have flowered into admiration, except their lessons were beggaring me.

Since my own research fund had expired, I asked questions and took notes. "A thing I don't quite understand, Boston Beau, is how you can afford to pay Mr. John twenty-two million credits for the privileges. I mean, you're paying *him* to sell *his* tickets."

Boston Beau scratched his chin, looked up, and did some mental calculations. When he was finished, he looked back at me. "How much did the show take in last season—about twenty, twenty-five million?"

"About that."

He nodded. "Say that you are a customer. You come to the ticket window to buy your two-and-a-quarter-credit ticket. You hand me—the ticket seller—a ten- or twenty-credit note; let's say a ten. Now, I give you four and three quarters credit back—"

"No. You'd owe me *seven* and three quarters."

He raised his brows. "I'm disputing that, Warts. I owe you seven and three quarters, but all you get is four and three quarters."

"How . . . ?"

Boston Beau grinned. "If after all your research you have a tenner left, I'd be pleased to take you over to Ten Scalps Tim and have him show you how it's done."

I glowered at the grifter for a moment. "No, I don't think so."

Boston Beau nodded and smiled. "See? Look at how much you have already learned." He clasped his hands together. "Now, just about everyone who goes to the show will have set money aside for it, and it's always in big bills. Maybe one out of twenty customers pays with the exact change. That means that, after deducting the amount I have to pay Mr. John—the two and a quarter credits—my profit is three credits. It's even more for larger bills. The standard short on a twenty is eight credits, and on a fifty is twenty-two."

"But, what happens when the customer counts his change and finds it short?"

"By then the line behind has pushed him out of the way, or if it hasn't, a couple of the boys working with the shortchange artist will shoulder him away from the window. Then, when the sucker puts up the big holler, the man at the window says he should have counted his change before leaving the window." He held out his hands. "I mean, it is not reasonable to expect the ticket man to pay such an unfounded claim—a guy just walking up and saying, 'Hey, you gave me the wrong change.' The crowd shouts the guy down, he gets embarrassed and usually walks off. If he persists, puts up a big enough squawk, or threatens to bring in the coppers, I'll take him aside and pay him off to keep him out of our hair."

"But, still, the amount you paid the Governor—"

"I'll clear as much out of the ticket windows as the show does, without the same expenses. Of course, that doesn't count the games—and the dips. All in all, on a planet such as Ahngar, my associates could clear thirty or forty million in a third of a season. I expect to double that on a planet as wealthy as Chyteew." He grinned and flashed his gold teeth. "And just think, they've never seen a show before." He closed his eyes, leaned back in his couch and said with a touch of ecstasy in his voice. "Ripe. *So* ripe."

TEN

15 JUNE 2144.

The day before we made orbit around Chyteew, I stormed into the Governor's office. "How . . . how can you turn those . . . those . . . grifters loose on those people? We'll ruin Chyteew for circuses forever!"

O'Hara rubbed his chin, then nodded. "How is your education coming along, Warts?"

"Mr. John . . ." I flapped my arms about for a bit. "I can't see why you are doing this! We could have at least broken even on the season, and the Monarch won't press for his money. You know that."

He shook his head. "One blow-down, one fire, a couple of blown dates—that's all it would have taken to wipe us out. I couldn't risk losing the show. That's why I had to take them on. There's another reason." He frowned and clasped his hands together, then shook his head. "But that's personal." He held out his hands and shrugged. "Should I have risked the show, Warts? Throw this all away, just because of a few scruples that together wouldn't buy a bale of hay for the bulls?"

"I . . . I don't know!"

I stomped out of there, walked up to the family quarters at the center of the ship, thinking to talk to Duckfoot. When the door to his quarters opened, Diane, Queen of the Flying Trapeze, was standing there.

"Warts."

"Where's Duckfoot?"

"He's down in the canvas shuttle." She stepped out of the doorway. "Come in. You seem worried."

I entered and the door closed behind me. "I am."

"Is it something to do with the tops?" She pointed at a couch and I sat. In front of me, Sweetie Pie was dangling from the overhead by her teeth. Diane nodded at her daughter. "Sweetie Pie is working on an iron jaw act. If she gets it down, the Director of the Ballet says she can join this season."

I gave a weak smile to the girl, then turned to Diane. "It's about these grifters Mr. John's taken on."

"What about them?"

"Is this a time for jokes?" I snorted. "They'll ruin the show, that's all!"

While Sweetie Pie lowered herself from the overhead, Diane seated herself across from me and smiled. "I'm certain that the Governor wouldn't do anything to harm the show, Warts. It's his life."

"He's doing it. Maybe he can't see it."

Sweetie Pie walked over and stood in front of me, hands on hips. "Duckfoot says the Governor knows what he's doing, and if that's what Duckfoot says, then that's what we say."

I stood, went to the door and stopped. "Blind loyalty such as that earned the Pendiian monarchy several beheadings!"

Sweetie Pie held up her nose. "Warts, are you planning on taking off Duckfoot's head?"

"Bah!" I stomped out of there, blazed my way through the corridors to the main sleeping bay, then flopped on my cot, frowning until my bumps collided.

The show was everything to the Governor. He had been with the thing as a poor, insignificant tent show back on Earth, and he had pioneered the star road. To save that, I suppose the Governor would even kill. But taking on the grifters would destroy the show's reputation, which would mean a falloff in customers, more clems with the towners, and eventually being frozen off planet by most or all of the profitable stands that the show had developed. We had all heard how the lucky boys had upset things on Ahngar, and it was only by the grace of the show being off planet that the grifters didn't taint the show.

Even so, the Monarch's representative came to O'Hara to ask what could be done about it. Well, the Monarch's problem was solved. But now we had the disease, and soon it would launder the people of Chyteew.

While I was fuming away, Fish Face Frank Gillis, the kid show director, came into the sleeping bay. He saw me, then looked around to see if anyone was within earshot. Satisfied that he would not be overheard, he walked over and sat on a built-in bunk opposite mine. "You look a little upset, Warts."

I turned my head and studied Fish Face. His large, half-closed eyes, along with his thick lips and chinless face, appeared calm. "You don't, which is kind of strange, considering why you quit."

Fish Face nodded. "That's because I made up my mind to do something about it. Can't stand grifters—never could. When the show puts down on Chyteew, I'm going to fix the slick gentlemen."

I sat up and faced him. "What are you going to do?"

Fish Face looked around again, then looked back at me. "I'm going to need some help. You in?"

I frowned. "I don't know. What—are you . . . are you going to holler *copper*?"

He lifted a finger and held it in front of his mouth. "Shhhh! Are you trying to get our heads massaged with tent stakes?"

"But, calling copper?"

Fish Face leaned forward. "I can't think of any other way to save the show. If we can get to the coppers on Chyteew and have them put the arm on the grifters at the first stand, maybe too much won't be made about it."

I looked down and shook my head. "I don't know, Fish Face. If anyone found out about it, we'd be poison on an O'Hara lot for the rest of our days."

He reached out a hand and clamped it on my arm. "You're a trouper, Warts. You know it's the right thing to do. Are you in?"

I thought hard, then swung my legs up and stretched out on my bunk. "What do I have to do?"

Fish Face nodded, then got to his feet. "The *War Eagle* from the advance will be up to report to the Governor as soon as we make orbit. We'll go back with her planetside and drop off at the first stand along with the twenty-four-hour man. Then we go into town and see what we can do."

ELEVEN

15 JUNE 2144.

As luck would have it, as the *War Eagle* docked with the *Baraboo*, Boston Beau Dancer decided to join us on our trip planetside, "to size up the local sucker stock" as he put it. No one on the *Baraboo*, except the advance and the route man, had ever been to Chyteew before; and Boston Beau wanted to get the lay of the land. Fish Face and I were friendly because we didn't want to give ourselves away. It was not easy. At the lot near Marthaan, we bid Tick Tock goodbye; and then the three of us set out on foot toward the tall buildings. The Asthu, the natives ruling Chyteew, are built along the general proportions of an ostrich egg, although considerably taller, with thick, blunt-toed legs and thin, four-fingered arms. Several times, walking down one of the many business malls in Marthaan, Boston Beau deliberately stepped in front of one of the egg-shaped creatures. The Asthu would bump into Boston Beau, utter a rapid, incomprehensible apology, then waddle on.

Boston Beau would grin and mutter, "Ripe. *So* ripe."

I frowned at him after he had bumped into his fourth pedestrian. "Why are you doing that?"

He cocked his head at the push of the crowd working its way into a business exchange. "Look at their eyes, Warts. Small and practically at the sides of their round head-ends. They can't see directly in front. Can you imagine what a man like Jack Jack can do to these people?" He cackled, then waved goodbye to us as he followed the push into the business exchange. "I think I'll check out what they like to do with their credits."

We waved back, then I stopped Fish Face and turned toward him. "Can you imagine what Boston Beau's gang will do here?"

Fish Face nodded without changing expression. Then, he pointed toward one of the creatures dressed in white belts who appeared to be directing foot traffic at one of the mall intersections. I felt slightly sick when I realized that the Asthu needed traffic cops to keep pedestrians from running into each other. "There's a copper. Let's find out where his station is."

We walked up to the egg in white belts and I began. "Could you tell me where the police station is?".

I was standing directly in front of the officer, and he rotated until he brought one of his eyes around to face me. It went wide, then he staggered backwards a step. "Mig ballooma!"

"Police station?" I tried again.

Slightly recovered, the officer took a step toward us, scanned with one eye, then the other. "Egger bley sirkis."

"What?"

The officer pointed at me, then at Fish Face. "Sirkis, sirkis, dether et?"

Fish Face poked me in the arm. "Listen, he's saying 'circus.' "

The tiny mouth on the egg rapidly became much larger, then the entire body dipped back and forth. "Sirkis! Sirkis!" As the bodies began piling up at the intersection, the officer reached beneath one of his white belts and pulled out a red-and-white card. "Sirkis!"

I looked at it, then turned to Fish Face. "It's an advanced reserve ticket for the show." I turned back to the officer and nodded. "Yes, circus. Police station?"

He tucked the card back under his belt, then held up his hands. "Nethy bleu et 'poleece stayshun' duma?" A lane of traffic mistook the officer's hand gesture for a signal and began piling into the cross lane flow. "Gaavuuk!" The officer scanned around once, then waded into the bodies, shouting, pointing, and shoving. After a few minutes of this, traffic began flowing again, and the officer returned. He pointed at a door a few paces from the corner. "Agwug, tuwhap thubba."

I pointed in the direction of the door. "Police station?"

He held up his arms again in that gesture that was probably a shrug, thereby causing the halted lane to pile into the cross lane again. "Ah, Gaavuuk! Nee Gaavuuk!" Back he went to untangle the bodies. Fish Face pulled at my arm and pointed at the door.

"I think we'd better go before the copper comes back. Think that's the station?"

I shrugged. "Let's try it anyway." We walked the few steps to the door. On the door was painted a variety of incomprehensible lines, dots, squiggles and smears. Toward the bottom was spelled out: **English Spoke Hear**. I nodded, then turned to Fish Face. "It's an interpreter." I pushed open the door and we entered a cramped, windowless stall. In the back, behind a low counter, one of the egg-shaped creatures was leaning in a corner.

Fish Face tapped me on the shoulder. "Is he asleep?"

I walked over to the counter and tapped on it. "Excuse me?" No response. I knocked harder. "Excuse me, do you speak English?"

The egg opened the eye facing me, started a bit, blinked then went big in the mouth. "SIRKIS!" He stood and reached under the wide brown belt he wore and pulled out an advanced reserve ticket. "Sirkis!"

I nodded. "Yes, we're with the circus." I turned to Fish Face. "Stretch Dirak and the advance have done quite a job." I turned back. "Do you speak English?"

The mouth went big again as the eyes squinted. "English spoke here."

"What's your name?"

"Name are Docco-thut, well sirs." Docco-thut dipped forward in the good egg's version of a bow.

I smiled. "We need an interpreter."

"English spoke hear."

"Yes, can you come with us? We want to go to the police station."

Docco-thut rotated a bit, went down behind the counter and came up again carrying a book. He held it up to one eye and began paging through it. "Police . . . police . . . hmmm. Regulation of community affairs . . . community . . . community, ah . . . hmmm . . . station . . . hmmm." Docco-thut put the book down and faced an eye toward me. "You want to operate a radio?"

Fish Face placed a hand on my shoulder. "Let me give it a try." He wriggled a finger at Docco-that. "Come with me."

Docco-thut pressed a button, part of the countertop slid open, and he walked through the opening. He followed Fish Face to the door. Out in the mall, Fish Face pointed at the traffic cop. "Police."

Docco-thut aimed an eye at Fish Face. "You want police radio?"

Fish Face shook his head. "Take us to the police's boss."

Docco-thut went back to the book. "Boss . . . circular protuberance or knoblike swelling—"

Fish Face took the book. "Allow me!" He found the definition he wanted, faced the book at Docco-thut, then pointed with his finger. "Boss. Supervisor, employer."

Docco-thut nodded his body. "You want control unit of traffic persons. You all I take for half credit."

I reached into my pockets and found them well laundered. "Fish Face, you have any money?"

Fish Face pulled out two quarter credit pieces and held them out to Docco-thut. Docco-thut took them, then shook his whole body. "You no account have?"

"Account?"

The body nodded. "Credit Exchange. You no account have at Credit Exchange?"

Fish Face and I shook our heads. Docco-thut shook his body

again, then turned around. He studied the mall for a few
moments, then began walking. I came up beside him. "Are we
going to the control unit of traffic persons?"

Docco-thut pointed at a box set into the wall of a few steps
away. "Exchange." He stopped at the box, pushed the two
coins inside, then spoke to it. "Docco-thut, temay, ooch, ooch
soog, temay, dis, ooch; simik cho." He turned from the box.
"Now, control unit of traffic persons."

TWELVE

15 JUNE 2144.

It became clear, after much talking and numerous references
to *English As She Is Spoke*, that traffic persons are concerned
only with traffic; they are not coppers. The boss traffic person
at the control unit directed Docco-thut to take Fish Face and
me to the local crime rectification unit. The boss crime rectification person was a tough-looking egg wearing a blue belt.
Fortunately Tuggeth-norz, as he was called, managed to scare
up an interpreter at the station with a little more experience.
We bid Docco-thut a fond goodbye; and laid another credit on
him, which he promptly dumped into one of those exchange
boxes before leaving the station. In way of parting, he held up
his advanced reserve ticket and said, "At sirkis, see you."

After the boss copper and his interpreter pulled their tickets
and showed them to us, we got down to the business at hand.
"Tuggeth-norz, there are grifters working the show."

The interpreter, Goobin-stu, waddled around for a bit, then
asked me. "What are 'grifters' please?"

I held out my hands. "Grifters—dips, shorters, card sharks,
shell workers . . ." I could tell from the interpreter's expression
that I wasn't getting through. "Do you know what a pickpocket
is?"

Goobin-stu whipped out his own copy of *English As She Is
Spoke*, then flipped through the pages, came to the proper page
and read. He opened his eyes wide, then studied both Fish Face
and myself. Putting down the book, he turned me around and
started jabbering at Tuggeth-norz, pointing at my hip pocket,
more jabbering, in went his hand pulling forth my billfold,
more jabbering, then Goobin-stu returned my billfold. As I
replaced my billfold, I turned and faced the box crime rectification person. Tuggeth-norz's eyes became very tiny as he clasped
his arms around his middle. Then, the eyes grew wider and he
held up his hands and jabbered at Goobin-stu. The interpreter
turned to us and said, "Is not crime."

"What?"

"Is not crime picking pockets. Tuggeth-norz says it not in law."

I scratched my head. "Do you mean your law never got around to making picking pockets a crime?"

Goobin-stu held up his hands. "Why should it? No pockets."

I looked around the station room. The Asthuians there all wore the blue belts, but no pockets. I turned back to Goobin-stu. "Well, where do you keep your money?"

"Money?" He then made a honking sound, jabbered at Tuggeth-norz, who then joined him. When they stopped honking, the interpreter shook his body. "We keep money in the Credit Exchange. If we did not, we would have to carry it in our hands." He honked again.

"Well, what about crooked games? There will be crooked games at the show."

Blank stares. Goobin-stu held up his hands. "Crooked games?"

"Games of chance, dishonest."

Goobin-stu scratched at the side of his head, shook his body, then held up his hands. "So?"

On the way back to the lot, Fish Face and I radiated gloom. Fish Face kept shaking his head. "I don't believe it; I just don't believe it." He turned toward me as we walked up to the front yard entrance. "You mean those eggs don't have a word for 'honest'?"

I nodded. "Which means that they don't have a word for 'dishonest.' " I shook my head. "Which means that anything dishonest is not a crime."

Fish Face kicked a small stone. "Which means that Boston Beau and his gang are going to make coin like they owned the mint."

I followed the stone with my eyes, then looked up to see Ten Scalps Tim's gloomy face peering from behind the bars of the ticket window. There was no line in front of the cage but the lot behind the ticket wagon was crammed with honking Asthuians being directed by white-belted traffic control persons. Latecomers were presenting advance reserved tickets at the gate and were being passed through. We nodded at the gate man, then moved onto the lot toward the sideshow. The Asthuians were listening to spielers, moving into shows and coming out from other attractions. But something was wrong. No one was selling any tickets. Fish Face and I walked up to Motor Mouth, the spieler for the Great Ozamund. He had just concluded his patter, pointed with his cane at the entrance to the show, and leaned forward on his stand as he watched the crowd of honking Asthuians pushing to get into the tent.

Motor Mouth turned away and saw Fish Face and me. "Did you ever see anything like it? They can't understand a word I'm saying, but they stand and listen. If my performance is enthusiastic enough, they go in and watch the show." He smiled and said in a lowered voice, "I don't mind telling you that my spieling is pulling in a bigger crowd for Ozzie than old Electric Lips across the way is getting for Zel."

I looked at Madam Zelda's spieler and duly noted the smaller crowd observing Electric Lips' performance. I turned back to Motor Mouth. "Why aren't you selling tickets?"

He shrugged. "The Governor's orders. These folks don't carry money." Then he shook his head. "Mr. John says we can trust them for it."

I looked up and down the midway. "Where are the grifters?"

Motor Mouth shrugged. "Gone, I guess. They weren't getting any business." He stood. "Got to get back to work, Warts. By the way, Mr. John said he wanted to see you two when you came back on the lot."

I nodded, then Fish Face and I left the midway and headed for the office wagon. Mr. John was sitting on the stairs observing the Asthuian lot lice and chuckling to himself. When he saw us he got to his feet. "Well, you two, are you going to have an army of coppers dropping on us?"

I grimaced while Fish Face shook his head. We came to a stop in front of him, then I folded my arms. "Mr. John, what's going on? Why aren't the kid shows selling tickets, and where are the lucky boys, and—"

O'Hara held up his hands, then rubbed them together. "One at a time, Warts." He looked at Fish Face. "Good to have you back."

Fish Face nodded. "I'd like to hear some answers, too, Mr. John."

O'Hara smiled, clasped his hands behind his back, and bounced back and forth from his toes to his heels. "Well, about the sideshow tickets, they don't carry any money. What they'll do is keep in mind what they owe, then the next time they pass one of those credit exchange terminals each one will transfer the proper amount to the show's account."

I scratched my head. "Are you sure you can trust them?"

"Why, yes, Warts. I didn't believe it when Rat Man first gave me the information on this planet, but here it is. They simply have no conception of dishonesty, stealing, cheating. Also, they are not what you might call impulse buyers. Everyone who wanted to attend the show made up their minds when the advance went through and bought reserved tickets."

"What about the grifters?"

O'Hara's grin evidenced that he was approaching the favorite part of his revelations. "To be sucked in by a grifter, you have to have a little grifter in your soul. Something for nothing is something these folks just don't understand."

I rubbed my chin, then nodded. "You can't cheat an honest man—or Asthuian." I nodded again. "The show is going to make a bundle on Chyteew, isn't it?"

"Looks that way."

I pursed my lips. "And the money you got from Boston Beau is still yours."

He shrugged. "I lived up to my part of the bargain."

"Is that it?"

O'Hara bounced on his toes and heels some more. "Well, the Monarch of Ahngar did offer to discharge the rest of the amount owed on the *City of Baraboo* if I'd get the slick gentlemen off his planet—" The Governor looked up, then smiled as he saw Boston Beau Dancer approaching.

"Mr. John." Boston Beau stopped, nodded at Fish Face and myself, then turned back to the Governor. "What about at the end of your tour on Chyteew? Can my boys get transportation to Vistunya?"

The Governor nodded. "As we agreed, if at the conclusion of our stay on Chyteew you wish to renew your offer, I will accept."

Boston Beau raised his brows, pursed his lips, and cocked his head to one side. "Another twenty-two million credits?"

O'Hara nodded, then opened the door to the office wagon. "That was the agreement." He smiled. "See you then." He entered the wagon and closed the door. Fish Face chuckled and walked off.

Boston Beau shook his head, turned, and began walking slowly toward the front entrance. I just couldn't resist. "Hey, Boston Beau!"

He turned back and glowered at me. "What."

I made the longest, most disgusting slurping sound that I could manage. The slick gentleman stared at me for an instant, then he smiled, waved, and left laughing.

IN THE CART

THIRTEEN

14 APRIL 2148.

Enroute to H'Dgva, the first planet of O'Hara's Greater Shows' tour of Tenth Quadrant planets. The last star system containing an inhabited planet was passed twenty-four days ago, and it will be another twenty days until we reach H'dgva. Today we will cross the border between the Ninth and Tenth Quadrants—the first star show ever to do so. . . .

Jon Norden, Chief Engineer for the circus ship *City of Baraboo*, sat slumped at his bridge station studying the match indicators for the ship's Bellenger pods. The mass transceivers had been cranky ever since the show left its laying-up grounds on Badner. With the pods in operation, the *Baraboo* crossed distances at several times the speed of light, while theoretically moving no faster than two hundred kilometers per hour. Without the pods—something Jon felt in his bones might be a distinct possibility—the *Baraboo* could make a maximum of six thousand kilometers per second under emergency impulse power. He didn't even want to think about the thousand centuries or so that it would take to get back to civilization at that speed. But that was their only option if the pods malfunctioned. Unmatched Bellenger pods, if used, would atomize the ship, leaving O'Hara's Greater Shows nothing but a memory and a cloud of subatomic particles.

Jon completed his fourth computer check on the pods, pursed his lips, then looked around at the long, low rectangle of the ship's bridge. In the center of the bridge stood a small, cloth-draped table. Before the table, Wall-eyed Mike Ikona, the ship's Boss Porter, prepared the crystal and champagne for the line-crossing ceremony. On the other side of the table, toward the front of the compartment, Bald Willy Coogan occupied his place in the Chief Pilot's chair, while standing next to Bald Willy was the Governor. John J. O'Hara kept his eyes toward the forward view ports almost as though he were searching for the border by sight.

Turning back to his instrument panel, Jon rubbed his chin and frowned. All indicators read green. Everything was fine. Not even a minor adjustment had been needed for the past three hours. Jon rubbed his chin again. Maybe things were just a little *too* fine. He reached forward and punched his comm for the rear engineering section. "Animal, you there?"

"I'm here, Pirate. Watcha want?"

Jon smiled at the nickname. Everyone with a circus had to have a special name, much as clerics on Earth adopted names when they joined priesthoods. Pirate Jon had gotten his when he led his fellow workers at the Arnheim & Boon Conglomerated Enterprises orbiting shipyard in securing the *City of Baraboo*—some might say stealing—for the show. Jon drummed his fingers on the armrest of his swivel seat. "Animal, get a crew down to the pods. I want the access ports pulled and both pod assemblies gone over with microscopes."

"I don't see anything down here. You have a reading?"

Jon shook his head. "Just a bone tickle. Tell me what you find."

"Engineering's putting on quite a party for crossing the line. My boys will sure hate to miss it."

"So, sign on and troupe with another show." He chuckled. "I'll save you some of that sparkle juice."

As the Second Engineer signed off, Jon wondered about the crew of riggers, welders, mechanics, and technicians that had followed him when he stole the ship from the yard. Karl Arnheim, the A in A&BCE, had tried to have them all arrested, and failing that, he had blackballed them from one end of the Ninth Quadrant to the other. The few who had tried to obtain shipbuilding work at various stands had always come back. The freeze was on, but never a complaint, never a regret.

"You look a little down in the mouth, Pirate."

Jon turned his head and looked up. "Oh, hi, Mr. John."

"I heard you tell Animal to check out the pods. Something wrong?"

Jon turned back to his instruments and shrugged. "Just a feeling. We've had so much trouble with them this far, I'd sleep a lot better if Animal had a look."

O'Hara nodded. "You're the engineer."

Jon rubbed his chin again, then turned his chair to face the Governor. "Mr. John, the grapevine says we're touring the Tenth Quadrant because Karl Arnheim is running us out of the Ninth. How much truth is there to that?"

O'Hara looked down, then faced Jon. "A lot. For the past three years he's been buying up every little one-horse show he can get his hands on—even forcing some to sell. In another two or three years, A&BCE will probably have a complete monopoly of Ninth Quadrant star shows."

Jon frowned. "Not if we stuck around he wouldn't. We opened up the Quadrant for the star circuses, and some of the crew think we ought to stay in the Ninth and slug it out with Arnheim. We've whipped him every other time he's tried something."

The Governor chuckled. "Yes, we have." His face grew serious. "But I'm not in business to fight, Pirate; I'm in the entertainment business." He held a hand out toward the front view ports. "There's thousands of planets out there just itching to see their first circus, and neither of us will live long enough to play them all. The Universe is big enough for this show and the Abe Show. All we have to do is move over a little bit. The price of not moving over is higher than I want to pay."

A loud pop resounded throughout the bridge, causing all heads to turn in the direction of the Boss Porter. Wall-eyed Mike held up the green bottle. "One minute to the Quadrant line." Wall-eyes turned and called to the bridge conference room.

Bald Willy stood up from the pilot's chair. "Everything on automatic, and let's do some damage to that jug of Wall-eyes'."

O'Hara clapped Jon on the shoulder, turned and went to the table. Jon studied the panel for a second, then flicked on the automatic alarm systems. He gave the panel a last look, then swung his chair around, stood and joined the others in the center of the bridge.

The bridge crew was joined by the non-bridge personnel from the conference room that the Governor had invited for the ceremony. Iron Jaw Jill, Sweetie Pie, and her mother. Duckfoot would be down cracking a keg with the roughnecks while Pony Red would be with the animal men in the menagerie. Kristina the lion lady, Madam Zelda, Pretzels the female contortionist, Fish Face. . . . Wall-eyed Mike held out a thin-stemmed lead-crystal glass filled with a bubbling, light golden liquid. When all of the persons on the bridge had gathered around the table and held glasses, the Governor looked at his watch for a few moments, then looked up. "That's it; we've crossed the line." He held up his glass. "To the season."

"To the season," they all repeated, then sipped from their glasses. As Jon swallowed, then raised his glass for a second sip, every alarm on his engineering panel began screaming.

His glass fell to the deck as he rushed back into his station chair and quickly scanned the instruments. He didn't need to look; he knew everyone on the bridge would be at their stations. He punched the comm for the pilot's station. "Willy, it's the pods. They're going out of match." Jon's fingers flew over the buttons. "I can't arrest it." He punched for the aft engineering section. "Animal!"

"This is Lefty, Pirate. Animal's up in the portside pod mount."

"Get them out of there! We're going to dump the pods!"

"What?"

"You heard me! Get them out of there. We don't have more than a couple of minutes!" Again Jon punched for the pilot. "Willy, I can only give you another two minutes of light drive, then we're going to have to dump the pods. You'd better get us headed to the nearest star and hope like Hell there's a habitable planet around it."

The Governor rushed to the pilot's station. "What about it, Willy?"

The pilot's fingers flew over the keyboard of his console. "The nearest star is . . . four light-years . . . *no data*?" He looked up at O'Hara. "We're already off the major trade routes. If we go to this place, we'll never be found."

"What about the distress beacon?"

Willy shook his head. "I already tried it. It won't jettison." He raised an eyebrow and looked at O'Hara. "It has to be sabotage."

O'Hara felt the color drain from his face. "Can we make it to a trade route?"

Willy shook his head. "We'd need light for at least eighteen minutes to make it to a trade route." Again he shook his head. "Still, if we head toward this star we'll be even further out of the way."

O'Hara scratched the back of his neck, then thrust his hands into his pockets. "Willy, if you're right about this being sabotage, we'd better do what we can about getting everyone off of this ship, and as soon as possible. Head for the star. Does it have a name?"

"No."

As Willy swung the ship to the right, the Governor walked over to the engineering section. "What about it, Jon?"

"Looks bad." He pointed at a readout. "Matching is already over critical. We heading for safe ground?"

"Yes. Willy said the nearest star is about four light-years away."

Jon did some mental calculations. "Then if I can keep the pods on another two and a half minutes, we'll be within impulse range." He punched for the aft engineering section. "Lefty. Is Animal's crew out of the pod yet?"

"Lefty here, Pirate. Everybody but Animal is out. The rest of the crew is standing by to close up the port."

"Never mind about that. Get them out of there, and when Animal gets out, seal off the compartment."

"Right."

Jon studied the readouts, flicked switches, and sweated. "Nothing's slowing it down, Mr. John. It's like every safety interlock in the joint has been shorted out." He punched again for the aft engineering section. "Lefty, run up that pod mount and chase Animal's butt out of there! We're running out of time!"

"Pirate . . . wait! Here he comes now, and he's pulling someone with him!"

"I thought you said the rest of the crew was out of there."

"I did, and they are. This is someone else. Have to go and help Animal. I'll call back when we have the compartment sealed off."

Jon watched the mismatch readout climb from the orange into the red. He punched the comm for the pilot's station. "Willy . . . how close are we? I have to pull the plug pretty soon."

"Almost there, Pirate. About twenty-five billion kilometers—"

"Pirate, we're out and the compartment's sealed!"

Jon slammed his right palm against the emergency pod jettison panel and a loud slam shook the ship. A row of red lights blinked on Pirate's panel as the impulse attitude correction systems attempted to push the wallowing ship on course. "It's the dorsal rear docking port . . . the *Blitz* must have been sheared off." He flicked switches and the screen above his panel showed the half-crippled advance ship struggling to get under power. The starboard pod was nowhere to be seen, but the port pod revolved dangerously close to the craft. "C'mon, Stretch. Get that crate under pow—" The screen went white, then dead.

O'Hara shook Pirate's shoulder. "What's wrong with the screen? Why can't we get a picture?"

Pirate watched as a row of red lights blinked off, signaling the successful sealing of the dorsal port. "The receptors in the rear cameras . . . they're burned out from the flash."

"Stretch! What about Stretch?"

Pirate shook his head. "Stretch, Fisty, Razor Red, and the others . . . they never knew what hit them." Pirate punched at his panel. "Dorsal engineering. Anybody there?"

"Here, Pirate. This is Nuts."

"Damage report."

"Except for a few bloody noses, we're all right. My board shows the *Blitz* missing."

Pirate closed his eyes for a moment, then opened them. "They've been exed." He punched again at the panel. "Willy, how close?"

"Twenty-three and a third billion . . . take us close to twenty-eight days on impulse. I hear right on the *Blitz*?"

"Yes." Pirate punched again. "Animal?"

"I'm here, Pirate. Been listening on the net."

"Animal, who's that guy you pulled out?"

"It's hard to tell. He's been burned pretty bad. He was caught in the pass/repass field up near the pod. Lefty's trying to see if he can find some identification . . . okay, here it is." Jon heard paper crackling. "I remember. He's an engineer we picked up when we were laying up on Palacine. His name's Stake Killing—funny name."

"Spell it."

"S-t-e-k-t K-y-l-l-i-n-g. Wait . . . there's more paper in here." Jon and the Governor heard a long, low whistle. "Pirate, you'll never guess who this guy is."

Jon reached out a hand toward the comm switch. "Karl Arnheim. right?"

"Right, but—" Jon Norden punched off the comm, then looked at O'Hara.

The Governor lowered his eyebrows a few notches. "How did you know it was Karl Arnheim?"

Jon leaned back in his chair. "Stekt Kylling. It's Norwegian for roast chicken." He shook his head. "And we always thought old Karl didn't have a sense of humor." He punched for aft engineering. "Animal, I want your crew to go over every rivet, nut, bolt, and connection in this ship, inside and out. There's no telling what else he buggered up, but you can count on it not being easy to find. Remember, he owned the outfit that built this ship." Pirate punched off, then looked at the Governor. O'Hara was staring at the dead screen, his eyes bright, a fist held to his mouth. He lowered his hand and looked at Pirate.

"Could he have died before he damaged anything else?"

"I doubt it, Mr. John. He knew enough to bypass our monitors and safety interlocks before throwing the pods into mismatch. Had to know he'd die if he remained in the pass/repass field more than ten seconds. I don't think he'd do that unless he was sure our number was up too."

O'Hara nodded, then rubbed his eyes. "I'll be off the bridge for a half hour or so, Pirate."

"Where will you be—in case we need you?"

The Governor lowered his hand. "I'll be at the family quarters telling . . . well, telling them." He turned slowly and left the bridge.

Pirate punched in another code and the screen came to life with a display of the *Baraboo's* general schematic. "Somewhere in there old Karl has left a few more surprises for us."

FOURTEEN

ROUTE BOOK, O'HARA'S GREATER SHOWS 15 APRIL 2148.

Enroute to star system 9–1134. Fuel tanks for impulse and maneuvering power ruptured. Still maintaining forward speed, relative to g–1134, of 6000 kps, but will need both forward and maneuvering power for course corrections and to make orbit, always supposing there is something there to orbit. Oxygen regeneration system sabotaged, reducing capacity to twenty percent. Water recycler sabotaged, all outside communications are out. . . .

Bone Breaker Bob Naseby, the ship's surgeon, looked across Karl Arnheim's blackened corpse at the Governor. O'Hara was studying the body, his face a reflection of the many unanswered questions that tormented his mind. He looked up at the surgeon. "Bone Breaker, why did he do it? We're nothing compared to A&BCE, and he could have hired all the talent he needed to destroy this ship. He had everything. Why'd he do it?"

Bone Breaker looked back at the corpse. Why did he do it? "Some people believe themselves in control of things. Movers and shakers." The surgeon shrugged. "I think you shook his faith in that. He's had three years since that stunt he pulled on us back on Mystienya fell through to stew about it. There's that, and Karl Arnheim was a very sick man. The brain scan I did shows a tumor located on the frontal lobe."

"He was crazy?"

"Well . . . perhaps that might be one way of putting it. The tumor is small, but I'm certain that it contributed to his behavior." Bone Breaker looked at O'Hara. "If he had had medical treatment, he could have had this fixed with a three-day stay in a hospital." He looked back at the corpse. "But first he would have had to admit that something had control of him, then he would have had to find the three days."

O'Hara nodded and smiled. "Not Karl Arnheim. He would have given you his left leg before he'd give you a day of his time."

"Well, he's not in control anymore."

O'Hara frowned. "Don't you bet on it. The air's already getting so thick you can taste it, and we still haven't figured out how to maneuver once we reach that star system—if we reach it." He nodded toward the corpse. "Karl's still running this show—for the time being, at least."

Jon Norden entered the sick bay, nodded at Bone Breaker, then turned toward O'Hara. "We have a problem. We've figured out how to rig the shuttle engines to operate from the bridge, which will give us at least some maneuverability once we reach that star system. We've got a lot of lightening up to do for it to work. But about the air. Pony Red—"

O'Hara frowned. "No one in a circus is going to be understanding about killing off the animals. Especially not the Boss Animal Man."

Pirate Jon held out his hands. "I don't want to kill them, but do you realize how much air just one of the bulls uses? We won't last more than another two or three days running our air at twenty percent, and then the animals will be dead anyway. But everyone else will be dead as well."

"What's Pony Red done?"

Jon lowered his hands. "He's sealed himself in the menagerie shuttle along with the led stock and exhibits. He threatens to cut loose if we try and force the docking port."

O'Hara cocked his head toward the door. "Let's go."

Pirate Jon followed the Governor out of the compartment into the main corridor leading to the portside shuttles. At the end of the corridor, O'Hara noticed three men standing at the sealed port to the menagerie shuttle. The Governor nodded at the three as he and Pirate Jon slowed to a stop before the port. Jon nodded at one of the men. "What's he say now, Goofy?"

Goofy shook his head. "He won't open up, and to tell you the truth, I don't blame him."

"Did you cut off the air?"

Goofy nodded. "He's running off of the shuttle's supply right now. With all the bulls and things in there he can't last more than two, three days."

One of the other men, Fatlip Louie, pulled at his namesake, then looked at Jon and O'Hara. "He's got respirators in there—special ones for the animals. I bet he could drag it out another day or two with them." Fatlip raised his eyebrows at the Governor. "Say . . ."

O'Hara grabbed Jon by the arm. "What about the shuttle air supplies and the respirators? Can we make it figuring those in?"

Pirate Jon pulled a computer from his belt and performed a series of calculations. He studied the results, pursed his lips, then repeated the series. He looked up at O'Hara. "Mr. John, according to my figures, using every possible air source and supply, including all of the respirators and vaccum suit supplies, and supposing that the regenerator on the ship remains operating at twenty percent capacity, and supposing that everyone takes it real easy the rest of the way, we might make it with nothing to spare." He shrugged. "Maybe."

O'Hara nodded, then turned to Goofy Joe. "Tell Pony Red his animals are off the hook."

Pirate Jon shook his head. "Mr. John, leaving the animals alive gives us no safety margin at all."

O'Hara nodded at Goofy Joe. "Tell him." He turned his head toward Jon. "Think about something, Jon. Why were the Bellenger pods buggered such that we had time to jettison them before they tore the ship apart? Not only that, but long enough to allow us to get within impulse range of that star system? Why did Karl Arnheim rig the air regeneration system to lose only eighty percent capacity? Why didn't he knock it out altogether?"

Jon shook his head. "What's your theory?"

"It's no secret that Karl would like to see this show destroyed." The Governor nodded. "I think it would appeal to Karl's sense of irony if he had us destroy ourselves." He turned and walked toward the bridge. As he left Jon and the others at the docking port, he turned his head and spoke over his shoulder. "We keep the animals, and everything else. Whatever else happens, this show survives!"

ROUTE BOOK, O'HARA'S GREATER SHOWS
27 APRIL 2148.

Enroute to star system 9–1134. Air stale, water short. Lightening of ship still in progress. Artificial gravity turned off to consume less oxygen. . . .

In the main sleeping bay, Motor Mouth swallowed against the free fall, then pushed himself over to Electric Lips' bunk. The usually florid-faced spieler was a touch of green around the gills. He looked over at Motor Mouth floating beside his bunk and grimaced. "Put your feet on the deck, Motor Mouth."

"Why? There's not much point in free fall."

Electric Lips glowered at his colleague. "Put your damned feet on the deck! Keep floating around like that and I'll aim my first load of cookies at you!"

Motor Mouth pulled himself to the deck. "Bone Breaker's spacesick pills aren't helping?"

"If God meant man to be in space, He wouldn't have given us stomachs." Electric Lips shook his head. "I can't get any sleep. When I close my eyes it's just awful, and so I keep them open. I swear my eyeballs are getting dusty!"

Motor Mouth cocked his head toward the other end of the sleeping bay. "I have something to get your mind off of your belly. Unstrap and come with me."

"Unstrap? You, my gum-flapping friend, are ready for the white rubber lot. I'd sooner rip out my tongue!" The image created in Electric Lip's mind at his most recent comment deepened his green. "Leave me, Motor Mouth. Leave me die in what little peace I can muster."

"Get up, Lips. Quack Quack's pretty down about the advance being exed. We ought to cheer him up. Come on. It'll give you something to do besides think about—"

"Silence! Don't say it!" With feeble fingers Electric Lips began pulling at his strap buckles. "Lordy, what I wouldn't give to be in jail right now." He rose, and together they pulled their way to the end of the compartment. Near the bulkhead, jammed between a conduit and a locker, they found the press agent, Quack Quack. He was staring at the dark wall of the locker, lost in thought. Motor Mouth pushed off from a bunk, caught the handle of the locker, then pushed himself to the deck.

"Hi, Quack Quack."

Electric Lips gulped, pushed off from another bunk and caught the conduit, thereby swinging himself around until he slammed into the bulkhead. He bounced, and—still holding onto the pipe—he swung back toward the locker where Motor Mouth grabbed him by his coat tails, then pulled him to the deck. As Motor Mouth helped Lips jam himself between the end of a rack of bunks and the lockers, Quack Quack shook his head.

"You two ought to look into putting your trunks in Clown Alley."

Electric Lips stopped his eyes from rolling, swallowed again, then aimed a sickly grin at the press agent. "You look a little down at the corners, Quack Quack. The Mouth and I decided to cheer you up . . . urp!"

The press agent shrugged. "I appreciate it, boys, but I guess I'm past cheering up. I should have been with Stretch and the boys on the advance. When the *Blitz* went . . . well, I'm just a little past it."

Motor Mouth frowned, then held out his free hand. "Lips and I have a disagreement. He says Buttons Fauglia pulled that Brighton number, but I say it was you."

Quack Quack turned to Lips. "Sorry Lips, but that was mine."

Electric Lips frowned at Motor Mouth, then turned back at Quack Quack. "I guess I have it fuzzy. Maybe you could refresh my memory?"

The press agent looked back at the locker wall. "That was a few years ago, wasn't it? That was back before I was in politics, and before I worked for that publicity firm in Chicago. I was with the Bull Show out of Glasgow, and we were stuck in Brighton. I mean, we didn't have penny one to put in the fuse box. Governor Bullard was near ready to dissolve the show, since we'd only been up for three nights and near playing to ourselves. Bullard's used to do two, three weeks at a stand like they do over there.

"Anyway, the customers just weren't turning out. The Governor he comes to me and says that we have to get the gillies to the tent; either that, or it's in the cart. Well, I thought on it some. I'd passed out the usual readers to the local papers, but editors won't use releases from a circus mediagent unless they're really starved for copy. If you remember, that was about the time that Northern Ireland lit up again and finally became a part of the Republic. The papers were squawking about that something terrible and we could have burned down the show and not gotten a line in print."

Motor Mouth nodded. "Those are cold days, true. Had a few like that with the Old One in Peoria. What did you do?"

Quack Quack rubbed his chin. "Well, you know that the trick is to get free space in the papers without the editors knowing it. They're always on the prowl for stunts, and you have to be on sharp toes to keep ahead of them. Well, I had a talk with Split Straw O'Toole. He was a trick shooter we had that was watering bulls while we were in England. About then the folks in Old Blight wouldn't have been too keen on us billing any shooter named O'Toole, if you know what I mean.

"O'Toole had kin up there in Ireland, and he called to make

a plant. That afternoon the constabulary up there happened upon a plan to raid Brighton and ex the Bull Show. Seems that the IRA was accusing us of being spies, and that justice needed doing. Now, it didn't matter that it had been four years since the Bull Show had toured Ireland. No one saw that, or even looked for it. The first thing was a screaming editorial in a Brighton paper that came out along with the story. Then, Governor Bullard had a press conference where he spat defiance at the blackguards who would attack a harmless show.

"Well, before you know it, the local citizenry turned out to show their support, but after a few speeches were made in Parliament, we had a couple of regiments standing guard on us, and buying tickets, too." Quack Quack shook his head. "From there on the tenting season was making coin. The story went in front of us and grew by the mile, allowing each local editor to vent spleen on his favorite patriotic subject. Next season we toured the Republic and just turned the story around a little, and the same thing when we toured the north. In the north, the IRA was after us, or the British depending on the town; in the Republic it was the Ulstermen after us, then back to the Old Blight with the IRA hot on our heels. We milked that stunt for three seasons until those papers finally realized just whose flag it was they were waving."

Motor Mouth cocked his head to one side. "Quack Quack, those shows over there; they call it tenting instead of touring or trouping, don't they?"

"Yes. I always liked what they called jobs over there. Tent Master is what they called the Boss Canvasman. And do you know what they call canvasmen?"

Electric Lips shook his head. "What do they call them?

"Czechs."

Motor Mouth frowned. "You mean like what you write out for money?"

"No. There was a town in a country called Czechoslovakia that did nothing but supply canvasmen to the European shows. So, they called them Czechs." The press agent turned toward Lips. "What are you studying on?"

Lips looked up smiling, his stomach forgotten along with Quack Quack's misery. "I heard you use a phrase that I've heard the Governor use every now and then. In the cart."

Quack Quack nodded. "In trouble. The shows over there use it."

"Wonder how that came to mean being in trouble?"

The press agent pursed his lips. "I think it comes from the

days of the Black Plague. They used to move carts through the streets to haul away the . . . dead." He returned his glance to the locker. "They'd call out 'Bring out the dead!' and then you'd haul your wife, your father, or whoever had died during the night . . . so when you're in the cart . . ."

Motor Mouth turned to Electric Lips. "That was terrific, Lips. I might even say inspired."

Lips frowned. "I'm sorry." Lips saw Motor Mouth going green. "Mouth, what's the matter?"

"Get me . . . a . . . bag!"

At the other end of the main bay, Weasel, the holder of the juice joint privilege, lay strapped in his bunk, licking his dry lips, and dreaming of enormous lakes of cool, clear water. He felt a hand shake his shoulder, the lakes disappeared, and he opened his eyes at a frown. Looking back was Wall-eyes Mike Ikona, the Boss Porter. "What'n the hell'd you do that for, Wall-eyes?"

Wall-Eyes held out a plastic squeeze bottle filled with a pink liquid. "Here. It's to drink."

Weasel raised an eyebrow. "Forget it. That stuff looks too much like pink lemonade."

"It is. We found five hundred gallons of it frozen in the ship's freezer."

Weasel shook his head. "I sell it; I don't *drink* it!"

"You'd better. There's not much else until they get the condenser rigged."

Weasel stared at the plastic bottle. "Why's it in a ketchup bottle?"

"You rather chase the stuff around the bay? C'mon, we got these from the grab joint supplies; they've never been used."

Weasel took the bottle, stared at it for a long moment, then inserted the nozzle into his mouth, making a face. He gave the bottle a squeeze, then removed it as he swallowed. His eyebrows went up and he smacked his lips. "Hey, that's not bad!"

Wall-eyes smiled. "You make a good product, Weasel. We're melting the stuff down in the pressure cookers, but we couldn't find your property lemon, so no floaters."

Weasel sipped again at the bottle, then shrugged. "What the hell, Wall-Eyes." He reached under his pillow and pulled out a bright yellow lemon. "This was supposed to last me the season, but what the hell—let's splurge."

*   *   *

Pirate Jon adjusted his pressure suit as he pulled his way toward the number ten shuttle. As he approached the docking port, he saw a small crowd of roughnecks gathered there. They stood silently, heads hung down. Pirate Jon stopped, noticed the red light on the lock cycle, then turned to the nearest canvasman. "Carrot Nose, why's number ten under vacuum?"

"The crew's out there dumping the main top." Carrot Nose snorted. "You ordered it."

Pirate Jon frowned. "I know, but they were supposed to wait for me. Who's bossing the cargo gang?" The faces gathered around the port grew noticeably longer. "Goofy?"

Goofy Joe rubbed his hand under his nose and sniffled. "Duckfoot."

"The Boss Canvasman? He doesn't know the first thing about moving cargo in free-fall. He's not even suit-trained."

Fatlip Louie gave a bitter chuckle. "The Boss Canvasman says if anybody's going to dump the old rag, it's going to be him. I wasn't going to argue with him."

Pirate Jon moved to the lock cycle. The shuttle side was open. He pressed the button to close the shuttle port, but the red light remained on. He turned to Goofy. "He's jammed the shuttle port open."

"Duckfoot don't want any interference. You got to understand, Pirate, that to Duckfoot, that old rag is as much a part of his family as Sweetie Pie or the Queen."

"We have to dump it boys, and everything else that we can. With the tops, sticks, rigging, blues, spool wagons, cats, and everything else in those shuttles gone, that'll be eight-hundred-plus tons less that the engines have to push against to make course corrections. . . ." He looked around at the faces. "There's something else. What is it?"

Fatlip shrugged, then shook his head. "Duckfoot, he looked awful different when he went in there." He looked at Pirate. "With the back doors of that shuttle open, and the old rag sailing off behind to who knows where . . ." Fatlip shook his head. Goofy Joe placed a hand on Fatlip's shoulder and looked at Pirate.

"Fatlip was going to say that it wouldn't take much for Duckfoot to jump out after the old rag, just to keep it company."

Pirate bit his lip as he smacked the lock cycle in frustration, then he pushed away. "I can't hang around here; there are other shuttles to be unloaded." As he made his way down the corridor, he saw Diane and Sweetie Pie heading in the opposite direction. He pulled up short as they stopped next to him.

Sweetie Pie's eyes were red. Pirate looked at Diane. "You heard?"

"Yes."

Pirate hung his head and averted his glance. "Maybe it'll be all right . . . I'm sorry."

Diane reached out a hand and placed it on Pirate's arm. "It's not your fault. Duckfoot has to do what he has to do." Diane looked down the corridor. "We ought to be waiting by the port." She released his arm, then the pair moved toward the number ten shuttle.

Pirate Jon pushed into a cross-corridor, then at the center of the ship he took another cross and moved to the dorsal passageway. As he reached the number one shuttle port, he found Warts, the route book man, waiting. The bumpy Pendiian turned his head in Pirate's direction. "Ah, I have found you."

"So?" Pirate pulled himself to a stop.

"The Governor sent me to tell you that the cally-ope stays. Everything else on the flying squadron can go, but the horse piano stays."

"That thing weighs almost four tons!"

The Pendiian shrugged. "I only bear the bad news, Pirate. I didn't devise it." Warts lowered his voice. "As far as I am concerned, the horse piano should be the *first* thing to go."

Pirate frowned. "Are you crazy? You have a vacuum inside that lumpy skull? Ditch the cally-ope?"

Warts shrugged, then pushed off. "Tender ears and an unfortunately refined taste in music are my only excuses."

Pirate turned into the open port, and amidst the forest of lashed wagons, cookhouse, and kid show equipment, Dr. Weems sat at his calliope, fingering the keys to a silent song. The Doctor looked up as Pirate approached. "I was just saying goodbye, Pirate. I've played many a ditty on these pipes."

"Well, say hello again. Mr. John says that it doesn't get dumped."

Dr. Weems' eyes grew wide. "The truth? Tell me, Pirate, do you speak the truth?"

Pirate nodded, then sighed. "But that's four tons I'm going to have to carve out of something else."

Weems clapped his hands together, then scratched his chin. "Pirate, you know you could lighten this thing up a bit if you drained the water out of the boiler."

"Water? That's right! How much is in there?"

"A hundred and twenty gallons . . . why?"

"Why didn't you say something? You know how short of water we are."

Weems shrugged. "I never thought of it for drinking. That stuff's pretty nasty. It's an iron boiler, you know."

"We can clean it up. A hundred and twenty gallons—that's another day on the company's ticket! More!"

The intercom signal sounded, and Pirate pushed his way to the docking port. He pressed the switch as he came to rest. "Pirate in number one."

"Pirate, this is Goofy outside of number.ten. They're closing up the shuttle doors. Thought you'd want to know."

Pirate switched off and pushed his way into the corridor. In moments he found himself pulling up to the number ten docking port. The lock was cycling, and as he came to rest, the hatch opened and a huge suited figure emerged. The ugly, unhelmeted head was Duckfoot's. Sweetie Pie pushed off and wrapped herself around the Boss Canvasman. "Hey!" He looked around at the grinning faces. "What's this?"

Diane moved next to Duckfoot and planted a kiss on his cheek. "This is just a welcoming party."

Duckfoot raised his eyebrows, then lowered them into the darkest of glowers. "You . . . you punks thought I was going to . . . *jump*? You think a show's nothing to me but a few yards of cloth?" He pushed away from the port, scattering his welcoming committee into the bulkheads. Sweetie Pie hung on and Diane kept up. She looked into Duckfoot's face and saw the tears. They entered the cross corridor toward the family quarters. He pulled up in the center of the cross corridor, placed one arm around Sweetie Pie and the other around Diane. "I sweat it. I swear I saw the old rag wave goodbye."

Jingles McGurk looked with disgust at his empty office. All of his furniture had been unbolted and tossed out along with his carefully kept ledgers, records, readers, and computer terminal. One thing remained to be removed—the shoulder-high safe bolted to the deck in the corner of the compartment. One and a half tons, it had to go. But first, Jingles had to open it to allow the cargo crew to cut the bolts from the inside.

Jingles pushed away from the bulkhead and came to rest against the brightly decorated safe door. He sighed, placed his left palm against the sensor plate, then punched in the combination with his right forefinger. A whirr, a click, then Jingles pulled open the door. Banded sheafs of credit notes and bags of coin floated weightless inside. He reached inside, pulled forth a pack of bills, then smiled as he broke the band and pushed the bills into the air. Pack after pack, he pulled them from the safe, broke the bands, then threw them into the air where they hung, drifting lazily in the air currents. After loosing the bills, Jingles opened the coin bags and emptied them by swinging the bags around his head. The safe empty, Jingles looked at the compartment, the air filled with bills and whirling coins. The treasurer smiled, pushed off from the deck, and somersaulted into the center of it.

"Wheeeee!"

FIFTEEN

ROUTE BOOK, O'HARA'S GREATER SHOWS 1 MAY 2148.

Enroute to star system 9–1134. Seven days to the star itself. Four planets can be easily seen, with three of them having orbits close enough to the star to make them uninhabitable. First course correction using the shuttle engines a total failure. Lisa "Bubbles" Raeder passed away. Kid show crew held services prior to her burial at space. Waldo Screener, the Ossified Man, has not been located after several intense searches, and is presumed to have joined his wife. . . .

Jon Norden tightened the last nut on the fuel connection, then rolled over onto the deck. "That's it."

"We hope."

Pirate Jon raised his head and looked at the Animal, sitting on the deck, his back against the bulkhead. Jon sat up and pulled himself across the deck until he leaned against the bulkhead next to his second engineering officer. "Animal, are you thinking about how we're going to have to hold this thing in orbit until the shuttles get free?"

Animal shook his head. "No. There's a lot of ways to die, and this one has to beat rotting away in bed as an old man."

Jon closed his eyes and leaned his head back. The thick air made his lungs gurgle slightly. "What then?"

"Look, Pirate. When we make orbit and everyone gets off on the shuttles except for the skeleton crew, air won't be a problem anymore—neither will water."

"So?"

"That'll give the crew time enough to repair the deep space communications—maybe even the emergency signal beacon. Anyway, we should be able to call for help after a few days."

Jon nodded. "That's what we're hoping. We can do it if we

can get these shuttle engines to work together making a good orbit."

"I've been thinking—or trying to think—the way old Karl would. There's not another star system within fifty light-years of this one, and I'll bet you anything this one has a habitable planet."

"Why?"

"I think Karl wants to maroon the show. Allow the show to make it down alive, then just let the circus piddle away. How long would it take for a bunch of people trying to survive to forget all about circuses?"

Jon shook his head. "If we get things working again we won't need to answer that."

Animal coughed, then nodded. "That's the way I think old Karl figured it too. You can't maroon someone if he can still yell for help."

Jon opened his eyes and looked at Animal. "You think Karl has another trick up his sleeve for us?"

Animal nodded, then let his head ease back against the bulkhead. "That's what I think."

"We've checked out practically every circuit, nut, bolt, and spring. What's left? What could we have overlooked?"

"I don't know." He shook his head. "I just don't know. We've run checks on everything possible . . ."

Jon frowned. "What is it?"

Animal moved his head forward. "The equipment we've been doing the checks with. Karl had enough smarts to bugger up your monitor so you wouldn't know what was going on until the pods had to be blown. What if he did the same to the other monitor and test equipment?"

"How can we check that out? Karl knew enough to reseal the engineering monitoring access doors."

Animal shrugged. "So, we unseal everything and go over it until we find something."

Jon closed his eyes, took a deep breath of the stale air, then pushed himself to his feet. "Let's get started."

Pony Red Miira returned from the number three shuttle's bull bay and shook his head as he sat down next to Waxy and Snaggletooth. "I know they kept the gravity on in the menagerie shuttle to keep from panicking the animals, but I wonder if it might be better to turn it off."

Snaggletooth shook his head. "They couldn't take it, Pony. At least they're quiet."

Waxy looked over at Pony. "How's Lolita?"

"The air's getting her. She's on the juice right now, but I'm afraid she'll suffocate if she lies down."

Waxy shrugged. "Take her off the juice, and she'll kick out the sides of the shuttle. The Governor know?"

Pony shook his head. "Mr. John's got enough on his mind. Snaggletooth, what about the cats?"

Snaggletooth shook his head. "All of them, the ones left, have got the wheezes. I don't figure them to last more'n two, three days."

They all looked up to see Kristina the Lion Lady enter the menagerie shuttle. She smiled at the three. "Almost seems odd to be under gravity." She cocked her head toward the back of the shuttle. "Pony, I'm going back to see my kids."

"Sure."

The three waited in embarrassed silence until Kristina had made the turn and had disappeared between the lashed-down cage wagons. Waxy rubbed his nose, then leaned back against a straw bale. "Kris grew up with them cats. Her momma used to make them dance the hoops, remember?"

Snaggletooth nodded. "Sure. I remember when Momma Kris's old man got clawed. What was his name?"

Pony frowned. "Charlie. Wasn't with us long, was he?"

Snaggletooth shook his head. "Those cats're gonna die, Pony. Kris won't take it easy."

Pony raised his eyebrows and nodded. "At least the horses and most of the bulls are holding up. Too bad about the apes—" Seven shots in quick succession deafened the three animal men, startling the animals into howls, roars, and screams. Before the three had made it to their feet, an eighth shot slammed against their eardrums. Pony rushed between the cage wagons, saw Kristina crumpled on the desk, then stopped as he saw the lions in their two cage wagons, limp and dead. He stooped over, turned Kristina over on her back, then noted the eight-shot Kaeber in her hand, and the tiny hole in her right temple.

Grabbit Kuumic, Boss Property Man, held the bulb box in his hands and frowned at Waco Whacko. "I dunno, Waco. We're supposed to dump all this stuff to lighten the ship."

Waco stared at the Boss Property Man with dark-circled brown eyes. "I don't want the bulbs, Grabbit; just the box."

"Well, what do you need it for?"

Waco's hands shot out and grabbed the box, pulling it out of Grabbit's grasp. "You want to know?" He opened the box, removed the six main lighting array bulbs, and let them float in the air. "If you want to know, come with me!" Grabbit turned and followed the snake charmer into the main center corridor toward the family quarters. Waco pulled himself into one of the doors lining the corridor. Grabbit stopped at the door and looked into the compartment. Strapped down on four cots, five to a cot, were Waco's twenty snakes from Ssendiss. They all looked asleep. Waco went to one of the cots and stroked one of the snakes. "Hassih, I have the box."

The snake opened its eyes, emitted a hiss, then closed them. Waco hung his head, then opened the box. He reached into the coil of one of the snakes, withdrew an egg, placed it into one of the box's compartments, then moved on to another snake. Grabbit frowned. "What it is, Waco? Are they all right?"

"They're dead . . . all of them, now. It's the air."

Grabbit shook his head. "I'm sorry, Waco. What about the eggs? Is there something I can do?"

"No." Waco went to another snake and withdrew another egg from deep in the reptile's coil. "All I needed was the box. I can't have those eggs floating around in here; they'll get damaged."

"What'll you do with them, Waco? How long do they take to hatch?"

Waco placed another egg into the box. There were five of them, fist-sized and bright blue. He closed the box and held it with both hands. "The way we reckon time, Grabbit, these eggs will take close to two hundred and seventy years to hatch. Whatever happens, I have to see that they get taken care of. I promised them." He turned his head toward the dead snakes.

Grabbit shook his head. "Waco, you'll be long gone by then. Who's to take care of them when you're in the big lot?"

"My sons and daughters, and their sons and daughters."

"You married?"

"Not yet. But I will be." He turned toward the dead snakes, closed his eyes, and shook his head. "I promise these eggs will hatch, Hassih, Sstiss, Nissa . . . all of you. You won't be forgotten."

Grabbit pulled his way out of the doorway and left the snake charmer alone.

SIXTEEN

ROUTE BOOK, O'HARA'S GREATER SHOWS
2 MAY 2148.

Enroute to star system 9–1134. Six days to go. Artificial-gravity power-supply has been rigged to crack water, releasing oxygen. This has helped the breathing some, but leaves us even shorter on water . . .

Peru Abner Bolin looked up from his bunk to see the Clown Alley gang gathered around. He turned to Cholly. "What is this, Cholly? A wake?"

"Peru, maybe we can get the gravity turned on in here, or at least we can move you to the menagerie shuttle—"

"No, no. Boys, the breathing's a lot easier without the gravity."

"Can't Bone Breaker do anything?"

Peru Abner slowly shook his head. "What's ailing me, Cholly, is something only a time machine could fix. Bone Breaker's all out of 'em." The old clown closed his eyes, then turned his head toward Cholly. "That Mutt and Jeff routine Ahssiel and I did . . . wasn't that a corker?"

Cholly nodded. "I wish the little plug was here right now." Peru Abner frowned. "I don't mean in this fix, Peru. But he'd want to be here with you."

"The boy's a prince, Cholly. He's got responsibilities." Peru Abner smiled. "Bet he'll make a dandy Monarch when his time comes. Can't you see him holding court dressed in motley?"

Cholly shook his head. "You were a pair, all right." He ducked as Stenny missed a handhold and went careening into a bulkhead. Peru Abner reached out a hand and shook Cholly's arm.

"It's too bad you can't do your number in free fall, Cholly. It'd be a sidesplitter."

Cholly raised his brows and smiled. "Peru, you never liked my act. You neat clowns never did go for tramps."

Peru Abner turned down the corners of his mouth and shook his head. "Jealous, that's all. The customers laugh at my stuff—my sophisticated stuff—but those belly laughs you got, Cholly; boy, did I envy those." The old clown flew into a coughing spasm, then quieted down as his eyelids grew very heavy. "I always liked your act, Cholly. I'd like to see it again."

Cholly shook his head. "I don't feel very funny."

Peru Abner reached out a hand and grasped Cholly's arm. "What we do is art! For fun we play cards, cut up jackpots, get drunk. When we perform, that . . . that's for the soul. Perform for me, Cholly." He raised his eyes to the rest of the Joeys gathered around his bunk. "All of you. I want to see all of you. Go on. Make fools of yourselves."

Cholly paused for a moment, then, with neither gravity nor makeup, he pushed away from the bunk, steadied himself in midair between two upper bunks, then began his poor soul act, depicting the tramp that never succeeds but has an everlasting flame of hope in his threadbare soul. The other Joeys went into their pratfalls and comic dramas, and in seconds the entire performance was chaos mixed with gales of laughter as clown after clown collided with either bunk, coworker, or bulkhead. Cholly tried, but he could not maintain the deadpan expression that had become his trademark. He laughed until the laughter brought tears to his eyes, then he steadied himself and pushed toward Peru's bunk. He caught the railing, then shook his head. "Damn, Peru, can we get free-fall planetside? This is great! If they have artificial gravity, maybe we can figure out an artificial free-fall for the breakout . . ." Cholly looked at Peru's face, eyes still open, his face relaxed, but smiling. "Peru?" He shook Peru's arm. The great clown had died.

ROUTE BOOK, O'HARA'S GREATER SHOWS
3 MAY 2148.

Enroute to 9–1134's planet. Second attempt at course correction successful, but leaving shuttle fuel low. We should intercept the nameless planet on the 8th. A name-the-planet contest is being conducted to raise spirits. The Governor suggested "Momus" after the ancient Earth god of ridicule. One of the bulls, Lolita, died under tranquilization. The Governor's health is failing as well. . . .

Warts Tho looked up from writing in the route book and glanced around the bridge at the crew manning the stations. Pirate Jon, strapped into his chair, was asleep, his head back. Bald Willy hung over his console, his only movement being a chest heaving for air. Since the communications bank was dead, the chair before it was empty. The Pendiian shook his head and looked at the screen above Pirate Jon's station. The tiny planet had grown noticeably larger. The blue-white orb had small polar ice caps, large landmasses, and small oceans. Water covered only fifty percent of the surface. It would be a dry place, but habitable. The planet had no moons—not even one.

Warts closed the route book and stuck his pen in his jacket pocket, entertaining thoughts of the foolish sailor who went down with his ship while completing the ship's log. He unbuckled himself from his chair, tucked the route book under his arm, then pushed toward the bridge's entrance. He took a last look at the screen and was startled to see that a pile of twisted wreckage was crossing the *Baraboo*'s path. "Pirate!" Warts pushed himself to the Chief Engineer's station and slapped Pirate's back. "Pirate! Wake up!" He turned to the pilot and shouted to the pilot. "Bald Willy! Do you see that ahead?"

Bald Willy looked around at Warts, then looked up at the screen. He turned back and punched in a code to illuminate his own screen. Pirate looked up, rubbed his eyes, then looked again. "I'll be a bull's backside. It's the *Blitz*." Sparks came from part of the wreckage. "Willy, it's under power! See the attitude correction jets?"

"Got you, Pirate." Willy punched at his console, then shouted into it. "Marbles, where are you?"

Pirate cut in. "Willy, the radios are still out."

"Yeah, but Marbles can read code. See that flashing light in the middle of that mess—just forward of the dorsal shuttle?"

Pirate squinted at his screen. "Yeah . . . I can just make it out. That looks like code, too." He shook his head. "How'd Stretch ever push that nightmare this far? When the pods went, they must have blown him quite a distance."

Warts waited until Marbles Mann, the ship's Chief of Communications, came on the bridge. He pulled himself over to Bald Willy's side. "What's up?"

Bald Willy nodded at his screen. "See that flashing light?"

"Yes. It's code . . . *Baraboo* . . . answer . . . wake up . . . hey rube . . ." Marbles looked at Bald Willy's console. "Where's the button for the forward docking lights?" Willy pointed to one of a row of square, orange buttons. Marbles talked as he stabbed at the button. "Jerkface . . . is . . . that . . . you?"

The flashing from the *Blitz* ceased for a moment, then resumed. "Marbles . . . you . . . pick . . . great . . . times . . . to . . . sleep."

"What . . . is . . . your . . . condition?"

"How . . . do . . . we . . . look . . . stop . . . plenty . . . broken . . . bones . . . stop . . . no . . . one . . . dead . . . stop . . . all . . . in . . . sleeping . . . bay . . . for . . . party . . . when . . . it . . . hit . . . the . . . fan."

Warts pushed away from Pirate's chair and headed toward the Governor's quarters.

*   *   *

The Governor's door hissed open and Warts stuck in his
head. The compartment was dark. "Mr. John? Mr. John?"

"Who . . . who's that?" The voice was very small and weak.

"It's me, Mr. John, Warts." He pushed into the compartment. "It's Stretch, Mr. John. The *Blitz* is back!"

"Say it . . . say it again, Warts."

Warts pulled up to the Governor's bed and turned on the
small reading lamp. The Governor's face was chalk-white, thin,
with large circles under half-closed eyes. He was straining against
his straps. "The *Blitz*. Stretch and the advances are back."

"How many dead, Warts?"

"None!"

O'Hara relaxed and let his head go back onto the cot. "That's
. . . good news." He closed his eyes and nodded. "Can the
Blitz make light speed?" He looked at Warts. "What about it,
and its communications? Can it transmit on deep space?"

Warts placed a lumpy hand on the Governor's arm. "Willy's
finding out about that now."

O'Hara gasped, then coughed. When his lungs quieted down,
he turned his head toward the Pendiian. "Warts?"

"Yes, Mr. John?"

"Thank you . . . thank you for coming to tell me."

"I thought you'd want to know right away."

"How does the *Blitz* look?"

Warts shook his head. "Looks pretty banged up. I didn't
even recognize it when I saw it."

O'Hara frowned, then nodded. "You been keeping up with
the route book?"

"Yes."

The Governor closed his eyes. "How long have you been
with the show, Warts?"

"This is my fifth season—well, it would have been—"

"It still will be."

Warts shook his head. "I don't understand."

O'Hara sighed, then coughed. Quiet again, his breath came
in short gasps. "I don't think . . . we're getting out of this one,
Warts. Maybe the crew can keep the ship in orbit . . . maybe
they can fix the beacon. Now that the *Blitz* is back, maybe . . .
maybe our chances are better." He shook his head as he coughed.
"If we get stuck on the planet, the show is in for the toughest
season it ever saw. No audience . . . hard work, scrabbling to
survive. It'll die, Warts. The show . . . the *circus!*" O'Hara
looked about, his eyes darting back and forth in their sockets.
"Warts? Warts?"

Warts squeezed the Governor's arm. "I'm right here, Mr. John."

O'Hara relaxed a bit. "We've got O'Hara's Greater Shows on board this rocket to Hell . . . the circus. The best of all the circuses . . . that ever existed." O'Hara's head rocked back and forth. ". . . the circus'll just fade . . . away. . . ."

"Mr. John?" Getting no answer, Warts leaned over the Governor and shook his shoulders. "Mr. Jo—"

The Governor's right hand shot out and grabbed Warts by the back of his neck, then a strong arm pulled the Pendiian's head next to O'Hara's lips. "Warts . . . never . . . never let these people forget who they are. Never . . . let them forget. . . ."

The hand relaxed, then the arm went limp and floated in the air. The Pendiian stared at the Governor for a long moment. Then Warts pushed away from the bed and came to rest against the Governor's desk. He turned on the light then and looked for the route book. He found it hovering at the foot of the Governors bed. He retrieved it, moved back to the desk, then opened it.

3 MAY 2148.

Enroute to Momus. *Blitz* has returned with all hands. John J. O'Hara has passed away.

AFTERSHOW

Horth Shimsiv, Ninth Quadrant Admiralty Officer, Investigations Division, turned the last sheet of the huge, hand-bound volume, then looked up at the young human dressed in black-and-white-diamond-patterned robe. "Well, what happened then?"

The young fellow roused himself from a doze, rubbed his eyes, then stood and joined the officer on the other side of the adobe shack. "What was your question?" He held out his hand.

The officer frowned and reached into his pocket for some of the little copper things they used for money on Momus. Taking several, he dropped them into the fellow's hand. "What happened after this? I'm here to investigate the actual accident."

The young fellow walked to a rough plank shelf containing several similar volumes and pulled one down. He turned and placed it before the officer. "What you read was the *Book of Baraboo*. You said you wanted to know about the ship. This volume is the first *Book of Momus*. I think it tells about the landing."

The officer frowned. "You don't know?"

The young man blushed. "I'm but an apprentice priest, Officer Shimsiv. Perhaps you would like to speak to the Boss Priest of our order, Great Warts."

"Warts?"

The young man nodded. "He is the last living member of the company that flew on the *Baraboo*. Please, come this way." He turned and walked to the back of the room, and halted next to a black-and-white-diamond-patterned curtain. Horth Shimsiv pushed his bulk to his feet, relaxed his tail, and straightened his uniform as he approached the door and came to a halt next to the apprentice priest. The young man lifted the curtain and stuck in his head. "Great Warts?"

"What is it, Badnews?" The voice was high-pitched and cracked.

"The officer from the Admiralty Office wishes to speak to you."

"Send him in; send him in."

Horth followed the apprentice into a small, dark room. In the back of the room sat a tiny Pendiian dressed in the familiar black and white diamonds. Before the old priest's comfortable wicker chair was a low table upon which were three cards: two jacks and an ace of hearts. "I've read the first book, Mr. Warts, but I still haven't learned what I need to about the actual crash."

The Pendiian leaned back in his chair, and held out his hand. Horth glowered, then dropped some coppers into it. "Well, thank you, officer . . . ?"

"Horth Shimsiv."

"Yes. Sit. Sit."

Horth found a rude wooden stool before the table and seated himself. "What about the crash?"

Warts nodded. "A sad day and a proud day."

"Meaning?"

The Boss Priest flipped over the three cards, then moved them around. When he stopped, he left them in a straight line, then looked at Horth. "Care to buy a chance on finding the ace?"

Horth frowned. "No thank you. What about the crash?"

Warts sighed. "Well, you know the *Baraboo* made orbit?"

"The book didn't say, but I assumed something of the sort."

Warts nodded. "Well, when the shuttles were loaded and on their way to the surface, the crew on the *Baraboo* must have found out whatever Karl Arnheim's last surprise was. As soon as we left, Pirate Jon was going to try and put the ship into a permanent orbit with the computers. The surprise must have been in there, because the ship dove and burned in the atmosphere before the first shuttle touched down." The Pendiian looked down and shook his head.

"What then?"

Warts looked up, collected his thoughts, then nodded. "Well, the shuttles hardly had any fuel. We couldn't do any fancy formation flying, so we went down when and as we could. Four of the shuttles did land together near here next to Tarzak. Four of them landed in different places up north, a couple landed west of here, and one went clear across the water to the next continent." The Pendiian shook his head. "Took us three years to get back together again. The parades started looking good after that."

"Parades?"

Warts raised his brows, then laughed. "Parades. Why, twenty minutes after our first shuttles touched down, we made formation and went on parade." He leaned forward as though he were explaining something to a mentally arrested child. "That's what O'Hara's always does after it makes a stand." He leaned back and smiled. "The service—the parade—the next year was better. We had a road cut to Miira by then, so we had the rubber mules—elephants—in the formation."

Horth shook his scaled head, then frowned at the Boss Priest. "I've seen cultures orient themselves around numerous things—making religions out of them. But . . . they were survival things with laws concerning food, sex, social organization. But, a *circus?* I've looked around this town a little, and everyone is either a clown, an acrobat, a magician, or something else. Keeping up these skills and passing them on, in addition to trying to feed, clothe, and shelter yourselves these past fifty years, must have wrought terrible hardships upon you. Why? Why did you do it? A circus, of all things. Why?"

Warts rubbed the bumps on his chin. "I thought you said you read the first book."

"I did. Still, I don't understand."

Warts studied the officer for a few moments, then shrugged. "It's a disease."

Horth sighed, then got to his feet. "Well, thank you, Mr. Warts. If I need more information we'll be sending someone down." The officer bowed, turned, then left the room.

Badnews held up his hand. "Great War—"

"Shhh!" Warts waited a few moments until he could hear

Horth's footsteps on the gravel path outside. "Now, my boy; what was it?"

Badnews frowned. "I've never seen one before, Great Warts, although I've read of them in the Books. Was that a rube?"

Warts rubbed his bumps, then nodded. "Yes, my boy, that was a rube." The old Pendiian pushed up the sleeves to his robe and flexed his fingers. He gathered up his three cards and put them down, face up. "And there's a whole shipload of them up there. Pardon me while I brush a little rust off of my game."

THE SPECKLED GANTRY

BY JOSEPH GREEN AND PATRICE MILTON

The red-and-gold Florida sun was just above the horizon when Davin Flynn reached his current work-site on the fifth level. Though the cloudless sky promised scorching heat later in the day, it was still cool this early in the morning; he hoped to finish this big patch by noon, then move into the shade. On the way down yesterday at quitting time he had noticed a really rusty area on an overhead beam next to the empty elevator shaft. That would be a better place to work during the worst of the heat.

Davin pulled the wire brush from his left-side wire holster and the paint scraper from the right one. The big steel I-beam he straddled was still moist with dew, hard and cold to a thinly fleshed bottom protected only by worn cotton pants. He started removing rust, scraping hard with the blade and finishing with the brush.

Davin soon noticed that his right arm felt okay today, but the arthritis in his left was getting worse. The linament he faithfully rubbed over arms and legs every night provided very little relief, but he kept using it anyway.

He worked hard for four hours, until he reached an area where the red paint was still firmly attached. His legs were almost numb with fatigue. Slowly he eased himself backward along the beam to the platform, then got to his feet. The overtaxed leg muscles spasmed and knotted; he hastily sat down again and kneaded them with his trembling hands, cursing the pain.

When he could move freely again, Davin opened a rusting can of zinc chromate. With the scraper he cut through the thick layer on top, and checked the contents. Still usable. Just a little thinner. . . . He poured paint and linseed oil into his mixing bucket, stirred vigorously. The gooey yellow-green substance resisted at first, then absorbed the oil and gradually turned fluid.

Davin filled his small can from the larger one and let it hang from the special hook on his belt. Sitting on the beam again, he worked his way out to the clean area and started painting, beginning at the most distant prepared area and working backward. The sides of this beam were barely rusty, and he had not scraped them; he painted both anyway. There was plenty of zinc chromate. He had discovered 400 one-gallon cans in an old POL locker in the deserted Cape Canaveral industrial complex.

It was too bad he couldn't get his hands on some of the "miracle paint" NASA had discovered during the Apollo Program. It had been used on the Golden Gate bridge in the early seventies, proving so resistant to salt and wind that it lasted three times as long as the conventional rust inhibitors. Yes, if he had a hundred gallons of that . . . as it was, new spots seemed to break out as fast as he painted old ones on this ancient steel tower.

"Hey, ol' man, you gonna' fall an' break your crazy head! You got nothin' better to do?"

Davin looked down in annoyance, but it faded when he recognized Leo Welch, Maria's boy. Leo seemed a little different from the other young people. He was one of the few who would listen to an old man retelling the exploits of the Space Program. Most got up and walked away when Davin started talking.

Leo climbed the stairs to the fifth landing, strong young legs making easy work of it. He was naked except for dungaree shorts, bronzed to a golden brown, muscular and sturdy as a youthful Spartan. The painting he could do, if he could be persuaded! . . . Davin shook his head, telling himself to forget it. No young man with such looks was going to spend his time working when he could be chasing girls instead.

Leo squatted easily on his haunches without sitting on the beam, looking around with interest. "Use'ta come up here sometimes when I was a kid," he said, pointing up at the old Payload Changeout Room. "My buddies met up there; 'sgot a great view. Say, you really done a lot o' work here. Are you keepin' up with the rust?"

Davin grinned at the friendly young man. "More than keeping up. I'm gaining. About another year and I'll be able to start work on one Crawler. After that, at least one check-out bay in the Vehicle Assembly Building." He looked to the southwest, where the giant bulk of the famous old building dominated the flat marshy land of Merritt Island. The blocky monument to Man's first trip away from Earth towered fifty-two stories high, a rusting monolith, the largest building in the world when it was constructed.

Leo looked doubtful. "I heard you say that before, but you don't ever seem to get caught up here." He looked around, scanning the peaceful water of Mosquito Lagoon to the north, the narrow neck of the Banana River just visible to the south. A freshening breeze blew in off the Atlantic, bringing a welcome touch of coolness. But it also brought salty vapor, the prime enemy of bare steel.

"Mama told me you didn't have any breakfast again this mornin'," Leo went on. "Don't you know that ain't good for you? A man needs his food."

One of the problems of living off the neighbors was that they knew when you ate. Sometimes there were bits and scraps of food in his little shack, more often not. "I wasn't hungry," Davin said, quite truthfully. He was seldom hungry, no matter how little he ate.

"Yeah, but you gotta keep up your strength. I'm going fishin' this afternoon. You be sure an' get back early, before the rest of the family gobbles it up."

Davin nodded. His young friend was quite right. To work, he must eat.

"You been scrapin' and paintin' on this old tower a long time now," Leo went on earnestly. "Why you botherin'? The Space Program ended before I was born. It ain't comin' back."

"Don't you say that!" Davin's voice held real anger. Leo looked away and shrugged. The older man softened his tone. "Believe me, Leo, someday one of the Space Shuttles stored in the VAB will be sitting upright on the Launcher Platform again. You'll live to see the mighty Crawler lift up the Platform, Space Shuttle and all, and bring them both to this pad. The computers will hum with their millions of data bits flashing back and forth, the oxygen and hydrogen tanks over there will be filled, and the old pumps will send the supercold fluids pouring into the Shuttle's expendable big tank. Someday men will again walk on the moon!"

Leo gave him a troubled look, one Davin had no difficulty interpreting. It said he was sixty-eight years old, maybe senile, a useless old fart who climbed around this abandoned steel wreck every day when he should be fishing instead. All the decaying equipment at this scene of past glories was falling down around his ears, while he tried to stop the onrush of time with a little scraping and painting. The Space Program was long dead. He should let it rust in peace.

"Well, I got to go. Don't you fall, now." Leo rose with muscular grace, and headed down the stairs. Davin saw one step bend beneath his weight. Leo nimbly hopped to the side, walking near the risers for the rest of the way.

Davin sighed. That rotten stairstep was chromate yellow. He had cleaned and painted it long ago.

Forcing himself to his feet, Davin stretched the stiffness out of his old joints. Then he carried the equipment and paint to the second floor deck, and started work on the rusty floor beam overhead.

He scraped and painted for the rest of the day, scarcely noticing he had missed lunch again. An hour before sunset he stopped. His hands were trembling so badly he could no longer hold his tools. That was due to lack of food, not fatigue alone. He placed paint cans and tools in an equipment room on the first floor and headed home, walking.

A few hundred yards north Davin stopped and turned, looking at the odd shape of the old Rotating Service Structure, the very special gantry designed for Space Shuttle launches. It was speckled from top to bottom with yellow-green blotches of zinc chromate. The tower that reared up adjacent to it was from one of the three Mobile Launchers used in the Apollo Program. It had been shortened, modified, and permanently installed at the pad for Space Shuttle launches.

The Launcher Platform now sitting on the pad was so large, he remembered, that tour guides pointed out to visitors how a baseball diamond could be laid out on one. The enclosed base itself was two stories high. It too had been adapted from the older Mobile Launcher.

The gantry looked as though it had contracted some form of mechanical leprosy, but at least it was still whole. Left to the unloving rain, sun, and salty wind, it would have fallen by now. He alone had kept the skeletal tower erect. It waited with mechanical patience to embrace another Space Shuttle, to hold the shuddering, fire-belching creation of Man's most advanced scientific knowledge in tender embrace. It waited to be brought back to life and use.

Davin turned away and walked north, eyes wet . . . and heard a familiar humming, whistling sound, followed by a hollow *thwaack!* A low heavy body burst from the brush almost at his feet, squealing madly. An arrow protruded from the hog's side. Another *thwaack!* sound, and a second arrow sprouted just below the black pig's thick neck.

The panic-stricken animal ran directly into Davin, knocking him down. Before he could regain his feet three bronzed young men had jumped from concealment, one with bow drawn back. The third arrow missed. The wild pig kept going, disappearing into thick brush fifty yards away.

The hunters ran fleetly after their prey. Davin tried to roll out of the way, but only succeeded in tumbling into the legs of the leader. He went down in a heap, and the second one then tripped over the two of them.

The third hunter, a little behind his companions, managed to leap over the tangle on the ground and keep going. He started around the brush pile concealing the hog.

Davin was hauled roughly to his feet, held erect before an angry young face. "Why the hell you always in the way, old man? We coulda got that pig if he hadn't seen you comin' and hid!"

"I'm—I'm sorry! Didn't know you were here!" Davin managed to gasp. The bronzed giant shook him until the old shirt tore, letting Davin fall to the ground again.

"You're useless, old man! You don't hunt, you don't fish. I oughta save the people from havin' to feed you." He fondled the hilt of his knife suggestively.

Davin knew this young man well, as he knew them all. Cory Desar, the son of the headman, was quite capable of murdering him and tossing the skinny corpse into the brush to feed the hogs.

"Please don't, Cory. My work—I have to keep the gantry in good shape. We'll need it again someday! Don't—please don't hurt me."

"Oh, you and that damn useless junkpile!" The anger was replaced by contempt and disgust. "It's dead, stupid! Don't you know we're never goin' back to that kind of life?"

"*Hey! I found the pig!*" came a distant shout, followed by a shrill squealing, abruptly cut off.

"Tomorrow morning I want to see you goin' out with the fishermen. Or tomorrow night you don't eat." Cory saw the stricken look on Davin's face, and the hard expression softened slightly. "Listen, Granpop, I know you're the last one left here who actually saw the big rockets flamin' off into nowhere. But those days are gone, man, gone forever. Don't you know we wouldn't build things like that again even if we could?"

Cory turned and started after his companions, breaking into an easy lope. His type would as soon run as walk.

It was still a half-mile up the coast to the collection of shacks Davin's little group called home. Most of the adults were coming in from the daily hunt for food as he arrived. All hands but his were filled with the usual clams, oysters, swamp cabbage, and horse bananas. They would be glad to hear there would also be roast pig.

Davin looked toward the Welch shack, and saw Leo cleaning a large trout. Several more were roasting over an open fire. He walked that way, sitting down on the wooden bench outside the flimsy structure.

Marie Welch gave Davin a tired smile, and served up a plate of fish and cabbage. He ate mechanically, not caring about the taste. It would give him strength for tomorrow.

In 1976, while the USA celebrated its great heritage of freedom from both need and bondage, Davin had stood on Cape Canaveral and watched demolition experts shatter two old gantries no longer in use. That fateful image had gone out on national television news, and from there around the world. Davin had stood, tears in his eyes, and made himself a solemn promise: No such desecration of Mankind's highest achievements should ever happen again.

Davin looked south to the splotchy tower, standing tall in the evening twilight. This visible symbol of the apex of human civilization had to be preserved. Tomorrow he would tackle that really bad area where the roof had almost rusted through on the upper deck. Tomorrow. . . .

THE NANNY

BY THOMAS WYLDE

I

Eismann woke up eighteen years too early.

He woke up panting, and the lights were on already. There was something wrong with the gravity; there wasn't any.

Surely, he thought, there ought to be *some* gravity.

The lid on his sleepbox was open and he heard two things: a high whistling sound like the air running out, and a faint clicking sound like an alarm bell tired of ringing.

Eismann's mouth was crackling dry, as evil-tasting as a mummy's cigar. His headache was increasing, but from somewhere deep inside, where his training was stored, came an urgent warning about the air pressure. . . .

He thought: The world is destroyed, or I wouldn't be here now.

It was an odd thought, and he searched his memory for help.

The last day. There had to be a Last Day. And a last *minute*, when they came for him, when his luck ran out—when everybody's luck ran out—but he couldn't find it.

He looked around. The room was familiar and anonymous—merely a small compartment, softly lighted. A jail cell, probably (he thought). There was a meal slot—not yet used—and another hole (he suddenly remembered) that would take his wastes and send them indirectly back to the meal slot. Tidy, but disgusting. Part of the game. (What game? he wondered.)

The alarm bell was still ringing—clicking, anyway—and Eismann figured it was about time to look into the matter.

He rolled painfully out of the sleepbox and floated free. He followed the whistling sound to a hole in the corner, down at deck level. Air was escaping through the hole at supersonic speed, passing out into interstellar space.

Space. I'm in space. Therefore the world is destroyed. . . .

The leak was small. Apparently something had hit the ship at the bulkhead. He guessed most of the damage was "below" him in the evacuated compartment where the eggs were stored.

The eggs . . . ?

Damn it, he thought. Why the hell didn't they leave him something to remind him what the hell was going on? A simple comic book, anything to jog his sleepy brain cells.

So—he was in interstellar space with the eggs, therefore the world was destroyed.

"And I only am escaped alone to—"

Job's messengers, he thought. But there were *four* of them. There are supposed to be two of *us*.

The other sleepbox was less accessible—the cramped shuttle didn't allow side-by-side arrangements. Eismann ignored for the moment the airleak—God knew how long it had already been leaking—and dove across the compartment for the second sleepbox.

There was the desiccated body of a man inside. The face was gone, but the name on the jumpsuit was familiar. It was Mackay, one of the meditechs at the orbital station—

Eismann suddenly remembered the station, how the ten of them had been in readiness, working the spy cameras and the laser downlinks, evaluating data, waiting suspensively for the Big Blowup.

—Mackay, the man everyone thought was a nark or a NASA spy. He must have been the one who put Eismann in the sleepbox and hooked him up. Then he tried to get himself set. And failed.

Things must have been pretty hectic at the end. A mutiny, maybe, or sabotage—anything to get free of the station and on the way. They had been pretty vulnerable up there, drifting along in the center of several laser cannon sights.

Eismann lowered the lid on the sleepbox. So much for his partner. Fine. Nobody liked the guy anyway.

You saved my life, he thought. Excuse me if I don't thank you right away.

He wanted to find out how bad things were first.

Eismann got busy.

He sealed the leak with some plastic gunk from a repair locker. In ten minutes the oxygen was steady at .3 atmospheres.

It was too late for his head or his raw throat. He went looking for the medicine dispenser and got some aspirin and something sour to suck on.

The alarm bell continued to click, so he checked the mission status board. It was then he found out he had awakened eighteen years too early.

There was no gravity because the deceleration burn was sixteen years away. He was still in the long coasting part of the trip.

Things were starting to drift back to him.

The mission—his crushing responsibility: in the event the world was destroyed, he and his ship were to leave the solar system on the small but not insignificant chance he could locate a habitable planet where the specially created and fertilized eggs could be brought into adulthood. A new race of Man, preserved and safe to start again.

It was Eismann's duty to raise the fortunate members of this new race, to nurture, and teach them, to protect and parent them—he was their Nanny. And he didn't even *like* children.

Now he was awake eighteen years too early, eighteen years before the first planet checkouts. Unless he could get his sleepbox working again, he'd have to hang around those eighteen years, losing his vitality all the while, waiting for the ship to reach the star system and analyze the first stinking, long-shot planet. And *if* it was habitable, he'd pop the eggs—twenty at a time—into the mechanical wombs.

A new generation every nine months—and there were twenty generations of eggs aboard. Enough colonists to go up against whatever a hostile planet could hit them with, enough warm bodies to survive the inevitable setbacks. Enough, maybe, to reestablish Man in the galaxy.

It wasn't going to be that easy.

Eismann found out why he was awake eighteen years early: whatever collided with the ship had damaged the liquid gas tanks. He came awake because his sleepbox had run low of coolant and triggered emergency revival procedures. There was no going back.

The same system supplied coolant for zygote storage.

Twenty generations of the last hope of Man were going to rot in the next compartment. The world *was* destroyed now, utterly.

(And I only am escaped alone to tell thee. . . .)

All right, Eismann. Heads up. There has to be *something* you can do.

He wedged himself in front of the computer terminal and began typing.

In ten minutes he'd transferred twenty eggs—ten each male and female—into the twenty wombs. As each zygote was encapsulated and monitored, he learned if it was alive or dead.

He had go to through a hundred eggs to find his twenty.

But they were the best twenty on the DNA lists, the most able-to-survive of an already impressively talented collection of genetically manipulated zygotes.

The cream of the crop, he thought.

(The proud Nanny . . .)

My twenty babies—you've got the Iceman on your side. We'll make it yet.

When he began asking some tougher questions, the computer kicked out an alarming message apparently left for him:

How do you like that, Eismann? You bastard sinner! How many more bombs are there? You're so smart—you know what Man needs to survive—you figure it out!

So it hadn't been a collision after all. A bomb.

There had been fanatical opposition to the so-called Egg Trip. (Who says Man may survive God's wrath?)

On the other hand, there were those who just hated Eismann—the Iceman—as they watched him move up the Last Man Alive List. Maybe they thought he moved up too fast, especially after Kathy's death.

Eismann shook his head slightly, more like a shiver. It had been an accident, but half of them thought he'd done it on purpose. In any case, the result of that midnight car crash was obvious: when Kathy died his stock rose. Now he was free, unattached (and unscratched)—a bona fide One Way Man. Kathy had been on that list too. . . .

Eismann cleared the message on the computer screen. There would be plenty of time to hash over the Good Ol' Days.

Back to work, sinner.

The ship's course had been thrown off by the explosion, but corrective burns had already been made. They were back on course, coasting at .2 speed of light.

Food was plentiful—some five years' worth for 135 persons of varying ages and requirements, enough surely to maintain twenty-two souls for eighteen extra shipboard years. No problem, except . . . except the food was all dehydrated. Of course.

Any planet capable of supporting humans *had* to have *some* water. That was basic. And the children were not to be born until such a planet was already underfoot.

He checked the life-support systems, checked the crucial water supply. . . .

It was this way: the water recycled through the food/waste systems, and though the original plan called for Eismann to be up and about for only a few months prior to a landing, there was enough reserve water to make his stay quite comfortable.

But twenty children? Ultimately twenty-two adults?

No way.

Too damned much protoplasm, that's all.

Eismann looked at the computer screen readout, pondering the twenty numbers arranged in two neat columns.

"Some of you guys," he said—the Iceman Cometh—"have got to go. Sorry."

Which ones? Easy: let the computer decide. The big question: *how many?*

Eismann asked.

Eighteen.

Well, hell . . . there was no point in arguing. He had to jettison eighteen eggs. He said, "Adam and Eve time."

Then he thought: Why one each? Why not two females?

He could nearly double the chances of Man's survival if he grew himself a couple wives.

He asked the computer to list the two best females. Hmmmm. No hurry, really.

Three hundred eighty eggs were dead or dying in the ruptured storage compartment. Nothing he could do about that. It's true he had a water shortage, but that problem wouldn't become acute for years, really.

Oh, God . . .

He had a vision: twenty nervous little girls, all lined up, a shadow passing overhead—the Iceman, brother—touching eighteen blonde heads, one by one, yanking them out of line and over to the waste disposal maw, which was so small he'd be forced to butcher . . .

No! The decision had to be made *now*, while the eggs were still microscopic abstractions. He took a deep breath and let it out slowly.

Two females, then. Or one of each. . . .

Then it occurred to him that by the time he'd have to report for stud duty he'd be over sixty.

What if I'm not fertile?

Fertile . . . infertile . . . that thought set off an old memory. Something they said during the long, boring pre-mission discussions . . . those cold men (the real Icemen) . . . a solution to an old cultural problem . . . uncles and nieces . . . the question of ostensible incest . . .

They had supposed he'd be among the young population in better, younger shape, his aging severely retarded by the sleepbox.

They wanted a clean start with this population—his filthy, contaminating genes were not allowed. He was, after all, just the bus driver.

So they sterilized him, even *before* Kathy's death.

God, he really moved up the list *that time*. The staff admired (and hated) him for his decision. Boy, they said, you really *do* wanna be the Last Man, don't you? He just smiled coldly—the Iceman—then they hated (and envied) him all the more. At that cynical time nobody considered the possibility Eismann really *cared* about the future of Man. Oh, well . . . ancient history.

Okay, back to square one: Adam and Eve. It was a story he could tell Adam when he was old enough to appreciate it.

On second thought, better not. By that time the dude might be willing—and certainly able—to deck his old Nanny. . . .

Eismann selected the two eggs, designated one of the pair of emergency water tanks for their use, then prepared to empty the remaining wombs. He hesitated again.

He knew (*damn it!*) that success of his mission demanded he wait as long as possible. Any birth defect could be disastrous. One sudden infant death (if there were only two in the running) would mean defeat; utter, hopeless defeat.

He *had* to let *twenty* fetuses come to term. He *had* to wait at least until their first birthday before selecting the fortunate two. One-year-old babies would not be conscious of his intent. They would not suffer. . . .

He *knew* what must be done.

This was why they'd chosen him (the Iceman). Hard decisions had to be made. Hadn't he demonstrated he was up to it? (That accident with Kathy worked—horribly—to his advantage. He knew it—and it made him wonder.) They needed a hardcore *survivor* to run this mission, and that's what they got. Congratulations, suckers. . . .

Yeah, he knew what had to be done. But he could not face the horror of that delayed selection. It was simply too gruesome.

Eismann the Iceman. *My ass* . . .

He reached out and dumped the eighteen eggs.

Now there are just the three of us.

Three of us, plus two each one-hundred-liter water tanks. He called up a water-inventory display. There was only one code on the screen. He fiddled with the computer, asking after the second water tank.

It took several minutes to find out—then more minutes to check and confirm—that the second tank was empty. Apparently he'd dumped it with the eighteen zygotes.

Babies and bathwater . . .

He stared at the computer screen. No question about it: there was now only enough water for two full-grown adults, plus a little extra for emergencies. Case closed.

It was clear that before the eighteen years were up there would only be two humans aboard the ship.

Eismann wouldn't be one of them.

Did I do that? he wondered. Or was that another of the "bombs" they promised? Does it matter now?

He and the computer got together on a little calculation. Assuming the two kids grew at the optimum rate, there'd come a time when the three of them would have to say their good-byes. Say seven or eight years after birth. . . .

Eismann sighed and went on with his chores. He had to do something about Mackay's mummified body, so he bagged it in plastic and shoved it into the trash compactor.

His finger hesitated above the RUN switch.

"Well, Mackay, you did your job. And you almost made it yourself. Maybe I'd have got to like you after a few years. And maybe not. As for thanking you—well, let's just say I'm still thinking about it." Then he pushed the button and drifted away.

"See you in nine years. More or less."

Eismann slipped into the webbing of the inoperative sleepbox, his day's work done. He investigated his personal locker (which some NASA joker had named *Eisbox*) and found a desiccated cigar. Felicitations & Bon Voyage, sucker. He unwrapped the cigar, broke it in two, and began to chew on one stale end. He knew he couldn't light it, but this was better than nothing.

After a minute he realized he felt pretty good. The Big Trip was underway—and under control. The Earth was—well, screw the Earth. *He* was the Earth now. Man still had a chance. NASA would have been proud . . . not that he cared. He was the Iceman, right? He didn't need anybody to *approve* his actions, right? Isn't that right (damn it)?

Settle down, Eismann. You done good. Now shut up.

He stretched out and thought a long time about the kind of tapes he'd leave behind for the benefit of Mankind. Instructions on how to start up a new human colony . . .

If only he *knew* how.

II

Eismann had plenty of time to reacquaint himself with the particulars of the mission.

He was on his way to Alpha Centauri.

There had been a lot of discussion during the planning stages of the mission, a lot of rather bitter argument. The mission was obviously a one-shot deal—all or nothing.

From the start, though, Alpha Centauri was the logical choice. Not only was it the closest—and hence the shortest trip—but the star system contained one extremely close copy of Sol, plus a lesser star of some possibilities. The chances of finding an Earth-type planet in this area was estimated as high as ten percent. Virtually the best bet going.

Man's lifeboat was a hastily thrown together patch-up job, a reworked third-generation space shuttle. For years they'd been siphoning off antimatter from the busy weapons labs, putting together enough for the deceleration burn. Then they used every resource—huge chemical rocket drop-off boosters, matter/antimatter reactors, and a close-solar whip orbit—to get the shuttle on its way.

They'd set him going at .2 cee. The deceleration burn would be a slow, matter/antimatter burn at about one-tenth gee. Two years of deceleration. Total trip time: twenty-two years.

With luck.

Eismann spent a few hours exploring what parts of the shuttle he could get into.

Most of the cavernous payload bay was filled with electromagnetic matter/antimatter fuel tanks. The rest was food—with automatic retrieval—then seed, nitrogen-fixing soil bacteria, fertilizer, and too little water. This whole area was sealed off.

The cockpit was crammed with extra life-support equipment and the planetary analysis experiments, but there was still enough room to pull himself into the one pilot seat left. He looked out the window.

The shuttle still faced forward—to be turned around before the deceleration burn—and Alpha Centauri was a visual binary dead ahead. At .2 cee the orange B star was shifted to blue, the yellow A star to blue-violet. Visually the change was not nearly so dramatic, since normally invisible infro-red light blue-shifted into the visual to make up for the lost reds and oranges. The stars seemed tinged with blue-green, but he gave up trying to make sure when his eyes began to water.

Though planetary entry would be automatic, the actual landing of the shuttle was too problematical for total computer control. There'd be oceans—not much reason to land if there weren't—and he'd try to put the ship down in a shallow, protected bay.

It was going to be tricky. Space shuttles, because of their ambivalent natures, always seemed to land too damn fast. He touched the controls and picked up a static charge of stage fright, as though the landing were coming up in *minutes* instead of—

He laughed suddenly, spraying out soggy flakes of his chewed-up cigar.

The landing was eighteen years off; plenty of time to—

He stopped laughing.

Well, it was not *his* problem, the landing . . . but how would *they* handle it, his kids? How the hell could they spend the last ten years of the trip without him—and then know how to make the landing?

He had spent years learning to pilot the beast, and there was no guarantee *he'd* remember enough, despite programmed rehearsals.

What the hell chance would *they* have?

He began to wonder if he was even *supposed* to succeed. Had they picked him in order to *make sure* the mission failed? He'd been the Iceman all his life—forced into the role by the accident of his name. Was that a clue? Had they seen some flaw, smoothed over by his unconscious role-playing, that they *expected* to break him apart?

He'd already *failed* to meet the egg-selection problem head on. Now here he was thinking up excuses to stay alive (the essential pilot)—at the expense of the entire mission.

Was he acting out his fatal weakness, just as someone high up in mission planning suspected he would?

The note had threatened him with more bombs. Maybe they meant *him*.

The ultimate doomsday device—all he had to do was reach out and caress the control board, flicking a few inappropriate switches, and the mission would be over. Mankind would be dead. All very sanitary.

It would save a *lot* of trouble.

Eismann suddenly reached out and snapped on the VHF radio. He'd never even thought to check. What if the Earth was *not* destroyed? What if this was all just a . . . a what? A joke? A prank? A damned expensive prank.

The speaker hissed uniformly as the radio scanned for signals. Nothing.

Let's see, he thought. I've been on my way four years—or so the computer says—at .2 speed of light. Earth is directly behind me (more or less) about eight-tenths of a light-year away. Commlink delay time 19 months and change—that's a strain on snappy conversation.

Turning in a *specific* channel would require some calculation. The red shift of a 50 MHZ signal coming out of a rapidly receding Earth would be about ten megahertz. If he tried to broadcast—but no, there was no point in that. He was too far away; it was too late.

So, he was alone. Probably. There'd been rumors about another shuttle headed in another direction. And the Soviets might have set something up—if there'd been time. It was all speculation. *He* was alone, at least, and the radio was silent. (He declined to aim his directional antenna at anything but the Solar System. For the moment he didn't want any big surprises.)

Better not to think too hard about any part of this. Not now, not yet. He'd have years to brood about the mission, to decide if he really wanted to go through with it.

Eismann climbed out of the cockpit and drifted back to the sleepbox.

In the two activated wombs the bodies formed, without hope and without despair, cell upon cell, the heirs of Man.

III

Eismann sweated in the elastic bicycle, nearing the end of his second exercise hour.

"How's that?" he said, shaking sweat out of his eyes.

The twins—the mechanical wombs had disgorged them precisely ten minutes apart—clung to the webbing of the sleepbox and watched quietly.

Ten months old, naked—as was Eismann nowadays—and already attentive, already clinging like bald monkeys to the webbing, swaying in zero gee. They seemed amused.

The only time they cried was just *before* fouling themselves. He decided they were afraid of the whining hand vacuum he chased them with, collecting their wastes. He'd *conditioned* a pre-evacuation fear. He wondered what Freud would have made of it. He hoped it wouldn't scar their psyches too badly.

He came out of his exercise corner and floated through the cool air toward them. He jammed the green hunk of soft plastic in his mouth (the lone cigar had long since been chewed to pieces).

He decelerated on the webbing and poked the boy in the gut. "How ye doing, guy?"

He couldn't bring himself to name the children. It was simply too *momentous*. He'd let the kids name themselves when they were old enough to know what names were for.

"You too, girl," he said, fingering her head.

The twins were tiny, very frail.

In zero gee they got no exercise just hanging around. And they were too young to learn any of the special zero-gee routines that he performed so religiously.

He stared at them, and they back at him, their eyes large and trusting. They never complained.

He shook his head at them and smiled sadly.

Every day he had an impulse to strangle them.

"What am I getting you into?"

They looked ordinary enough, despite zero-gee frailty. Eismann kept expecting to see signs of their genetic superiority. The eggs and sperm cells that produced the frozen zygotes were rumored to be illegally manipulated—superclean, recessive gene weeded, piggy-backed, quadruple-stranded DNA—it was never clear exactly what had been done. The idea was to compensate for the colony's severely limited gene pool. The mission planners couldn't have known *how* limited it was going to be. These kids, and their children—there was no telling what might develop.

Anyway, it was not his problem.

He held out his forefinger and the little boy took it, floating away from the webbing.

"You're light as a feather, my friend. You know that?"

The little guy reached back as his "sister" reached out. Now both babies floated free from the sleepbox webbing, hand in hand.

Eismann pulled his finger away, and the twins floated before his face, watching.

He felt the sweat going off his body, going into the air, going ultimately into the water retrieval system and back into the reservoir.

He thought a lot about the water in that reservoir.

Every gram the babies gained came from that reservoir, water permanently removed from the cycle.

"How long before you're on your own, hunh?"

And then what will you do?

The twins refused to exercise.

They'd whine and complain (*now* they complained) and bounce off the ceiling a few times. It was easy to catch them, the room was so small, but he hated to force them into the elastic bike if they were so set against it.

Five years old, and heavy into anarchy. Same old story.

The girl was Kathy, a name she insisted had to come from him. He regretted it now. Maybe she'd change it later.

The boy was Ice. He had insisted on taking Eismann's name, calling himself variously "Eismann II" and "Eismann too."

Eismann urged him to change it, but the kid would have at least part of his name. (*Nobody* wanted his first name: Horace.) Eismann thought calling him *Mann* was too pretentious, so they settled on *Ice*. He hoped that, too, would change with time.

Time . . .

At the rate they were growing—*slowly*—the damned deadline kept moving back.

He brooded about it, but it was not something they discussed, though the kids seemed emotionally and mentally ready to take on any load. It was phenomenal, really, how quickly they developed in that area.

They both spent hours before the computer screen: Q&A.

Eismann spent a lot of time querying the computer himself, trying to find out exactly what had happened on Earth. But there was nothing, no current history readout to augment his vague memories of heightened tension in the world. He so utterly failed to remember the final day—the moment when they actually came for him—that he wondered if perhaps they didn't fiddle with his mind. Maybe there was something built into the sleepbox to blank his memories. Did that make sense?

He had a theory. The events leading up to the Last Day of the Earth—pathetic, outrageous, prideful and greedy as they must have been—were likely to cast doubt on the worthiness of Man to continue as a species in the universe. Maybe they wanted to prevent him from prejudging Man. They probably cursed the flimsy technology that kept them from eliminating him altogether. They had to trust him completely. Too bad.

Now they counted on him to—

"That's not right," he said, wedged in front of the computer keyboard.

"They" no longer counted on him. "They" were long gone. If "they" existed still on Earth, if there was any bombed-out remnant of human life on that diseased, dying planet, Eismann doubted any of them even knew of this mission—or would care. "They" had their own problems.

No, the only people who counted on him now were the twins. They required his help, *demanded* it. And for now, they got it.

The artificial "day/night" cycles continued to pile up as the years drifted past. They settled into an unending series of routines: the bedtime routine, when Eismann tried to remember stories to tell them, invariably choosing something too childish or too adult for them—the twins were alternately bored or baffled; the "work" routine, when he tried to get them to help with the housekeeping of the shuttle, vacuuming and filter cleaning and checking the status of life-support systems. The computer kept up a steady drizzle of preventive maintenance jobs for them, but the twins only worked hard on things they'd never done before, like calibrating the instruments that analyzed the waste/food cycle for impurities. And finally, there was the "play" routine, when Eismann tried to sneak in some organized exercise for the twins—a plan they saw through from the earliest attempts, escaping with zestful ease and generally causing more work for Eismann than it was all worth.

And what, exactly, was it all worth? He didn't know. The "importance" of the mission waxed and waned on its own routine schedule, as if tied to some remnant of tidal force in Eismann's mind. Some days the responsibility squashed him flat, on others it exhilarated him. Most of the time it meant nothing at all; the "mission" floated high above his consciousness, like a wispy cloud in a clear blue sky—it could safely be ignored because there would be plenty of time to think about it later. He was surprised, every now and then, to remember he hadn't yet come to a conclusion: was human life worth preserving?

There were adventures to mark the passage of time. When the twins were six or so, Eismann woke up with a toothache. After weeks of enduring the throbbing pain he decided he'd have to pull the tooth. He searched through the shuttle tool kit and found a pair of pliers, but they looked awfully unwieldy. Consulting the computer he located an excellent set of dentist's tools—complete with crash-course cheat sheet instruction manual—but the storage code indicated the pack was stashed deep within the cargo hold and not available to him. It would be the pliers or nothing.

The twins floated nearby, amused and interested in this novel activity. "Whatcha going to do, Eismann?"

"This is serious medical business," he said.

"We know."

Ice nudged Kathy and reached for a bulkhead gripbar, grinning. Anything to break up the routine, even "serious medical business."

Eismann wedged himself into the vanity before the stainless-steel mirror. He probed awkwardly with the pliers. Somewhere somebody was giggling.

There was no trouble finding the right tooth—he had only to tap it gently to send a ghost-nail through his lower jaw—but figuring out how best to grip the thing was a problem. The pliers weren't shaped right for a smooth yank outward. He'd have to pull the tooth upward.

Kathy clung to his forearm, her mood locked into his, now dark and gloomy. He positioned the pliers over the tooth and gently squeezed. He pinched his gum and involuntarily jerked his arm, his eyes blinking tears. Kathy hung onto his elbow. "Push off!" he told her, but it must not have sounded right with a pair of pliers in his mouth. She held on, looking concerned. A moment later the pliers' grip was right and he yanked hard.

The tooth broke in two and the pliers slipped, smacking his upper molars at the gumline. He yelled and jerked his hand away, accidentally biting his knuckles. The pliers swung out and smacked Kathy on the arm, sending her flying across the compartment where she smashed into the cockpit ladder.

Eismann roared in pain and regret and pushed off after her, trailing small globules of bright red blood. Kathy had bounced by then, and Ice—who had stayed clear throughout—pushed off in a trajectory to intercept. Eismann got to her first. Her eyes were wide with fright and pain, and he cursed himself as he assessed her injuries: a broken left ulna where his pliers had struck, and a broken right femur where she'd hit the ladder. He felt small hands tighten painfully about this throat. "Leave her alone!" screamed Ice.

"Leave *me* alone, goddamnit!" he yelled back, sending a necklace of darkening blood over his shoulder. He finally had to put Ice in the Place, an area in the center of the compartment, out of reach of bulkhead or handhold. Ice would be stranded there until Eismann came for him.

Eismann consulted the computer Medifax file, then gave

Kathy a half-ampule of Demeraid before setting the fractures. She cried slowly as he worked, mumbling her apologies for getting in his way. Ice struggled and twisted in the Place, screaming to be set free. Eismann ignored him. Ice was naked, of course, so he had nothing to throw, nothing to use as reaction mass. He was stuck good and he knew it, and his frustration was a torment to them all. He made sure of that.

After he'd put Kathy to bed—and after assuring her he didn't blame her for any of this—Eismann went to talk to Ice. "It was an accident, damn it," he said, slurring his words a little as he worked his tongue around an aching mouth. The bleeding had stopped, but the pain was more real than the steel in the shuttle's superstructure. And he had yet to face the other half of that broken tooth, still anchored in his throbbing jaw.

Ice stared at him sullenly. "Let me go."

Eismann took a breath. "*She* forgives me."

"She can if she wants."

"My tooth hurts."

"That's too bad."

Eismann stayed by the wall, out of reach. Ice floated motionless in the Place, hands on his hips.

God, he's pissed, thought Eismann. And not afraid to show it. Not like me.

"You want to protect her," Eismann said.

"Of course."

"She's not your *sister,* you know."

"Yes she is!"

Eismann looked away. It was too early to go into *that.* He said, "It doesn't matter. You should protect her. But not against *me.* You have to know I'll never want to hurt her. Never."

And the thought: but I haven't decided yet, have I? I may even *kill* her, kill *both* of them. Isn't that right? Isn't that still a possibility?

His hand whipped out and grabbed Ice by the ankle. He spun him around and aimed him at the sleepbox where Kathy floated, her frail limbs splinted and gunked in fast-setting plastic. He pushed him—gently. "Go to bed, Ice. And don't worry. But don't forget, either. Something's bound to happen someday. I want you to be ready."

Then he squirmed into the cockpit to brood. Every few seconds, in a motion he seemed powerless to control, his tongue dragged across the jagged fragment of his broken tooth and probed its soft, ultrasensitive center. And every time he did that his head shivered with a pain of almost stunning intensity.

And each time he felt that exquisite pain he vowed never to do it again. But he couldn't stop himself, no matter how hard he tried, no matter how bad the pain got. Amazing, he thought.

Absolutely amazing.

About a year later they had a little party. The computer had said: ten years to go.

"Ten years till *what?*" asked Ice, teasing.

The twins were seven-and-a-half—a pair of loud-mouthed *runts*.

That day Eismann told them about the journey to Alpha Centauri. But they'd known all along (computer Q&A).

They knew about *everything*.

Ice said, "Got the latest update, Eis*mann*. At our present rate of growth, the water reserve will become critical in five-and-a-half to six years."

"I can hardly wait."

Kathy wouldn't talk about it, but neither would she cry.

Ice said, "Me and Kathy are supposed to keep Mankind alive."

"It's a big responsibility."

Ice laughed, echoing Eismann's short, ironic chirp. "Maybe not."

"What do you mean?"

Ice toyed with one of the spherical "cupcakes" Eismann had struggled to bake for the celebration. The sugar-coated globe wobbled as it spun, a bite out of one side. "The thing is," said Ice, "nobody asked *us*. What if we don't want to?"

Eismann shrugged. This was not the time to argue about it. So the kid had doubts.

Welcome to the club.

They spent a lot of time, singly and in groups, watching TV and movies on the monitor. Nearly a quarter of the inventory was available to them, the rest in "deep storage" (a phrase that continued to infuriate Eismann every time it appeared on the computer screen).

The twins liked the old movies best—westerns like *Red River* and *The Wild Bunch*, war flicks like *Casablanca* and *A Guy Named Joe*, comedies like *The Philadelphia Story* and *The Awful Truth*. These were Eismann's favorites, the ones he always used to watch on the late show on TV back in the World. The twins took to them automatically.

They had little interest in the more modern stuff, the porno snuff comedies of the '90s, or the early made-in-space spectaculars from the turn of the century.

Their TV selections were likewise vintage: "Leave It to Beaver," "The Mary Tyler Moore Show," and "Spuds Pozo!"—all shows that were already in reruns when Eismann was a kid. The newer stuff just didn't captivate them.

Maybe the twins were getting a biased notion of what the world had been like; maybe they were learning it was a better place than it had been. So what? They'd need all the optimism they could get when they set out to build a new world.

If, thought Eismann, this little experiment lasts that long.

He understood now that the sleepbox had been designed to do more than preserve his vitality and conserve the consumables. According to the flight plan he'd have come awake with very little time left and a hell of a lot to do. He was supposed to be far too busy to think. Too busy to *doubt*.

But the landing was still eight years off.

One "game" they played was called Shuttle Landing. They took turns going through the computer simulations, responding to mock emergencies, scoping out hypothetical landing sites, gaining points toward a goal of "Safe Landing."

Kathy was the best "pilot"—a fearless barnstormer. It even began to look as if the twins *could* handle the landing by themselves.

Of course the transition to "real" time was a killer, but Eismann knew that there was precedent. Ninety years earlier, when aircraft were single-seaters, would-be pilots packed what advice they could carry and went up to solo on the first try. If they crashed, they flunked.

If Kathy crashed the shuttle . . . Man flunked out forever.

Still, it was the only chance. . . .

When he was ten-and-a-half, Ice came to him and said: "You screwed up, Eis*mann*."

"That right?"

"Kathy and me should never have been born."

"Don't be pessimistic," said Eismann dryly. But how could they *not* be, living with him. "All the eggs were spoiling. I had to do something."

"You could have opened the egg storage compartment to vacuum and kept it in the shade. They'd have kept frozen, you know."

Eismann just stared at him.

"You could've kept *all* the eggs frozen until we got to Alpha Centauri. That way we wouldn't have the water problem, you know?"

Eismann knew, and his face grew hot with realization of what he'd done. He'd doomed them all—almost certainly—by setting up this train of events. Sure, there'd been a bombing—that wasn't his fault. But his first reaction at that moment of crisis was wrong. He'd had other options. Christ, it might even have been possible to reactivate his sleepbox.

There was no point in trying now. It was too late, and he had the twins to look after. His children. His doomed children. Some goddamn Nanny he'd turned out to be.

He didn't have to say a thing. He could tell by the amused expression on Ice's young face that he'd been caught. One more thing to think about in the horrible years to come.

Ice floated away. He never mentioned it again.

On their fourteenth birthday the twins came to him with a plan.

Eismann was edgy. He exercised one hour three times a day, checked the water level *four*. Soon, soon . . .

There'd been no more of the promised "bombs" in the system. Maybe the threat was an exercise in psychological warfare.

He stayed alert. The next critical phase was coming. . . .

"Listen to this," Ice said. "In fifteen months or so we'll begin our deceleration burn, right?"

"I told you not to use that word," Eismann said. "There is no moon; there are no *months!*"

Ice looked at Kathy and smiled. "If I say one and a quarter *years* he'll just say—"

"Get on with it!" Eismann said. He was nervous.

Ice explained slowly. They—the twins—were afraid of the coming deceleration. Afraid of the one-tenth-gee bogey man that had been coming to get them all of their lives. Nothing they had read or dreamed about gravity, real or artificial, had made them eager to experience its unrelenting grip. They wanted no part of it.

"You can handle it."

"We can *learn* to," said Ice, "if we must. But we'll never make it on a planet, Eis*mann*. Never."

But they had a plan.

And the Iceman wept when he heard it.

"You have to promise," said Ice, staring hard at him, staring right through him to where the heart of doubt and fear stirred miserably.

Kathy nodded. "You have to."

Eismann felt himself dwindling beneath the force of their commitment and the somber weight of their sacrifice. There was no way out. He whispered, "I promise."

IV

It was close, but they made it. And Eismann got to keep both his legs. Ice was right; he'd need them.

The shuttle was already within the orbit of Alpha Centauri B and closing in on the A star, the heavier of the two. B had passed apastron before the mission was launched, and now was still poking along the slow side of its eighty-year orbit.

(The C star, also called Proxima Centauri, was way the hell off somewhere, and in any case was not under consideration as a suitable star.)

Alpha Centauri A got picked mainly because it was currently closer. It was also pure yellow again, now that the ship had lost nearly all of its wavelength-shifting speed.

Eismann turned forward in the observation bubble and looked back along the way he'd come.

Sol was the brightest star in Cassiopeia.

Eismann dropped down into the main room. He was well used to the one-tenth-gee thrust (used even to living on the back wall), and he was anxious to get even heavier. His muscle tone was good (he'd worked long enough getting it), and his bone calcium was fair.

He was sixty-two—a skinny, bald old man. He felt great.

His brood looked up as he hit the wall (floor).

A dozen babies, ranging in age from one month to one year.

All the children of Ice and Kathy—and twenty more in the wombs.

All parentless now, except for their aging Nanny.

Ice's plan was simple and inevitable.

The twins would never live to walk the new planet—should one be discovered—but their children could. Their children, most of them, would be born in the planet's gravitational field. A dozen more would be brought there at a very early age—and out of an already one-tenth-gee inertial field. Most would adapt easily.

And Eismann must be ready to land and attempt the adaptation to full gravity. It was—after all—his job, his mission.

Ice and Kathy matured and supplied the fertilized eggs for the twenty wombs. (Eismann never discussed sex with either of the twins, but he agreed—gratefully—to Kathy's request for a private corner. Ice took full charge of the tricky egg-gathering phase, acting quite dispassionately. The Iceman saw his unconscious tutoring at work here—and it scared him . . . but in other areas the twins proved remarkably warm and generous. Eismann hoped he'd contributed some part of this, too.)

The twins were of slight build, Kathy too frail even to bear her own children. It was probably a miracle she matured sexually at all. But then, she *had* to.

They both suffered quietly in the one-tenth-gee deceleration field. Kathy, especially—her broken femur had not set properly. When Eismann watched her limping and saw the unconscious gimace of pain that tightened her pretty face, he wanted to cry.

Have I done *any*thing right? he asked himself. Anything at all?

"Here comes old Gimpy," she'd say, bouncing off the floor. She'd laugh and Eismann would think of Kathy, his Kathy. They looked the same in his mind now, indistinguishable, equally loved, equally mourned.

I'm haunted by a trillion trillion ghosts, he thought. The ghost of every creature that leapt, swam, or crawled on a dead planet once called, briefly, Earth.

There are a million ghosts in orbit around every cell of my body. I am aswarm with the dead.

On some days he felt very . . . *thick*.

Before the end, as the water level sank below the minimum, sacrifices had to be made. It was agreed both that Eismann should remain whole and that the fetuses be given priority in the fight for protoplasm. The twins gave up their almost useless legs.

Then, the final egg implanted, they gave up everything else. They went together.

Eismann was three AUs from Alpha Centauri A when he spotted the planet.

Automatic equipment monitored A and B and predicted planets by orbital perturbations. Eismann looked where the computer told him and there it was—1.04 AUs from the A star, moving in a rather complicated series of precessing ellipses.

Eccentricity of the orbits varied, but even the worst-case prediction from the computer was acceptable.

Besides: green forests and blue oceans under cloudy but transparent skies. And oxygen . . . yes, it would do.

The ten-to-one longshot had paid off.

Eismann made a slight course change—the third in as many days—then held his breath and shut down the main drive. He spent several nervous hours manipulating the remaining plasma of antimatter fuel (using the remotes, of course). The ejection capsule used the fuel to power the electromagnetic bubble that kept the anti-matter isolated. When the fuel ran out, the field would collapse—but by then there should be little anti-matter left. Just enough to blow the capsule to pieces.

Eismann watched the beaconed capsule accelerate away from the shuttle. He hoped nobody would come across it before the anti-matter was gone—it was a hell of a discourteous package to leave drifting about.

Far too dangerous to risk bringing to the planet with him. Unless—

That would be funny, he thought. If the whole damned planet was made of anti-matter—what a great joke on me!

Rather unlikely now: if the planet were anti-matter it would be almost certain the suns were too. But the shuttle was already caught in the swirl of their stellar winds. If those particles were anti-matter, his ship would have been eaten away by microdetonations by now.

So—not to worry. Plenty of other problems to keep him occupied.

The planet was coming up rapidly. There was only going to be one landing attempt, anti-matter or no. There wasn't enough fuel left to orbit the planet—the bomb-induced course corrections eighteen years ago had seen to that—no time to scour the planet for safe landing sites. Or airports. . . .

On the last day Eismann lit off the main chemical engines and emptied the propellant tanks in less than three minutes. After that there was barely enough time to get the shuttle turned for a headfirst entry. He was coming in too damned fast, but there was nothing he could do about that now. He'd have to dive right into the atmosphere and skip his momentum away.

Too deep a bite, and that would be it—meteor time. Too shallow and he'd skip right back out, on his merry way to nowhere. Eismann gnawed nervously on his plastic teething ring. Then he grinned.

Here's where I earn all that back flight pay.

Well, not quite yet—computers were still running the show. The shuttle pitched slowly upward until Eismann could no longer see the planet out his cockpit window. The sky was black and sprinkled with constellations, their patterns familiar, yet slightly distorted. He was not so *very* far from home.

It was peaceful up there. The only sounds were those of air fans and the hiss of an ink-jet printer making hard-copy log entries. Eismann tightened his harness straps, eager for something to do. There was still no sense of motion, save the flickering readouts of the radar altimeters. The radios were quiet, so far.

All the Space Traffic Controllers must be on strike, he thought. He started to laugh, then stopped.

I'm an old man, he thought suddenly. Too old to start something like this.

The shuttle quivered, and a ripple of fear swept his body. A row of white and green status lights flickered amber for a moment, then settled down.

Eismann shut his eyes and listened to the rush of surging blood in his ears. I *am* too old for this.

In fact, he thought, I am the oldest living astronaut.

Hell, I'm the oldest living *any*thing.

And I don't want to die. Not now, not after—

The shuttle shook and bounced, porpoising on the invisible, almost nonexistent air. Alarms gonged softly; again the board lit up red. Two control computers overloaded and shut down; they tried to reset, failed, and put themselves on hold.

That's the plan, he thought abruptly and with horrible certainty. The final "bomb" in the system. They'd rigged the shuttle computers to blow the landing. So close and yet—

Eismann reached out and took the stick.

The shuttle reacted badly to his touch, yawing immediately to port and beginning a slow clockwise roll. By the time he'd corrected the ship's attitude his whole body shook with every thudding heartbeat.

My God, I am going to die. We are all going to die.

I should not be in this pilot's seat, he thought desperately. Kathy was twice the pilot I was.

Which Kathy? Either one, damn it.

Both dead now, what does it matter?

(And I am escaped alone to tell thee.)

Christ, I *am* the survivor type all right. But the best man doesn't always win, brother. There are other factors.

(They couldn't take the chance drugs or poisons would contaminate the water supply as their tiny legless bodies entered the system. "There is no other way," said Kathy, turning her back, offering her frail neck to his muscular hands. It was worse than he could have imagined. And afterward . . .)

The best Men he'd ever known—Kathy and Ice—were dead. He'd seen to it. The hell with logic. *He'd* killed them, just as he'd killed Kathy, his Kathy.

And now he'd finish the job, wreck the shuttle, and kill them all. Kill himself, kill the babies, kill Man.

All he had to do was nudge the stick downward a half centimeter.

Is this why they chose me?

If the babies knew, if they understood . . .

(The babies were strapped each-to-each like link sausages and tucked into his sleepbox. If they cried he couldn't hear them. They trusted him.)

We could die now and no one would ever know, he thought.

But the shuttle steadied up and straddled its imaginary flight line. He was still in control—for the moment. No "bombs," just nerves.

The atmosphere was thicker up there than expected. Maybe there'd been a lot of stellar activity lately, warming up the air and pumping it higher. The first of how many surprises?

He began to torture himself with a litany of possible disasters.

What if there's no ozone layer? The ultraviolet will cut me to pieces. Or what if the soil kills all my seeds? And what if the native plants are inedible or poisonous? Or what if the air is crowded with lethal bacteria or viruses? Or the forests thick with ravenous beasts? What if I trip over my shoelaces and bust my skull?

The shuttle vibrated harshly in the thickening air. The sky was blue-black, the stars hazy. Daylight failed quickly as the shuttle raced into the nightside of the planet. The red-orange glow of the heatshield tiles blossomed ominously around the windows.

Within minutes he was in the shadow of the planet, and all he could see was the ship on fire. His hand tensed on the stick.

I used to like this part, he thought. Flying . . .

Flying the shuttle, flying *anything*. But that's all over now. This will be the last time, the last flight.

For twenty-two years Man had been an interstellar race—for the duration of this one voyage. Man at his apex.

In half an hour the Space Age would be over, the Dark Ages rebegun. Or maybe there'd be . . . nothing.

The final flight.

All those years of training—of playing the Game with Ice and Kathy—they would all pay off in the next few minutes. Or not.

He saw their faces, their smiling, determined faces. They wanted this to happen. They'd given up everything for this to happen, sacrificed everything so Eismann could put his cargo safely on the ground of this new planet. Why?

What did they know about Man? How could they care about His preservation? The only man they ever knew was Eismann. What about him convinced them Man was worthy of staying alive?

Nothing, he thought. Not a damned thing.

No, they did it for *me*. So *I* could live. So I could pace the fresh earth of this new planet, chomping on my silly plastic pacifier, watching their children grow up.

They did it for their old Nanny.

It was *personal*.

Then Eismann realized why he couldn't waggle the stick and end the Final Flight in a futile blaze of light. It was personal. He had a cargo to deliver, the precious children of his oldest friends. He had *promised* them, and now he'd have to keep his promise—even if no one would ever know.

Especially if no one ever knew.

It was something Men did.

Eismann wiped his eyes. The fiery glow of the shuttle's nose and belly flared brightly and the cockpit groaned and muttered. Cooling fans picked up the pace. They were still fifty miles high.

"I'll do my job," he said. "I'll make you proud, or rip my guts out trying."

I'm one hell of a meteor, he thought suddenly, as he blazed across the night sky.

I wonder who's watching? I wonder what they think?

Invaders from Earth, coming to *getcha*. One bald old Nanny and his vicious gang of Earth babies.

God help you, here we come.

HITCHHIKER

BY SHEILA FINCH

"Go ahead on the dump, Atlantis."

Ellen Devon maneuvered down the row of hastily set-up folding chairs, her movements made clumsy by the four layers of clothing she'd donned against the December cold. Hearing the loudspeaker, she felt her stomach knot. Plagued by a series of small mishaps and changes of plan, Atlantis had earned the nickname "hard-luck shuttle" on this flight.

"Dump complete, Joe."

Of most concern had been a glitch in communications while Jackie was on EVA. Then had come the last-minute change of plan when a tropical storm blanketed the cape, and now a computer malfunction that was delaying landing at Edwards. Ellen couldn't rid herself of the uneasy feeling there was more to it than NASA was admitting.

"Stand by one."

To the east, the mountains stood out starkly black against the pale mauve of the dry lake; the sky over the California desert turned the unbelievable shade of crayon pink a child might choose to illustrate sunrise.

"No joy there, Atlantis. Try the dump again."

Patrick Kelly slid into the seat beside her, holding two Styrofoam cups of coffee. "Here—this'll get the blood circulating. How do you feel?"

He was handsome enough to be a Hollywood playboy, yet she knew he had the instincts of an ambulance chaser. "Are you going to report my answer?"

He gave a short, barking laugh. "If it's interesting enough to my readers, maybe."

"At least you're honest."

"Okay. All balls on that one."

Surprisingly, Ellen thought, considering the short notice of the shuttle's change of landing plans, there was a small crowd of people here, NASA personnel and their families. But then crowds always gather at a disaster site—

What was the matter with her? She glanced at Kelly, sipping coffee as if there were nothing wrong—and perhaps there wasn't.

"What kind of satellite was Jackie supposed to repair?"

"Huh?" he said. "Oh, a scientific one. In polar orbit, studying the solar wind's interaction with Earth's magnetic fields. Why?"

She shrugged, not sure herself why she'd asked. He gave her an odd look, then returned his attention to the scalding coffee.

"Atlantis, we'll see you at TDRS at four plus one."

"Where's Tidris?"

"What," Kelly said, "not where. Tracking Data Relay Satellite."

She imagined the note he'd make for his column: *Astronaut's twin sister ignorant of crucial terminology.*

"Odd that they say 'see' not 'hear.' "

"We also still say 'the sun's rising,' " he said, nodding toward the east.

The loudspeaker that had been broadcasting a continuous stream of shuttle to mission control communications since they arrived was silent. She sipped her coffee and studied the NASA facility, trying to blot out the uneasy feeling in the pit of her stomach. Sixteen miles off the highway, it looked like another small, unimportant airport—a runway over the flat dry lake bed, hangars, an office building or two, a group of house trailers for temporary office space. Next door, on the strip at Edwards, F-100s practiced takeoffs and landings. The scene reminded her of air shows their father had taken them to every summer in the Midwest. She remembered the displays of jet engines, the flight simulators Jackie was so absorbed in, the film strips the Air Force recruiter always showed that she watched over and over again. It had been obvious, even while they were still in junior high school, which twin was going to make a name for herself, and where.

"Did anything—unusual—happen when Jackie worked on the satellite?"

"The video link broke down. You know that."

"You're the press. I thought—"

Kelly was silent for a long while, as if he were replaying the sequence of events in his memory. "They reported some magnetic turbulence when the shuttle approached the satellite. But that was from ten kilometers out, so it probably had nothing to do with anything. What's making you so jumpy?"

"Just nerves, I guess."

She wondered if Jackie was disturbed by the delays. But it had been a long time since Ellen had allowed herself to be close to her sister, to know with that intuitive bond identicals sometimes have what her twin's reactions would be to anything. How much had he suspected when he called her? Ellen was familiar with his column, *Kelly's People*; he went for the jugular in human relationships. Why then had she accepted? Boredom in her own career teaching high school science? A lingering sense of regret over the split with Jackie? Or this unease that had been with her for the last three days?

"Atlantis, this is Houston. Do you read?"

Ellen stripped off the first layer of clothing, dumping the car coat on the next seat.

"More coffee?"

She shook her head.

"I'll be back in a minute—want to talk to someone." The columnist loped across the clearing toward one of the office buildings.

"Atlantis, how do you read?"

The mission itself had been billed as routine—repair of a satellite with a crippled energy system, a job needing Jackie's training in microcircuitry. Ellen had sat up past midnight hoping to see it on TV, her feelings a mixture of pride and bitterness that she would never confess to Kelly. The media called Jackie a heroine, for she'd apparently had a lot of trouble despite NASA's downplaying of the incident. The next morning the landing plans were changed, and Kelly called, seizing the opportunity.

"Atlantis, this is Houston. We have good news for you. Do you read?"

Why didn't they reply? She looked uneasily at the sky. Of course they weren't visible. They weren't even back in the atmosphere yet. Now the sun was up, it was getting warm; she removed the sweater, leaving a shirt over the tee. On top of one of the buildings, a large radar tracking dish caught her eye.

"Loud and clear, Houston."

"The analysis of the GPC 2 dump was clean. We're clearing you for de-orbit burn—"

She jumped as Kelly touched her arm.

"Won't be too much longer now. In the meantime, how'd you like to speak to your sister?"

She stared at him. "What—?"

"I've got friends in high places!" He grinned. "Literally. Maybe we can swing something. Come on."

If he thought he was going to get an emotional reconciliation scene out of her, she decided, he was in for a surprise.

The communications room was guarded by a stiff-faced airman, holster bulging conspicuously at his waist. Kelly flashed a pass and he let them through. Inside, she had a déjà vu of the airport control tower she'd sat in with her father when Jackie was soloing, but this had more computer screens.

"—an old L-5 friend," Kelly said. "Guess I never explained I'm a closet space enthusiast."

She shook hands briefly with an older man, whose white hair contrasted starkly with his mahogany skin. Missing the name Kelly had spoken, she read his ID tag, Colonel James Gardner. The leaden feeling in the pit of her stomach was growing. It was more than nervousness at the thought of finding something to say to her twin after all this time.

"—may not be possible," Gardner was saying. "Major Devon hasn't been on the air in a while."

"Anything wrong?" Kelly's journalistic antenna was up immediately.

"Probably means nothing. But Atlantis had trouble on this one. That's off the record, by the way."

The voice of Houston came in, clearer than over the public loudspeaker. *"Elapsed time: twelve days, four hours, twenty-three minutes, five seconds."*

Cold welled up through Ellen's body. She clutched the back of a chair. A feeling of *wrongness* flooded her mind—

She scrubbed at her forehead, pushing the sensation away.

"Just have to wait and see." Gardner stopped as another transmission came in.

"Go to page 1-6 of the manual, Atlantis."

Jackie was in trouble, she knew. As children, they'd always known when something happened to the other. They were used to phantom sore throats and painful knees that the other had bumped. They'd shared each other's emotions, the frustrations and heartaches of their love affairs, though Jackie had always been more popular with boys and teachers than her sister. Then Jackie had gone on to a glittering career in space, and Ellen was left grading papers for Physics 1. There'd been little to say to each other after that, and few shared perceptions. Now, suddenly, there was this gnawing danger—

"Colonel?"

He looked at her over his shoulder. Behind him figures raced on a CRT.

"What *really* was wrong with the satellite Jackie repaired?"

Seconds passed and she was aware of every head in the room turning to gaze at her.

Gardner took his time, his dark face unsmiling. "Fluctuation in the solar cell output—it's the first satellite with big solar panels we've put in polar orbit. Worked fine for a couple of weeks, then shut down. Sudden and unexplained energy drain. Happened more than once."

"Was it working when my sister rendezvoused with it?"

He nodded. "But it was due to go AWOL again right about then. That's why we sent her—to see what was causing it."

The room suddenly lurched under her feet. She had the vertiginous sensation of spiraling downward at tremendous speed—

"Ellen?" Kelly touched her arm. "Are you all right?"

"Bathroom—" she managed.

Someone led her down a corridor, and waited while she went inside. She leaned over the toilet, but nothing came up.

Later, she allowed herself to be persuaded to lie down. Sleep came almost immediately—she'd been up since 3:00 a.m. to get here on time—but was fitful and disturbed by dreams she forgot as soon as she woke.

The sun was high over the dry lake bed when she sat up, but she shivered with cold and reached for her sweater.

Kelly pointed out the observation window. "She's on her way."

The radar dish on the roof opposite tracked slowly east to north. Colonel Gardner led the way outside; she followed with Patrick Kelly.

Across the dry lake bed there was a line of tiny shapes under a brooding dust cloud, and an occasional flash from a windshield. The shuttle's delayed landing had given people time to jam the public viewing area. At the landing site, a line of support vehicles waited, hydraulic lifts, firefighting equipment, a gigantic fan to vent the shuttle's noxious exhaust from the landing area. Nausea twisted again in her stomach.

"There it is!" Kelly exclaimed.

A tiny bright speck had appeared in the unflawed blue dome over the base. Kelly pushed field glasses into her hands. In the lens, the speck revealed its deltoid shape. As she watched, it emitted three short bursts of white exhaust as if it were about to type its own arrival data on the sky.

"Hey, you're trembling," he said. "Don't be afraid. The shuttle handles well."

"You don't understand—"

Now the chase plane behind Atlantis was visible. The sonic boom cracked across the quiet desert morning.

She gripped his arm. "Something's terribly wrong."

"If it were, they wouldn't let Atlantis down till they'd found it."

"It's Jackie—something's happened. She shouldn't be allowed —Jackie should be quarantined."

Kelly looked at her, his expression hard. "Back off, Ellen! I know what it meant to you growing up in Jackie's shadow. I did my homework. But you can't allow jealousy to ruin her triumph. She's earned it."

Atlantis was lined up for landing. Without warning, the barrier Ellen had erected against further humiliation gave way, and her mind opened up. Not in years had she felt this close to her sister, maybe never.

I'm here, Jackie!

She had a sharp image of Jackie, arms outstretched to her twin. Something else—

*Cold, dizzying vastness—

*The clutch of inchoate menace—

She broke away from Kelly's restraining hand and bolted through the gate. The shuttle touched down. Behind it, the chase plane gained altitude again.

"Ellen, come back!"

Running, she realized the futility of it. Atlantis had landed more than a mile away—distances were deceiving here. She'd never make it in time. She'd waited too long.

Someone was gaining on her, and she half turned, expecting Patrick Kelly. It was Colonel Gardner.

"Tell me what it is," he said. She slowed but didn't stop. The black man jogged beside her. "I'm listening to you."

"You wouldn't understand."

"Try me."

"It's my twin—"

"I had an identical twin once," Gardner said. "I knew the moment his plane was shot down in Vietnam."

She pulled up short, panting, and stared at him. His expression mirrored the pain she felt. She nodded briefly and told him what she knew.

When she was done, he pulled out his transmitter. "Gardner here. Code: Mayhem. Repeat, Code: Mayhem!"

Ellen peered through the double chickenwire screening of the Faraday cage. Jackie had lapsed into a coma. She'd descended the shuttle's steps with help from the shuttle's commander, collapsing the moment her feet touched the ground. But by then the truck-sized emergency medical vehicle had come racing up in a cloud of dust, and men swathed in outfits that resembled moon landing suits had gathered her up and disappeared with her into the portable isolation unit. The rest of Atlantis's crew seemed untouched, and after the doctors were through examining them they went on to debriefing.

The first three days had been chaotic.

Every instrument brought into Jackie's vicinity reacted wildly. Whatever it was that had happened to Jackie as she repaired the crippled satellite, it disrupted the functioning of anything using electricity. The first computer monitoring her vital signs burned out crucial circuits ten minutes after being activated. The second and third—state-of-the-art machines on loan from JPL—malfunctioned repeatedly. She herself jerked and lunged about the room like a maniac, then collapsed into near lifelessness only to revive suddenly and writhe and twist again.

They'd constructed a Faraday cage around her hospital bed in the isolation unit to shield themselves and the instruments from the surging electromagnetic disturbance that was Jackie Devon.

"Can't you *do* something?" Ellen asked, gazing at the temporarily lifeless form of her twin. Whatever was wrong with her had left her in peace, although comatose, for the past six hours. "There must be some drug—"

"Even if we ever do find bacteria floating free in space—and we haven't yet—it's highly improbable they'd find conditions on Earth to their liking," Dr. Alvarado, head of the space medicine team told her, obviously annoyed Gardner had given her the clearance to stay.

"NASA used to worry about that, back when Glenn and the others were riding the rockets," Kelly said. "But we know more now."

"You can't be certain, though, can you?" she said.

Ellen—

Jackie's voice?

The isolation unit dissolved in a dazzle of urgent light.

*Geometries of fire like burning glaciers—

*Something primeval whirling in terror—

As swiftly as the experience came over her, it vanished.

"It's got Jackie!" She clutched Colonel Gardner's arm. "There's something in Jackie's mind! I can *feel* it."

"That's not possible," Alvarado said. "And how could you know, in any—"

Gardner gripped her shoulders, steadying her, his dark eyes assessing her thoughtfully. "But you just might, I think. What do you feel?"

"Nothing I can put into words. Something jagged—spiraling—burning—like lightning—"

"If you're right—" Gardner left the thought unfinished. "My guess is it's some phenomenon dependent on energy. That would explain the periodic shutdown of the satellite. Your sister was there when it was—well—*feeding*. We designed the mission so she would be."

Jackie lay sprawled across the bed like a rag doll. Heavily shielded waldos snaked cautiously toward her to take their readings. Gardner huddled with the scientists over their instruments, conferring.

Kelly steered Ellen outside the mobile unit to a chair at the foot of the steps. The desert air cooled rapidly as sunset approached.

"They're not telling me everything," she said shakily.

He glanced at a guard just out of earshot. "I found out what happened after they brought Jackie back to Atlantis—after she gained consciousness. For a while, she was okay. Then everything she touched began to malf."

"The shuttle's computer problems—"

"Yeah."

"But why the secrecy?"

"They couldn't be sure the Russians didn't have a hand in it. Antisatellite weapons and such."

"There must be something—"

"They've tried almost every experiment in the book."

"They're not going to let you tell this story to your readers, you know. It'll be classified."

"We all take risks. This is mine."

She propped her head with her hands and stared at the ground.

"What're you getting from her now?"

She shook her head. "Nothing. It comes and goes."

"Ms. Devon?" Colonel Gardner emerged at the top of the steps. "Get some rest. There's nothing you can do here for a while."

"That *thing*—it's not an 'effect'—it's a parasite."

"I rather tend to believe you. But whatever it is that hitched a ride to Earth in Major Devon's body, it's not going to give up easily. We don't have much choice but to wait."

"And what happens to Jackie in the meantime?"

Ellen!

This time she was certain. "Look—it may sound silly, but Jackie needs me."

"We can't allow you inside the protective shielding."

He was afraid she'd be contaminated and bring it out, she knew. "All right. But I have to be near her."

Gardner led her back to the Faraday cage. The unit was jammed with doctors, scientists, technicians of many specialties. Men wearing protective suits were just emerging from the open cage; the scientists used the dormant periods to move equipment in or out, hoping to find the magical combination. So far, nothing had worked. Behind them, Ellen saw a trail of cables and voltage meters.

Without warning, disturbance broke out in the cage. Jackie's body bolted upright on the bed and flung itself across the room at the departing men. They barely managed to get the door shut in time as she fell to the floor.

*Prismatic yellow light—coalescing into ice—

*Danger! The stench of burning flesh—

Giddily, she staggered against the wire shielding of the cage. The link between them was strong, pulling her toward Jackie, compelling her to touch. At the distant edge of awareness she felt Gardner's hands gripping her shoulders, holding her back.

She clenched her teeth as icicles lanced through her skull.

"What is it? Tell us," Kelly urged.

Through the mesh she saw the jerking, zombielike figure of Jackie struggling to its knees. The eyelids flew open and for a second she was caught by the blue gaze.

Home—go home—

She fought down the horror that climbed into her throat. *No. You're not my sister. You're a parasite.*

Thought rushed over her: Humans shared their bodies with so may entities already—mitochondria, chloroplasts, bacteria. What was one more?

She dared not allow herself to think like that.

Jackie now lay crumpled awkwardly in a corner like a mario-nette with broken strings.

"What have you done to Jackie?" she cried aloud.

But the link was fading, as if the being that struggled so hard to control the human body it had entered was depleted by the effort.

Help—

Sorrow overwhelmed her, a sense of something captive and despairing.

"It doesn't understand!" she screamed, writhing in Gardner's grip. "It wants to get out, but it doesn't know how!"

Then—void where the link had been a moment earlier. But just before the silence closed in, she had a brief, vivid image of a curtain of energy, rippling with blue light. It vanished, leaving her drained.

She allowed Gardner to lower her onto a couch and didn't protest when a medic approached to administer a trank.

"Northern lights," she said, as the shot took her down into darkness. "But why would it live in the aurora borealis?"

Around 5:00 a.m., Kelly brought her soup and a glass of milk. Gray winter light was beginning to push its way through the mobile unit's small windows. She felt sticky, in need of a shower. He sat with her, coaxing her to eat. However this turned out, she thought, he'd get some kind of story. But that was unfair. It wasn't journalism alone that kept him here.

"You're not half as sadistic in the flesh as you are in print."

"Illusion only, fair lady."

"Which one?"

"Try me and find out?"

"Forget it!" But she was smiling again. "Tell me what they're saying about that *thing*."

"Well—I'm out of my depth here!—there's a constant drizzle of electrons into the ionosphere at the geomagnetic poles—"

"From the solar wind," she explained. "When the wind is strong, the electrons plow deeply into Earth's atmosphere, interacting with the plasma. We see the excited oxygen atoms in high latitudes as the aurora borealis."

"Thanks, Teach! Anyway—"

"We've always known there were strong, unexplained electri-cal currents in the aurora—"

"—that's the energy source. This—whatever—suddenly found an unexpected delicacy in its own backyard, and it learned to harvest the satellite's solar power cells."

"So it kept coming back to—eat—the stored electrical energy?"

"Seems that way. They think it didn't know enough to stay out of Jackie when she made contact while it was getting its fix. But it did recognize the power pack she wore to maneuver."

Depression welled in her. "All it wants to do is go home."

"The sixty-four-thousand-dollar question is how. Best we can hope for is that it'll die of energy starvation eventually."

"And if it dies, what happens to Jackie?"

He looked at her with sudden insight. "It's always been a love-hate relationship for you, hasn't it?"

Ellen pushed the soup away unfinished.

Gardner, who had also spent the night on a nearby couch, judging from his rumpled uniform and the bags under his eyes, looked up from the computer as she approached.

"There are too many answers we don't have," he said, before she could ask her question.

"Why do you take such risks?" she said bitterly. "You knew there was something terribly wrong with that satellite. Why did you send my sister into danger?"

"If we hadn't," he said gently, "then for sure we'd never have known. I know it's a frightening situation, but you must remember your sister took the risk willingly."

"*It's* frightened too."

She was struck by the irony. The first alien humans had ever encountered, and they had no choice but to wait for it to die. Would there be anything left of Major Jacqueline Devon afterward?

"There's got to be something you could try," Kelly said.

"We've tried about everything," one of the scientists replied. "It's packing a terrific punch in voltage—tough to deal with."

There was pain in his voice. Ellen glanced at him. Gordon Chen. She remembered when Gardner introduced them Chen had said, *I feel responsible for Major Devon. It was my experiment she was trying to salvage.*

"It's learning fast," Gardner told them. "Already it knows enough not to enter the equipment we've used against it—just to guzzle the energy from it."

"That implies it's sentient?" Kelly put in.

"Maybe. At least, intelligent. There's a subtle difference. Sentience means self-awareness. Dogs are intelligent, but we doubt they have a sense of self. Dolphins, and chimps, who knows? As far as extraterrestrials are concerned and how we deal with them, it's an important distinction."

"But what kind of thing can live without a body, for Chrissakes?"

"We have to reevaluate our scenario for the evolution of possible life-forms," Chen said. "What this represents is an electrical ecology. Something we never thought of. And—think of the *size* of the auroral zone! How far out from Earth it extends. The tremendous amount of energy pouring in from the sun. My God! And it's ancient—there's been ample time for a whole chain of life-forms to evolve."

"Interesting to speculate how far up the chain this one is!" Kelly said dryly.

"Or how big," Gardner said. "Remember, Atlantis measured turbulence ten klicks out. That was the entity's signature. So the question is, did *all* of it enter Major Devon? And if not, what does that fact mean?"

"How the hell are we supposed to deal with something like that?" Kelly asked.

"We'd better *learn* to deal with these things—safely—if we want to continue using polar orbits," Chen said.

Inside the Faraday cage, Jackie twitched on her knees. Slowly now, one foot extended and she rose, swaying, grasping the bed for support.

"Notice how its control of the host body is improving?" one of the doctors said. "It's learning to do *that* too."

"If it doesn't kill her first—" Dr. Alvarado murmured. In the face of massive evidence, he seemed to have reluctantly accepted the parasite theory. "That last EKG was bad news."

"You're looking at this the wrong way," Ellen said. "Trying to zap it, kill it, you'll only succeed in killing my sister as well. What we need is to get it out."

"We've tried that," Chen said. "It's an electrical current itself, so we ought to be able to catch it with some kind of a conductor. But, trouble is, there were some pretty good conductors in the satellite, and it's used to them—knows how to avoid getting into them."

"And it seems to prefer being inside a living entity," Gardner added. "Maybe because it's using her to communicate."

"Then you have to fool it. Try something new, something that wasn't on the satellite. Isn't there something it won't recognize, that it'll get sucked into too fast to avoid?"

Gardner and the scientist stared at her. Then Chen's face flushed.

"My God!" he said.

* * *

"Ready, Ellen?"

She nodded, clenching her fists to keep herself from trembling. In the cage, through cold fog rising from the liquid helium, she could see the body of her sister stumbling around again, eyes closed, one foot clumsily stepping on the other. She couldn't bear to watch.

"Remember—get her to put her hand on it. She *must* make contact." Chen indicated the makeshift rig, hastily assembled from one of JPL's cannibalized computers.

"Maybe we should wait—when it drops her again—get a glove on her?" one of the medical specialists muttered.

"No time! She's weakening fast," Alvarado said. "If she goes into ventricular fibrillation—"

She could feel the thing's panic now.

Out!—out!—

There were no guarantees it would work. No guarantees, even if it did, that Jackie would survive. *All right. Do as I say.*

Emotion engulfed her. Homesickness! It was like a child or a small animal, she thought. Thrashing about in terror, it only succeeded in getting further entangled in the trap.

She was the only one who knew, the only one who could communicate with it, and she'd been cast in the role of its betrayer.

Home—dying—

She couldn't do it.

If she didn't do it, Jackie would surely die.

She had a memory then of their last year in high school, Jackie with the lead in the school play, Jackie on the softball team, Jackie with five offers of dates for the senior prom, Jackie winning the scholarship to MIT.

Near the door of the Faraday cage, the coiled wires of the cryotron waited, wreathed in fog. She shivered in the extreme cold, despite the sweaters and boots they'd made her wear.

No one could blame her if she wasn't telepathic after all.

"Look at the way it's moving *now!*" a voice murmured behind her.

Her sister's hand moved purposefully—smoothly—to brush a lock of hair away from her eyes.

She caught Kelly's gaze and he nodded. We all take risks, Kelly had told her.

Come toward me, Jackie. Trust me.

Step by step she directed the halting progress of her sister's body. Painfully she urged, cajoled, bullied, *pushed* the limp hand up.

Fingers uncurled slowly—reached out—
Now!

A microsecond before the comatose astronaut's hand touched the surface of the superconductor, a spasm wracked her. The blue lips parted and a cry emerged, halfway between a growl and a scream. Something flashed across the gap. Jackie toppled to the floor.

"Down the drain!" a technician exclaimed jubilantly, looking up from the gauges she'd been monitoring. "We got it! Look at those needles spin! No way it could resist the pull of that negative field."

"It won't get out of there in a hurry!" Chen smiled with relief. "As long as we keep the superconductor at extremely low temperature—something we can't do on a satellite yet—the current will flow around it forever."

Alvarado's medical team hurried inside the cage.

Ellen found tears streaming down her face. "It asked for help."

Colonel Gardner glanced at her, understanding. "You had to do it, to save your sister."

"It wanted to be free, to go home."

"This is only the beginning, Ms. Devon."

"Not a very glorious one!"

"We've got a lot to learn."

"If Jackie lives—" Kelly began.

"You realize, I can't allow you to tell this story," Gardner warned.

"Win some, lose some," the columnist said. "It'll be worth it."

Toward sunrise—the same improbable pink flush over the dry lake she'd first seen the day Atlantis landed—Jackie's eyelids fluttered. Pulling away from their sympathy, Ellen opened the door to the cage.

Then she hesitated. If her sister lived—

"Jackie?"

DEAD RINGER

BY EDWARD WELLEN

There is a bodie without a hart, that hath a toong, and yet
   no head;
Buried it was, ere it was made, and lowde it speakes, and
   yet is dead.
   —*Riddles of Heraclitus and Democritus* (London, 1598)

1

When he and his son reached Fifth and Chestnut, Nolan
Stedman caught sight of the Bell through the light-streaked
glass of its pavilion. He thought of a crack and looked forward
to voicing it. Franklin would turn on him all the scorn a ten-
year-old could muster for a bad pun the ten-year-old had not
come up with first. Meanwhile, Nolan smiled watching Franklin
take in the activity: Philadelphia's streets filling with all the
inhabitants thereof; street vendors breaking out small flags,
inflating balloons, readying bagels on shopping carts liberated
from supermarkets, proclaiming hot dogs, chili dogs, and pop
from three-wheelers. Nolan shuddered at a delicacy that seemed
unique to Philly, pretzels with mustard on 'em, but Franklin
showed no such compunction toward the stomach.

Nolan felt the Fourth of July tingle in the air. And vibes from
himself, inner reverberations of heartbeat and blood pressure,
now that the caper was at hand.

His present state brought to mind an embarrassing moment
of his own childhood when he had been unable to contain
himself: to-do did things to kids. Better be beforehand. "Did
you go to the bathroom yet?"

Franklin sidelonged him world-wearily. "I went to the bath-room yet."

Smarting off. Smartass.

"Then you're ready to recycle yourself?"

"Huh?"

Nolan gestured toward a cart that had a cool aura. "Like a refill?"

Thursday's child was thirsty. "An orange crush?"

Nolan sprang for an orange crush. Soda and liplicking erased the mustard mustache the pretzels had given Franklin. Nolan grinned. Nell'd kill him if she knew the junk food he'd let their son put away. What the hell, once a year; and every kid was a garbage disposal unit.

After the last dying gurgle, Franklin dropped the bottle into the nearest recycling bin. Without waiting to be told. Nolan looked up at the sky and aimed his thought at Nell's orbit. I must be doing something right.

Franklin had caught the vector. "Thinking of Mom?"

Nolan smiled and nodded. A touch guiltily; thinking of himself too and still tasting bile though nearly a dozen years had passed since the Space Shuttle program dropped him. He took Franklin's hand. "Let's go, son." It came out gruff.

Minimizing his limp, he headed them onto the mall. They cut across green with the spring worn out of it and tagged onto the line leading into the glass pavilion. They moved along, stop-and-go, keeping their body spaces, with—but not of—the group. Behind them a baby, frontpacked on its father, cried a tentative, testing cry. Ahead of them two nuns, like thumbs of praying hands, leaned together but apart; one with a very red face talked rapidly; the other waved a black-gloved hand calmingly.

Father and son followed them inside—and there it was. It stood hanging at floor level from its yoke in the dusty sunlight in its glass pavilion in Independence National Historical Park. Eighty parts copper, twenty parts tin.

It rang out a hush. The visitors clustered around it like fish gaping at a diving bell that had come down to them in their depths. A plush rope held them back, but their hands could reach out over and stroke the Liberty Bell.

Proclaim liberty throughout all the land unto all the inhabitants thereof. —Lev. 25:10.

It had to proclaim liberty silently. Rivets or spot brazings kept the crack from spreading.

"Well? Is the Bell all it's cracked up to be?"

Franklin turned his head slowly and gave his father the anticipated pitying look.

Nolan let his head fall forward heavily to acknowledge the weight of Franklin's scorn. Then he unbowed his head and tightened his mouth. The attendant, in National Park Service ranger uniform, was urging folks to move along and make room for more. Time to pull the caper.

He gave Franklin another chance to score off him. "Can you count one to a hundred?"

One corner of Franklin's mouth twitched but his face stayed grave. "A snap. One . . . two . . . a hundred."

"You rat-fink." Nolan leaned near for Franklin's ear only. "When I give you the high sign, a tap on the shoulder, you start counting to a hundred—a full chimpanzee count, buddy—while you walk over to the far side of the pavilion. When you get there, turn and face this way, and when you reach a hundred, start crying. Say something like, 'Where's my daddy?' Got it?"

Franklin looked wounded. "I'm not a wimp."

Nolan sighed impatiently. "It's only a diversionary move. If you can come up with something just as effective but more manly, fine."

Franklin blinked, then nodded. "Okay." His eyes took on a shine and he whispered, "What're you going to do?"

"You'll see when it happens." Nolan straightened and looked around. The group at the Bell was starting to yield under pressure from tourist backup. "Nothing to be afraid of. Don't let the noise spook you." He tapped Franklin's shoulder.

Mouthing numbers, Franklin edged away from the Bell through a temporary parting of nuns. Nolan watched him. The actual count didn't count: it was just to keep Franklin too busy to look conspiratorial.

Facing the Bell again, Nolan reached into his pants pocket for the charge. His hand curved ready. But when Franklin's diversionary move came it took Nolan as much by surprise as it did everyone else.

Crash. Then bloody murder of a yell. Nolan swung around with the rest. Franklin lay writhing on the floor. Beside him, a toppled standard holding an arrow pointed now to the floor. Franklin sat up and bent forward to touch an ankle. He stopped short with a wince. "Ow! I broke my leg."

It fooled the others and—for the second—Nolan too felt a stab of alarm. Then Nolan flashed back to himself as a kid limping along on a make-believe lame leg, to the crickety whistling of his corduroys, in a play for sympathy or a stab at

drama ("Who is that bravely suffering boy?"). Kids made
natural actors. That later life could make mock real, that a
stupid accident providing him with a real limp had ended Nolan's career as a shuttle pilot, was something to repress.

As others sprang into talk and the attendant into action,
Nolan slipped the charge and a ball of adhesive out of his
pocket, stepped stiffly over a plush catenary, stuck the charge
inside the Bell along the crack in the soundbow, lit the fuse,
and was back over the rope without challenge from anyone.
Perfect misdirection. Everyone had turned toward Franklin and
had surged to see.

Barang!

The quantity if not quality of decibels proved gratifying. The
long-dead cracked Bell sounded a loud dull cracked note. A
nun shrieked and black-gloved hands fluttered heavenward,
scared crows. People of all feathers scattered and made scarce,
seeking the sanctuary of outdoors. The frontpacked baby cried
fiercely; just the noise would have stunned it, the father's jump
had given it a contact scare.

"Nothing to worry about, folks. Don't panic." But Nolan
talked to the glass walls.

Only he and Franklin remained inside the pavilion. Franklin
stood jittering happily on his miraculously healed leg. A ranger
stared in at them as at fish that had dirtied the tank.

Nolan had a qualm or two, his heartbeat undulating to the
sound of a nearing siren. "Stand still," he told Franklin, and he
smiled and nodded reassuringly to the ranger. He tried to make
light. "What's white and black and has fuzz inside?"

Franklin pointed to a police gumball maneuvering closer.
"That!"

And there *they,* really, were. The Philly cops answered the
squeal in force. They wore riot helmets and carried Perspex riot
shields. They ran ready with nausea gas, tear gas, rubber bullets, and water hoses. Eighty parts copper, twenty parts tintin-
nabulation. A bullhorn directed them in the sealing of all escape
routes.

The cops pushed the swelling crowd and even the privileged
TV camerapersons and press photographers well back. Nolan
strained to spot Maggie McGee. He'd tipped her off there'd be
a story at the Bell today. "Fireworks, Maggie. Unscheduled
fireworks." He'd hoped she'd cover it in person, fly in from
Washington aboard her channel's chopper. But now the trigger-
happy cops, not the media, were his concern. Moving slowly,
he took out his ID card and pinned it to his Hawaiian shirt.

"Franklin."

"Yes, Dad?" Franklin seemed suddenly solemned by Nolan's tone.

"Make no sudden moves. Understand?"

Looking puzzled, Franklin nodded.

Guns drawn, the cops swarmed carefully in. Nolan and Franklin gave themselves up, Nolan raising his hands slowly and Franklin following suit.

"Turn around, keep your hands high, spread your feet, lean against the wall."

They didn't assume the position fast enough to satisfy one young longhaired cop. Growling, he whipped his pistol at Nolan's temple. Disbelief kept Nolan from tilting his head away in time. The sight raked flesh; blood trickled into his left eye.

Nolan tried to speak calmly and pleasantly, though aggrievedly. "Easy, officer. That was uncalled-for. We're not resisting."

The cop growled again but did not strike again.

A husky cop patted Nolan down. His hand froze on the bulge in Nolan's pants pocket. "What's this?"

This, standing out in stark outline along the thigh of Nolan's tight jeans, had a rodlike look. Nolan could see that it might seem a stick of dynamite.

Before Nolan could answer, the longhaired cop touched his gun to Nolan's neck.

Nolan did not move, did not even breathe.

The husky cop reached in and tugged out a sheaf of paper that rubber bands held in tube shape.

The gun at Nolan's neck relaxed. Nolan felt free to speak. "Press releases, officer."

"You on some sort of First Amendment kick? You belong to some terrorist group?"

"Neither, officer. What I did—"

The husky cop shoved the press releases back down. "Save it, the lieutenant's coming. He'll read you your rights."

Nolan smiled reassuringly at Franklin. Up to now, law 'n' order had meant nothing more serious personally to Franklin than "Keep Off the Grass." Now the kid looked worried.

Even so, he appeared let down when none of what the crime shows had led him to expect took place. No skin search, no handcuffing, no fingerprinting.

Before it came to all that, the jut-jawed lieutenant in charge read Nolan's ID. He glared at Nolan in scorn but spoke with some respect. "So you're the Beady Eye."

Nolan didn't mind the nickname, but it would help now if

he stood on his spelled-out dignity. "Bespeaker of the Department of the Interior. This was a test of security measures."

The lieutenant nodded sourly. "A test."

Nolan shrugged righteously. "Nothing wrong with your people's response, but it was response, not prevention. The harmless firecracker could just as easily have been high explosive."

The lieutenant eyed him stonily. "So?"

"So I proved my point: the Liberty Bell needs more protection from terrorists and other crazies."

The lieutenant nodded, a glint in his eyes as he held his gaze on Nolan. "And other crazies, yes."

That flushed color; Nolan felt the heat of it. He touched a fresh facial tissue to his temple. It came away pink; the bleeding had begun to stop.

The lieutenant locked eyes with him. "Looks like you hurt yourself pulling this stunt."

Nolan broke the gaze to glance at the longhaired young cop. Nolan's mouth tightened. Then he met the lieutenant's eyes again. "Looks that way."

With a satisfied shake of his head, the lieutenant turned away and called off the squeal.

Wait, Nolan wanted to tell him. *Listen. Sometimes a guy has to use unorthodox means to get his message across, resort to the offbeat to bring needed change.* But the lieutenant had gone with his people. Nolan smiled brightly at Franklin.

"Well, we did it."

"Yeah." That came out late and leadenly.

Nolan flushed again. Had he gone too far, misused his son, lost respect? Dammit, there he went again, worrywarting, making moles out of nothing. Of course Franklin wasn't disowning him; the kid merely felt beat after all the excitement.

Nolan's gaze shot to rangers examining the Bell. He knew they had found no damage, but they glanced his way accusingly. No, just curiously.

Now TV camerapersons and press photographers, unleashed, huddled around the rangers. The rangers thumbed them at Nolan. Reporters surrounded Nolan and Franklin, shouting questions that canceled each other out. No Maggie McGee—if she had been there she would have shoved herself politely to the forefront—but someone from Channel 3 had showed.

Nolan had counted on making the most of the photo opportunity, get his message across with a few choice quotes about vigilance, but now he made it short and sour. He drew the tube of handouts from his pocket, thrust it at the nearest outstretched

hand, and while the newsgatherers fought for copies he grabbed
Franklin, said, "Let's get out of here," and somehow they did.

2

They drove back to Bethesda and reached home on the hour.
Nolan voiced the TV on and the default station, Channel 3, lit
up.

As usual, the anchorperson smilingly declaimed headlines
while tantalizing snatches of clips flashed by. Nolan braced
himself for something on the order of DINGBAT DEFACES DING-
DONG, but nothing screened about the Liberty Bell, the BDI,
or even Philadelphia. No shot of Nolan and Franklin in the
glass pavilion, no flashing police cars, no crowds waving at the
camera, no "Unexpected fireworks at the Liberty Bell in Philadelphia this morning."

Momentous announcements from the White House preempted
the news. The biggest headline-grabber, the banner event, was
President Dodge's lifting the secrecy lid on the previous administration's shenanigans, uncovering Cabinet members' conflicts
of interest, breaches of security, taking of bribes.

Miffed that this should break just now, Nolan turned away.
He didn't switch off but he tuned out.

Then Franklin was tugging at his arm. "There you are, Dad!"

For a split second Nolan thought it was indeed him on the
screen; he grinned back at his image. Then the words of the
talking head registered and he knew he had never spoken them.
His look-alike was making a statement, as a ranking member of
the select committee, about the Ins' investigation of the Outs'
misdeeds. "—and we promise to ferret out the betrayers of the
public trust and to prosecute them without fear or favor—"

"Look closer, Franklin. That's cousin Bob." He felt slightly
miffed again. "Can't you see he's older than me?"

Franklin nodded dutifully but spoke doubtfully. "Ye-es."

Nolan could never get over how different the polished conservative Senator Robert Stedman, Jr., was from the fascinat-
ingly reckless Bob Stedman the younger Nolan Stedman had
looked up to as a kid.

But what gave with the Bell story? Why not even minimal
coverage? He waited till the newscast ended to make sure there
was no mention, then went to the phone.

Maggie McGee sounded philosophical when Nolan's call caught
her at her office. Philosophical that he wasn't calling to suggest
a date; he had been going out with her when he met Nell, and
she had never given up hinting that she was still available. And

philosophical about the buried story. Sweetly so; the rustle of a wrapper and the talking with a full mouth told him she was putting away one of her quick-energy candy bars. "Happens."

"But why just now?"

"Conspiracy theory? Uh-uh. I do buy politics theory. The White House, all same all departments including Interior, saves items to release when needed. Ranges from appointments and signings, making it seem the Chief's on a working vacation, to announcements of note, burying unfavorable publicity."

Nolan smiled with perverse satisfaction. "Then I must've struck a nerve."

Maggie laughed glutinously. "Grow up, Nolan. Don't flatter yourself. Lax security at the Liberty Bell ain't what's moving and shaking the movers and shakers. Must be a really big shoe getting ready to drop. 'Swhy I'm at my desk now, trying to reach my sources and find out what's really cooking, and I'll get back to it soon as you get off the line."

"I'll get off right now. Sorry I troubled you."

"Aw, did I hit you where it hurts? Next time we meet I'll kiss it and make it well." She made it sound suggestive.

Nolan felt suddenly uncomfortable, with Franklin in earshot. He mumbled something, anything, and hung up.

He looked at his watch. Five hours to kill before calling Nell. He turned to a bored-looking Franklin.

"Let's have a snowball fight."

"Snowballs? On the Fourth?"

"When will you learn to stop looking at your father as though he's crazy when he makes a perfectly sound statement?"

"Sound?"

"Echo in here. Yes, sound. Sound goes with the Fourth. The Bell may not ring out, but firecrackers go off. And we can throw snowballs if we have snowballs, and we have snowballs. Follow me. Walk this way."

Nolan shambled like a gorilla, knuckles almost to the floor. A glance back showed Franklin aping him. In the kitchen, he dug deep in the deep freeze and brought forth a plastic bag of snowballs.

"The snows of yesteryear, son. Poor François Villon was too parochial in time and space to know about the icecaps, much less the marvels of modern engineering." He got a grip on a ball and squeezed it through the plastic. "Too marvelous. Or marbelous. Better let them thaw a bit before we have at one another."

Even after a ten-minute wait in the outdoor sun, the cores

remained icy. He stationed himself, with his dozen snowballs, and Franklin with his, twenty paces apart and took care to miss Franklin. Franklin did not show the same concern and the palpable hits stung.

"My own flesh and blood bloodies my own flesh." Nolan ducked one last time and gratefully watched the last of the spent snowballs melt on the grass into mirrors of the sky.

They lay on the lawn and gazed skyward.

"Dad, do you believe in UFOs?"

"Sure."

"You do? Did you ever see one?"

Nolan made up a story on the spot. "Hard to say. I may have—then again I may not have. When I was your age, we had a dog— "

"Clangor," Franklin prompted. "Basset."

Nolan frowned. For this story he needed another dog. Keep Franklin off-balance. Stop the kid from getting hooked on labels, let alone becoming a know-it-all able to call him on details he couldn't justify or even remember. "No, this one was Clinger, a bulldog. Before Clangor's time. Well, sir, this one day Clinger and I were out on the lawn—"

"At your Uncle Bob's place in Vermont."

Nolan had been on the point of making that the local habitation, but he shook his head. Insistence on precision made for verisimilitude—and kept the beloved snot off-balance. "Sorry. This was the open space in the park next to the county office building. I was waiting for Uncle Bob, though. To pass the time, I threw a Frisbee for Clinger to catch. Now, you wouldn't think a little old fat waddly bulldog would be good at that, but let me tell you old Clinger excelled, pure excelled."

"Gee."

"Well, sir, this particular day we were alone on the lawn and I was sorry nobody else was around to watch old Clinger excel himself. Got the Frisbee every time in one powerful leap and held it in his sure jaws. Now, here comes the strange thing. I've never told anyone about this till now. Well, sir, I took the Frisbee for the last time from Clinger and turned away from him and walked thirty paces before turning to throw again. When I did turn, I couldn't believe my eyes. But my eyes insisted there was no mistake. They said I was seeing another Frisbee sail out of the blue on a trajectory that would buzz it by Clinger. As I said, no one else was there on the lawn with us, so who could have thrown it? The county office building was too far away from us for the Frisbee to have come from there, even if someone had stood on the roof and thrown the Frisbee with all his—or her or its—force. No, sir, it just could not have been—and yet there it was." He left Franklin space for a gee.

"Gee!"

"Well, sir, old Clinger wasn't sitting down on his haunches studying about where the Frisbee came from. No, sir, old Clinger got set to catch that Frisbee. Now, as I stared at the Frisbee, it hit me that that Frisbee was like no Frisbee I had ever had anything to do with. That Frisbee had tiny little lights all around its rim."

Nolan gazed through Franklin thoughtfully. "Looking back, I'm not so sure they were rim lights after all. They might've been tiny little windows, showing that the Frisbee was hollow and lit up inside. Flight deck and cabins, you know."

Franklin's eyes bugged satisfactorily. "Gee!"

Nolan nodded. "Well, sir, I had sense enough to realize this Frisbee wasn't a Frisbee. 'Clinger,' I yelled, 'don't jump!' " He shook his head. "Too late. Soon as the thing came in Clinger's range, Clinger made a mighty leap and clamped his powerful jaws on the thing. 'Clinger,' I yelled, 'let go!' But once Clinger had a hold Clinger wouldn't let go. Sure, it must've surprised him when his weight and momentum failed to bring him and the Frisbee back down to the ground, but he held on. The Frisbee seemed to shudder with the impact and stall in midair for the fraction of a second, then little tiny rocket engines fired and the craft took off like a, like a shot."

"Gee!"

"Ten gees at least. Well, sir, talk about keep on keeping on, old Clinger held on holding on. It was a saucer-sized flying saucer, was what it was, and it carried poor old Clinger up, up, and away."

"What happened then? He did come back, didn't he?"

Nolan shook his head sadly, too moved to speak. It took him a moment to summon his voice. "Never came back. Well, sir, I couldn't bring myself to tell Uncle Bob the truth about Clinger's disappearance. To tell *you* the truth, I had begun to doubt that I had seen what I had seen, even with affidavits from my eyes, and I knew very well nobody else would believe me, so I told Uncle Bob that Clinger had chased after a squirrel. When they gave Clinger up for lost they got me Clangor."

"But what do you think happened to Clinger? Did the aliens take him to their home world?"

Nolan spread his hands as though feeling for and weighing just and unjust rain. "We can only speculate. However, if you study your star charts you'll see Sirius, the Dog Star. Even though the chart doesn't specify the breed, doesn't come right out and say Bulldog, I somehow *know*. To me, Sirius will always be Clinger."

Franklin stared at him. "But, Dad, Sirius was there long before—"

"Hey, look at the time. Let's hurry indoors and make that call to Mom."

Nolan let Franklin dial Spacelab's code number and Nell's extension.

"Nell Packard here."

Her voice always surprised Nolan, though it had been this deep for almost ten years. The Pill tended to lower the vocal register, as female singers had learned. Franklin had been an accident; sperm had whipped past a defective coil, setting back her career the space of the balloon months of her pregnancy and the deflated month after parturition, and motivating her to switch to the Pill to prevent another viable accident.

"Hi, Mom."

" 'Lo, Franklin. Your dad with you?"

"Uh-huh. Guess what."

"I give up. What?"

"We bombed the Liberty Bell!"

"That's nice."

Franklin rolled his eyes at Nolan. Nolan kept his face blank, but he knew what Franklin meant and he knew how Franklin felt. Mind on her mission, Nell often did not process messages from home.

Nolan leaned in to speak past Franklin into the mouthpiece. "We bombed, period."

"Wow. That sounds interesting. I'm glad my two guys are having fun."

Even tight-beam linkups and scrambling circuits would not keep talk secret and sacred. So, even though they would not have got mushy anyway, awareness of other ears made for constraint and inanity.

"Loads of fun. What about you? How much time have you for lazing?"

"Nolan! You know I can't talk about that."

Her sudden anger stunned and then angered *him*. Then he saw how they had both gone wrong. Her preoccupation with the hush-hush new laser weapon she was working on had led her to take *lazing* for *lasing*. He swallowed the reply he had been about to make.

He tried to patch it up. "Oh, come on now, Nell, it can't be all work. Everyone has to goof off once in a while. Why *can't* I say I hope you take time out, at least for the view?"

Nell's turn to regroup. It didn't take her long to catch on. "Sorry. Maybe I need to join Workaholics Anonymous. But I do look down almost every pass, and I do think of you all the time."

"Goes double." He cleared his throat. "When are you taking the shuttle back down?"

"It's scheduled for the twenty-second of this month." She cleared her throat. "Well, take care fo yourselves."

"You too. Have a nice orbit."

"Thanks. Love you, Nolan; love you, Franklin." She threw them a vocal kiss. "*Mmmmuh.*" Dry run for a wet dream.

He lay in bed alone remembering them alone together on that ski slope eleven years ago. Trying to impress her before their marriage, he had sped over the rise ahead of her, veered toward a sapling, and bore down on it. The sapling seemed slight enough and supple enough to bend way over before him, let him ride over it, and then whip upright in his wake, leaving her with the puzzle of how his skis swept by on either side. The tree bent way over before him all right, but a bough snagged his belt. He never figured out the mechanical forces involved, he knew only that he wound up twisted on his back with a snapped legbone. First his unnecessary bravado caused him to break his leg, then his stupid machismo caused him to compound the break. He shoved to his feet so Nell would find him upright when she caught up with him, only to have the leg fold under him when she did come upon him. Nell spoke no wounding words and did what needed doing. She lashed their skis into a travois and hauled him down the slope, got Nolan into the car and to the hospital. When months later he reported at Kennedy Space Center, the gimp washed him out of the Space Shuttle program. NASA was tightening its belt, trimming down; when it came to who'd stay and who'd go the fittest had the edge.

Burning again with remembered shame, he fell asleep. Snow filled his dreams. A kid—himself? Franklin?—made a snowperson, then attached a snow penis to make it a snowman, but some-body came along and expressed outrage and knocked off the penis.

3

Bright and early, Nolan feinted a punch to Franklin's jaw. "Put up your marquises." He ducked a roundhouse right. "The Kayo Kid. Okay, that's enough working up an appetite. Besides, you're getting too good."

They made breakfast, ate it, fed Pearl Diver II+ the dirty dishes, and Nolan drove Franklin to summer day camp.

The Fourth had fallen on a Wednesday and even Washington couldn't stretch that either way into a long weekend, so government offices were nominally open on the fifth. After dropping Franklin off, Nolan phoned ahead from his car while making for the Department of the Interior.

The Interior Secretary's secretary sounded user-friendly but said firmly that the Interior Secretary was busy and in any case a caller needed an appointment set up long in advance.

Nolan said just as firmly, "Not the BDI when on a matter of importance. I'll be there in fifteen minutes."

After the Big Ripoff of 1998, Congress had institutionalized whistleblowing. Now each department of government had its ombudsman, its Bespeaker, with direct access to the Secretary. If the Bespeaker felt the Secretary to be unresponsive or corrupt, the Bespeaker had the right to go over the Secretary's head to the President. If the Bespeaker felt the President to be unresponsive or corrupt, the Bespeaker had the right to go over the President's head to the People.

The Secretary's secretary gave Nolan no more guff and when he got there she greeted him with a cold courtesy she had caught from her boss and buzzed him in.

Nolan had never found much interior to the man. Now there was only a stiff exterior of unwilling patience.

SecInt listened with the hum that was his busy signal, then pursed his lips as though thinking something sour about whistleblowers. But he did not pooh-pooh Nolan's public theatrics in Philly as puerile.

"No big problem. If you feel security's lax, and a national treasure's at risk and people might get hurt in the unlikely event of a terrorist attack, we'll install metal detectors."

"Metal detectors would not screen out plastic charges."

"Then what do you suggest? That we store the real Bell in a vault and display a hologram of it?"

Nolan felt sure SecInt had set that up to knock down; still, he could not keep from pulling his head back to duck a roundhouse right. "That should be the last resort. The people have a right to the real thing, the thing itself."

"Then what? Do we pour plastex around the Bell, seal it inside a cube of the stuff?"

Nolan felt the joy of battle. He and this guy would always be poles apart, polemics together. "Hardly. People should feel free to feel freely, be able to touch the Bell, have hands-on experience of their heritage."

"Agreed. So?" SecInt's eyebrows knitted. "You bespeak a problem, and that's your duty, but what happens when there's no solution?"

"There's always a solution."

"Problematical. But say that's so. In this case, the only solution I see raises a problem of its own. More guards. More guards mean bigger payroll. But I have a budget. I have to stay within my budget."

"We can have tighter security without adding guards. I'm thinking of state-of-the-art mind-scanning."

Something flashed in SecInt's eyes, quickly dulled. "That's new and untried."

Nolan shook his head. "I've looked into it or I wouldn't have brought it up. It works."

"Fill me in."

"Before peole got near the Bell, they'd pass through scanners. Significance-probability mapping would tell whether the brain signals were in the hostile-thoughts range. A silent alarm would go off, guards would move in and rush the person away."

SecInt's frown signaled hostile thoughts. "What if terrorists programmed a moron, or brainwashed a drugged or hypnotized normal, and sent such a person in to do the job?"

Nolan was proud of SecInt. "Good question." That made him prouder of himself. "There'd still be an overlay of the wrong pattern. The very programming is hostile in intent, and it would show up as abnormal brain activity for that person."

SecInt pointed an aha! finger. "How coould the mindscreener—mindscanner?—tell what's abnormal for a person? We have no data base covering everyone."

"Not yet. And I hope we never do. But the mindscanner can demodulate the carrier wave, giving us a statistical-probability handle on the information wave."

SecInt smiled a smile that remained enigmatic till SecInt himself defined it. "Pardon the ironic smile. The Bell symbolizes freedom, proclaims liberty. Doesn't what you're suggesting run counter to what this land stands for, to all we hold dear?"

Nolan blinked. He thought hard before he answered. "What price freedom of thought? Sometimes we have to protect ourselves from ourselves. A society of individuals has the right to protect society against individuals. The body politic can't let its hand cut off its nose to spite its face. All I know is, we're beset by terrorists foreign and domestic." He leaned forward to be confidential and persuasive. "The BDT told me mindscanners will soon be in place at airports to detect would-be hi-jackers, mad bombers, and even smugglers. She's sounded out Supreme Court watchers and the consensus is mindscans will prove Constitutional. So it would be safe to go with mindscanners. And they'd be cheaper than extra guards."

SecInt gave off his busy signal for a long moment. Then, "If the device can fit into my budget it's certainly worth considering." He leaned forward, ready to push out of his chair. "Anything else on your mind?"

Nolan shook his head. "Not at the moment." He stood up. "Thank you for your time."

SecInt waved that away. But he did not say, "My pleasure."

4

Nolan's tickler file reminded him monthly to check up on how faithfully Interior stepped up security for the Bell. In August, a call to SecInt brought assurances that a survey of mindscanner practicality was in the works. In September, he learned that SecInt had appointed a committee to review the survey. During October, Interior studied the committee's report. In November, Interior solicited bids for mindscanner installation. During December, Interior studied the proposals. January saw the awarding of the task and the signing of the contract. On February 1, SecInt himself phoned Nolan.

"The mindscanner's in place. No publicity to mark the deed: undesirable for the public to be overly mindful of it."

Nolan told SecInt, and himself, "Well done."

On February 2, he got a call from Maggie McGee. "Happy Groundhog Day."

Uh-oh. Was he going to hear innuendoes about holes? "Good to hear from you, Maggie. What's new?"

"Our Philly affiliate has it that some crackpot snuck in during the night and spraypainted the Liberty Bell yellow. He phoned our office saying he did it because President Dodge is too soft on our foes. Trouble is, the National Park Service, on orders from Interior, denies the incident took place. But the Bell Pavilion did open late this morning, and our Philly filly says if you look real close at the Bell you can see signs of hasty scrubbing."

Nolan felt a swift kick in his guts. Even as he got all worked up about the Bell, he asked himself why. The Bell, sure, but more than the Bell. It had become personal. More than wrath at duty derelict, at promises unkept, or his sense of gestalt incomplete, of an undertaking clamoring for closure. Something midway between perseverance and perverseness: stubbornness. Bulldog Stedman.

"Hello? Nolan? About the alleged incident and Interior's unforthcomingness—any comment? This *is* your bailiwick."

How much ground does a groundhog hog? "Just say that the BDI says security measures are supposed to be in place, and that he will be looking into what went wrong—if anything did go wrong."

"Good enough for the record, I guess." Her tone grew inviting. "Off the record, when are you going to come out of your hole? I have some good stuff, some corks to pop, and—"

He pressed his beeper to beep. "Sorry, Maggie, got to take another call. Be talking to you soon again."

After Maggie clicked off, Nolan got through to SecInt's secretary.

"Sorry, sir, he's out at the moment and can't be reached. But he thought you might call, so he left a message for you."

She played it for him. SecInt's voice seemed unconcerned. "To answer your questions, yes, the system's in place but the technicians have yet to hook it up; and no, that won't take long."

Nolan programmed his tickler file to nudge him to follow through.

Good thing he did; happenings between February and June took his mind off the Bell.

Bad thing he did; damned bedside tickler pinged for attention last evening of Nell's Earth leave, itself an unscheduled bonus event thanks to her need to get fitted in an improved EVA suit.

It was a careful rapture, because of Franklin in the next room, and they had just agreed that, next time, they would have to get away by themselves. That would help them try to work things out. They had grown more and more constrained during their get-togethers and they knew they had things to work out. At the moment, though, they did have something going for them, and they were in a clinch, faces so close that they had to shut their eyes to visualize one another, when the ping came on the bedside monitor.

Nell opened an eye and stared at the message. She pulled away, and when Nolan opened his eyes she pointed.

TIME TO GO SEE HER.

"I thought at first it was the reminder that I shuttle back to Spacelab today, but it seems to be for you."

Nolan grinned. "Your rival." Then, as Nell stiffened, he hurried to explain. "It's the Liberty Bell. I want to check on her security. To bell-ringers, a bell is a she."

Nell smiled and leaned to kiss him, one hand pulling her hair back out of the way. "My bell-ringer."

Three hours later he and Franklin saw her, Nell in shrinkwrap jeans, off on a flight to Florida and a shuttle launching back up to Spacelab. For some reason, after the accident that barred him from an active part in the shuttle program, he always found some reason to duck attending actual liftoff of a shuttle.

They all waved so long, then Nolan dropped Franklin off at summer day camp and on this day in the last week in June, nearly one year after he and Franklin had bombed the Bell, he flew to Philly and the Bell.

Changes there were. A cyclone fence ringed the mall and the glass pavilion. At the new gate he spotted the mindscanner. If you didn't know what you were looking for, you'd pass the mindscanner's guileless housing by without a second glance.

A short line at this hour on this day. As the Bell reeled him nearer he thought thoughts of hate. Not hatred for the Bell—that would have been hard to feign—but hatred for SecInt and the unresponsive and obstructive bureaucracy SecInt stood for—and that was easy to feel. More than enough to set the mindscanner silently shrieking.

He passed the mindscanner. Nothing happened. The door of the glass pavilion did not snap shut to keep him out. No guards rushed up to grab him.

"Please keep moving, sir."

He stood stiff with rage, holding up the line. If ever the silent alarm should go off, now was the time.

A guide did step to his side. "Sir, aren't you feeling well? Come inside and sit down."

That held out hope the mindscanner had worked after all, but the hope didn't last. This was no ruse to take him quietly. The guard seemed genuinely solicitous about him; she sat him down, gave him breathing space, and even stood ready with an oxygen whiffer.

Beyond anger, Nolan felt sadness. He gazed at the Bell. If

the Bell could have tolled it could have tolled any of a number of happenings—birth, marriage, death; alarm, rebellion, victory— but whatever it tolled it would have tolled the passage of time.

His mind shot to SecInt and ilk. What was with these people? Didn't they know life's only real currency was time? Why didn't they do their job? Why did they waste time?

SecInt had stalled and lied. Why?

Nolan felt just sore enough to go over SecInt's head to the President. Better not go off half-cocked, though. Not that he was beholden to President Dodge. He had a lifetime post. A Bespeaker served not at the will or whim of any administration. But maybe he should touch base with the BDS.

5

Fabian Piel, Bespeaker for the Department of State, had trademarks: eyepatch and the grooved cheeks of a carved eb- ony mask, making him a favorite of cartoonists. Nolan and Fabian had been friends ever since Nolan had called him on the eyepatch. It had suddenly struck Nolan that Fabian wore the eyepatch sometimes over the right eye and sometimes over the left eye. "What's the idea? Why do you wear that thing?" "Because I want to see." Nolan had blinked. "See what?" "No, see who and see how long and see whether. See who catches on, and see how long it takes the who, and see whether the who will speak up about it. You've known me a year. Took you till now to get wise. But you spoke right up. So that evens out, gives you a respectable score. To answer your why, childhood amblyopia started me on the eyepatch. I don't really need it now, of course, but—" He shrugged and Nolan laughed, and that was the end of that and the beginning of their friendship.

Today, the eyepatch covered the right eye. A grin unpleated the grooves in the cheeks. "Still walking the path of righteous- ness?"

"Following your footsteps."

"Makes me feel like the guy who looked back to see a bear sniffing his footprints. 'You like tracks? I'll make more.' How are Nell and Franklin?"

"Fine, thanks." There was no one to ask Fabian about in return. "Let me tell you about something that doesn't ring true."

Fabian sat back unmoving, unpatched eye shut. He seemed lost in reverie or asleep, but Nolan knew he listened. Nolan had a feeling that the other eye stayed wide open looking through the black silk veiling it.

Nolan finished, caught himself leaning forward into Fabian's silence, and leaned back. "Well? How does it compute?"

Fabian's talk had a way of taking a few degrees of digression. Would it now? It would.

The unpatched eye opened but looked past Nolan. Fabian spoke dreamily. "Computers are turning the cosmos into machine-language soup. Long way to go, but they're busy busy busy. Like the Peripatetic Pipsqueak."

"What in hell is that?"

"Cosmologists are all wrong about the Big Bang. It was, and always is, the Peripatetic Pipsqueak. All began with one lone subatomic particle. Nothing else anywhere. But it had a spin on it, and that created curvature. Took time, though time had so little meaning that it was the same as instantaneous, but eventually it caught up with itself—or met itself—and caromed, giving off its strike note and its hum note. Well, sir, that one particle has been doing its darnedest to stitch together the universe. One dot all over the place warping and woofing itself into the Great Tapestry. The experiential world's a self-seeing photon screen that seems fixed at the speed of light. And all of it the nearest thing to nothing busy making itself into the nearest thing to something."

Nolan smiled but narrowed his eyes at Fabian. When Fabian Piel most digressed he most made a point. "Meaning?"

"Are you making whole cloth out of nothing? A Bespeaker must ask himself or herself if he or she has an ulterior motive for targeting someone."

Nolan felt himself redden. "If I see the need to act should I search my soul before I take action? Hamlet was Hamlet, but Denmark did smell of something rotten."

Fabian opened his mouth, then closed it.

Nolan gave a tight smile of encouragement. "No, go on."

Fabian's shoulders moved, not so much a shrug as a loosening up. "Ask yourself about yourself. Can you be sure you're not trying to prove yourself to Nell and raise yourself in your son's eyes?" Fabian sat in darkside profile, but could have been casting a sidelong glance at Nolan through the patch. "Nell foremost, and that could be your big problem, a self-fulfilling prophecy. More you try to gain assurance of worth from Nell, more you make her ill at ease. That tends to drive her farther away—and *that* makes you try harder to prove yourself to win her back." He faced Nolan.

Nolan's cheek pulsed. He'd asked for it. Should've remembered that Fabian once worked as a private eye, heading his own agency before the Congressional Commission tapped him for bespeakership, that Fabian's doctorate was on motivational research. Nolan felt his face give off waves of heat as his mind flashed back to the fuzz flourishing the gun. To prove a point, father had imperiled son. He felt the heat mount. Dammit, though, he had been doing his duty. And the Bell still stood at risk.

He tried to keep his voice even. "I have no illusions about myself, but—"

"That's your greatest illusion."

Nolan winced. "Okay, but I'm not imagining that the Bell has zero security."

"But you have doubts about what to do next, or why come to me?"

Nolan found himself grinning suddenly. "I've never had to go to the President yet and I guess I needed the moral support you've just given me."

Fabian grinned back. "My pleasure."

6

The Bespeakerphone on the desk in the Oval Office answered on the tenth ring. President Dodge's voice showed a mix of curiosity and annoyance. "Yes?"

Nolan identified himself as the BDI and asked for an appointment for that afternoon.

A pause, then, "Let's see. The Iranian ambassador, the President of United Korea. No. I'll fit you in between the U.S. Spelling Champ and the Vienna Boys' Choir." That put him in his place. "Two thirty." Sounded like a dental appointment. "I'll notify the East Gate."

"Thank—"

Click.

"—you."

A terrorist bomb had weakened the power grid. Though the White House had its own power, its lights burned dim in sympathy. An usher led Nolan along a murky corridor. As they passed an open doorway Nolan caught an Army major glancing out from behind a desk and doing a double take. So it didn't surprise him when he heard quick soft footsteps and felt a tap on his shoulder.

Before Nolan could turn, it was all over. The major had whispered his piece and headed back to his office. "Bob, the

Four Committee has to meet about the Bell. Tonight, same time, same place."

Nolan smiled. Not the first time someone had mistaken him for his cousin. He made to tap the usher's shoulder, get the usher to wait while he went back to straighten the major out. Then the words sank in. The major would be Major Marshall Sixtus, the President's military attaché. What did the major and Bob have to do with the Bell? Nolan let his hand fall short of the usher's shoulder.

They reached the Oval Office.

Nolan, despite himself, hit a brace on coming into the presence. President Sally Dodge was Black Irish—the map of Ireland with a little burnt Cork around the eyes where sleepless nights had bruised the skin. Her loose sweater did not point up the fertility symbols. On the other hand, she did not wear trousers. Definitely not one of the boys. Frost hair framed a face that knew it would be on stamps and coins long after it faded from today's media. Joan of Arc. Eve of battle.

She got up slowly and unsmilingly. She eyed him, he thought chauvinistically, as if he were tracking up a floor she had just mopped. Her eyes measured him. Suddenly she smiled the famous crinkly smile.

She pointed a finger at him. "Aren't you Commander Packard's spouse? Didn't you used to be involved in the space program too?"

"Guilty." As always when someone made the identification he felt the tips of his ears burn. Nell had kept her last name but he always told himself it never really got under his skin as long as the quizzer didn't call him Mr. Packard.

"And you're the image of Senator Stedman. You his younger brother?"

He made his standard response. "Cousin twice removed—but I keep coming back."

Her laugh was more an acknowledging "Aha" than a "Ha-ha."

Nolan dug his nails in his palms. Be businesslike. Save your kidding for yourself and Franklin. Mistake to be facetious in the Oval Office.

President Dodge confirmed this with a glance at the digital clock on her desk. "Let's get on with it." Meaning "Let's get it over with." She gestured him to a chair. "What do you know that I don't and should?"

Nolan briefed her on the Bell's lack of security, on SecInt's failure to set the mindscanner to work.

President Dodge's finger put Nolan on hold, then got SecInt

on the videophone. She cut into the image's flowery hello. "Why isn't the mindscanner monitoring visitors to the Bell?"

"It has to do with Operation Let Freedom Ring."

"What the hell is that?"

"We plan to give the Bell its voice back. This anniversary it will ring out the way the founders meant it to. This entails unimpeded access to the Bell for precise measurements."

Dodge frowned. "We're talking about *the* Liberty Bell, right?"

"Right, Ms. President."

"The Liberty Bell is cracked, right?"

"Right again, Ms. President."

"You're not planning to fill in the crack or recast the Bell?"

SecInt galvanized in horror. "Of course not, ms. the crack's too sacred."

"My view exactly. Well, then, won't a cracked bell sound a cracked note?"

"Ah, that's where computer simulation comes in, ms. We've been feeding into the computer the Bell's specifications—metal makeup, soundbow's size and shape, clapper's size and shape. Tricky business getting asolutely accurate measurements—even with, or maybe I should say especially with, laser calipers. Technique requires readings in the zillions. We take unobtrusive automatic readings around the clock. The technical term is statistical stochastics. The mindscanner would interfere with the calipers' sensors. We're nearly there, though. And once we have it all in the computer, come the Fourth the Bell will ring out its true note. Can you imagine the effect, the sensation?"

Dodge looked thoughtful. "It's a powerful symbol, all right. And if we can bring it to life . . ."

SecInt pounced on that. "The perfect way of putting it, Ms. President. Why, let's use the motto: *Bringing life to a symbol and a symbol to life.*"

"How sure are you it will work?"

"I can all but guarantee it. All that worries me is the time element. That's why we've been keeping the operation hush-hush. Be national letdown if we announced it now and then failed to bring it off in time for this year's celebration."

"How does it stand?"

"Looking good. But we're holding up word till we're certain. No point putting you and your office on the line till the ringing program is operational."

"Thanks. I like these surprises." She gave a curt nod. "You have till the day before the Fourth to get the mindscanner in working order." She flipped him away imperiously. Her asperity carried over to the nuisance who had brought the news. "Anything else?" Meaning, Any other volcanic anthills?

Nolan felt himself hesitate under her gaze. Then he went for broke. "I think if you call Major Sixtus in he can add something."

She frowned. "What's he got to do with the Bell?"

"Right. That's the question to ask him."

Still aiming her frown at Nolan, she pressed a button.

Major Sixtus did another double take on entering; he registered that Nolan was not Bob, shot a look of blame at Nolan for resembling Bob, then recovered, all in a flash. He stood still without seeming stiff.

Dodge gave no sign of noticing the double take. "Major, I've just been talking with SecInt about the Liberty Bell. Were you aware of Operation Let Freedom Ring?"

"Yes, ms." A modest cough. "In point of fact, I suggested it to Secretary Odmow."

Dodge cracked a smile. "You keep surprising me, major." She sighed and leaned back. "Tell me about it."

He told her substantially what SecInt had told her. Major Marshall Sixtus seemed in total command of himself. He had a discreetly knowing air whenever he looked from Pres. Dodge to her visitor. If you knew suzerain like I know suzerain . . . Nolan caught on. From Major Marshall Sixtus's point of view, Bespeaker Stedman and even President Dodge were mere walkons in the epic drama starring Major Marshall Sixtus.

He was good. By the time he finished he had Dodge over her mad and looking forward to pressing the button that would set the Liberty Bell ringing and to taking spotlighted bows for Operation Let Freedom Ring.

Dodge glanced at the clock. "Can't keep *Gemütlichkeit* waiting." She looked at her appointments sheet and grimaced. "Damn. Then there's the trade balance to take up."

Nolan got up and nodded gravely. "A matter of great import."

He kicked himself, but Dodge had already tuned him out.

She rose, absently shook hands again with Nolan, then shuffled some papers on her desk.

Nolan and the major left the Oval Office together. They walked the dark corridors in less-than-companionable silence. Nolan strove to minimize his limp and keep pace with Sixtus, match Sixtus's swinging stride. He felt he had come across as foolish and even wimpish in Dodge's eyes, as one given to overreacting and to overestimating his own importance. His face twitched. The Pathetic Pipsqueak.

He shot a glance at Sixtus's impassive face. He had no doubt that dreams of glory unfolded in Sixtus's mind. And Sixtus no doubt had no doubt of seeing many of them come true. And with good reason. Man must be five years younger than Nolan and already stood closer to wielding real power than Nolan would ever get. Nolan knew he would never want to ask Sixtus for a favor.

They neared the usher's station. Nolan felt a sudden urge to apologize to Sixtus for his unbecoming officiousness.

But Major Sixtus spoke first. Before giving Nolan over to the usher, Major Sixtus delivered his parting shot in a conversational tone. "Watch what happens next time you try to put me on the spot. Have a nice day, Mr. Packard."

Nolan stared after the major's back till the usher throatcleared her presence. As Nolan went out he heard a pitch-pipe sound and high voices find their places.

7

Nolan picked Franklin up at summer day camp. He drove with an absent smile, inclining his head as the twig bent his ear.

"And so I told Sandy she knew what she could do with her old— Hey, we're not heading straight home. Oh, boy! We going to do something?"

"That's nice. Um, I mean, that's right. I have business to see to, so I'm leaving you with Mrs. Oeppel. You like her."

"Yeah, but . . ."

"Be only for a few hours." Nolan went on, but more in the nature of thinking aloud. "Maybe I'm fantasizing. Maybe it's all a Gilligan hitch."

"What's a Gilligan hitch?"

"Navy slang. A Gilligan hitch is an imaginary knot in an imaginary rope." No noose is good noose, a hangman's not, to string yourself up with. Damn limp had done the Indian rope trick with the NASA hitch, vanished his hoped-for space career, destined him to become Bespeaker Stedman pulling on the Liberty Bell's nonexistent bell rope and making waves of silence. Fate took career decisions, career moves, out of your hands. "Here we are."

He'd phoned ahead to make sure Mrs. Oeppel would be home and available, but he waited while Franklin pressed the chime push, waited till the door opened on Mrs. Oeppel's cheery face, waved back to both Franklin and Mrs. Oeppel, waited till the door closed on Franklin. Only then did he feel free to tackle the Gilligan hitch.

*   *   *

He phoned Maggie. "Would you know Senator Bob Stedman's whereabouts?"

Maggie knew all the bodies, cold and warm. If he hadn't felt leery of kidding with her, because that might lead to her believing he had more on his mind than calling her for information, they could have done an Abbott and Costello routine (Hugh's on first, Watt's on second, Ware's on third, Wenn's at short, Wye's at bat, Howe's the catcher . . .). He set a businesslike tone.

That, however, put her off; right away she had a bargaining chip on her shoulder. "Why don't you ask his office?"

"Because I don't want his office to know I'm asking."

"What's up?"

He told her about Operation Let Freedom Ring.

"Okay, Nolan; sounds like something I might could use. Tell you where you *won't* find the distinguished junior senator: the Senate chamber or his S.O.B. office. He'll be ducking a vote in the late-night session on the bill to let American Express handle Social Security the way Blue Cross handles Medicare. Quite an exodus. Issue's too hot for most senators; they're hiding out—a lot of them with their lovers." Her tone softened. "Speaking of shacking up—"

He overrode that, pretended he hadn't heard it. "Thanks for the information, Maggie."

"Anytime."

He caught the overtone of "and not just anytime a story's in the offing." Maggie knew he was a one-woman man. Why did she come on so strong now? Did she sense better than he what was happening between him and his one woman? She wasn't wrong in one thing—if Nell and he drifted farther apart, then maybe he would give Maggie a tumble.

Covering the hotels was out, even by phone. Bob'd use a nom de register. But Senator Robert Stedman, Jr., resided here in Bethesda. That made staking out Bob's home a sensibler way to waste time. But it stood, or lay back, in the most exclusive part of Bethesda. No curbside parking allowed, not even for deliveries. That made staking it out a problem.

Nolan drove slowly past the Georgian Tudor place. The garage door's windows showed a car inside. Bob was divorced and had no children, had but one car as far as Nolan knew. A cleaning person would have left his or her car in the driveway. True, Bob could have a lover, and the car could be the lover's, but Bob had changed mightily since his wild young days. These days Senator Robert Stedman, Jr., had a discreet life-style. Take it that this was Bob's car and that Bob was home.

How would Fabian Piel have handled this stakeout in his PI days? Would he have parked in someone's driveway a few houses down the street? Nolan tried this, but a venetian blind blinked vertically and sections of a face looked out, and Nolan pulled away. Would Fabian have kept circling the block? Nolan tried this, alternating right and left turns to pass Bob's house from different directions. At least dusk kept falling, turning the Maverick darker shades of blue that might make it appear different cars. And Nolan alternated high and low headlight beams with each pass.

At 7:22, Nolan was coming into the street for the fortieth time when the garage door rolled up and Bob's Ambassador limo backed out.

Nolan braked, waiting to see which way the limo would swing.

It arched away, indicating that once it straightened it would head toward Nolan.

Nolan reversed to behind the crosswalk and crouched below the windshield. He peered as the limo slid past, Bob at the wheel. Nolan allowed him a hundred-meter lead, then followed. He kept his distance, letting an occasional car come between, and tailed the limo into Washington.

Nolan eased up on the gas as Bob swung onto the ramp down into the new Oporto complex. Nolan gave Bob a minute to park, then drove into the underground garage in time to see the elevator door close. He took the visitor's slot next to Bob's limo. He worked toes, ankles, and knees to loosen up. He still got out stiffly and still felt kinks in the bum leg when he walked toward the elevator. Though the place looked new and bright, just knowing yourself to be underground made it dank and dark, just knowing you stood on someone else's turf made it ominous.

As he studied the wall directory alongside the elevator another car pulled in and parked in a visitor's slot. Nolan put the car and its driver on subliminal hold while he ran his gaze down the list. What name would ring a bell?

Odmow, 1512. That would be *the* Odmow, SecInt. All other names hanging silent, take it Bob called on Odmow.

What did a snoop do now? To get the elevator to move, you had to pick up the intercom phone, punch the tenant's directory number, identify yourself so the tenant would buzz you in. At least he knew Bob, Odmow, and Sixtus were in cahoots.

So? All Washington was in cahoots against itself. These particular cahoots had to do with the Bell, but why the Bell? Not for its intrinsic worth. Way back in the early days of the Republic, those stuck with the useless thing even tried to sell it for scrap—and found no takers. Over time, though, it had gained value as a patriotic symbol. If these conspirators added luster to it, more power to them. He felt suddenly asinine: tilting at windmills without Don Quixote's excuse of nearsightedness.

The driver of the car that had followed his in stood waiting politely for him to use the intercom phone. Nolan shook his head and gestured the handing over the priority. The man gave an acknowledging nod, lifted the phone off the hook, and punched 1–5–1–2.

Nolan, about to turn away and head for his car, froze. He took his first real look at the man. Scruff him up some, give him a honky's idea of dreadlocks in place of the careful love-curl, thin him a tad, erase a few lines, and he was the spitting image of a front-page troublemaker of a decade and a half ago. Nolan tried to capture the name of that terrorist who had gone into hiding.

The man smiled at Nolan and stuck his free hand into his jacket pocket in an attitude of casual patience. But he had the kind of smile that makes you look to see if your fly's open.

Nolan cast his eyes again upon the directory, trying to keep them from zigzagging as violently as his thoughts.

The hum of connection, then Odmow's voice answered. "That you, Wolpy?"

That was the name. Wolpy Rubb. Nolan held still. What dealings did SecInt have with a still-wanted fugitive? Why would Rubb surface here and now?

Rubb spoke conversationally into the phone. "Got it, my man. I'm bringing up a guest."

Nolan's head whirled so fast his eyes had to play catch-up.

Rubb's hand came out of the pocket holding a neat little .22.

Odmow hummed. "Guest?"

"The Beady Eye himself. I tailed him here."

Nolan went cold.

How long had Rubb been following him?

Odmow's ruminating hum rose slightly in pitch. "No violence, please. Very well, come on up. Don't ring off till I buzz you in."

Nolan already had a buzz in his ears—blood-surge—and did not catch the intercom's. But the elevator door opened and the automatic waggled Nolan toward the elevator.

Rubb hung up and followed Nolan in.

The door closed and they rode up in companionable tableau. When the car stopped and the door slid open the .22 gestured Nolan out and to the right, to where the door of SecInt Odmow's suite stood ajar in halfhearted invitation. The .22 prodded Nolan in.

8

Nolan felt his shoulder muscles tighten. He pushed the door wide and stifflegged into SecInt Odmow's grave hum. As always, it surprised Nolan that Odmow showed no open animosity despite their run-ins over the environment and the nation's natural resources and treasures. Maybe Odmow always felt sure of triumphing in the end.

"Welcome, Mr. Bespeaker." Odmow frowned at Rubb. "Put that thing away."

Rubb put the .22 away but shut the door and stayed between Nolan and the door.

Like a good host, Odmow inclined his head toward an archway into a paneled and bookcased living room. Major Marshall Sixtus, sitting at ease in civvies, glanced over a cocktail glass at Nolan. It might have been light on the liquid that put a glitter in Sixtus's eyes.

But Nolan was seeking himself, and there by the window he stood. Bob faced the window but his head twisted enough to show him to be looking not out through Thermopane at the illuminated spokes of Washington's thoroughfares raying out like the Statue of Liberty's crown but rear-viewing the room.

Nolan might have been staring in the mirror at himself as he would appear ten years from now if he lived. Bob looked back at him from that angled vantage somewhat more wryly.

Bob turned from the window. "Hello, Nolan."

"Hello, Bob." The familiar face, the family face, looked suddenly strange. Nolan had known at the time only that the old senator, Uncle Bob, had used all his influence to bail Bob, Jr., out of some sort of trouble. "So you were really in with Rubb during those years when you dropped out?"

Bob smiled. "A wild and crazy guy."

Nolan caught himself smiling back.

Sixtus emptied his glass and rang it down on the coffee table like a gavel. Nolan had been wondering how long it would take before Sixtus exerted ringleadership. "Our careers prove there's a time for the direct approach and a time for the approach devious. This is the season for directness. Before we start, Mr. Packard won't mind your patting him down."

Rubb gave Nolan a nod. "Assume the position."

Nolan faced the wall and spread-eagled himself leaning into it. The wall breathed his heat back at him. He stared at a gold plaque inscribed to SecInt Odmow by the country's best chemical polluter.

Rubb frisked him, emptying Nolan's pockets and putting the contents on the coffee table.

Out of the corner of his eye, Nolan saw Rubb whisper into Sixtus's ear, get a nod, then whisper into Bob's ear and hand him something that clinked.

Then Rubb spoke to Nolan. "Okay, Beady Eye. You can peel yourself from the wall."

Nolan shoved himself erect, brought his feet together, and turned.

Bob's gaze met Nolan's for a moment, then slid away. Bob spoke to his partners. "I'll be back soon. You guys carry on. Marsh has told me most of the details already."

As Bob left, Rubb spoke to Sixtus with a nod at Nolan. "Where do we stash this in the meanwhile?"

"Lock him in the bathroom."

Rubb raised an eyebrow. "The door locks from the inside only. What good's that?"

Odmow hustled toward a closet. "I know just the thing." He reached a carry-on bag down from the closet shelf, unzipped the bag, and drew out a contraption. "Here's a lock I use on my hotel-room door when I travel."

Robb's .22 gestured Nolan to the bathroom, then held him up while the free hand reached in to switch the bathroom light on. "Maybe I'd better check out what-all's in there. Beady Eye might try something."

Sixtus smiled coldly. "If he wants to OD on aspirin or cut his wrists with a razor blade . . ." A shrug finished the thought.

Odmow shook his head. "He'd be out of luck. I have no aspirin and I use an electric shaver."

Sixtus's matt-black eyes flashed disappointment, then diminished Nolan to nothing. Nolan read in those eyes Sixtus's dream, Sixtus's wish: it was Marshall Sixtus at play in a world where everyone else had the life and will of a toy soldier.

Rubb waved Nolan into the bathroom.

Odmow hummed to himself fitting the contraption to the jamb. "Goes on like so."

The door closed and Nolan heard the contraption click into place. The knob turned and the door shook but there was no real give.

A happy hum. "There. See how it holds?"

Sixtus's voice cracked the whip. "We've wasted enough time. Let's finalize the details so there'll be no slipups."

His voice and their footsteps diminuendoed and only a faint murmur came through one wall of the bathroom.

9

Under the medicine cabinet and above the sink a drinking glass rested in its holder. Nolan took the glass and put its mouth to the murmuring wall and flattened his ear against the bottom of the glass. Sixtus's voice and Sixtus's words came through.

". . . will close the pavilion down on the third to raise the Bell off the floor so it can swing freely. Regular National Park Service crew rigs a bell rope and tests it. Wolpy, with a technician's ID, wires the clapper and the soundbow so the program switches on when the clapper strikes the soundbow."

Rubb sounded bored. "Still don't see why we can't simply flick a switch here without all that both—"

"You know how faulty lip sync destroys a film's illusion? How it is when they dub a foreign film and you see the words don't match the mouth movements? If we're going to pull off this job, everything has to mesh, be in semantic phase. We're out to grab people on the gut level. They have to know, have to feel in their bones, that the Bell rings true. That's how we get control: through the sound, through the sense of the sound. The sound penetrates the brain, it becomes a structure in the nervous system. Semanticists call this a meme."

"Thought you said it would be something like hypnosis. Mass hypnosis."

"Call it hypnosis, brainwashing, conditioning, behavior modification, odylism. By any other name, it would be what it does. I call it a wordless command, an unspoken catchphrase, that imprints itself in the mind. You've heard of the Knock-of-Fate notes from Beethoven's Fifth that spelled out V for Victory to the Free World in WWII? That was a meme. Well, our meme is a psychological pattern of Wagnerian harmonics I've worked out on computer. If this meme could spell itself out, it would say, 'Believe in me, no matter what. I'm the true freedom—the freedom to obey.' Each individual will internalize it idiosyncratically but all will be open to it, feel born again. They'll respond to the first voice that commands them, like newly hatched geese following the first mother surrogate they see. So I have to be ready to imprint immediately. For it to work, the Bell-ringing must look authentic, leave no space for a flicker of doubt." A determined, command-decision pause. "That clear?"

A grunt and a hum seemed to satisfy Sixtus. "Good. That should get us control of all who tune in, which will be more than enough for an orderly takeover of all governmental functions. Even those who don't tune in will feel the vibes, which will leave them susceptible to later imprint. Now for the hookup to accomplish all this. We beam the Bell's reconstructed note to an artificial Earth satellite with a parametric solid-state microwave amplifier. The signal comes back down to transmission towers. The towers project enormous amounts of radio frequency energy. This energy seeks out any metal surface—your furnace, your toaster, the fillings in your teeth, your vacuum sweeper, your house siding, your rain gutter, your electric blanket, and of course your radios and televisions. Then too, there's the old Project Sanguine. In case Sanguine's before your memory, that was something the Navy tried to float in the Midwest."

Nolan's mouth twitched. *Something the Navy tried to float in the Midwest.* Sixtus hadn't come up with that one on purpose. Revolutionaries are usually so intense they don't seem to have much sense of humor.

"Sanguine was supposed to transmit orders to nuclear submarines if all else got jammed or taken out. Sanguine's buried grid is still in place, and we tie that in as well. The transmitting antenna will radiate the ELF—extremely low-frequency—electromagnetic wave. Even the deaf will feel the vibes—and for them we'll have a close-captioned command."

A hum from Odmow. "*We'll* pick 'em up too. So we have to remember—"

"To use the earphones I gave you. They play white noise set to nullify the Bell's note. We'll be the only ones immune. One thing more—"

Nolan heard a ringing.

Odmow answered it. "Bob? Everything go smooth? Great. Hold on, I'll buzz you in."

Nolan took his ear from the glass and the glass from the wall. He restored the glass to its holder. Time to think about breaking out, getting away.

They were all out of their skulls, of course. What did the four silly bastards think they were doing?

Nolan went cold. He knew what they thought they were doing: brainwashing America, and perhaps the world if other countries picked up the event. Nolan went subfreezing. Who was he to say they couldn't pull it off?

Yesterday, one silly bastard, Hitler, had brought the world to the brink. Today, one person in a key spot could take over the world.

And today, now, one person—a silly bastard in his own right and in his own way—had to stop these other silly bastards.

Somewhere down where words had their beginnings and the mother tongue had been licking him into shape, *silly bastard* made a delayed association with *sap*. Sap made a blindingly flashing association with *sock*. Nolan slipped off a shoe long enough to remove the sock.

He filled the toe of the sock with the bar of soap from the soap dish. Soap only personal size, but hardly vitiated. Sock only ankle length, but enough for a knot and a hold. He swung it. A sap. He hung it at his belt, under his jacket.

The medicine-cabinet mirror showed him baring his teeth in a smile. Just like Bob's. The smile widened grimly.

He dusted a distinguished touch of a talcum powder on his hair at the temples. The mirror showed him an indubitable Bob. He opened the cabinet. His gaze shot to the electric shaver and to a blister package of antacid tablets.

The package backing was a cardboard-foil laminate. He stripped off the foil, folded it lengthwise several times, then forced it down over both prongs of the electric shaver's plug, piercing the foil at the two points and seating the foil firmly. "Here goes." He set his teeth and plugged the cord into the wall socket.

A faint pop, crack, or sizzle, and the bathroom light went out.

Were the hall and living room on the same circuit? The hallway at least was; no light showed now under the door. A surge in the wall murmur spoke for the living room.

Odmow's voice bounced nearer along the hall. "I'll reset the tripped switch."

Nolan pulled the plug out and waited for the lights to come back on.

A triumphant hum. "Aha: easy."

Nolan gave Odmow time to return jauntily to the living

room. Then Nolan plugged the short-circuiter in again. Again darkness.

With an irritated hum Odmow brought light back to the world.

Again Nolan brought darkness.

Nolan started to bring his sapping arm around. He stopped, and heard himself say, "One second, Bob. Tell me, why are you in this wacky thing?"

Bob faced him slowly. He spoke softly. "I have to go along because of past associations. There's a lot you and the world don't know about me that those who knew me back then could expose." He had a nervous habit of buttoning and unbuttoning his jacket. He jerked his head toward the living room. "We were terrorists together. Then we saw the light. The way to reach our goal of bringing down the government, all governments, was to go intravenous—IV. That's why we called ourselves the Four Committee. Sixtus and Odmow hid by going public. Those aren't their real names. They took names off gravestones and built new identities. The Feds hadn't made *me*, so I stayed me and let Dad clear my name. After he died and I won his seat, I got Sixtus his appointment to West Point, backed Odmow for the Cabinet, and even put in a good word for you as Bespeaker. Wolpy is Wolpy; we couldn't do much with him."

From the living room Sixtus's voice summoned Bob.

Bob called back he was coming. He unbuttoned his jacket one last time. He gave Nolan an earnest look. "Nolan, for God's sake behave and nothing will happen to—"

Nolan swung the sap hard to override his queasiness.

Sock!

It connected well. Bob's startled eyes rolled up and he went limp.

Nolan dropped the sap to catch Bob and lower him to the floor. Nolan pulled Bob's jacket off and thrust himself into it.

He smoothed himself down and breathed deep and stepped out of the bathroom. He glanced down the hallway into the living room.

Odmow was the only one visible through the archway and at the moment faced where Sixtus would be sitting behind the cocktail table.

Nolan made a quick study of the contraption to see how it worked. He slipped it off the door but held it seemingly in place as he closed the door. An edge-of-the-eye glance showed him Odmow looking his way.

Nolan fiddled with the travel lock, then nodded to himself in satisfaction and turned away from the door, his body hiding that he brought the travel lock with him as he lowered his hands. His left hand held the lock behind him, his right hand gave Odmow the O-for-okay sign. Odmow nodded, and gestured to the empty seat beside him. Nolan started that way, concentrating on not limping.

When he reached where the hall branched toward the front door he raised a finger to sign one minute and veered.

Once out of Odmow's view, he let his limp go hang in favor of speed. He made it to the front door of the suite and had it open before he heard the first stir.

He stepped out, slipped the travel lock over the edge of the door, slammed the door shut, and secured it with the travel lock.

The shaking of the door quickened his heartbeat. He told himself to take it easy. The lock should hold.

He reached the elevator, pressed the button, and tried to think ahead calmly as he waited.

A hammering began. They were knocking out the pins of the door hinges. They would be out in less than a minute.

Stedman's law. Elevators stand waiting at your floor when you don't need them, are at their farthest and holding when you're in a hurry. He strode away from the elevator to hunt the door to the fire stairs.

He spotted the exit just as the door of Odmow's suite lifted off its hinges and swung inward.

The elevator car pinged its arrival as Rubb shoved through to the corridor. His gun fixed on Nolan.

Nolan weighed the distance to the fire stairs against the distance to the elevator. The stairs were nearer, but the elevator was faster in the long run. He made a dash for the open elevator.

A searing blow to the left arm spun him half around. The sound of the shot filled the corridor and rang in Nolan's ears. Nolan twisted himself back around and hurled himself into the elevator as another shot that just grazed Bob's jacket rang out. He stabbed the garage-level button. The door slid shut, the elevator car started downward. Inertia held him upright, then he let rubbery legs take on the curvature of the four-dimensional space-time continuum and sit him on the floor. He hadn't reckoned with Rubb's recklessness, but he could forethink only so far.

The throbbing present demanded attention. Bob's lemon jacket showed the spreading bloodstain in nice contrast. The bullet seemed to have gone clean through the flesh of his left arm, missing the bone, but he had to stop the bleeding. He pulled Bob's show handkerchief out and wadded it down through the armhole into the sleeve to press against the arm.

To show how bemused he was, how much in shock, he did not move fast enough to get up and out when the elevator stopped and the door opened at the garage level. The door almost shut on him and he would have started back up toward Odmow's floor if he had not caught himself and the door in time. He held it and forced it back and squeezed out. Still leaning his weight to hold it open, he slapped the breast pockets of Bob's jacket for something, anything, and reached in and came out with a ballpoint pen. He held one end to the jamb and, arm throbbing and quivering, slowly let up on the door till it hit the other end of the pen. Carefully, he let go of the pen. The pen remained in place, holding the door open. The UP arrow stayed lit but the elevator stayed jammed.

Still bemused, still orienting himself, he made for the slot to the right of Bob's stretch limo. Another car took up the space where he had left his Maverick.

A momentary sense that the universe had dropped away from under him. Wait; Bob had gone out for a while. Bob must have taken the limo; when he came back he had to find another slot. That's why the Maverick was now on the other side of Bob's Ambassador.

For all the good it did Nolan. He had left his belongings on Odmow's cocktail table, his car keys among what he had emptied his pockets of.

Why hadn't he taken up a useful trade like hotwiring cars?

He snapped his fingers: he wore Bob's jacket. He patted the pockets; a satisfying hard feel and a heartening dull clank. Good old Bob. Nolan came out with car keys. He made for the Ambassador. He heard a faint sound from the limo. Sounded like the pinging of a cooling engine. Only natural. The universe was back in place.

He unlocked the Ambassador's door, slid in, and fitted the ignition key. He backed out of the slot and drove up the ramp and out of Oporto.

11

Where to? Hospital? Gunshot wound meant police report meant disbelieved explanation meant footless delay. Who'd take the flaky BDI's word against that of the likes of the White

House's Sixtus, Interior's Odmow, and the Senate's Stedman? More pressing to pick up Franklin before the Four Committee could think to snatch the boy as a hold over Nolan. He headed toward Bethesda.

First priority, meanwhile, warn the President about the conspiracy. Nolan grimaced foreseeing the job he would have convincing Dodge that her military aide planned to take over the United States and the world. With a sour smile he picked up the car phone and rang the code number of the Bespeakerphone.

The recorded voice that answered was not the voice of Sally Dodge.

"This is Major Marshall Sixtus. President Dodge is presently unavailable. At the beep, leave your message. President Dodge will get back to you as soon as possible. Thank you."

At the beep, Nolan's mouth still hung open. Had Sixtus already made President Dodge a prisoner in the White House? More likely, Sixtus had simply snuck a call-forwarding chip into the President's Bespeakerphone. Nolan hung up without saying word one.

That left Nolan with the media option. Bespeakers had the right of eminent estate, the power to claim access to print and electronic media.

He took up the car phone again and dialed Maggie McGee's home number.

Her canned voice told him that dunning was against the law but that all news leads would be gratefully received.

She should love a juicy conspiracy.

At the beep, he briefed her answering machine on the Four Committee conspiracy to subvert the Liberty Bell's reconstructed ringing to meme the populace into subjection. He named the Four and suggested that Maggie check them in depth for terrorist background. He rang off just as the limo pulled up at Mrs. Oeppel's.

He honked the limo's horn. It played a superpatriotic bar of "The Stars and Stripes Forever."

Mrs. Oeppel's front door opened but Franklin did not burst forth. Mrs. Oeppel kept the door leashed while she looked out. Good for Mrs. Oeppel. She didn't recognize the car and wasn't about to send Franklin out. But Nolan groaned at the thought of having to get out and go up to the front door.

He groaned again when he got out. Stedman's law. You always bump the injured part. He sidled to the front door to keep Mrs. Oeppel from seeing the bloodstained sleeve of Bob's jacket.

Mrs. Oeppel smiled and took the chain off the door. "Oh, did Franklin forget something?"

Nolan blinked. "Back up, Mrs. Oeppel. What do you mean did Franklin forget something?" He tried to squeeze his gaze past Mrs. Oeppel. "Sorry I'm a bit late. Where's Franklin? *He* can say whether or not he forgot something."

Mrs. Oeppel batted her eyes. " 'Where's Franklin?' " She looked beyond him to the limo, then stared at him. She spoke as to a not-too-bright ten-year-old. "You were here an hour ago, Mr. Stedman. You picked up your son. You drove up in your blue Maverick and honked your horn and Franklin ran out and got in and you drove away."

His jaw dropped. He turned to face her more fully.

She saw the bloody sleeve. "Oh, my! You haven't gone and got hurt in an accident?"

He felt suddenly woozy and rested his bad leg a step higher than the other.

Mrs. Oeppel dropped her gaze. "You know you have only one sock on?"

Bob had called for the kid. Bob had snatched Franklin.

But Bob wouldn't harm Franklin. Bob was his cousin, his more than cousin. After that drunk driver—who of course came out of it without a scratch—swerved into Dad's car and killed Mom and Dad dead and Nolan went to live with Uncle Bob and Aunt Betsy and Cousin Bob, Jr., Bob and Nolan had been like older brother and younger brother.

Still, there were times. Like when seventeen-year-old Bob, Jr., took seven-year-old Nolan for a spin in Bob, Sr.'s, new Coupe de Ville and banged it up and Bob, Jr., turned to Nolan and told him, "I got out to take a leak and you released the brakes; I sprinted alongside, grabbed the wheel and swung the car into a tree to save you and the car from diving into the lake. I don't want Dad to think I let him down. You won't tell him I was at the wheel." "I know better." There must have seemed just enough ambiguity in Nolan's answer to make Bob narrow his eyes and twist Nolan's arm, though Nolan set his jaw to keep from crying out. "You'd better know better."

Nolan's queasiness grew. Bob, however reluctantly, belonged to the tight little ruthless bunch that planned to trash the world. Why should the well-being of a ten-year-old, however close kin, standing in the way stand in the way?

Mrs. Oeppel's mouth had been moving and sound had been coming out.

Nolan reached back to catch a few of her words that had

gone by him. "No, I'm fine, Mrs. O. I did get shaken up a bit, but it's not as bad as it looks. Still, I do need rest, and I think I'll get that, starting now."

Her mouth moved again and sound came out, but he mustered a mustard-eating grin and turned with a wave of his good arm and limped bravely to the limo.

12

He pulled away, trying to catch up with his thoughts. He hadn't escaped after all. As long as the Four Committee had Franklin, they had Nolan. The Four Committee would expect him to realize that about now and would count on him to call them.

Before he agreed to anything, he'd have to make sure Franklin was alive and well. They'd have to let him ask Franklin a question only Franklin could answer.

He could ask: "What did you write in the snow?" Once, Franklin had stomped big block letters in the snow on the front lawn: HI MOM. With the Spacelab's hi-res scope Nell could make that out. She might even scribe a quick HI back with her laser on low. They had phoned her to look down during the next pass, but duty, some pressing business aboard the craft, had kept her from getting a fix and looking till orbits later, when the words had blurred into meaninglessness under the sun. But Franklin might have repressed that memory.

Question, question. Got it: "Frisbee catches dog. What's the dog's name?"

Hope sprang Clingerlike. Maybe Franklin had slipped away from Bob. If so, Franklin would head home.

Nolan headed home while using his Bespeaker's access code to get Odmow's unlisted Oporto phone.

Odmow's cagy hum. "Yes?"

"Put Franklin on. I want to make sure he's all right."

Odmow's startled hum, then a muffled powwow, then Sixtus's voice took over smoothly.

"The boy's safe enough, but he's under sedation. Come back and we'll show him to you." The tone seemed to blend truthfulness and mockery.

"Sure. Expect me when you see me." Enough ambiguity to give Bob and the others to think. Before he had to listen to more, and answer, he rang off. Quickly, to put himself out of reach, he dialed the one number he could be sure would give a busy signal, that of Bob's car phone itself.

Home was just around the corner. Instead of making the

turn, he coasted to a stop on the street behind his. He parked at the curb so that the car overlapped two properties; each homeowner would think the visitor pertained to the other. He looked past his back neighbor's yard to his own house. He saw lights in the windows, but those a timer switched on to fool your denser housebreaker. He had one hope. Sixtus could have been lying, Franklin could have made it home after all.

Nolan got out of the limo.

In the stillness he heard again the ping from the car. Bob could use a tuneup.

Nolan cut across his neighbor's lawn to the rear of his own house.

Swiftly at first, then slowly. It could be worse to know than to not know. The throb in his arm and the lag of his leg told him, *No: lost cause*. The bastards were way ahead of him. They had his son.

Nolan set his jaw. Think too much and the hands lost their steadiness, the knees go liquid.

He kept to the shadow of the neighbor's hedge till he reached his own and scattered paraphernalia. The rear door answered his palm on the ID panel by unlocking and sliding open.

Nolan stepped inside and to one side. He stood listening. He heard only himself.

He made for the front and climbed the stairs. He listened again at the top. Thicker silence. He swallowed.

"Franklin? It's me. Daddy. It's really me. Are you there? It's all right to come out."

He listened once more. Only the dying echoes of his words.

The night light was on in Franklin's room. Nolan looked around at the cluttered emptiness. He picked up a long-forgotten *Mother Goose*. It cracked open at *Ding, dong, bell,/ The cat's in the well./ Who put her in?/ Little Johnny Green/ Who pulled her out?/ Great Johnny Stout./ What a naughty boy was that/ To drown poor pussy cat,/ Which never did him any harm,/ But killed the mice in his father's barn*. Sure. Ask the mice *their* hero's name.

Nolan headed for his bedroom and the dresser. He ought to come away from this with a fresh pair of socks at least. He opened the drawer but the dresser-top photo of Nell caught his eye and held him. What would he tell Nell? What could he tell her? That he had failed her and Franklin? His putting their son in jeopardy would lead to her coming down on him, his losing Franklin would finish their relationship.

He heard a car pull up out front. He forgot all about socks.

He stole a look out a window. The car door opened and Wolpy Rubb got out and looked up at the house. At this very window, it seemed. Nolan dashed downstairs and out the back and through the hedge and to the limo and drove away.

13

Fabian looked pleasantly unsurprised. "I knew it." He eye-balled Fabian up and down. "I knew one day you'd come to a bad end. You're wearing only one sock."

Nolan gave Fabian's naked eye both barrels. He showed his teeth in a primitive smile. "That makes us a pair."

Fabian helped Nolan out of Bob's lemon jacket and rinsed the bloody sleeve in cold water and left it to soak in some protein-dissolving solution. "You got off lucky."

"Very. It's only a crease."

"I meant your wearing a short-sleeved shirt means I don't have to cut away your shirtsleeve." Dried blood glued the wadded handkerchief to the wound and the bleeding began again when Fabian pulled the wad away. "Hold still." Fabian cleansed the wound and applied a nonstinging antiseptic that stung and dressed it with sterile gauze pads and paper surgical tape.

Bob's limo was down in the parking garage of the BDS's co-op apartment building, but Nolan had not felt really safe till Fabian Piel checked him over on the monitor and passed him into the apartment itself.

Fabian put the first-aid kit away. "Okay, give."

The toilet seat was up, sign of a bachelor, and Nolan lowered it and the lid and sat down and gave and Fabian listened.

"Man, you sure have been making big waves on the poor little Potomac." He sighed. "Go stretch out on the couch in the living room and I'll be with you in a minute."

It came to a long minute, but the doze Nolan fell into did him some good.

Fabian shook him awake and showed him the lemon jacket. "I blow-dried it and ironed patches on the inside of the entry and exit holes. Bad as new. Is this really what conservative junior senators from Maine wear these days?" He let Nolan struggle into it by himself. "You'd better get used to going it alone. If half what you tell me is true, you've got a tailless blind mouse's chance of belling the cat. I did a little cautious calling around. Nobody knows from nothing. It's only your word." He drew a deep breath as though about to proceed against his better judgment. "You want to rope the BDJ into this, ask her to find out unofficially what the FBI can come up with on the alleged snatching of Franklin?"

Nolan shook his head. "The Four Committee must have a line into the FBI."

"Do you have *any* plan?"

"I've been thinking." A lie. It had only now come to him. But maybe a molecular mole had been at work in his mind's underground. "Use our look-alikeness to get into Bob's SOB office. See what I can dig up to blackmail Bob into releasing Franklin."

Fabian closed his visible eye. "Please, I don't want to hear. I don't even want to think about it. All I asked was did you have a plan. I don't want to know the details." But his face worked. He was lining things up in his mind, getting everything straight. His visible eye opened but stared beyond Nolan, eye and eyepatch uniformly uninformative. "You're dealing with crazies. They may have genteeled themselves, but they're still crazies. Not that the rest of us are all that sane. Tell you, Nolan, I keep trying to get a handle on what it's all about and it keeps eluding my grasp. Nearest I can come to it, the meaning is the moving toward meaning. We keep trying to increase order, move from chaos to entropy, by means of information. To that end, computers grind away like the Sampo, the salt mill of the gods, turning the cosmos into machine-language soup." His words took on gospel intonation. "Yes, brother, I see something bigger yet at work. The gravitational pull of probable futures is stronger than that of the fulfilled past, the mass of things undone and forming greater than that of things formed and done with. Hallelujah. Heat death will come when past and future reach equilibrium and cancel out, leaving a vast waste of potential."

Nolan stared past Fabian. Through the window, the spotlit tip of the Washington Monument showed above the apartment building across the way like the needle of a gauge and no doubt oscillated minutely if you watched closely enough. For that matter, parallax would do it. Fabian could have fun moving the obelisk by switching his eyepatch.

Fabian's voice swung suddenly from uplifting evangelism to down-to-earthness. "How you going to get into the SOB this time of night, let alone into Bob's office?"

With a grin Nolan reached into the inside breast pocket of Bob's jacket and flashed gilt-edged plastic. "Bob's Senate ID card."

"Not enough. You still have to get past retinal scanning—the eyeprint has to match."

Nolan's grin faded.

But Fabian winked the unpatched eye. "You need cheaters." He put up a peace-sign hand. "I'm talking contact cheaters. I'm talking smart cheaters." He left the room and came back with a pair of contact lenses in a small unlabeled box. "Put these in and the built-in chips will fake out the retinal scanner. There's a nanosecond's window during which the chips will get a look at the file pattern, match it, and mirror it back." He handed the box to Nolan and walked to the window. "Don't see Paul Revere out there, 'The Americans are coming, the Americans are—' " He shaded the pane against the room light. "That apartment's been vacant for months. Still dark, but now there's a window open. I don't like that." He reached to the cord.

Nolan got up to see over Fabian's shoulder.

Fabian shoved, not taking the time to care that he shoved the wounded arm. "No, dammit, move to one side while I draw the cur—"

Zinggg-thwack!

Intensity gave it all slow motion. Nolan got his balance and turned with a delayed flash of anger at the shove. He saw glass shower and Fabian's head spatter. A dead man fell.

Flat against the wall to one side of the window, Nolan pulled the cord, shutting out the needle showing the world running on empty. He stared in shock at the still form. The eyepatch had blown off. Fabian stared back with two good dead eyes, beyond shock. A vast waste of potential.

Nolan picked up the phone, dialed 911, and reported death in a dead tone. He added that the shot had come from the building opposite the BDS's but that the assassin had no doubt fled.

"Yessir. Who is this?"

Nolan hung up.

He left with the briefest glance at Fabian. The eyes asked too many questions. *Why did you involve me? Will you avenge me? Can you get Franklin back? What will you tell Nell? Do you know what you're up to? Are you up to it?*

14

Likeness and Bob's ID card got Nolan into the mostly dark SOB and the contact cheaters got him into Bob's all-dark office.

He switched on the lights in Bob's inner office and went

through the desk and the files. Nothing of significance except that Bob liked to sneak a nip and a joint. And, of all things, a Bible.

With a half-smile wrying his face, Nolan scanned the walls. At the right of the framed picture of Bob Sr.—with time, how much Bob Jr. and Nolan had come to look like him, dammit; your own passing time was what haunted you—the wall seemed slightly soiled. Sign of use. Nolan grasped that side's edge of the frame. In grasping it your hand touched the wall and your oils darkened the paneling. He pulled. The framed picture swung away from a wall safe. Too solid a safe door for a jimmy. And too tricky for a Jimmy Valentine. An alphanumeric keypad took the place of a dial. Only way in was to puzzle out the association in Bob's mind when Bob had set the combination.

But Nolan knew now he had never known the real Bob. How could he hope to read Bob's mind?

Best bet was the obvious with a twist—the devious.

Nolan tried BOB, BOB JR, RS, RS JR, IV, FOUR, 4, FOUR COMMIT-TEE, 4 COMMITTEE, IV COMMITTEE. He tried IVY, INTRAVENOUS, INITIAL VELOCITY, IN VERBO. He tried STEDMAN and NAMDETS. He even tried CLANGOR; there *had* been a Clangor and Clangor had been Bob Jr.'s till Bob Jr. took up with the wild bunch and dropped out of sight for months, leaving the care and love of Clangor to Nolan. He tried CARRABASSETT; lot of associations there—Clangor had been a basset and Carrabassett was in Franklin County, Maine. Nothing paid off. He put his ear to the safe door and listened while he tapped the keyboard at random. No giveaway click of tumblers. Probably no tumblers, just a latch that would open at the right sequence.

Think. Maybe Bob had left some clue. The liquor and the weed meant highs. In the cloud of a high, Bob could grow forgetful. He might have foreseen the need to remind himself of the number.

Look. Nolan's eyes lit on the anomalous Bible.

Scrutinize. Nothing written on any flyleaf. He held the Bible by its winged-out cover and shook the great speckled bird. No slip of paper fell out. But he did spot one dogeared leaf, and this in the fourth book—Numbers. The turned-down corner came during Chapter 15.

Any highlighted passages? No.

Numbers. Number 15. Nolan returned to the safe and keyed 15. The safe stayed mum.

Back to the volume. What did the good book have to say for itself?

Nolan ran his eyes through Chapter 15 till they hit Verse 12. *According to the number that ye shall prepare, so shall ye do to everyone according to their number.*

He keyed 12. No click. He keyed 15:12. No damn good. It hit him that the original Hebrew ran the other way; he keyed 51, 21, 12:15, 21:51, 51:21. Good damn no.

Had to be another approach. He looked at the alphanumeric keypad. He had tried alpha, then numeric. Now try alphha again.

The fifteenth letter of the English alphabet is O, the twelfth is L. He keyed OL. Nothing. Hebrew again? *LO!* With a breathless sense of inevitability he keyed LO. *Click.* The safe door opened.

Nolan reached in and grabbed. A rubber-banded sheaf of slips bearing scribbled initials and figures should repay scrutiny and research, but Nolan had no time for such painstaking. He did pocket the sheaf. If it was worth stashing to Bob, it would be worth worrying about to Bob.

He found an offer on a lobbyist's letterhead: the hint of a political contribution in return for a vote in favor of handing Social Security administration to private business or for at least an abstention. He pocketed this.

A Walkman, looked like, but here the earphones plugged into a shirt-pocket cassette player. Nolan put a phone to an ear and switched the player on. No incriminating conversation, no illuminating notes, only a cryptic meaninglessness. Nolan kept listening, hoping the hissing-radiator, stridulating-cricket noises, sounds a tinnitus sufferer might hear, would grow into sense. They did not. He put it back, then took it out again and pocketed it. The noise made sense after all. This had to be the white noise Sixtus had spoken of that would counter the note of the Bell. Even if it was not, if it was worth safekeeping it was worth stealing.

Only other item a manila envelope. He unflapped it and shook out onto the desk a sheaf of clippings. All dealt with terrorist acts of fifteen years ago. Nolan stuffed them back into the envelope and shoved the envelope into an inside pocket of the jacket.

His ears quivered to the sound of stealthy footsteps the other side of the door. He closed the safe and swung Uncle Bob's portrait back in place. His eyes darted around. No other way out.

Why should there have to be? If that was not Bob himself, or others of the Four Committee, *he* was Senator Robert Stedman,

Jr. He drew himself up and put on a senatorial look as the door
whisked open.

15

Two men stood in the doorway. The majority whip and the
sergeant-at-arms.

The majority whip shook his head sadly but wore a big grin.

"Gotcha! You can't get out of this one. Jim here will twist
your arm if he has to, but I'm sure you'll come quietly. You
know when the jig's up."

Nolan had never danced the jig, but his mind whirled as
though he'd just spun out of a fast one. He tried to remember
the majority whip's name but came up blank, so merely smiled
ruefully and let them lead him down to the underground train.

The sergeant-at-arms noticed the limp. "Got a sore foot,
Senator Stedman?" He took a closer look. "Say, you don't
have a sock on that there foot."

Nolan took a look for himself. "Damned if you're not right,
Jim."

The whip was oblivious. "You're the last one I need, Bob.
We're going to have a vote and we're going to pass the bill.
You make the difference. Then we can adjourn and all go back
home for the summer. Just in time. Tomorrow's the Fourth; big
parade in my home state. Same in yours, I don't doubt."

They rode with Nolan to the Capitol and made sure he
entered the Senate chamber. The whip hurried to the dais to
whisper in the president pro tem's ear but Nolan stopped just
inside the door.

Where in hell did Bob sit?

Jim must've thought Senator Stedman was balking. His hand
scooped Nolan's elbow. "All the way in, Senator."

Nolan took a faltering step. "Maybe you'd better help me,
Jim."

"Oh, sorry, sir. Be glad to." He guided Nolan to Bob's seat.

The able senator from Texas was droning away, keeping the
quorum under, but a sense of things beginning to stir, of decision at hand, brought the members out of their drowse.

Nolan settled himself in Bob's seat and looked around—at
the yawning senators in the well, at the bored correspondents
and the few visitors in the gallery. Man, he could wake them
up. He had the ideal forum.

Hold up the vote, get the floor on a point of order or a point
of personal privilege or whatever parliamentary maneuver a
senator could draw on. Pull a Jefferson Smith and filibuster to

get the nation's attention, make public the Four Committee's threat to liberty, the Bell plot.

But the Four Committee held Franklin.

And even if Nolan got the floor, how long could he hold it before they shouted him down and the sergeant-at-arms and the Capitol police dragged the impostor off? Probably not long enough to voice a coherent and convincing warning.

Meanwhile it had come to a roll-call vote. Nolan rose at Bob's name to cast Bob's vote. He drew forth the lobbyist's letter and flourished it. He exaggerated Bob's Down East delivery for Bob's finest hour. Yankee Noodle put a feather in his cap and called it macaroni. Drawing on memories of Uncle Bob's eloquence, letting his sense of occasion carry him away, he expressed his indignation and horror at the blatant attempt to bribe him. "The Pine Tree State does not sell its votes. I cast a resounding nay."

That woke them up. It was the swing vote and doomed the measure. In the turmoil and tumult, with the chair yelling for order and senators clamoring for the floor, Nolan strode up the aisle toward the door. In passing, he handed the letter to the majority whip, who had turned a majestically impotent purple. Uncool Sam.

In the corridor, correspondents elbowed to corner Senator Stedman. For a moment Nolan hesitated, tempted to welcome their importuning, use them to break the bigger story. Then he thought again of Franklin, and grabbed the sergeant-at-arms and pointed him at the press. "Press 'em back, Jim."

Nolan made it to the underground train and rode it to the SOB. He reclaimed Bob's Ambassador and pulled out of the garage.

Hurry away. News of the vote, and realization Nolan had played Bob, would draw the Four Committee's firepower here.

Where to now?

Philadelphia, here I come.

16

If he headed the other way he might throw the Four Committee off for a time—but he would lose considerably more time. The car radio, even on the police band, made no mention of a stolen Ambassador, but that very silence seemed suspicious. The Four Committee must be using every agency to find and neutralize him. A clandestine APB would be out on the limo and a contract on him. He'd have to ditch the limo soon even if that meant making his way to Philly on shank's mare.

Meanwhile, he took the middle ground by picking U.S. 1 over 95 and the Baltimore-Washington Parkway. He stopped once to top the tank with Bob's credit card and to empty and replenish himself. He had no cash, but the automatic service station attendant added the soft drinks and chocolate bars to the gasoline tab. The Ambassador hummed along, putting Nolan in mind of Odmow, and made it through inner-city Baltimore with only a few evil eyes casting its way and only one brick bouncing off the trunk.

U.S. 1 again out of Baltimore. His arm ached when he held his hand on the wheel, it ached when he lowered his hand to his lap.

Approaching Bel Air, he spotted a chopper against the moon. Unlikely, at this hour, to be flying radio-station traffic watch. Route 22 offered itself just then, and he swung off onto 22.

The same or another chopper hovered over Havre de Grace. Nolan hid the Ambassador under a bridge till the chopper flashed out of sight. Either they had made him or they would soon make him. He had to ditch the Ambassador soon.

He heard his name as the radio faded in again: . . . *District of Columbia police would like to question Bespeaker of the Department of the Interior Nolan Stedman about the assassination, earlier this evening, of Bespeaker of the Department of State Fabian Piel. Authorities emphasize that the BDI is not a suspect, but they believe the BDI can furnish information vital to conduct of the investigation. . . .*

He had to ditch the Ambassador *now.* He followed his nose as much as his sense of direction and the slope of the land, heading down to the shore, to where the sweet stink of the Susquehanna met the salt stink of Chesapeake Bay, to the end of an abandoned pier listing into the dark water.

End of the line for the Ambassador. He got out, closed the door, reached in through the open window to release the hand brake.

For the rest of his life he would have bad dreams about this moment, would wake up drowning in sweat.

Releasing the brake would let the limo roll forward and dive into the river. He doubted the river was deep enough at this point to cover the limo completely. He hoped not. The splash might not raise immediate alarm, but come morning someone should spot the limo's rear bumper sticking up out of the water and mud and that someone should tip the cops. They went and told the sexton, and the sexton tolled the bell.

Divers wouldn't find BDI Nolan Stedman's body, but the

license plate would tell the cops that the limo belonged to Senator Robert Stedman, Jr. That might suffice for the Four Committee, lead them to believe he had drowned and washed away, let them feel they could free Franklin. But what counted now was freedom to reach the Liberty Bell.

He released the hand brake, and jerked himself away. The car started rolling, then stopped. The front left wheel had come up against a loose board that chocked it. His left arm lent little strength but he wrenched the board away and put the car on a roll again. As he straightened and stepped back, he heard the *ping!*

The trunk.

He unfroze himself and sprang to catch up with the front door. He leaned in and pulled the hand brake and kept pulling it till he thought it would snap off. If the brakes didn't hold, he would go into the water with the car.

The car came to a vibrating stop. It stood with the nose overhanging the river, the front wheels clinging by the skin of their tread. Another centimeter and it would have gone over taking Nolan with it.

Pier timbers groaned. Under the car's weight the pier settled, sharpened its angle. Soon, very soon, even with the brakes on, the car would slide into the drink.

Nolan leaned in farther to push the trunk-lid release. The trunk lid popped open. He pulled himself out and hurried shakily to the trunk.

A chill gripped him with trembling skeletal fingers.

Franklin.

Franklin on his side in a fetus curl. Franklin with tape sealing his mouth and tape binding his wrists together behind his back. Franklin with a tire wrench in the cramped fingers. Franklin twisting to glare at him in fright and fury.

Crack.

The pier's forelegs buckled, the car slid away from Nolan, taking Franklin.

No time to be careful or gentle. Nolan got hold of Franklin any old how.

Either he pulled the boy from the trunk or the trunk pulled away from them. The tire wrench clunked on the pier.

The new slant of the pier stepped Nolan forward after the car. He strained against this and tottered on the edge with his burden as the car went in. He fought to keep from falling forward and following it in as the car threw its sullen splash over them.

17

Franklin's weight made the arm hurt like hell but Nolan held his son. It was his bum leg that gave, collapsing him so that Franklin fell with him and landed on his lap. Nolan squirmed them a safer distance from the edge. Franklin let go of the tire wrench; it clunked on the sodden planking. Nolan peeled the tape from Franklin's mouth and wrists.

Franklin croaked something. Poor kid's throat must be dry and sore.

Nolan bent to listen. He had trouble finding his own voice. "What?"

"Are you you?"

"I haven't been myself lately, but I'm your father. I'm Nolan Stedman."

"You're wearing *his* coat."

"Cousin Bob's, you mean?"

Franklin nodded. "I know it wasn't you before. I got in the car and I saw you were Cousin Bob. Cousin Bob said he was doing you a favor, picking me up and taking me to you, because something came up you had to take care of. On the way, he stopped at a drugstore and came out with a Coke and gave me some tablets to drink with it. He said they were vitamins, because you would be busy and he would be busy too and the two of you might forget to feed me. I told him Mrs. Oeppels made me a snack and anyway I could look out for myself, but he said take the damn pills and wash them down. And I did, and I got sleepy, and when I woke up I was in the dark and all tied. I knew I was in the trunk of a car—the rubber and gas and oil smells—and every once in a while I heard a car start up and go away or come and shut off. I couldn't yell, or move much, and I felt around and got hold of a tool and I tried to bang on the trunk lid. Then the car went for a long ride, a lot of long rides. And every chance I got I banged. It was hard, because every time I banged, the tool got away from me and I had to find it and get hold of it all over again. I kept banging, though, but nobody answered. Till now."

Nolan squeezed Franklin to him.

"Dad, you're hurting me."

Quickly Nolan eased up. "Sorry, son."

"That's all right, Dad."

Nolan looked at the limo's rear end sticking up out of the river. "We'd better get going." First he had to see if he could stand. He made it to his feet. Okay. Had to be okay. He helped Franklin up. "Think you can make it?"

Franklin nodded and took a few wobbly steps. Nolan watched
him, ready to catch Franklin if the legs gave. But Franklin's
squirming in the trunk to find the wrench and bang on the lid
seemed to have kept the circulation going. Franklin would
make it.

Nolan picked up the tire wrench and took it along.

Franklin eyed him. "Is that for if we run into Cousin Bob?"

Nolan hefted the wrench. "I guess it would come in handy
for that. But I had something else in mind." Like bashing into a
store and its cash register or breaking open a parking-meter
coin box. But why tell Franklin that till he had to?

"Why did Cousin Bob do that to me? I thought he liked me."

Nolan looked away, at dawn beginning to transfuse the darkness. "I'm sure he does like you. But he's in with some bad
men and they're planning a bad thing. I'm in their way, so Bob
kidnapped you to get a hold over me."

"What kind of bad thing?"

Nolan sketched it for Franklin as they poked along dark
streets, away from the waterfront and toward the center of
town. "Understand now?"

"I think so." Franklin looked around at the strange yet
familiar heart of another city than his own. "Where are we,
Dad?"

"Havre de Grace."

"Where are we going?"

"Philadelphia." First to Wilmington, then to Philly. But before first, the fare. Money makes even shank's mare go. "Ah."
He had spotted an automatic teller. "Wait one."

He put Bob's bank card in the slot. The screen asked him to
enter his Personal Identification Number. Conservation of energy, if not elegance, called for Bob to stick with his office-safe
open sesame. LO. But the keypad was numeric only. Nolan
entered 1215.

On the money. On the PIN money. The screen welcomed
him. Nolan rubbed his hands, warming up to withdraw the
limit. But now the screen flashed: SORRY, THERE WILL BE A
SLIGHT DELAY. KINDLY WAIT.

Nolan turned away from the automatic teller. He took Franklin's elbow and urged the boy along. "Walk, don't run, but
walk fast." Bob must have notified the central computer the
card was stolen.

They rounded the corner. Up ahead, a squad car—on a
silent approach down the street paralleling the automatic teller's—
cast its flashes ahead of it. Nolan looked for cover. Only solid

brick buildings shoulder to shoulder, no nice dark alleys. He hurried them to the nearest entrance and glanced through the glass door. Mailboxes lining the outer hallway indicated an apartment building. Before the squad car made the turn into this street, Nolan pulled Franklin inside.

"Cover your eyes." He swung the wrench at the light bulb. Faster than unscrewing the bulb.

Shards showered them and the foyer went dark. They watched the squad car speed by and squeal around the corner leading back to the automatic teller. Nolan opened the door and hurried himself and Franklin away.

18

A Santa Claus in reverse, a wino filling a green plastic sack with deposit containers he scavenged from garbage cans, oriented himself by the neon of a bar, took bearings, and directed them to the bus terminal.

Behind Nolan's back the wrench twitched in Nolan's hand. The bulging sack, if you cashed its contents in at the nearest twenty-four-hour supermarket's refunding machine, represented fare-and-a-half to the next town, if not to Wilmington. How much bad could he do in the name of doing good? If there seemed no other way to save the world, could he bring himself to tap an inoffensive innocent on the head? He thanked the man and hurried Franklin and himself away.

The bus terminal housed sleepers on benches and floor. Nolan scanned the posted schedules and fares. They had three hours to kill and nineteen dollars to raise.

He studied the vending machines. They seemed vulnerable to the wrench hooked in his belt under Bob's jacket—but not without waking the sleepers. He would have to pick a coin box on a quiet dark street. He started to lead Franklin out again into the night. Sight of a Seven-Up dispenser stopped him. Franklin hadn't complained about thirst but the poor kid would be dying for a drink.

A thought struck Nolan. He turned to Franklin. "By any chance do you have any change?"

Franklin dug down and rooted around. "No change, Dad."

Nolan's hand closed on his thought of the wrench. He continued toward the door. "Let's go."

"But I do have something left over from my allowance, if that helps." Franklin almost apologetically pulled out a crumple of bills.

Nolan's gaze swept the sleepers for the glint of an eye.

"Don't flash that in here." He moved the two of them into the men's room. It was filthy but empty. He counted the money. God bless allowances kids got these days. With a grin he dropped the wrench into the wasterecycler.

With a groan, the wasterecycler upchucked the wrench. The WR's recorded voice reproved him. "Unsuitable matter. Seek a heavy-duty disposal unit."

"Sorry, I wasn't thinking." Nolan picked the wrench up and jammed it behind the hand drier, which had no voice to protest in. He patted Franklin's face with its streaks of dried tears and grime. "Let's unmatter suitably and wash up. Then we'll squeeze in somewhere for a snooze till our bus comes."

19

Nolan flipped a fifty-cent piece. "Heads she loves me . . ." He watched it spin in slow motion; the Liberty Bell engraved on it, when viewed from the side, had the shape of a Space Shuttle seen head on. Then somehow he was aboard the gigantic Liberty Bell Space Shuttle, Nell was with him, and with a surge they had liftoff, and with another boost they reached orbit. Then Nell got into her EVA suit and went through the chamber and out the hatch and blew him an airless kiss and floated away toward Sirius. Nolan frantically goosed the Liberty Bell Space Shuttle in an effort to follow Nell, but it ignored Nolan's attempts at control and dropped him to Earth instead. That was not a good dream, and he half awakened out of it. Dream something better. He skiied smoothly, gracefully, showing off for Nell. He swallowed the bell curve of a mogul by holding himself upright till he got to it, then letting his legs draw up under him and leaning forward from the waist so that at the crest he crouched, then stretching straight till at the hollow between moguls he was again upright. Nell clapped. The sound started an avalanche. Nolan woke up fighting his way out of snow. But it was white daylight and the bus had just pulled into the terminal.

He shook Franklin awake only after the last of the other passengers got off the bus. Nolan himself had dozed in fits and starts and felt unrefreshed and, rubbing his stubble as he limped down the aisle ahead of Franklin, unpresentable.

But looks ranked low in the scheme of things. Forestalling the Four Committee had top priority.

Several passengers had paid the DO NOT PLAY RADIOS OR TVS sign up front no mind, and all had got a repeated earful of the remarkable news about the reconstructed ringing of the Liberty

Bell scheduled for eleven. His heart jumped. What time was it now?

He glanced at his wrist, but the last known address of the watch was Odmow's cocktail table. He stopped to ask the bus driver.

"Ten-fifteen. Right on the nose." She grinned at Franklin. "Going to see history in the making?"

Nolan answered for Franklin. "That's right. Which way from here, and how far?"

"Oh, you'll make it in plenty of time. Three blocks that way, turn right one block, and you'll hit Fifth. The Bell's at Fifth and Chestnut."

"Thanks."

"Watch your step getting off."

Nolan, helping Franklin down the high last step, saw her make her last notations. Nolan and Franklin were already only two tickets in her rubber-banded stack.

In spite of himself, Nolan smiled watching Franklin take in the activity: Philadelphia's streets filling with all the inhabitants thereof; street vendors breaking out small flags, inflating balloons, readying bagels on shopping carts liberated from supermarkets, proclaiming hot dogs, chili dogs, and pop from three-wheelers. Everyone celebrating freedom, not knowing that freedom, including the freedom to cheapen freedom, was at stake.

Nolan felt the Fourth of July tingle in the air. And vibes from himself, inner reverberations of heartbeat and blood pressure, now that the showdown was at hand.

He squeezed Franklin's shoulder. "Have to go to the bathroom before we leave the terminal?"

Franklin shook his head. "But I'm *starving*."

Nolan dug down for the change from buying their bus tickets with Franklin's allowance. "Here. Get yourself a no-chol hotdog and a lo-cal soda." That left one thin FDR dime that he put back.

"Aren't you hungry?"

Nolan's stomach growled on cue. "No."

He watched Franklin flag down a motorized dispenser working the fringe of the crowd, slot his money, and make his choice. Franklin gobbled and guzzled, then remembered his manners and offered Nolan some. He looked anxious when Nolan took him up on the offer. Nolan held himself to a token bite and a token sip.

"Thanks. You finish the rest while we keep moving."

Franklin looked relieved. "I guess you really aren't hungry."

"Maybe it's because I have other things on my mind."

Franklin glanced around at the people they moved with before whispering stagily, "The Liberty Bell caper?" He craned to see if he could see the Bell yet. His eyes brightened in anticipatory nostalgia for the scene of the crime.

Nolan nodded. "Think you're up to creating another diversion?"

"Sure." The way Franklin looked at his empty pop bottle and the greasy napkin from the hotdog, and the fact that he did not dispose of them, told Nolan that these items would play a part.

Under a tree that created an eddy, an old black woman sat on a folding stool and smoked a thin brown cigar and fanned herself. The TV in her lap and the face on the screen caught Nolan's eye.

He drew himself and Franklin near. "Mind if we watch?"

"Be my guest."

". . . Maggie McGee, coming to you live from Philadelphia. And Philadelphia is alive—with excitement. Yes, folks, in just a few minutes—at eleven o'clock, to be exact—the Liberty Bell" —the TV cut from Maggie's face to a closeup of the Liberty Bell—"cracked though it is, and mute for centuries, will, through the magic of computer simulation, ring out on this Fourth of July. In the words inscribed on the Bell itself, words from Leviticus 25:10, it will 'proclaim liberty throughout all the land unto all the inhabitants thereof.' "

The screen cut from the Liberty Bell to a shot of Maggie McGee against the background of the Channel 3 television van.

And far across the swarming sward Nolan spotted the real live Maggie and her van and her camera crew and her Tele-Prompter, all a knot in the streaming grain of the crowd.

Her TV persona went on, but not a word or a hint about the Four Committee conspiracy.

She would have tipped off the administration right away, through someone she thought she could trust, while demanding dibs. Maybe she wasn't breaking the story yet because someone had ordered her to hold off, the better to trap the conspirators. That was the best-case scenario.

But she wasn't all that great an actress; he read only her normal bubbliness, not an effervescing of a deeper suppressed excitement. It worried him. He had to assume the worst, that Maggie had informed the wrong someone. He felt a chill in the sunlight, a cloud of the mind. What if Maggie had given up on him, had transferred her hots for him to his look-alike Bob, had tipped Bob off? No, no; that way lay paranoia.

He tapped Franklin's shoulder and pointed to the screen. "You see Maggie McGee?"

Franklin nodded.

Nolan lifted Franklin to look over the pointillist stipple of heads. "See the van way over there? That's where she is now." He lowered Franklin to the ground and spoke softly. "That's our rendezvous point. After you make your diversion, head for the van, tell Maggie who you are, and say you're going to wait inside for me. I'll meet you there as soon as I can. Got it?"

"Got it."

Nolan nodded his thanks to the woman. She nodded her acknowledgment. Nolan started himself and Franklin toward the glass pavilion.

Franklin tugged himself free. "One second, Dad." He darted back to the woman and spoke to her. Her fan stopped, she looked at Franklin, then at Nolan, shrugged, and handed Franklin something from a pocket. Franklin darted back to Nolan's side. "Okay, Dad." He showed Nolan a disposable lighter added to the empty bottle and the greasy napkin.

Nolan grinned tightly. "So that's your diversion. A simulated Molotov cocktail."

"You got it, Dad."

My son the terrorist. A budding Wolpy Rubb. The need was now, the game was for real, for keeps; but he'd have to make sure after this was all over—if it turned out right and he had the option—that Franklin grew up to be one of the good guys.

They edged as near to the glass pavilion as they could and peered through the cyclone fence. The Bell hung off the ground now; a rope tailed from it.

And two hefty rangers were getting ready to ring it. Each took a turn of the rope around the wrist. A man with a photo ID badge pinned to his white coveralls crawled out from under the Bell. At a nod from him, the rangers pulled. The Bell swung. At the top of its swing, he raised a hand. They hung on, holding the Bell so. The man in coveralls stooped under the bell to check the clapper's contact with the soundbow. He backed out, straightened, and made the O sign. The rangers let the Bell swing back to still center. They unwrapped their wrists and stood easy.

The man in coveralls closed his tool box and stepped out of the glass pavilion. Nolan saw his face.

Wolpy Rubb.

Nolan turned and, keeping Franklin in front of him, moved the two of them away from the fence and deeper into the crowd.

He gave Rubb time to come out of the fenced-in area and head wherever Rubb was heading. Nolan chanced a tiptoe stretch and spotted Rubb climbing into the cab of an Interior Department maintenance truck parked in an official space. Rubb and the truck sat there.

That vantage would give Rubb a view of the Bell in the glass pavilion, but now the crowd would block Rubb's view of the gate. Nolan moved Franklin and himself back toward the gate.

Nolan stared through the fence and the glass of the pavilion. The rangers stood stiffly aware of their place in history and of the pool camera focused on them and the Bell.

To reach the Bell, and rip out the wiring so the clapper would not close the circuit when it struck the soundbow, seemed to Nolan the easy part. The rangers would be rapt, wrapped up in their task, hung up in the rope. But even if they stopped him short of ripping out the wires, just disrupting the proceedings enough to put the Bell and its simulated note out of sync might keep Sixtus's meme from taking.

Getting through the fence and to the glass pavilion would be the hard part. Nolan grimaced; he had himself to thank for that.

The mindscanner.

His own security measures blocked his way.

He caught himself shaking his head, and set his jaw, then caught Franklin watching him and saw Franklin's jaw set. The Stedman look, the Clinger spirit.

Nolan smiled a smile he didn't feel. "Time for the diversion, son." He gave Franklin a *Go!* pat.

Franklin smiled tensely back and edged away along the fence.

Nolan made for the gate. A ranger inside the fence saw him approach and said patiently and tonelessly that there was no admittance till after the ceremony.

Just then Franklin's pop bottle glittered in a high arc over the fence, the greasy paper-napkin wick flaming.

"A terrorist bomb!" Nolan put hysteria in his voice. "Everybody run!"

Voices picked up the alarm and everybody ran, some this way, some that. Through the milling, Nolan saw Franklin head for the television van.

Inside the fence, two rangers rushed toward where dry grass

had caught fire, and began stomping. One ranger remained irresolutely at the gate.

Nolan pointed a few points away from the van. "There he goes! The man in the plaid bib overalls!"

The ranger opened the gate and ran the way Nolan pointed in pursuit of elusive plaid bib overalls.

Nolan slipped inside. The gate funneled him toward the mindscanner's guileless housing.

To fake out the mindscanner, he thought thoughts of love for the Bell. He wished the Bell only the best. His heart yearned toward the Bell. Whatever he did to the Bell he did for the Bell's own good.

The mindscanner must have sensed his wish that the Liberty Bell fail to ring. The mindscanner could not tell whether his intent boded ultimate good or ultimate bad for the Bell. It knew only that the brain signals were in the hostile-thoughts range. That was good enough to bode immediate bad for the Bell. The mindscanner gave the alarm.

Red LEDs flashed on ranger belts. Ranger hands shot to stunner holsters. Ranger eyes vectored toward the gate.

Nolan felt a flash of indignation. No Bell Oblige. Why had the mindscanner rejected him and passed Rubb?

Do the mindscanner justice, whatever Rubb's level of hostility toward the American ideal of liberty, Rubb would be *wanting* the Liberty Bell to work. Nolan wanted it *not* to work, so fairness did not enter into the equation.

Rangers came running before Nolan could make it through the gate funnel. They cut off the way to the Bell, got set to draw on the hostile intruder.

Nolan had to stay free. His bad leg gave under him as he turned, but he pulled himself around and limped out and away and made himself scarce in the milling crowd.

The crowd cut him off from Maggie's television van—and from Franklin, if Franklin had made it to the van. Franklin would have to look after himself for a few minutes more. Nolan had to get to a phone.

21

One block over on Fifth he found a public phone. He felt eyes on him; really it must have been a sense of movement. He looked up. A woman in a third-floor window of an apartment house watched him as he put the dime in the slot and punched O and then Nell's Spacelab code. The computerized voice clicked in. "May I help you?"

"Nolan Stedman making a collect call, person-to-person, to Nell Packard."

"Thank you."

The ringing gave way to Nell's voice. "Yes?" Preoccupied, even harassed.

"Is a Nell Packard there?"

"Yes, here just happens to be one."

"A collect call from a Nolance Tedman. Will you accept the charges?"

"Will I what? Nolan, really. I haven't time for games."

"Will you accept the charges?"

"I accept the charges."

Nolan didn't wait for the computerized voice to give him the go-ahead and get off the line. "Nell, listen—"

"How's Franklin? I didn't hear from him yesterday."

"He's fine." God, I hope he's fine. "Now, listen. Not much time. I'm dead serious." Why did that put him in mind of Clinger? Another persister, but another loser. "Are you going to be passing over Philly soon?"

"Um. Not *over*, but it'll be in line of sight in fifteen minutes. Is this to tell me not to miss the ringing of the Liberty Bell? You needn't've worried. We got word, and of course we're tuning in. Everyone united: very patriotic. What a spectacular way to mark the Fourth!"

He let out a breath he hadn't known he was holding. "It's this pass or never."

"What is? What are you talking about?"

He heard himself tell her about the Four Committee and the perversion of Operation Let Freedom Ring, and his voice sounded hollow and his words seemed wild. Then he heard himself wait.

Nell said nothing.

"Do you understand, Nell? I can't do anything at this end to stop Sixtus. It's up to you. The laser beam. Aim it at the Liberty Bell in the glass pavilion."

"Nolan, Nolan. Do you know what you're asking me to do?"

"I'm asking you to save the country, to save Franklin."

"Nolan, don't. You don't have to prove anything."

"Dammit, Nell, I'm not trying to prove anything. I'm trying to save everything."

Something between a sigh and a sob. "How do I know—"

"That I'm not cracked? You don't." He caught himself on the point of saying, Trust me. Trust my judgment. He would have been begging her to do what Sixtus's meme would order everyone to do: Believe in me. He spoke slowly and clearly. "Trust my love for you. Trust your love for me."

Nell said nothing.

"Maybe I'm asking too much. I know how you slaved to get where you are. I know you think I resent your work, and I guess I do envy you. Why should I expect you to stake everything on my say-so?"

Nell shouted nothing.

"It's your decision. But whatever you do, Nell, I'll always love you." Hang up, dammit. Say nothing more. Anything more would strike the wrong note. Still, he had to add, "For your own sake, don't tune in the sound." He hung up, but he found it hard to open his hand and release the phone, his grip had tightened so.

He looked up. The woman in the window looked down expressionlessly. From somewhere in the room behind her the glow of television flickered. Not all channels would carry the ceremony. This was probably a commercial break during her favorite soap opera. Even if she didn't watch the ceremony at the crucial moment, she would get the vibes of the tainted Bell note from the steel skeleton of the building, from her refrigerator, from the fillings in her teeth. Even if she, and others like her around the world, the reality-tuned-out ones, somehow escaped the note of the Bell, would they make any difference?

As he limped quickly away he wondered if the woman noticed that he had only one sock.

22

"That's him. That's my dad." Franklin, on the lookout for him, got him past the cordon and into the van.

Maggie McGee stared at Nolan. "You look like hell. What's going on? Your kid's been trying to tell me about some conspiracy having to do with the Bell."

Nolan stared back. "I explained it all to your answering machine."

"That explains it. Yesterday my answering machine caught a glitch and lost all messages."

Score another point for the Four Committee.

How could he hope to make the unbelievable believable?

Nolan patted himself, felt the reassuring bulges, reached in and drew out the envelope full of clippings about decade-and-a-half-stale terrorist acts and the sheaf of slips bearing initials and figures. He handed them to Maggie and briefed her.

Maggie shook her head in helpleessness. "Even if all this

checks out, it's too late." She jerked her head at the bank of monitors.

The anchor man in Washington was saying, according to the closed captions for the hearing-impaired, "And now we go live to the Oval Office."

President Dodge sat at her desk and poised a finger over a button. Someone here in the van raised the gain. "Fellow countrypersons and peoples of the world, it is my great honor and privilege to make the Liberty Bell ring out at last and give voice to its message of freedom for all."

Nolan looked to the console to see some way of wresting control and telling President Dodge to hold everything, but the knobs and switches were a mystery to him. He had lost. He snatched from the pocket of Bob's jacket the earphoned minicassette player. He switched it on and gave a quick listen. The hissing-radiator, stridulating-cricket noises shut out everything else. At least one person here would not hear the Bell. "Franklin, put this on."

Then, while Maggie watched and went pale and big-eyed, he covered his own ears with his hands. A useless gesture, but when you had nothing else to fall back on, useless gestures had their use.

With a pang of wry consolation, he had a thought that might have been a meme, Fabian Piel's legacy to him. *Don't feel so bad. It's all happening to happenstances of atoms, to fleeting patterns of particles.*

The monitor that showed what went out over the air split its screen. The left half showed President Dodge's finger coming slowly down to the button, the right half showed the Bell beginning to swing.

In the right half, a searingly bright beam shot down at a slant from the sky. It pierced the glass, struck the Bell dead center and sliced through. The Bell fell apart; the two rangers flew backward holding to the sheared rope as though unpinning a tail from a donkey.

In her half of the screen, President Dodge sat frozen, finger still pressing the button, staring into a small monitor showing the split-screen action. Into that half, Major Marshall Sixtus, arching from soles to eyebrows in triumph, thrust himself. He removed his protective cassette earphones and leaned over President Dodge to speak into the mikes on her desk.

"You have heard the Liberty Bell ring. This is President-for-Life Sixtus, proclaiming a New Order and a New Day—"

That was as far as he got. Secret Service agents pounced on

him. They dragged him out frothing and screaming, "But you have to believe in me!" An obvious nut case. That half of the screen went blank.

The scene at the glass pavilion took full screen. Rangers stood looking down at the two halves of the Liberty Bell. One touched the nearer half and jerked back his hand and sucked his fingertip.

Maggie pressed her tiny earphone more tightly into her ear, evidently got word to cover the breaking story, and projected for the mike in her cleavage to pick up. "This is Maggie McGee, coming to you live from Philadelphia, where something has just happened to the Liberty Bell. We're trying to learn just what happened. At the moment, we can say only that we saw what you must have seen: out of a clear sky, what looked like a bolt of lightning struck the Bell. Let me take you to the glass pavilion of the Liberty Bell to assess the damage and learn the cause." She left the van to do her job.

Nolan followed her on the monitor as her cameraperson tracked her through the gate and to the pavilion.

He swelled with love and pride. Nell had come through. His ears still rang with the Bell's eloquent silence.

"What happened, Dad?" Franklin had the earphones in his hand. "Is it all right to take them off now?"

"It's all right, Franklin. I took my spare set off too."

Nolan whirled. Bob Stedman had climbed into the van.

Nolan stepped in front of Franklin. "Hello, Bob."

"Hello, Nolan. You have a charmed life."

"Yes. Fabian Piel died in my stead."

Bob nodded at Franklin. "I'm glad the boy's all right. I was afraid he'd have used up the air in the trunk by now."

Nolan saw Franklin's eyes swing back and forth between the cousins. He gave Franklin a reassuring smile, then faced Bob grimly. "What are you doing here? It's your turn to be on the run."

Bob nodded. "I know when I've lost." He did have a look of calm resignation. "But Wolpy Rubb doesn't: Rubb thought he spotted you going into this van. He's very angry: curiously, he blames you for sabotaging the Bell. He wanted to blow up the whole van, but I told him to let me check it out. I'll go back and tell him he thought wrong. But from now on you'd better look over your shoulder."

He turned, then stopped as though at an afterthought and faced Nolan. "Oh, would you mind giving me back my jacket?"

Nolan worked himself stiffly out of the jacket.

Bob gave him a strange smile. "So Rubb didn't miss you after all."

Nolan glanced at the bandage on his arm. He spoke flatly. "He just winged me, but he plugged Fabian Piel."

Bob nodded. "Yes, he does a better job with a telescopic sight." Bob shrug-fitted himself into the lemon jacket. He gave Nolan the strange smile. He said again, "You have a charmed life."

Then he stepped slowly down out of the van.

Zinggthwack.

The impact shoved Bob out of sight to one side of the doorway. Nolan pushed Franklin deeper into the van and strained to listen.

He heard cop shouts. "I spotted the sniper! Guy with white coveralls in the Interior truck." "Get him! He's the same terrorist who blew up the Bell."

Small-arms fire, squealing tires, a crash, silence. And when Nolan looked out he saw the blazing wreck of the Interior Department truck.

Closer home, wine stained the lemon jacket. Nolan stared down at the twisted sprawl of his dead look-alike and shivered. Send not to know for whom the bell tolls. That's how I'll look when I'm dead.

It was all over. He had spoken from the van with President Dodge and with Nell, and in the van with the cops, and with Maggie to the people.

The story still preempted regular scheduling, and Maggie McGee was summing up, reading from her fact sheet. "The Liberty Bell is not gone. There are fifty Liberty Bells. Each state capitol has a replica of the Liberty Bell—an exact likeness down to the crack . . ."

Franklin tugged Nolan's arm. He pointed down and whispered into Nolan's ear. "You know, Dad, you have only one sock on."

Nolan nodded gravely. "I'm my son John." He squeezed Franklin's shoulder. "Don't look down. Look up." He looked up and Franklin followed his gaze. "Somebody up there likes us."